Praise for Cheryl Williford and her novels

"Well done and will have you rooting for a [happily-ever-after.]"
—*RT Book Reviews* on *The Amish Widow's Secret*

Praise for Diane Burke and her novels

"Burke's story [is] about the power of love…"
—*RT Book Reviews* on *Hidden in Plain View*

"Will keep you guessing until the end…"
—*RT Book Reviews* on *Bounty Hunter Guardian*

"[A] fascinating story of hidden identities and forbidden love, creating a page-turning mystery."
—*RT Book Reviews* on *Double Identity*

Cheryl Williford and her veteran husband, Henry, live in South Texas, where they've raised three children, and numerous foster children, alongside a menagerie of rescued cats, dogs and hamsters. Her love for writing began in a literature class, and now her characters keep her grabbing for paper and pen. She is a member of her local ACFW and CWA chapters, and is a seamstress, watercolorist and loving grandmother. Her website is cherylwilliford.com.

Diane Burke is an award-winning author who has had six books published with Love Inspired Suspense. She is a voracious reader and loves movies, crime shows, travel and eating out! She has never met a stranger, only people she hasn't had the pleasure of talking to yet. She loves to hear from readers and can be reached at diane@dianeburkeauthor.com. She can also be found on Twitter and Facebook.

CHERYL WILLIFORD
The Amish Widow's Secret

&

DIANE BURKE
Hidden in Plain View

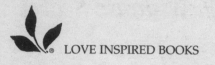

LOVE INSPIRED BOOKS

Recycling programs for this product may not exist in your area.

ISBN-13: 978-0-373-83893-6

The Amish Widow's Secret and Hidden in Plain View

Copyright © 2016 by Harlequin Books S.A.

The publisher acknowledges the copyright holders of the individual works as follows:

The Amish Widow's Secret
Copyright © 2015 by Cheryl Williford

Hidden in Plain View
Copyright © 2013 by Diane Burke

CONTENTS

THE AMISH WIDOW'S SECRET

Cheryl Williford

This book is dedicated to the memory of my grandfather, Fred Carver, who encouraged me to reach for the stars, and to my Quaker great-grandmother, Clarrisa Petch, who inspired me.

Acknowledgments

To my patient and understanding husband, Will, who read and critiqued way too many manuscript chapters and blessed me with honesty. To my eldest daughter, Barbara, who graciously gifted me with fees for contests and conferences. To the ACFW Golden Girls critique group, Liz, Nanci, Jan, Zillah and Shannon: you are loved. To Eileen Key, the best line-edit partner in the business. To Les Stobbe, my wonderful agent and mentor; to my amazing Love Inspired editor, Melissa Endlich, who believed in me; and last but not least, to my Lord and Savior, Jesus Christ, who has opened many doors, enabling this book to be written and published.

Take delight in the Lord, and He will give you your heart's desires. Commit everything you do to the Lord. Trust Him, and He will help you. He will make your innocence radiate like the dawn, and the justice of your cause will shine like the noonday sun.

—*Psalms* 37:4–6

Chapter One

It was the most beautiful thing she'd ever seen.

Sarah Nolt couldn't resist the temptation. *Gott* would probably punish her for coveting something so fancy. She allowed the tip of her finger to glide across the surface of the sewing machine gleaming in the store's overhead lights.

She closed her eyes and imagined stitching her dream quilt. Purple sashing would look perfect with the patch of irises she'd create out of scraps of lavender and blue fabrics and hand stitch to the center of the diagonal-block quilt.

"Some things are best not longed for," Marta Nolt whispered close to Sarah's ear.

Sarah jumped as if she'd been stung by a wasp. A flush of guilt washed over her from head to toe. "You startled me." She shot a glance at her lifelong friend and sister-in-law—the two had grown up together and had even married each other's brothers. Had Marta seen her prideful expression? All her life she'd been taught pride was a sin. She wasn't convinced it was.

Compared to Sarah's five-foot-four frame, Marta

appeared as tiny as a twelve-year-old in her dark blue spring dress and finely stitched, stiff white prayer *kapp*. Marta's brows furrowed. "It is better I startled you than your *daed*, Sarah. He's just outside the door waiting for us. He said to hurry, that he has more important things to do than wait on you this morning. Did you do something to irritate him again? One day he'll tell the elders what you've been up to and—"

"And they'll what? Call me in for another scolding and long prayer, and then threaten to tell the Bishop how unruly a widow I am?" Sarah turned for one last look at the gleaming machine and moved away.

"If they find out about you giving Lukas money, you'll be shunned. You know they're looking for someone to blame and wanting to set an example since he ran away with young Ben in tow. Everyone believes they've joined the *Englisch* rescue house. The boys' father is beyond angry. Nerves have become rattled throughout the community. People are asking who else is planning to leave."

"I'm not joining if that's what you're thinking. I wasted my time by looking at a sewing machine I can't ever have. I dream. Nothing more. How can that fine piece of equipment be so full of sin just because it's electric and fancy? It's made to produce the finest of quilts."

Sarah shoved back a lock of hair and tucked it into her *kapp*. "Last week an *Englisch* woman used one of the machines for a sewing demonstration. My heart almost leaped out of my chest, Marta. You should have seen the amazing details it sewed. It would take a year or more for us to make such perfect stitches by hand. *Daed* needs money for a new field horse. If I had this machine, I could make quilts more quickly and sell them to the *Englisch* on market day. I could make enough money to keep my farm and eat more than cooked cabbage and my favorite white duck."

"All you have to do is ask for help, Sarah. You are so stubborn. The community will—"

"Rally round? Tell me I must sell Joseph's farm because a family deserves it more than a helpless widow. *Nee*, I don't want their help."

"Careful. Someone might hear you."

Marta had always tried to accept the community's harsh rules, but today her words of mindless obedience angered Sarah. "I *will not* ask for help and will not be silent. Will *Gott* finally be satisfied if He takes everything dear from me, including my dreams?"

"*Ach*, don't be so bitter. Your anger comes from a place of pain. You need to pray. Ask *Gott* to remove the ache in your heart." Marta took her hand and squeezed hard. "Since Joseph died you've done nothing but stir up the community's wrath. You know what your *daed's* like. He'll only take so much before he lets the Bishop come down hard on you. You can't keep bringing shame on the Yoder name."

"I don't care about my *daed's* pride of name. Is his pride not sin too? I am a Nolt now, not a Yoder. I'm a twenty-five-year-old widow. Not a child. I will make my own decisions. You wait and see."

"*Meine liebe*. The suddenness of Joseph's death brought you to this place of anger and confusion. Don't grieve him so. His funeral is over, the coffin closed. It was *Gott's* will for Joseph to die. We must not ever question, Sarah. Joseph was my older brother, but I'm content to know he's with the old ones and happy in heaven."

Memories of the funeral haunted Sarah's sleep. "I'm glad you are able to find peace in this rigid community, Marta. I really am. But I can't. Not since *Gott* let Joseph die in such a horrible way. To burn to death in a barn fire is too horrible. What kind of *Gott* lets this happen to a man of faith? This cruel *Gott* has *nee* place in my life." Sarah sighed deeply. *Will I ever be happy again and at peace?*

She reached out a trembling hand and grabbed a card of hooks-and-eyes and threw it in the store's small plastic shopping basket that hung off her wrist. She added several large spools of basic blue, purple and black thread and turned back toward Marta, who stood fingering a skein of baby-soft yarn in the lightest shade of blue. "Do you have something you want to tell me?"

"Nee." Marta's ready smile vanished. "I'm not pregnant. *Gott* must intend for me to rear others' *kinder* and not my own."

Marta had miscarried three times. Talk among the older women was there would be no *bobbel* for her sister-in-law unless she had an operation. Sarah knew the young couple's farm wasn't doing well. There would be no money for expensive procedures in *Englisch* hospitals for Marta, even if the Bishop would allow it.

Sarah said, "I wish—"

"I know. I wish it, too. A baby for Eric and me. And Joseph still alive for you. But *Gott* doesn't always give us what we want or make an easy path to walk."

Heavy footsteps announced Sarah's father's approach. Both women grew silent.

"Do you realize the sun is at its zenith and a man

grows hungry?" Adolph Yoder's sharp tone cut like a knife. The short-statured man rubbed his rotund stomach and glared at his only daughter.

Sarah straightened the sweat-soaked collar of her father's blue shirt and smiled, trying hard to show her love for the angry man. "I'm sorry, *Daed*. Time got away from us." Sarah gathered the last of the sewing things she needed and tried to match his fast pace down the narrow aisle.

Her father stopped abruptly and turned toward her. His blue eyes flashed. "You must learn to drive your own wagon, daughter. Do your own fetching. Enough time has passed."

"Ya." Sarah nodded. He turned away and moved toward the door. She thought back to the times she'd begged him to teach her the basics of directing a horse or mending a wheel, but nothing had ever come of it. He had always been too busy trying to be both *Mamm* and *Daed* to her and her younger brother, Eric. She blamed herself and her mother's sudden disappearance into the *Englisch* world on her father's angry moods. Once again she wished her *mamm* had taken her with her when she'd left Lancaster County.

Joseph would have been happy to teach her to drive, but *Gott* had taken him too soon. Bitterness swelled in her heart, adding to the pain already there. Tears pooled in her eyes and slid down her cheeks as she thought of him. She brushed them away, not willing to show her pain.

Moments later the familiar woman at the checkout line greeted Sarah as she might an *Englisch* customer. "Hello, Sarah. How are you today, dear?"

"Gut, and you?"

"Oh, I'm fine as I can be," she responded. "You're buying an awful lot of thread. You ladies planning one of your quilting bees?"

"*Nee,* just stocking up." Sarah emptied the small basket on the counter and began stacking the spools of thread.

"Well, you let me know if you need someone to help sell your quilts. I'll be glad to place them in the shop window for a small fee. You do beautiful work. You should be sewing professionally."

Distracted by her thoughts, Sarah tried hard to follow the older woman's friendly banter. "*Danke.* I'll speak to the Bishop's wife and see what she says, but I don't hold much hope. There are rules about selling wares in an *Englisch* shop. You know how strict some are."

"Yeah, I do." She patted Sarah's hand.

Sarah's father walked past and glanced at the two women. He hurried out of the shop, letting the door slam. His bad mood meant problems for Sarah. When riled, he could be very cruel. She had no one to blame but herself for his bad attitude today. She knew he grew tired of her lack of control and rule breaking. People were openly talking about her. She had to learn to keep her mouth closed and distance herself from the *Englisch*.

Sarah hurried out of the store and trailed behind Marta. Fancy *Englisch* cars dotted the parking lot. She made her way to her father's buggy parked under a cluster of old oaks.

He stood talking to a man unfamiliar to Sarah. The man turned toward her as she approached. He wore a traditional blue Amish shirt, his black pants wrinkled and dusty, as if he'd been traveling for days. The black hat on his head barely controlled his nest of dishwater-blond curls. Joseph had been blond and curly-haired, too. Memories flooded in. Her heart ached.

Men from all around the county were coming today. The burned-out barn was to be torn down and cleared away. The man standing next to her father had be one of the workers who'd traveled a long distance to lend a helping hand. She often disapproved of many Amish ways, but not their generosity of heart. Helping others came naturally to all Amish. She honored this trait. It was the reason she'd helped the neighbor boys get away from their cruel father.

"Sarah," Marta called out and motioned for her to hurry. Sarah picked up her pace.

"Come, Sarah! Time is wasting," her father called out.

"Ya, Daed."

The tall, well-built man smiled. She was struck by the startling blueness of his eyes and the friendly curve of his mouth. His light blond beard told her he was married. She gave a quick smile.

Marta stepped forward. "This is Mose Fischer, Joseph's school friend. He came all the way from Florida to help us rebuild the barn."

Mose Fischer took her hand. The crinkles around his eyes expressed years of friendly smiles and a good sense of humor.

Sarah wasn't comfortable with physical contact, but allowed him to take her hand out of respect to Joseph. She returned his smile. "Hello. I'm glad to meet you." She meant what she'd said. She was glad to meet him. She'd only met her husband's sister, Marta. Meeting

Joseph's childhood friend made her feel more a part of his past life.

Adolph put his hand on Sarah's shoulder. Touching her was something he rarely did, especially in public. "Sarah loves *kinder*. Perhaps you'd like her to care for your young daughters while you work?"

"If Sarah agrees, I'd like that very much." Mose Fischer seemed to look deep into her soul, looking for all her secrets as he spoke. *Why hadn't his wife come to Lancaster with him?* "I'd be glad to care for the *bobbles*, and I'm sure I'll have help. Marta seldom gets a chance to play with *kinder* and will grab at this opportunity."

Marta nodded with a shy laugh and smiled. "Just try to keep me away."

"How old are the *kinder*?" Sarah grinned, happy for a chance to be busy wiping tiny fingers and toes. She'd be much too preoccupied to fret or watch the last of the barn come down.

"Beatrice is almost five and Mercy will soon be one. But, I warn you. They miss their *mamm* since she passed and can be a real handful." Pain shimmered in his eyes.

"I'm sorry. I didn't know you were a widower. You were very brave to travel alone with such young daughters."

"We came by train from Tampa, but my memories of Joseph made all the effort worth it. I didn't want to miss the chance to help out his widow."

"Where are you staying?"

"Mose and the girls will stay on my farm, and so will you." Adolph gave Sarah a familiar glare.

"That's fine. I can stay in my old room for a few days, and the girls can sleep with me." Sarah nervously straightened the ribbons hanging from her stiff white prayer *kapp*. Since she was in deep mourning, her father knew she wanted to continue to hide herself at her farm, far away from people and gossip. "If that suits you, Mose." She held her breath. She suddenly realized she needed to be around the girls as much as they needed her.

Dressed in a plain black mourning dress and *kapp*, her black shoes polished to a high shine, Mose could see why Joseph had chosen Sarah as his bride. There was something striking about her, her beauty separating her from the average Amish woman. She tried to act friendly, but he'd experienced the pain of loss and knew she suffered from the mention of Joseph. Greta had been the perfect wife to him and mother to his girls. After almost a year, the mention of her name still cut deeply and flooded his mind with memories.

"I hope they're not a handful for you." A genuine smile blossomed on the willowy, red-haired woman's face. She looked a bit more relaxed. The heavy tension between Sarah and her father surprised him. Surely Adolph would be a tower of strength for her. She'd need her father to lean on during difficult times. Instead, Mose felt an air of disapproval between the two. He'd heard Adolph Yoder was a hard man, but Sarah seemed a victim in this terrible tragedy.

"I'll bring the girls around in an hour or so, if that's all right."

"*Ya.* I'm not doing anything but cooking today. The girls can help bake for tomorrow's big meal." Sarah smiled a shy goodbye and followed Marta into the buggy. She pulled in her skirt and slammed the door.

Through the window she waved, "I look forward to taking care of the *kinder.*"

"Till then," Mose said, and waved as the buggy pulled onto the main road, his thoughts still on the tension between father and daughter.

Walking came naturally to Mose. He set out on the two-mile trip to his cousin's farm and prayed his daughters had behaved while he was gone. Dealing with her own grief, he wasn't sure Sarah was up to handling the antics of his eldest daughter. Four was a difficult age. Beatrice was no longer a baby, but her longing for her dead *mamm* still made her difficult to manage.

The hot afternoon sun beat down on his head, his dark garments drawing heat. He welcomed the rare gusts of wind that threatened to blow off his straw hat and ruffle his hair. Lancaster took a beating from the summer heat every year, but today felt even more hot and muggy. He would be glad to get back to Sarasota and its constant breeze and refreshing beaches.

A worn black buggy rolled past, spitting dust and pebbles his way. To his surprise, the buggy stopped and a tall, burley, gray-haired man hopped out.

"Hello, Mose. I heard you were in town."

I should know the man. He recognized his face but struggled with the name. "Forgive me, but I don't remember—"

"*Nee.* It was a long time ago. I'm Bishop Ralf Miller. It's been five years or more since I last went to Florida and stayed with your family. I've known your father for many years. When we were boys, we shared the same school. I believe you'd just married your beautiful bride when your father introduced me to you."

"My wife died last year," Mose informed him.

"Childbirth took her." Saying the words out loud was like twisting a knife in his heart.

"I'm sorry. I had no idea."

"There's no reason you would know,"

"*Nee*, but it worries me how many of our young people are dying. I assume you're here to help with Joseph Nolt's barn clearing."

"I just met his widow. Poor woman is torn with grief."

"Between the two of us, I'm not so sure Sarah Nolt is a grieving widow. One of the men at the funeral said they heard her say Joseph's death was her fault. The woman's been unpredictable most of her life. Her father and I had a conversation about this a few days ago. He's finding it hard to keep both farms going, and Sarah is stubbornly refusing to return to her childhood home. Joseph's farm needs to be sold. If she doesn't stop this willful behavior, I fear we'll have to shun her for the safety of the community."

Surprised at the openness of the Bishop's conversation and the accusation against Sarah, Mose asked, "What proof do you have against her, other than her one comment made in grief? Has she been counseled by the elders or yourself?"

"We tried, but she won't talk to us. She's always had this rebellious streak. Her father agrees with me. There could be trouble."

"A rebellious streak?"

"You know what I mean. Last week she told one of our Elders to shut up when he offered her a fair price for the farm. This inappropriate behavior can't be ignored."

"You've just described a grieving widow, Bishop. Perhaps she's…"

Bishop Miller interrupted Mose, his brows lowered. "You don't know her, Mose. I do. She's always seemed difficult. Even as a child she was rebellious and broke rules."

"Did something happen to make her this way?" Mose's stomach twisted in anger. He liked to consider himself a good judge of character and he hadn't found Sarah Nolt anything but unhappy, for good reason. Adolph Yoder was another matter. He appeared a hard, critical man. The Bishop's willingness to talk about Sarah's personal business didn't impress him either. These things were none of Mose's concern. He knew, with the community being Old Order Amish, that the bishop kept hard, fast rules. In his community she'd be treated differently. If she had no one to help her through her loss, her actions could be interpreted as acting out of grief. Perhaps the lack of a father's love was the cause of his daughter's actions. "Where is Sarah's mother?"

"Who knows but *Gott*? She left the community when Sarah was a young child. She'd just had a son and some said raising *kinder* didn't suit her. Adolph did everything he could to make Sarah an obedient child, like his son, Eric, but she never would bend to his will."

"I saw little parental love from Adolph. He's an angry man and needs to be spoken to by one of the community elders. Perhaps *Gott* can redirect him and help Sarah at the same time."

"We're glad to have your help with the teardown and barn-building, but I will deal with Sarah Nolt. This community is my concern. If your father were here, he'd agree with me."

Mose drew in a deep breath. He'd let his temper get the better of him. "I meant no disrespect, Bishop, but all this gossip about the widow needs to stop until you have proof. It's your job to make sure that happens. You shouldn't add to it."

"If you weren't an outsider you'd know she's not alone in her misery. She has her sister-in-law, Marta, to talk to and seek counsel. Marta is a godly woman and a good influence. If she can't reach her, there will be harsh consequences the next time Sarah acts out."

"I'll be praying for her, as I'm sure you are." Mose nodded to the bishop, and kept on walking to his cousin's farm.

But he couldn't help wondering, who was the real Sarah?

Beatrice squirmed around on the buckboard seat, her tiny sister asleep on a quilt at her feet. "I want cookies now, *Daed*."

Mose pulled to the side of the road and spoke softly. "Soon we'll be at Sarah's house and you can have more cookies, but if you wake your sister, you'll be put to bed. Do you understand?"

The tear rolling down her flushed cheek told him she didn't understand and was pushing boundaries yet again.

"*Mamm* would give me cookies. I want *Mamm*." An angry scowl etched itself across her tear-streaked face.

These were the times Mose hated most, when he had no answers for Beatrice. *How can I help her understand?*

"We've talked about this before, my child. *Mamm* is in heaven with *Gott* and we must accept this, even though it makes us sad." He drew the small child into his arms and hugged her close, his heart breaking as he realized how thin her small body had become. He had to do something to cheer her up. "Let's hurry and go and see the nice ladies I told you about. Sarah said she'd be baking today. Perhaps she'll have warm cookies. Wouldn't cookies and a glass of cold milk brighten your spirits?

"I only want *Mamm*."

Tucked under his arm, Beatrice cried softly, twisting Mose's heart in knots. His mother had talked to him about remarriage, but he had thrown the idea back at her, determined to honor his dead wife until the day he died. But the *kinder* definitely needed a woman's gentle hand when he had to be at work.

His mother's newly mended arm limited her ability to help him since the bad break, and now her talk of going to visit her sisters in Ohio felt like a push from *Gott*. Perhaps he would start considering the thought of a new wife, but she'd have to be special. What woman would want a husband who still loved his late wife? But he couldn't become someone like Adolph Yoder either, and leave his young children to suffer their mother's loss alone. Adolph's bitterness shook Mose to his foundation. Would he become like Adolph to satisfy his own selfish needs and not his daughters'?

Deep in thought, Mose pulled into the graveled drive and directed the horse under a shade tree. Sarah Nolt hurried out the door of the trim white farmhouse, her black mourning dress dancing around her ankles. She approached with a welcoming smile. In the sunlight her *kapp*-covered head made her hair look a bright copper color. A brisk breeze blew and long lengths of fine hair escaped and curled on the sides of her face. The black dress was plain, yet added color to her cheeks. Mose opened the buggy's door.

Beatrice crawled over him and hurried out. A striped kitten playing in the grass had attracted her attention. Mercy chose that moment to make her presence known and let loose a pitiful wail. Mose scooped the baby from the buggy floor.

Beatrice suddenly screamed and ran to her father, her arms wrapping around his leg. "Bad kitty." She held out a finger. A scarlet drop of blood landed on the front of the fresh white apron covering her dress.

Sarah took the baby and tucked the blanket around her bare legs as she slowly began to rock the upset child. Tear-filled blue eyes, edged in dark lashes, gazed up at the stranger. "Hello, little one."

Amazed, as always, that the tiny child could make so much noise, Mose watched as Sarah continued to rock the baby as she walked to the edge of the yard. Mose soothed Beatrice as Sarah moved about the garden with his crying infant.

Moments later Sarah approached with the quieted baby on her shoulder. "The *bobbel* has healthy lungs." She laughed.

Mose ruffled the blond curls on Mercy's head. "That she does. You didn't seem to have any trouble settling her."

"I used an old trick my *grandmammi* used on me. I distracted her with flowers."

Beatrice looked up at Sarah with a glare. "You're not Mercy's *mamm*." She pushed her face into the folds of her father's pant leg.

"I warned you. She's going to be a handful." Mose patted Beatrice's back.

Sarah handed the baby to Mose and dropped to her knees. Cupping a bright green grasshopper from the tall grass, she asked, "Do you like bugs, Beatrice?" She held out her closed hand and waited.

Beatrice turned and leaned against her father's legs, her eyes red-rimmed. "What kind of bug is it?" She stepped forward, her gaze on Sarah's extended hands.

Motioning the child closer, Sarah slightly opened her fingers and whispered, "Come and see." A tiny green head popped out and struggled to be free.

"Oh, *Daed*! Look," Beatrice said, joy sending her feet tapping.

Sarah opened her hand and laughed as the grasshopper leaped away, Beatrice right behind it, her little legs hopping through the grass, copying the fleeing insect.

Mose grinned as he watched his daughter's antics. "You might just have won her heart. How did you know she loves bugs?

"I've always been fascinated with *Gott's* tiny creatures. I had a feeling Beatrice might, too."

Mose's gaze held hers for a long moment until Sarah lost her smile, turned away and headed back into the house.

Chapter Two

Steam rose from the pot of potatoes boiling on the wood stove. The men would be in for supper soon and Sarah thanked *Gott* there'd only be two extra men tonight and not the twenty-five hungry workers she'd fed last night.

She glanced at the table and smiled as she watched Beatrice use broad strokes of paint to cover the art paper she'd given her. The child had been silent all afternoon, only speaking when spoken to. The pain in her eyes reminded Sarah of her own suffering. They grieved the same way—deep and silent with sudden bursts of fury. The child's need for love seemed so deep, the pain touched Sarah's own wounded heart.

Almost forgotten, Mercy lay content on her mat, a bottle of milk clutched in her hands. Her eyes traveled around, taking in the sights of the busy kitchen floor. The fluffy ginger kitten rushed past and put a smile on the baby's face. Sarah saw dimples press into her cheeks. If she and Joseph had had *kinder*, perhaps they would have looked like Mercy and Beatrice. Blonde-haired with a sparkle of mischief in their blue cyes.

Joseph's face swam before her tear-filled eyes. She missed the sound of his steps as he walked across the wooden porch each evening. His arms wrapped around her waist always had a way of reassuring her. She'd been loved. For that brief period of time, she'd been precious to someone, and she longed for that comfort again. Her arms had been empty but *Gott* placed these *kinder* here and she was grateful for the time she had with them.

"Would you like a glass of milk, Beatrice? I have a secret stash of chocolate chip cookies. I'd be glad to share them with such a talented artist."

"Nee," she said.

"Perhaps—"

"I want my *mamm*," Beatrice yelled, knocking the plastic tub of dirty water across the table and wetting herself and Sarah's legs.

Sarah stood transfixed as the child waited, perhaps expecting some kind of reprimand. There would be no scolding. Not today. Not ever. This child suffered and Sarah knew the pain of that suffering. She often felt like throwing things, expressing her own misery with actions that shocked.

Quiet and calm, Sarah mopped up the mud-colored water, careful not to damage Beatrice's art. "This would look lovely hung on my wall. Perhaps I could have it as a reminder of your visit?"

Beatrice looked down at her smock, at the merging colors against the white fabric, and began to cry deep, wrenching sobs. Unsure what else to do, Sarah prayed for guidance. She knelt on the floor, cleaned up the child before wrapping her arms around her trembling body. "I know you're missing your *mamm*, Beatrice. I miss my husband, too. He went to live in heaven several months ago and I want him back like you want your mother back."

"Did he read stories to you at bedtime?" Beatrice asked, her innocent gaze locked with Sarah's.

Their tears fell together on the mud-brown paint stain on Beatrice's smock. "Joseph didn't read to me, but he told me all about his day and kissed my eyes closed before I fell asleep." The ache became so painful Sarah felt she might die from her grief.

"My *mamm* said I was her big girl. Mercy was just born and cried a lot, but I was big and strong. I help *Grandmammi* take care of Mercy. Do you think *mamm's* proud of me?"

Sarah looked at the wet-faced child and a smile came out of nowhere. Beatrice was the first person who really understood what Sarah was living through, and that created a bond between them. They could grieve together, help one another. *Gott* in his wisdom had linked them for a week, perhaps more. Time enough for Beatrice to feel a mother's love again.

She would never heal from Joseph's death, but this tiny girl would give her purpose and a reason for living. She needed that right now. A reason to get up in the morning, put on her clothes and let the day begin.

The screen door banged open and Mose walked in, catching them in the warm embrace. Beatrice scurried out of Sarah's arms and into her father's cuddle. "Sarah likes me," she said and smiled shyly over at Sarah.

Mose peppered kisses on his daughter's neck and cheeks. "I see you've been painting again. How did this mess happen, Beatrice?"

"I was angry. I knocked down my paint water."

Beatrice braced her shoulders, obviously prepared to deal with any punishment her father administered.

"Did you apologize to Sarah for your outburst?"

"Nee." Beatrice rested her head on her father's dirty shirt.

"Perhaps an apology and help cleaning the mess off the floor is in order?" Mose looked at Sarah's frazzled hair and flushed cheeks.

"Sarah hugged me like *Mamm* used to. She smells of flowers. For a moment I thought *Mamm* had come back."

Sarah grabbed the cloth from the kitchen sink and busied herself cleaning the damp spot off the floor. She didn't know what Mose might think about the cluttered kitchen. Perhaps he'd feel she wasn't fit to take care of active *kinder.* She scrubbed hard into the wood. *Maybe I'm not fit to care for kinder.* She and the child had cried together. She was the adult. Shouldn't she have kept her own loss to herself?

"I'm sorry I made a mess, Sarah. I won't do it again. I promise."

Sarah looked into the eyes of an old soul just four years old. "It's time some color came into this dark kitchen, Beatrice. Your painting has put a smile on my face. There's no need for apologies." She smiled at the child and avoided Mose's face. She felt sure he'd have words for her later. She leaned toward Mercy, kissed her blond head as she toddled past, checked her over and then handed her a tiny doll with hair the color of corn silk. "Here you are, sweet one. You lost your baby." Sarah expected a smile from the adorable *bobble,* but the child's serious look remained.

Sarah scrambled to get off the floor. Mose stood over her, his big hand outstretched, offering to help.

She hesitated, but took his hand, feeling the warmth of his thick fingers and calloused palm. His strength was surprising. She felt herself pulled up, as if weightless. She refused to look into his eyes. She'd probably find anger there, and she couldn't handle his wrath just now. She'd be more careful to stay in control around the girls.

"You've broken through her hedge of protection." Mose leaned in close and whispered into Sarah's ear. She looked up, amazed to see a grin on his face, the presence of joy.

"I just—"

"*Nee*, you don't understand. You reached her, and for that I am most grateful."

Sarah didn't know what to say. She'd never received compliments such as this before, except from Joseph and her brother, Eric. Joseph had constantly told her how much he loved her and what a fine wife she made. Receiving praise from a stranger made her uncomfortable.

"I have supper to finish before my father returns. He likes his meal on the table at six sharp. If I hurry, I can avoid his complaints."

"I'm sure he'll understand the delay with two *kinder* underfoot."

"You don't know my father. He runs his home like most men run their business. I must hurry."

Sarah prepared the table with Beatrice trailing close behind. She let the child place the cloth napkins in the center of each plate and together they stood back and admired their handiwork.

Beatrice glanced around. "We forgot Mercy's cup."

"I have it in the kitchen, ready for milk." Sarah patted Beatrice's curly head.

"And the special spoon she eats from."

Sarah laughed at the organized child. Beatrice had the intensity of an older sister used to caring for her younger sister. "You'll make a great *mamm* someday," Sarah told her, moving the bowl of hot runner beans closer to her own plate. No sense risking a nasty burn from a child's eager hand.

"Do you think my *daed* will be proud of me?" Beatrice looked excited, her smile hopeful.

Sarah pulled the girl close and patted her back. "I'm sure he'll notice all your special touches."

"My *mamm* said… I'm sorry. My *grossmammi* said I was to forget my *mamm,* but it's hard not to remember."

Sarah's face flushed hot. How dare someone tell this young child to forget her *mamm*? Had her own mother missed her when she'd left the Amish community for the *Englisch*? She had no recollection of how her *mamm* looked. No pictures graced the mantel in her father's house. Plain people didn't allow pictures of their loved ones, and she had only childhood memories to rely on, which often failed her. If she brought up the subject of her mother to her father, there always had been a price to pay, so she'd stopped asking questions a long time ago.

"I believe remembering your mother will bring joy to your life. You hang on to your memories, little one."

A fat tear forced its way from the corner of Beatrice's eye. "Sometimes I can't remember what her voice sounds like. Does that mean I don't love her anymore?"

Sarah lifted the child into her arms and hugged her, rocking her like a baby. "*Nee*, Beatrice. Our human minds forget easily, but there will be times when you'll hear someone speak and you'll remember the sound of her voice and you'll rejoice in that memory."

Beatrice squeezed Sarah's neck. "I like you, Sarah. You help me remember to smile."

Sarah felt a grin playing on her own lips. Beatrice and Mercy had the same effect on her. They reminded her there was more to life than grief. She would always be grateful for her chance meeting with them, and Mose.

Bathed in the golden glow of the extra candle Beatrice had insisted on lighting before their supper meal, Mose noticed how different Sarah looked. Her hair had been neat and tidy under her stiff *kapp* earlier that morning, but now she looked mussed and fragile, as if her hair pins would fail her at any moment. He didn't have to ask if the *kinder* had been a challenge. She wasn't used to them around the house. He read the difficulty of her day in her pale face, too, and in the way she had avoided him the rest of the afternoon.

As if feeling his eyes on her, Sarah glanced up, a forkful of runner beans halfway to her mouth. Her smile was warm, but reserved. He needed to get her alone, tell her how much he appreciated her dealing with his daughters. He knew they were hard work. She deserved his gratitude. He'd worked hard on the barn teardown, endured the sun, but knew she'd worked harder.

"Beatrice tells me she had a lovely day." He smiled at his daughter's empty plate. It had been months since she'd eaten properly, and watching Beatrice gobble down her meal encouraged his heart.

Sarah and Beatrice exchanged a smile as if they had a secret all their own. "We spent the afternoon in the garden and drank lemonade with chunks of ice," Sarah said. "I learned a great deal about Mercy from your helpful daughter. She knows when her baby sister is hungry and just how to place a cloth on her bottom so it doesn't fall off. She's a wealth of information, and I needed her help." Sarah patted Beatrice's hand.

The child smiled up at her. "I ate everything on my plate. Is there ice cream for dessert?"

Mose found himself smiling like a young fool. Seeing his daughters back to normal seemed a miracle.

Adolph banged his fork down and dusted food crumbs from his beard. "There will be no ice cream in this house tonight. *Kinder* should be seen but not heard at the table. There'll be no reward for noise." He glared at Sarah, as if she'd done something terrible by drawing the child out of her shell.

"My *kinder* are encouraged to speak, Adolph. Beatrice has always been very vocal, and I believe feeling safe to speak with one's own parent an asset, not a detriment. I'm sure we can find another place to stay if their noise bothers you."

"There is no need for you to leave. I'm sure I can tolerate Beatrice's chatter for a few more days." Adolph frowned Sarah's way, his true feelings shown.

Mose fought back anger. He wondered what it must have been like to grow up with this tyrannical father lording over her.

As if to avoid the drama unfolding, Sarah pushed back in her chair and began to gather dishes.

"The meal was *wunderbaar*. You're an amazing cook," Mose said.

Sarah nodded her thanks, her eyes downcast, her hands busy with plates and glasses.

Beatrice grabbed her father's hand and pulled. "Let's go into the garden. I want to find the kitten." She jumped up and down with excitement.

Adolph scowled at the child.

Mose scooped Mercy from her pallet of toys and left the room in silence, Beatrice skipping behind. Seconds later, the back door banged behind them.

Mose heard Adolph roar. "You see what you did? Can I never trust you to do anything right?" Adolph walked out of the kitchen, leaving Sarah alone with her own thoughts.

Moments later the sound of splashing water and laughter announced a water fight had broken out in the backyard. Sarah longed to join in on the fun, but instead went for a stack of bath towels and placed three on the stool next to the back door and a thick one on the floor. Mose would need them when their play finished.

She peeked out the window, amazed to see Mose Fischer soaked from head to toe, his blond hair plastered to his skull like a pale helmet. Beatrice had him pinned to the ground. Water from the old hose sprayed his face. She'd had no intention of watching their play but was glad she had. Mose's patience with his daughter impressed her. Even young Mercy lay against her father's legs as if to hold him down so Beatrice could have her fun with him.

Their natural joy brought Joseph to mind. He'd been playful and full of jokes at times. It had taken her a while to get used to his ways when they'd first married, and she'd known he'd found her lacking. She'd soon grown used to his spirit and had found herself waiting with anticipation for him to come in from the fields. She missed the joy they'd shared. A tear caught her unaware. She brushed the dampness away and sat in her favorite rocker. Minutes passed. She listened to the *kinder's* laughter and then Mose's firm voice reminding them it was time for bed.

The quilt she was stitching was forgotten as soon as the back door flew open and three wet bodies rushed in. She laughed aloud as she watched Mose try to keep a hand on Beatrice while toweling Mercy dry.

"Would you like some help?"

"I think Mercy is more seal than child." He fought to hold on to her slippery body. Mercy was all smiles, her water-soaked diaper dripping on the kitchen floor.

Sarah rushed over and took the baby. The child trembled with cold and was quickly engulfed in a warm, fluffy towel. Sarah led the way to the indoor bathroom, baby in arms. Mose filled the tub with water already heated on the wood stove. Sarah added cold water, checked the temperature of the water, found it safe and sat Mercy down with a splash. Mercy gurgled in happiness as Sarah poured water over her shoulders and back.

"You're a natural at this." Mose spoke behind her.

Sarah reached around for Beatrice's hand and the child jumped into the water with all the gusto of a happy fish. Water splashed and Sarah's frock became wet from neck to hem. She found herself laughing with the *kinder*. Her murmurs of joy sounded foreign to her own ears. *How long has it been since I giggled like this?*

In the small confines of the bathroom, Sarah became aware of Mose standing over her. "I'm sure I can handle the bath. Why don't you join my father for a chat while I get these *lieblings* ready for bed?"

Beatrice splashed more water. Mercy cried out and reached for Sarah. Grabbing a clean washcloth from the side of the tub, Sarah wiped water from the baby's eyes. "You have to be careful, Beatrice." She held on to the baby's arm and turned to reach for a towel. Mose had left the room silently. She thought back to what she had said and hoped he hadn't felt dismissed.

The girls finally asleep and her father in his room with the door closed, Sarah dried the last of the dishes and put them away. Looking for a cool breeze, she stepped out the back door and sat on the wooden steps. Her long, plain dress covered her legs to her ankles.

Fireflies flickered in the air, their tiny glow appearing and disappearing. She took in a long, relaxing breath and smelled honeysuckle on the breeze. Somewhere an insect began its lovesick song. Sarah lifted her voice in praise to the Lord, the old Amish song reminding her how much *Gott* once had loved her.

"Dein heilig statthond sie zerstort, dein Atler umbgegraben Darzu auch dein knecht ermadt..."

No one except Marta knew how much she'd hated *Gott* when Joseph had first died. She'd railed at Him, her loss too great to bear. But then she'd remembered the gas light in the barn and how she'd left it on for the old mother cat giving birth to fuzzy balls of damp fluff. She'd sealed Joseph's fate by leaving that light burning. When she woke suddenly in the night, she'd heard her husband's screams of agony as he tried to get out of the burning barn. Her own hands had been scorched as she'd fought to get to him. She hadn't been able reach him and she'd given up. She'd failed him. He had died a horrible death. Her beloved Joseph had died, they'd said, of smoke inhalation, his body just bones and ashes inside his closed casket. She stopped singing and put her head down to weep.

"Something wrong, or are you just tired?" Mose spoke from a porch chair behind her.

With only the light coming through the kitchen window, Sarah turned. She strained to see Mose. "I'm sorry. I didn't know you were there." She wiped the tears off her face and moved to stand.

"*Nee.* Don't go, please. I want to talk to you about Beatrice, if that's all right."

Sarah prepared herself for his disapproval. She'd heard it before from other men in the community when she'd broken *Ordnung* willfully. The Bishop especially seemed hard on her. She sat, waited.

Mose cleared his throat and began to talk. "I wanted to tell you how much I appreciate your taking such good care of my girls. They haven't been this happy in a long time, not even with their *grandmammi*."

Sarah touched the cross hanging under the scoop of her dress, the only thing she had left from her mother. If her father knew she had the chain and cross, he would destroy them. "I did nothing special, Mose. I treated the *kinder* like my mother treated me. Your girls are delightful, and I enjoy having them here. They make my life easier." She clamped her mouth shut. She'd said too much. Plain people didn't talk about their problems and she had to keep reminding herself to be silent about the pain.

"Well, I think it's *wunderbaar* you were able to reach Beatrice. I've been very concerned about her, and now I can rest easy. She has someone to talk to who understands loss."

Understands? *Oh, I understand.* The child hurt physically, as if someone had cut off an arm or leg and left her to die of pain. "I'm glad I was able to help." She rose. "Now, I need to prepare for breakfast. Tomorrow is going to be a busy day for both of us. There is food to cook, a barn to haul away."

"Wait, before you go. I have an important question to ask you."

Sarah nodded her head and sat back down.

"I stayed up until late last night, thinking about your situation and mine. I prayed and prayed, and *Gott* kept pushing this thought at me." He took a deep breath. "I wonder, would you consider becoming my *frau*?"

Sarah held up her hand as if to stop his words. "I…"

"*Nee*, wait. Before you speak, let me explain." Mose took another deep breath and began. "I know you still love Joseph and probably always will, just as I still love my Greta. But I have *kinder* who need a mother to guide and love them. Now that Joseph's gone and your *daed* insists the farm is to be sold, you'll need a place to call home, people who care about you, a family. We can join forces and help each other." He saw panic form in her eyes. "Wait. Let me finish, please. It would only be a marriage of convenience, with no strings attached. I would love you as a sister and you would be under my protection. The girls need a loving mother and you've already proven you can be that. What do you say, Sarah Nolt. Will you be my wife?"

Sarah sat silently in the chair, her face turned away. She turned back toward Mose and looked into his eyes. "You'd do this for me? But…you don't know me."

"I'd do this for us," Mose corrected and smiled.

The tips of Sarah's fingers nervously pleated and unpleated a scrap of her skirt. "We hardly know each other. You must realize I'll never love you the way you deserve."

"I know how much Joseph meant to you. He was like a *bruder* to me. You'd have to take second place in my heart, too. Greta will always be my one and only love." Mose watched her nervous fingers work the material, knowing this conversation was causing her more stress. He waited.

She glanced at him. "I'd want the *kinder* to think we married for love. I hope they can grow to respect me as their parent. I know it won't be the same deep love they had for their *mamm*. I'll do everything I can to help them remember her."

"I'm sure they'll grow to love you. In fact, I think they already do." Mose fumbled for words, feeling young and awkward, something he hadn't felt in a very long time. He'd never thought he'd get married again, but *Gott* seemed to be in this and his *kinder* needed Sarah. She needed them. If she said no to his proposal he'd have to persuade her, but he had no idea how he'd manage it. She was proud and headstrong.

"What would people think? They will say I took advantage of your good nature."

Mose smiled. "So, let them talk. They'd be wrong and we'd know it. I want this marriage for both of us, for the *kinder*. We can't let others decide what is best for our lives. I believe this marriage is *Gott's* plan for us."

Sarah's face cleared and she seemed to come to a decision. She smoothed out the fabric of her skirt and tidied her hair, then finally took Mose's outstretched hand with a smile. "You're right. This is our life. I accept your proposal, Mose Fischer. I will be your *frau* and your *kinder's* mother."

Sarah paused for a moment, then spoke. "Being your wife brings obligations. I expect you to honor my grief until such a time I can become your wife in both name and deed, as a good man deserves." She looked him in the eye, seeking understanding. He deserved a woman's love and she had none to give him right now.

Mose smiled and nodded, gave her a hand up and stepped back. "I wish there was something I could do to help you in your grief."

Sarah didn't know what to say. Few people had offered her a word of sympathy when she'd lost Joseph. They'd felt she'd caused his death. "I'm fine, really. I just need time." She lied because if she said anything else, she would be crying in this stranger's arms.

"Time does help, Sarah. Time and staying busy."

She could feel his gaze on her. She hid every ache and hardened her heart. This was the Amish way. "*Ya*, time and work. Everyone tells me this."

"Take your time, grieve." He murmured the words soft and slow.

Her heart in shreds, she would not talk of grief with him, not with anyone. "I don't want to talk anymore." She moved past him and through the door, ignoring the throbbing veins at her temples. She would never get over this terrible loss deep in her heart. This unbearable pain was her punishment from *Gott*.

Mose wished he'd kept his mouth shut. He'd caused her more pain, reminding her of what she'd lost. Joseph had been a good man, full of life and fun. He'd loved *Gott* with all his heart and had dedicated himself to the Lord early in life. His baptism had been allowed early. Most Amish teens were forced to wait until they were sure of their dedication to *Gott* and their community, after their *rumspringa*, when they're time to experience the Englisch world was over and decisions made, but not Joseph. Everyone had seen his love for *Gott*, his kindness, strength and purity. He felt the painful loss of Joseph. What must Sarah feel? Like Joseph, she seemed sure of herself, able to face any problem with strength…but there was something else. She carried a cloud of misery over her, which told him she suffered a great deal. What else could have happened to make her so miserable?

He heard a window open upstairs and movement, perhaps Sarah preparing for bed. Mose laughed quietly. Was he so desperate for a mother for his *kinder* that he had proposed marriage to a woman so in love with her dead husband she could hardly stand his touch? They both had to dig themselves out of their black holes of loss and begin life anew. Could marriage be the way? He knew he would never love again, yet his *kinder* needed a mother. Was he too selfish to provide one for them? Would marrying again be fair to any woman he found suitable to raise his *kinder*? No woman wanted a lovesick fool, such as he, on their arm. They wanted courtship, the normal affection of their husband, but he had none to give. He was an empty shell. Mose looked out over the tops of tall trees to the stars. *Gott* was somewhere watching, wondering why He'd made a fool like Mose Fischer. Stars twinkled and suddenly a shooting star flashed across the sky, its tail flashing bright before it disappeared into nothingness. It had burned out much like his heart.

Chapter Three

Sarah's eyes were red-rimmed and puffy. She placed her *kapp* just so and made sure its position was perfect, as if the starched white prayer *kapp* would make up for her tear-ravaged face.

"My mother wore a *kapp* like that, but it looked kind of different." Beatrice clambered onto the dressing table's stool next to Sarah.

"It probably was different, sweetheart. Lots of Amish communities wear different styles of *kapps* and practice different traditions."

"How come girls wear them and not boys?" Beatrice reached out and touched the heavily starched material on Sarah's head.

"Several places in the Bible tell women to cover their heads, so we wear the *kapps* and show *Gott* we listen to His directions." Sarah wished she could pull off the cap, throw it to the ground and stomp on it. Covering her head didn't make her a better person. Love did. And she loved this thin, love-starved child and her sweet baby sister. She felt such a strong need to make things easier for Beatrice and Mercy. "Would you like to help me make pancakes?"

As if on a spring, the child jumped off the stool and danced around the room, making Mercy laugh out loud and clap her hands. "Pancakes! My favoritest thing in the whole wide world."

Sarah pushed a pin into her pulled-back hair and glanced at her appearance in the small hand mirror for a moment longer. She looked terrible and her stomach was upset, probably the result of such an emotional night. She'd lain awake for hours, unable to stop thinking about her promise to wed Mose. She'd listened to the *kinder's* soft snores and movements, thinking about Joseph and their lost life together.

Gott had spoken loud and clear to her this morning. The depression and grief she suffered were eating up her life. She'd never have the love of her own *kinder* if she didn't come out of this black mood and live again. But why would Mose want her as a wife, damaged as she was?

"Your eyes are red. Are you going to cry some more?" Beatrice jumped off the bench and danced around, her skirt whirling.

The child heard me crying last night. She forced herself to laugh and join in the child's silly dancing. Hand in hand they whirled about, circling and circling until both were dizzy and fell to the floor, their laughter filling the room.

A loud knock came and her father opened the door wide. "What's all this noise so early in the morning?"

Her joy died a quick death. "Beatrice and I were—"

"I see what you're doing. Foolishness. You're making this child act as foolish as you. It's time for breakfast.

Go to the kitchen and be prepared for at least twenty-five men to eat. We have more work to do now that the old barn is to be towed away. We'll need nourishment for the hard day ahead."

Beatrice snuggled close to Sarah, her arms tight around her neck. "This may be your home, but you're out of line, *Daed*. Close the door behind you. We will be down when the *kinder's* needs are met." Sarah looked him hard in the eyes, her tone firm.

Her father's angry glare left her filled with fury. She hated living at his farm, at his mercy. She longed to be in her own home two miles down the dusty road. She would not let him throw his bitterness the *kinder's* way. She'd talk to him in private and make things very clear. She'd be liberated from his control once she and Mose were married. But, right now she was still a widow and had to listen to his demands. But not for long. *Gott* had provided her a way to get away from his control.

"Come darling, let's get Mercy out of her cot and make those pancakes. We have a long day of cooking ahead of us and need some healthy food in our bellies."

"Is that mean man your *daed*?" Beatrice asked.

Sarah helped her off the floor. *"Ya."* She lifted Mercy from her cot and nuzzled her nose in the baby's warm, sweet-smelling neck. She checked her diaper and found she needed changing. Mercy wiggled in her arms, a big grin pressing dimples in her cheeks. She held the warm baby close to her and thanked *Gott* her father's harsh words hadn't seemed to scare the baby.

Watching her sister get a fresh diaper, Beatrice spoke, "Why is he so angry? I don't think he loves you." Confusion clouded Beatrice's face, a frown creasing her brow.

"Of course he loves me," Sarah assured her. But as she finished changing Mercy's diaper, she wondered. *Does he love me?*

The narrow tables lined up on the grass just outside Sarah's kitchen door didn't look long enough for twenty-five men, but she knew from experience they would suffice. She, Marta and three local women laughed and chatted as they covered the handmade tables with bright white sheets and put knives, forks and cloth napkins at just the right intervals.

As the men began gathering, Sarah placed heaping platters of her favorite breakfast dish made of sausage, potatoes, cheese, bread, onions and peppers in the middle of each table and at the ends. Bowls of fresh fruit, cut bite-size, added color to the meal. Heavy white plates, one for each worker, lined the tables. Glasses of cold milk sat next to each plate.

"The table looks very nice," Marta whispered.

"It looks hospital sterile." Sarah loved color. Bold, bright splashes of color. What would happen if she'd used the red table napkins she'd hemmed just after Joseph died? In her grief she'd had to do something outrageous, or scream in her misery. She longed to use the napkins for this occasion. Bright colors were considered a sin to Old Order Amish. *How could Gott see color as a sin?* Some of the limitations she lived under made no sense at all.

"We're plain people, Sarah. *Gott* warned us against adorning ourselves and our lives with bright colors. They attract unwanted attention." Marta straightened a white napkin and smiled at Sarah.

"I know what the Bishop says, Marta, but I think too

many of our community rules are the Bishop's rules and have nothing at all to do with what *Gott* wants. The older he gets, the more unbearable his 'must not's and should not's' get."

"Everything looks good," Marta said in a loud voice, drowning out Sarah's last comment. Bishop Miller's wife walked past and straightened several forks on the table close to Sarah.

Marta rushed back into the kitchen, her hand a stranglehold on Sarah's wrist. "Do you think she heard you?"

"Who?"

"Bishop Miller's wife."

"I don't care if she did."

"Well, you should care. I know she's a sweet old woman and always kind to me, but she tells her husband everything that goes on in the community, and you know it."

Sarah shrugged and looked out the kitchen window, watching Mose approach the porch and settle in a chair too small for his big frame. Her future husband wore a pale blue shirt today, his blond hair damp from sweat and plastered down under his straw work hat. Beatrice left the small *kinder's* table and crawled into her father's lap, her arms sliding around the sweaty neck of his shirt.

"That child loves her *daed*." Marta grabbed a pickle from one of the waiting plates of garnish.

"She does. It's a shame she has *nee* mother to cuddle her."

"I'm worried about you, Sarah. Lately all you do is daydream and mope."

Sarah considered telling Marta her news but decided against it. Marta would never approve of a loveless marriage. "Don't worry about me. I'll be fine. I like hav-

ing the *kinder* here. They've brightened my spirits. I've
never had a chance to really get close to a child before.
They can make my day better with just a laugh. They
are really into climbing, even Mercy. This morning I
caught her throwing her leg over her cot rail. She could
have fallen if I hadn't been close enough to catch her.
I'm going to see if someone has a bigger bed for her
today. She's way too active to manage in that small bed
Daed found in the attic."

Sarah grabbed two pitchers of cold milk and headed
out the back door.

"Is there more food? These men are hungry." Adolph
grabbed Sarah by the arm as she passed through the
door, his fingers pinching into her flesh.

"*Ya*, of course. I'll bring out more." She placed the
pitchers on the table and returned the friendly smile
Mose directed her way.

"See that you do," her father barked, as if he were
talking to a child. He moved down the table, greeting
each worker with a handshake and friendly smile.

Sarah hurried into the kitchen and grabbed a plate
of hot pancakes from the oven and rushed back out the
kitchen door, a big jar of fresh, warmed maple syrup
tucked under her arm. Her father was right about one
thing. The men were eating like an army.

The last of the horse-drawn wagons carrying burned
wood pulled out of the yard and down the lane, heading for the dump just outside town.

Mose grabbed the end of a twelve-foot board, pulled
it over and nailed it into the growing frame with three
strong swings of the hammer. A brisk breeze lifted the
straw hat he wore, almost blowing it off his head. He

smashed it down on his riot of curls and went back to work. The breeze was welcome on the unseasonably hot morning.

"Won't be much longer now," the man working next to Mose muttered. The board the man added would finish the last of the barn's frame, and then the hard work of lifting the frames would begin.

Sweat-soaked and hungry, Mose glanced at the noon meal being served up a few yards away and saw Sarah carrying a plate piled high with potato pancakes. She'd been in and out of the house all morning, her face flushed from the heat of the kitchen. Beatrice trailed behind her, a skip in her steps and the small bowl of some type of chow-chow relish dripping yellow liquid down the front of her apron as she bounced.

He laughed to himself, taking pleasure in seeing Beatrice so content. Sarah had a natural way with *kinder*. She'd make a fine mother.

"Someone needs to deal with that woman."

"Who?" Mose turned his head, surprised at the comment. He looked at the man who'd spoken and frowned. Standing with his hands on his hips, the man's expression dug deep caverns into his face, giving Mose the impression of intense anger.

"The Widow Nolt, naturally. Who else? Everyone knows she killed Joseph with her neglect. Bishop Miller might as well shun her now and get it over with. No one wants her in the community anymore. She causes trouble and doesn't know when to keep her mouth shut."

Mose mopped at the sweat on his forehead. "What do you mean, she killed Joseph? There's no way she's capable of doing something like that. The police said he died of smoke inhalation."

Stretching out his back and twisting, the man worked out the kinks from his tall frame, his eyes still on Sarah. "She did it, all right, *bruder*. She left the light on in the barn, knowing gas lights get hot and cause fires."

"I'm sure she just forgot to turn it off. People forget, you know." Mose knew he was wasting his breath. Some liked to think the worst of people, especially people like Sarah, who were powerless to defend themselves.

"Sarah Nolt is that kind of woman. Her own father says she's always been careless, even as a child."

"I believe *Gott* would have us pray for our sister, not slander her for something that took her husband's life."

"Well, you can stand up for her if you like, but I'm not. She's a bad woman, and I wouldn't be here today if it weren't for my respect for Joseph. He was a good man."

"He'd want you to help Sarah, not slander her." Mose threw down the hammer. His temper would always be a fault he'd have to deal with, and right now he'd best move away or he'd end up punching a man in the mouth.

The food bell rang out. He dusted as much of the sawdust off his clothes as he could. Still angry, he moved toward the long table set up in the grass and took the seat closest to the door. A tall glass of cold water was placed in front of him by a young girl. *"Danke."* He downed the whole glass.

"You're *welkom*," the girl muttered and refilled his glass. Mose watched Sarah as she served the men around him. She acted polite and kind to everyone, but not one man spoke to her. The women seemed friendlier but still somewhat distant. He saw her smile once or twice before he dug into his plate of tender roast beef, stuffed cabbage rolls and Dutch green beans. Sarah knew her way around a kitchen. The food he ate was hardy and spiced to perfection.

A group of men seated around the Bishop began to mutter. A loud argument broke out and Mose could hear Sarah's name being bandied about. Marta hurried past, her face flushed, and the promise of tears glistening in her eyes. Her small-framed shoulders drooped as she made her way into the house. Soon Sarah was out the door, her eyes locked on Bishop Miller who sat a few seats from Mose.

"You have much to say about me today, Bishop Miller. Would you like to say the words to my face?" Her small hands were fisted, her back straight and strong as she glared at the community leader.

Adolph shoved back his chair and stood.

"Shut your mouth, Sarah Yoder. I will not have you speak to the Bishop like this. You are out of line. You will speak to him with respect."

"My name is Nolt, *Daed*. No longer Yoder. And I will not be told to hush like some young *bensel*. If the Bishop has something to say, he need only open his mouth or call one of his meetings."

Mose rose. *Gott, hold Sarah's tongue.* She had already dug a deep well of trouble with her words. Her actions were unwise, but he would not stand by and watch her be pulled down further by her father's lack of protection. Let the Bishop show proof of her actions and present them in a proper setting if he had issues with her.

Bishop Miller's wife hurried to Sarah and put her arms around her trembling body. "Let us leave all this for today and have cold tea in the kitchen. We're all tired and nerves frayed. Today a barn goes up. It is a happy day, Sarah. One full of promise. Let us celebrate and not speak words that cannot be taken back."

Mose waited, wondering if Sarah would relent. She turned and stared deep into the eyes of the woman next to her. Moments passed and then she crumbled, tears running down her face as she was escorted away.

Mose watched the door shut behind the women. He longed to know if Sarah was all right but knew she wouldn't want him interfering. "What's going on?" Mose murmured to Eric, Sarah's brother.

"Someone has found proof that Sarah was the one who gave money to Lukas, a young teenager who recently ran away from the community."

"Money? Why would she do that?" They spoke in whispers, his food forgotten.

"I only heard a moment of conversation but it seems *Daed* saw her speaking with the boy's younger brother the day before Lukas took him and left for places unknown."

"That's not solid proof. Sarah must be given a chance to redeem herself."

"She'll get her chance. A meeting has been called, and I plan to talk to Bishop Miller before it comes around. I suspect she'll be shunned, but I have to make an effort to calm the waters. Lord alone knows what would happen to her if she's forced to live amongst the *Englisch*." Eric got up to leave, but turned back to Mose. "Marta's offered to look after the *kinder* at our house until tomorrow. Sarah is too upset to think clearly."

Tired from the long day of cooking and cleaning, Sarah lay across her childhood bed on the second floor of her father's house, her pillow wet from tears. She cried for Joseph, for the life she'd lost with him, and for the loneliness she'd felt every day since he'd died. She needed Joseph and he was gone forever.

Marta held her hand in a firm grip. "You mustn't fret so, Sarah. The children can stay with Eric and me tonight. Most likely you will be given a talking to tomorrow and nothing more."

"And if I'm shunned, what then? You and Eric won't be allowed to talk to me. The whole community will say I'm dead to them. Who will I call family?"

"Why did you give Lukas money? You knew you ran the risk of being found out."

Sarah sat up, tucking her dress under her legs. Marta handed her a clean white handkerchief and watched as Sarah wiped the tears off her face. "I couldn't take it anymore. Every day I heard the abuse. Every day I heard the boys crying out in pain."

"Did you talk to any of the elders about this?"

"I talked to them but they put me off, said I was a woman and didn't understand the role a father played in a boy's life." Sarah blew her nose and tried to regain control of the tremors that shook her body.

"But surely beating a young boy senseless is not in *Gott's* plan. Do you believe your *daed* would tell on you if he knew it was you who gave the boys money?"

"Of course he would, but he didn't know. I made sure he was gone the day I slipped money to Lukas."

"Then how?"

Sarah smoothed the wrinkles out of her quilt and set the bed back in order. "It doesn't matter now."

"How would you survive among the *Englisch*? You know nothing about them. Your whole life has been

Amish. I fear for you, Sarah." Marta brushed away her tears as they continued to fall.

A shiver ran through Sarah as she thought about what Marta said. She wouldn't be strong enough to endure the radical changes that would have faced her. Thank *Gott* for Mose's offer of marriage, for the opportunity to go to Sarasota and leave all this behind. But would he want to marry her if she was shunned and was she prepared for a loveless marriage? She feared not. *Gott's will. Grab hold of Gott's will.*

Chapter Four

❧

Sarah roamed through the small farmhouse, gathering memories of Joseph and their time together. She had no picture to keep him alive in her mind, only objects she could touch to feel closer to him.

A sleepless night at her father's farm, after her confrontation with the bishop, had left her depressed and bone tired.

Downstairs, she smiled as she picked up a shiny black vase from the kitchen window. When Joseph had bought it that early spring morning, he'd known he'd broken one of the Old Order Amish *Ordnung* laws laid down by Bishop Miller. The vase was a token of Joseph's love. It was to hold the wildflowers they gathered on their long walks in the meadows. The day he'd surprised her with the vase she'd cried for joy. Now it felt cold and empty like her broken heart. The vase was the only real decoration in the farmhouse, as was custom, but their wedding quilt, traditionally made in honor of their wedding by the community's sewing circle, hung on the wall in the great room.

In front of the wide kitchen windows, she fingered

the vase's smooth surface, remembering precious moments. Their wedding, days of visiting family and friends, the first time she'd been allowed to see the farmhouse he'd built with other men from the area. He'd laughed at her as she'd squealed with delight. The simple, white two-story house was to be their home for the rest of their lives. He'd gently kissed her and whispered, "I love you."

Moved to tears, her vision blurred. She stumbled to the stairs and climbed them one by one, her head swimming with momentary dizziness. On the landing she caught her breath before walking into their neat, tiny bedroom. Moments later she found the shirt she'd made for Joseph to wear on their wedding day hanging in the closet next to several work shirts and two of her own plain dresses.

Sarah tucked the blue shirt on top of a pile of notes and papers she'd put in the brown valise just after he'd died. He used the heavy case when he'd taken short trips to the Ohio Valley area communities to discuss the drought. In a few days she'd use it to pack and leave this beloved farmhouse forever.

Her dresses and his old King James Bible, along with the last order for hayseeds written in his bold print, went into the case. The Book of Psalms she'd given him at Christmas slipped into her apron pocket with ease. Her memories of him would be locked away in this heavy case, the key stashed somewhere safe.

Most of her other clothes and belongings would be left. She'd have no need for them now. Mose would take care of her. A fresh wave of anxiety flushed through her. She had no idea if she could go through with this marriage.

She thought back to Joseph and wondered what he'd think of the drama surrounding her. *He'd be disappointed.* He'd followed the tenets of the Old Order church faithfully. The rules of the community were a way of life he'd gladly accepted. Yes, he'd be disappointed in her.

She faced shunning. Bishop Miller preached that those who were shunned or left the faith would go to hell. Joseph was with the Lord. *I'd never see my husband again.*

A wave of dizziness caught her unaware and she grabbed the bed's railings to steady herself. Moments later, disoriented and sick to her stomach, she sat on the edge of the bed and waited for the world to stop spinning. All the stress had frayed her nerves and made her ill.

A loud knock came from downstairs. Sarah froze. She didn't want to talk to anyone, not even Marta, but knew she'd have to see her before she left. There were others in the community she'd miss, too. Her distant family members, her old schoolteacher, the friendly *Englisch* woman at the sewing store…all the people who meant everything to her. They'd wonder what really had happened, why she suddenly had disappeared, but she knew someone would tell them what she'd done. Her head dropped. A wave of nausea rolled her stomach, twisting it in knots.

The knock became louder, more insistent. She moved to the bedroom window. No buggy was parked out front. Perhaps one of the neighborhood *kinder* was playing a joke on her. She checked the front steps and saw the broad frame of a man. Had her father come to give her one last stab to the heart? It would be just like him to come and taunt her about her coming marriage to Mose.

"Sarah? Are you there? Please let me in."

Mose's voice called from her doorstep. He sounded concerned, perhaps even alarmed. Had something happened to one of the *kinder*? Why would he seek her out? He'd heard it all. He was an elder in his community. Even if he wasn't Old Order Amish and didn't live as strict a life as she did, but he'd be angry she'd given the boys money and would judge her. Still, he was a good man, a kind man. Perhaps he just wanted to talk to her.

The thought of his kindness had her rushing down the stairs and opening the heavy wood door Joseph had made with his own hands. She used the door as a shield, opening it just a crack. *"Ya?"* She could see a slice of him, his hair wind-blown, blue eyes searching her face.

"Hello, Sarah. I thought I might find you here."

She nodded her head in greeting.

"Are you all right?" Mose's hand rested on the doorjamb, as if he expected to be let into the house.

Sarah held the door firm. "I'm fine. What do you want, Mose? I have things to do. I'm very busy."

"I'm worried about you. You've been through so much."

"And none of it is your business," Sarah snapped, instantly wishing she could take back her bitter words. He'd done nothing but be kind to her. She missed the girls and wondered how they were, if Marta was still caring for them. She pushed strands of hair out of her eyes and searched his expression. She saw no signs of judgment.

"You're right. All this is none of my business, but

I am soon to be your husband. I want to help, if I can. Please, can I come in for a moment?"

On trembling legs, she stepped back to open the door all the way. "Come in."

Mose stepped past Sarah into the silent house. Sarah glanced around. Nothing seemed out of place. There was no dust, no evidence anyone even lived here.

He turned back to Sarah. "I tried to find you after everyone left yesterday. Beatrice was asking for you. *Kinder* don't understand why adults do what they do."

"I did what everyone is saying," Sarah blurted out, then offered a seat to Mose, but stood, swaying to and fro.

"Sit with me before you fall, you stubborn woman." Mose took Sarah's elbow, guided her to a wood-framed rocking chair with a padded seat and back rest. She didn't resist, but once down, her fingers went white-knuckled on the chair's arms.

Mose sat on the couch opposite her. "You said there was no misunderstanding. Did you give the boy money so he and his brother could leave the community as the bishop said?"

"*Ya.* I did."

"Why did you help them? They have a father who's very worried about them," Mose said.

"I'm sure he is concerned. He needs their strong backs to run his farm. They're better off away from him." Sarah stared into space, her features ridged, unrelenting.

"You've heard from them?"

She looked at him. "*Ya,* I did. They're staying with their sister, Katherine, in Missouri. She took them in after…" Her voice trailed off.

"After what, Sarah?" Emotions played on her face. Something was not being said. Mose felt sure she'd acted out of kindness. He hadn't known her long but felt sure she wasn't the type to interfere in other people's business, especially to separate a family.

Sarah drew in a ragged breath. "After the boy's father beat Lukas until he could barely move, that's what. His *bruder*, Ben, was getting older and had begun to talk back to his father, too. Lukas knew it was only a matter of time before his *daed* would use the strap on him. Lukas asked me to help them get away. I knew the boy was telling the truth about the risks of more violent beatings. They were in danger.

"Lukas's father is a harsh man and had taken to drink. He took his anger out on his sons when the crops failed or something went wrong. Lukas had made the mistake of asking to go on *rumspringa* with some of his friends in the next community, and his father had flown into a rage. This beating wasn't the first Lukas had endured, but it was the worst. He was often whipped with a cane. I could hear his cries for mercy blowing across the field that separates our land. Joseph and I had often prayed for the boys, asking *Gott* for a hedge of protection." Sarah swallowed hard and went on. "Joseph wouldn't stand for the whippings and had warned the father, even threatened to talk to Bishop Miller about the situation…but after Joseph died, the beatings began again."

Mose reached across and took one of Sarah's hands and squeezed. Her fingers were cold and stiff. "Does Bishop Miller know all this?"

Sarah jerked her hand back. "I tried to tell him many times, but he told me to keep my nose out of other people's business. He said men were supposed to discipline their *kinder*, but this wasn't discipline, Mose. This was pure abuse." Sarah pushed back her hair and gasped. "Oh, I'm sorry. I didn't realize my *kapp* was missing. It must have fallen off when I…" Her head dropped and she sat perfectly still.

"When you what, Sarah?"

"I almost fainted. I've been ill and forgot to eat this morning."

"You need to be in bed with someone taking care of you."

"*Nee*, that's not possible. The Bishop's called a meeting. I decided I must be there to defend my actions. I have to at least try."

Mose watched her as she spoke. He could see she was terrified of being shunned. Who wouldn't be? As strict as Bishop Miller was, anything was possible, including shunning. "I could speak to the Bishop and the elders and see if—"

"*Nee, danke* for offering, but I'd rather you didn't."

"He may still declare you shunned, even if we marry and you leave the community."

She paled a chalky white. "But…I thought if I left, all that could be avoided."

"*Nee*. I don't think he's feeling generous, but I could be wrong."

"Then shunned it is. I'll have to learn to live with it, though I don't know how."

Mose leaned forward, their gaze connecting. He meant it when he'd promised security, strength. Things she no longer had. "Don't fret, Sarah. *Gott* will make a way."

Sarah checked the position of her *kapp* and dreaded

the thought of what was about to take place this evening. Mose sat tall and straight, his hands folded in his lap, the picture of calm. She wished she had his determination. She was too emotional lately. Everything seemed so hard, as though she was climbing a hill, her feet sliding out from under her in slippery mud.

The moments ticked by. The room darkened as dusk surrendered to the shadows of night.

The heavy door to the bishop's chambers opened with a squeak. Sarah jumped.

Mose stood, pulling her up off the chair as he took his first step forward. She hesitated. He turned back to her. "All will be well, Sarah. Leave it to me. I will be your strength."

She knew the bishop. Doubt flooded in. She tried to clear her thoughts and prepare herself for the ugly confrontation.

An old wood table with chairs all around filled the small, stifling room. "Sit here, Sarah, and you there, Mose," Karl Yoder prompted, motioning to two empty chairs positioned at the middle of the table. The position would place them directly across from Bishop Miller. The elder walked with them toward their chairs. A distant cousin, she'd known Karl all her life. He'd been Sarah's favorite church leader growing up. She'd gone to him and his wife when life had gotten to be more than she could bear as a teenager. She wondered what he thought of her now. He looked stern, but flashed a smile, giving her hope.

Hands were extended to Mose as he greeted each man. He introduced himself to those who didn't know him. Sarah counted six men at the table. Sneaking a glance at Bishop Miller, she saw his jaw tighten. Just for a second their eyes met and she quickly looked away, only to notice her father sitting bent over in the corner of the room. She averted her gaze and looked down at the floor. Her hands gripped in a knot on her lap. She waited. Mose cleared his throat, the only nervous sound he'd made since they'd come into the room.

Ernst Miller, the bishop's son, stood. "This meeting is called to discuss the matter of Sarah Nolt."

Off to the side, Sarah's father rose, almost knocking over his seat. He blurted out, "I want to know why Mose Fischer is allowed to sit in on this meeting? He's not a member of our community. What's going on today has nothing to do with him."

"All will be explained in good time," Ernst assured him and motioned for Adolph to take his seat.

The high color in her father's cheeks told her he was in a fine temper and nothing they said would keep him calm.

"As I was saying," Ernst continued, his tone holding a slight edge. "We are here to discuss the recent actions of Sarah Nolt." His gaze drifted to Sarah.

She looked directly in his eyes. *Don't let him ask me about the beatings.* She had enough problems without stirring up a hornet's nest of accusations against her neighbor, accusations she couldn't prove.

"How well did you know Lukas and Benjamin Hochstetler?"

"Not well," she replied. "I knew they lived at the farm next to ours. They moved in several weeks after Joseph and I married." Bringing up Joseph's name set her heart pounding. She paused for a few seconds and then continued, "I used to take the boys drinks of cool water on hot afternoons when they'd plowed the field closest to our home."

"So you did get to know them well?" Ernst asked.

"Not really. They were always busy about the farm and I seldom left the house, so that didn't leave much time for socializing."

"But you spoke to them from time to time?"

"Yes, I did. I liked the boys. They were lonely, hard-working *kinder* and seldom saw people other than their fa—"

"How did you hear they had run away and ended up in Missouri?" The bishop spoke up, stepping on her last word. Ernst sat down, content to let his father continue.

Sarah pulled her feet under her skirt. *How do I answer this without digging up more dirt?* "I received a letter."

"A letter from Lukas?"

"*Nee.* The letter was from Benjamin."

The Bishop's voice rose. "Not from Lukas?"

"*Nee.*" Sarah shook her head.

Bishop Miller leaned forward on his elbows. "What did the letter say?"

Sarah couldn't help but smile, remembering Benjamin's barely legible scrawl. The note told about the joy he felt with his sister's family. "He said they had arrived in Missouri and that their sister was happy to see them."

"Did you know they were going to Missouri?"

"*Nee.* I didn't." Sarah was glad she could answer with honesty. Lukas had never told her their destination, only that family wanted them.

A man, someone Sarah was unfamiliar with, leaned over to the Bishop and spoke quietly in his ear. The man spoke at length. Each word seemed to last an eternity. Finally the man sat and Bishop Miller continued.

"Sarah Nolt. Did you give money to Lukas, knowing he planned to use the funds to leave this community?"

Sarah swallowed hard, preparing herself for what was to come. The truth had to come out, whatever the cost. "*Ya*, I did."

Loud conversation broke out amongst the men. Bishop Miller slammed his fist on the wood table to regain control of the room.

"You know what you're admitting to, what the consequences could be?"

Mose stood, surprising Sarah. "The only thing she's admitting to is helping the boys out of a life-threatening situation, nothing more. In all fairness, I think this question should be asked." He turned to her. "Sarah, why did you help the boys?"

The same poker-faced man leaned over and spoke to the Bishop again. A quiet barrage of words went back and forth before the question was asked by the bishop. "Why did you feel it necessary to help the boys, Sarah?"

The loud heartbeats in her ears made it hard for her to hear his question. She looked at Mose and he nodded, encouraging her to tell them her story. "Joseph and I made it a habit to sit out on the porch swing each evening. Right after the Hochstetler family moved into the old farm across the field, we often heard the sound of a child crying and a man yelling in anger. More than once Joseph hurried over to the farm and would come back red-faced with frustration. He wouldn't tell me what happened, but the child's crying always stopped."

"Did you ever ask Lukas about these times?" The man sitting next to the Bishop asked this question.

Sarah pulled on one of the strings to her prayer *kapp*, working out how she could speak without some kind of proof. "He told me his father often whipped him with a strap."

The bishop stood. "We spoke of this before, Sarah. You were told to stay out of this family's business. I spoke to the father myself. He said the older boy was rebellious and had to have these whippings as a form of correction."

Sarah looked up, holding Bishop Miller's gaze. "Did he tell you he beat Lukas so badly the child couldn't walk for a time? Or about the scars on the child's back from being whipped with a buggy whip? Would you have whipped your son in this manner, I wonder? Would you lock him up in a chicken coop for a week with nothing to eat but raw eggs?"

"*Kinder* are prone to lie, Sarah. We all know the problem you had with lying as a teen."

The bishop's voice cut into her like a knife. She'd cried out for help as a child, but no one had taken notice of her father's cruelty.

"I did not lie as a child, and I do not lie now. It's all true. I have no proof, but I have the satisfaction of knowing I helped rescue those boys from an abusive father, someone Joseph kept in line until his death."

Her father was out of his chair and leaning over Sarah in seconds. "Do you accuse me of abuse, too?" Fury cut hard edges into his face.

Mose rose and stood next to Sarah. "This is not the time to—"

"This is the perfect time to bring up this girl's past." Adolph bent low, shaking his finger in Sarah's face.

"This is all a lie, isn't it, Sarah? A lie about me and a lie about the reason you sent the boys away."

Sarah took in a deep gulp of air, stood and prepared for the worst. "I did not lie about you. You *are* cruel, Father." She faced him. Her heart hammered.

"I've lived this lie long enough. It is time for all to be made clear," Adolph yelled at the bishop.

Bishop Miller jumped to his feet and walked toward Adolph. "This is not the time or place, *Herr* Yoder."

"It is the perfect time, Ralf. I will not be silent and have my good name tainted by this girl. She is no longer my responsibility and I want no further contact with her. She brings back painful memories, memories I need to forget."

"Years ago we agreed—"

"You told me what I had to do, and I did it. But I will not be held responsible any longer. I have done my share of giving to this community when I married her mother, that pregnant Amish woman."

Sarah's body shook with cold. Blood drained from her face. "What are you saying, *Daed*?"

"Don't call me *daed* again, Sarah Nolt. I am not your father. Your father was an *Englisch* drunk."

The small room seemed to close in around Sarah. Everyone went silent. Their gazes shifted from Sarah to Adolph. Her father's hands clenched into fists. "I will not be shunned because of you, do you hear me, woman?" His balled fist pounded the table, startling everyone. "I did nothing but try to help a stranger in our midst, an Amish girl who was pregnant and desperate."

An ugly smirk grew on his face, narrowing his eyes and slashing his mouth. "The thanks I got for all my kindness was a spoiled *kinder* and a lying witch of a

wife who finally ran off with the same *Englisch* drunk
who got her pregnant."

He leaned in, his hands palm down on the table, fac-
ing Sarah. "You are their bastard child. I don't guess
you knew that, did you? I raised you as my own, but no
more. You've broken too many *Ordnung* rules and deserve to be shunned. I will not have my family's name
besmirched by your actions."

Sarah stood, her legs trembling out of control.

Adolph began to pace the room. "Eric is my son, my
blood. He makes me proud. But you!" He turned, his
bony finger pointing at her. "You bring me nothing but
shame. You are not my daughter by blood and the bishop
knows it." He moved toward Bishop Miller's chair and
stared directly at him. "You know I'm telling the truth.
Tell her." He turned back to Sarah. "You must go. Now."

Mose caught Sarah around the waist as she swayed.

"Come. Let me help you to the chair." He propped
her limp body against his. She groaned. He looked up,
his eyes sparking fire at Adolph Yoder. "You're an evil,
cruel old man. You don't deserve a daughter as fine and
loving as Sarah. All you know is hatred and cruelty. *You*
should be banned from this community, not this tenderhearted girl." He looked down at Sarah's bowed head
and wished he could strike the man who'd made her like
this. He believed problems could be fixed with prayer
and conversation, not violence. But today he yearned
for a physical release to his anger. He wanted to physically hurt him until Sarah's pain ended.

Bishop Miller and the community elders stood, their
chairs scraping back as they faced Adolph. "There was
no need for this, Adolph. I would never have let you
come to the meeting if I'd known you would act in this

manner," Bishop Miller said. "*Herr* Stoltzfus, go find Eric and tell him to come collect his father. We no longer have need of him at this meeting."

"You can't do that," Adolph blurted out. "I only said what was true." He glared at Sarah. "She's been nothing but trouble, that girl. I'm innocent of any wrongdoing. You all know I am. Everyone here knows who she really is, what she's done. I'll share none of the blame for her actions. Eric and I want nothing to do with her any longer. You must…"

"*Nee*, Adolph. I think you are mistaken. I do *not* have to listen to you." Red-faced, Bishop Miller spat out his words. "I want you out of this room and gone from my home."

"But…"

"You will leave or be shunned today. Do I make myself clear?" He sat and began to write in a ledger. "I declare there will be no shunning for Sarah Nolt this day, but she must leave the community as soon as possible. What she did was wrong, even if her actions were prompted by her love for these *kinder*. I should have listened to her when she came to me with her story. All of this could have been avoided."

Sarah lifted her head, shocked the bishop would admit fault of any kind. Tears cascaded down her pale face. Her voice shook as she spoke. "I wish no harm to come to my…to Adolph Yoder. Mose and I will leave here as soon as we are married. I hope to be allowed back into the community to see my brother and his wife sometime in the future, if you will allow it."

The bishop laid down his pen. "You can come back from time to time, Sarah, but you'll be watched closely. Your actions were just too foolhardy to be swept away.

Mose has informed us of your engagement. I'll arrange for one of the preachers to marry you before you go, but only because of my love and respect for his father and family."

Sarah rose from her chair. *"Danke,"* she murmured, swaying. She avoided looking into the bishop's eyes. Mose grabbed her hand and assisted her across the room and then quietly shut the door behind them.

Chapter Five

The freshly pressed blue cotton wedding dress hung on a plain wire hanger. Sarah put the still warm iron on the woodstove's burner and shoved the padded wooden clothes press back under the sink.

She took a glass from the kitchen cupboard Joseph had made and filled it with water. Tired beyond words, she pulled out a kitchen chair and sat. Her trembling hands covered her face. Warm tears slipped through her fingers. She would be married just hours from now. She'd prepare the same meal she'd cooked for Joseph on their wedding day and wear the same wedding dress she'd sewn for their special day. It was tradition.

Memories flooded in, choking her throat closed. Joseph had looked so handsome in his black suit and white shirt the afternoon they'd married. That bright morning all those months ago, she'd cooked several dishes for their wedding meal. Her heart light, singing old gospel songs, she'd hurried through the preparation.

The meal prepared, she'd dressed with care and anticipation. She'd slipped her homemade blue wedding dress over her head just moments before he'd rung the doorbell. Joseph had arrived with flowers picked from the field behind her father's farmhouse. Laughter and joy had filled the house as they'd eaten together. Later many people had come and filled the house with more love than she'd ever dreamed possible.

Marta's hand on Sarah's arm jerked her from her memories.

"I'm sorry, Sarah, but it's time. It's almost seven and we have to meet Eric for the wedding." She looked into Sarah's eyes. "You need to wash your face and remove all traces of red from your eyes. I know all this has been hard on you. I don't know how you can marry a man you don't love, but then I've not walked in your shoes. We all survive *Gott's* will the best we can."

Marta helped Sarah prepare, pulling her wedding dress over her head and letting the fabric settle around her hips.

"There, just right." Marta gave an appreciative sigh, adjusted the garment here and there and smiled. "I was worried the dress would be too small for you since you put on some needed weight. Thank *Gott* you did. You'd gotten so thin after—"

"After Joseph died?" Sarah finished for her.

"Well, yes…but you're back to your normal weight now and look *wunderbaar*. I'm so glad this day has finally arrived. I've been concerned for you for so many months."

"I've had to force myself to eat. Joseph would want me strong and living life to the fullest."

"But today is not about Joseph. This is Mose's day and you must put your memories of Joseph away now. He is gone. The grave is—"

"Closed. Yes, I know." She'd heard the phrase a hundred times, knew it was true, but somehow she couldn't put the memories of Joseph away, like he'd never existed. "Yes, I know better than anyone the grave is closed."

Marta sighed. "I don't mean to be cruel, but you must find a way to release Joseph. This marriage to Mose is for the rest of your life. If you don't settle these feelings for Joseph, you'll grieve yourself to death."

Sarah hugged Marta, something frowned on by her Old Order Amish community, but often shared by the two friends. She appreciated how hard it must be for Marta to say all these things about Joseph, her own dead brother. She'd loved him without limit. Somehow she'd found a way to release him to *Gott*. Sarah knew she had to find a way to do the same.

Forcing a smile, she rested her hands on Marta's tiny shoulders. "I'll get through this day and all the days to come. Mose has been so kind to me, so understanding. He deserves a wife who loves him. I will be true to *Gott's* plan and be the best wife I can be." Sarah took a deep breath and pushed it out. "Now, let's get this dress hooked up and go downstairs. We shouldn't keep Mose waiting any longer."

They worked the back hooks of the dress up together, Sarah twisting and turning, trying her best to close them at her waistline. "They just won't close here," she said, and they both laughed. "I guess I've gained more weight than I thought."

"Don't fret," Marta smacked away Sarah's scrambling fingers. "Your apron will hide the gap. No one will notice."

The dark mood lifted; both women smiled as Marta began to work on Sarah's long hair. "Your *kapp* must be perfectly placed. Every old woman at the service will be gauging and measuring."

Sarah looked into the mirror and wished the dark circles under her eyes would go away. "Will people come to the wedding?" Sarah wrung her hands.

"Oh, some will come out of morbid curiosity, some to mutter and make harsh comments, but the rest will be here for you because they love you. You must be prepared for what some might say and ignore them." She beamed at Sarah. "Now we talk only about good things, like how beautiful you look."

"Do you think Mose will approve of my dress? He may be used to finer things." Sarah fiddled with the waistband of her apron. *Please, don't let anyone notice my weight gain, Gott.*

"I think he'll be too busy being nervous to notice the shadows under those beautiful eyes of yours. Now, let's get going before Eric comes up to drag us to the house. It's good the service was allowed to be held at our home," Marta said. "Just remember the important people in your life will be there, and that's what matters."

"I need to pray," Sarah insisted, remembering the promise she'd made to *Gott*. She would put all she was into this new marriage. Mose deserved her loyalty and she had every intention of giving it to him.

They bowed their heads in reverence. Sarah closed her eyes. *Lord*, Gott, *please bless this union. It might be wrong to marry without love, but Mose and I need each other. Pour your favor on the wedding guests and bless the meal afterward. Give us your approval today. Help me get over this draining virus. I need to be strong for the girls as we travel to Florida. Help me to be a*

*good mamm to the kinder and an acceptable wife for
Mose Fischer. Amen.*

"You look radiant." Marta stood just behind Sarah
and adjusted the back of the prayer *kapp*, making the
placement perfect. "I've asked a few of the women
to take the baby up to the bedroom if she fusses, and
Beatrice has been warned to be quiet, or she'll find herself in bed with her sister."

Lingering for a moment, Sarah breathed deeply.
Marta finally put her hands on Sarah's back and pushed
her toward the door.

They walked slowly down the stairs and into the
great room, where benches were lined up in rows. The
sound of the back door shutting told her people were
still arriving. She looked around and smiled at the sight
of Beatrice sitting at the back. Mercy sat on the lap of
one of Sarah's cousins. The little girl chewed on a toy.
She took in their freshly washed appearance and plain
dresses and smiled. These little girls would soon be her
daughters. Her forced smile warmed to a happy grin.

She turned toward Mose. He looked handsome in his
borrowed black suit and newly purchased white wedding shirt. She watched with pride as he walked in her
direction. He moved with purpose, his demeanor calm,
so different from her high-spirited Joseph the day they
had wed. She knew so little about Mose Fischer, the
man who would become her husband in a matter of
minutes. He walked up to her and she suddenly felt shy
and as tongue-tied as a young, innocent girl. "You look
very handsome."

"So do you," Mose said, then quickly corrected himself. "I didn't mean to imply you looked handsome.
What I meant is, you look exceptionally beautiful to-

night." He laughed, but the sound came out edged with nerves. Perhaps he'd been thinking similar thoughts, that they barely knew each other. She accepted Mose's outstretched arm and let him lead her toward the back of the room.

A handful of people sat scattered around the room, somber-looking men on one side and their wives, most busy with restless school-age *kinder*, on the other.

Someone cleared his voice and Sarah jumped. Ruben Yoder, her distant cousin, came out of the room off to the left and stood at the front of the room, prepared to sing. In a fine tenor voice, he sang a single verse of an ancient song of praise, one she'd never heard before. The congregation sang seven stanzas of another old song from the Ausband. Sarah joined in, listening to Mose's voice for the first time.

Several songs later, *Herr* Miller, the bishop's son, stood and recited Genesis 2:18 from the King James Bible.

The hour of songs and scripture verses seemed to go on and on. Out of the corner of her eye, she saw Beatrice being led out of the room and through the kitchen door. The child had done well, waiting all this time for something interesting to happen before being sent away.

Bishop Miller came into the room, her brother, Eric, following behind him. Several of the other ordained preachers lined up. As Eric moved to take the song leader's place at the front, Sarah realized her brother would be performing the wedding service and not the Bishop. Eric had been elected as one of the community's new preachers a few weeks ago and she was so pleased she and Mose would be married by him.

Bishop Miller settled in a chair behind Eric. He

flashed Sarah a glance. Sarah felt Mose take her hand and squeeze hard, sending a silent message of reassurance. His hand felt warm, the rough calluses on the palm reminding her how hard he'd worked with the men to tear down the old barn and rebuild the new one in just a matter of days. She linked her fingers with his.

Sarah looked at her hand entwined with Mose's tanned fingers. Her pale skin looked so different from his brown skin. They were about to become united in the holy bonds of marriage and she didn't even know his favorite color or what foods he liked to eat. Feeling eyes on her, she glanced up and met his gaze. The iris of his eyes had gone a deep blue with emotion. He was taking this marriage ceremony seriously, and she had to do the same. She respected him beyond measure, but love? A new feeling stirred in her heart. Friendship could grow into love, could it not?

Mose stood and walked to the end of the bench. Sarah rose and stood by his side. Hand-in-hand they walked to the front of the room. Marta met her there and Mose's cousin, Eli Fischer, stood beside him.

Sarah watched her brother's mouth move as he spoke words over them, but had no idea what he said. In her mind she was standing with Joseph, answering the hard questions the pastors and deacons had asked about their loyalty and love for one another. She would answer as if responding to them. She pulled herself from her dream-like state and heard Mose speak.

"I will love Sarah with all my heart and give her my respect and loyalty until the day I die."

Eric turned her way, his face formal. His eyes met hers. "Will you be loyal to Mose and lean only on him for the rest of your life?"

Sarah turned toward Mose and held his eyes. "I will be loyal to you in all ways and let my love for you grow until my dying day."

Sarah brother's hand encompassed theirs. "The mercy of God and His blessings be on you today, and every day hence. Leave us now in the name of the Lord. I declare you now man and wife. What *Gott* has put together, let no man put asunder."

In a traditional wedding service, songs would have been sung now, but their marriage was anything but traditional. Months ago she'd been given the name Sarah Nolt. Now she would be known as Sarah Fischer. The name sounded strange to her, almost foreign.

They left the room and headed out into the dreary day. A strong wind blew and Sarah shivered. She tried to be excited for Mose's sake. He was a generous man, had rescued her. Thanks to him she could still be connected to her brother, Eric, and sister-in-law, Marta. She was the new bride of Mose Fischer, a fine man in good standing in his community. She'd have two beautiful daughters to care for and love. She turned to Mose and excused herself, a forced smile spread across her face. She should be happy, but she wasn't. Joseph's memory was always there. Memories of what she'd done and how he'd died. "I'll be right back and meet you in the kitchen, just before the meal."

Well-wishers interrupted her walk up the stairs several times, but she finally made it to the room and fell across the bed, her pent-up tears releasing.

Moments later, Marta rushed into the room, sat on the edge of the quilt-covered bed and took Sarah's hand in hers. "You didn't answer the door when I knocked."

Sarah wiped her tears away and forced a smile. "I'm sorry."

"Do you want to be left alone? I can come back in a bit and help you prepare for your trip."

"*Nee*, there's no need for you to leave. It's time I pull myself together and rejoin my guests, eat and say good-bye. Beatrice and the baby should be awakened. They will need to eat before we go."

"That's why I came in. Mercy's just up from her nap. Mose said to tell you he'd be back in a few minutes. He's got a surprise for you and seems very excited."

Sarah sighed. "He's been nothing but wonderful. I don't know what I would have done without him. He deserves so much better than me."

"*Ach*, I will not listen to such foolishness." Marta hugged her. "He is a fine man, I'll give you that. But you're a wonderful woman and will make him a great wife and mother for the girls."

"I pray you're right," Sarah said. "Where are the girls? Did Mose take them with him?"

"Beatrice insisted she be allowed to go. Seems she's been told about his surprise and can't wait to…"

Sarah grinned. Marta never could keep a secret. "She can't wait to what?"

Marta changed the subject abruptly. "I'll miss you when you're in Florida."

"I know, but its best we leave as soon as possible. My fath—" Sarah paused and corrected herself "—*Adolph's* inappropriate behavior played a large part in the Bishop's decision not to shun me. I don't want to risk him changing his mind at the last moment."

Not wanting to think about it anymore, she changed the subject. "Mose says his community is strict, but not old-fashioned. Gas and electric lights are allowed in the houses there and some carry cell phones for their businesses. I'm extra thrilled because I've heard women can own sewing machines, and you know I want one so bad."

"That's the brightest light I've seen in your eyes in a long time. I'm so excited for you. Who knows? Maybe Eric and I will head south and someday you'll find us on your doorstep."

Sarah laughed. It felt good to feel joy. "It would be wonderful if you did, but Eric will never leave his *daed*."

Sounds of the screen door slamming shut brought Marta to her feet. "You'll be needed in the great room. I have a feeling Beatrice is holding her breath until you get there.

"You're probably right." Sarah hurried down the stairs, toward the sounds of a giggling child.

"Sarah, come see," Beatrice called out just as Sarah walked past the front door and into the great room. Mose stood in the middle of the room, a huge bouquet of beautiful wildflowers in his hands.

"For my bride," Mose said.

Sarah wilted to the floor in a faint.

Chapter Six

"She's coming round." Marta sounded so far away.

Wisps of fog swirled and blurred Sarah's vision. Confusion rattled her thoughts, making her stomach clench with fear. *Where was she? What had happened?* She reached out a hand. She was lying on the braided rug she'd made months ago.

Something touched the side of her face. She opened her eyes and a man's face came into focus. Mose. He leaned over her, his brow knitted close together.

"Sarah, are you all right?"

She lifted her head and stared into his sky-blue gaze. Mose made her feel safe again. "Yes, I'm fine." But she wasn't. Dizzy spells had plagued her for days.

"She's been looking pale, Mose. She must be completely stressed out, and she's not eating regularly." Marta spoke from somewhere behind Mose.

He pushed a lock of hair back from her forehead. "Do you hurt anywhere?"

"*Nee.* I don't think so." Mustering all her strength she leaned on her arm and made an effort to get up, still muddle-brained.

Mose slipped his arm around her waist and eased her into a sitting position. "Don't move. Not until we know you're okay. You might have broken something when you fell."

"I'm fine. I don't feel dizzy. Everything just went a bit hazy for a moment, that's all. My stomach's been upset. It's stress, no doubt." Mose had shocked her, his tall frame standing in the great room, his hands full of wildflowers. For a moment he'd looked so much like Joseph.

Mose took the glass of water Marta handed him and placed it against Sarah's lips. "Drink this. It'll make you feel better."

She sipped and then quickly drank down the whole glass.

"You need to sit for a while until the dizziness passes." Mose put his hand on her shoulder. "When was the last time you had a proper meal?"

"I think it was yesterday, but I can't be sure. So much has been going on."

"You've been through a lot. It's no wonder you fainted."

"I'm fine now, Mose. Really." Determination had her pushing up off the floor with Mose's help. Sarah stood and found her footing.

Mose helped her into a chair. "I think a meal is in order, don't you?"

Sarah nodded and glanced around the room. Wildflowers lay strewn across the wide-plank wood floor. Forgotten, Beatrice stood ankle deep in the pile of stems and blooms, her tiny black shoes peeking out. She seemed frozen in time, her face a mask of horror, eyes wide. Tears streamed down her pale cheeks. Sarah made eye contact and Beatrice flew across the room, into her waiting arms, her eyes still rounded with fear. She leaned in and rested her head on Sarah's shoulder. Beatrice's hand patted her softly. In a rhythmic tattoo, she whispered, "You won't die. You'll be all better. *Gott* has made you my new *mamm*."

Marta hovered close. "Why don't I go get you something to eat from the meal outside? It will only take a minute."

Mose spoke before Sarah could respond. "That sounds like a good idea. Beatrice, why don't you go with Marta and make sure she gets Sarah some of her favorite sour pickles. You know how they help sick stomachs."

Pried out of Sarah's arms and led to the kitchen, the little girl shouted over Marta's shoulder, "*Nee*! Sarah needs me."

Sarah took in a deep breath and found a smile. "I'd love a plate of hot food, but only if you fix it for me." The child grinned as Marta carried her away.

"You looked like you needed a moment to regain your composure." Mose smiled, one tiny dimple showing in his right cheek.

"I did." Sarah nervously rubbed the soft fabric covering the padded chair. "It was the oddest thing, Mose. One minute I was fine, the next I was falling flat on my face. But I feel fine now, like nothing happened."

"You can't skip meals and expect to remain healthy. You have two small *kinder* depending on you now, and we have a long trip ahead of us. The girls can run healthy women into the ground." He laughed, a twinkle in his eye.

"I know. I don't know what I was thinking. It was very foolish of me."

Mose bent on one knee in front of her. "*Nee*, not even

the strongest person can experience the tragedies you've gone through and come out unscathed. Together we'll work our way through this."

"But your reputation will be sullied by our quick marriage."

"You're not to fret. I'm your husband now. You're my wife and the mother of my *kinder*. I will always be here for you. Joseph would have wanted it this way. I feel honored to have you as my wife." He smiled so tenderly Sarah almost broke down. Her lip quivered as she took the rough hand he held out to her. She grasped it, their fingers entwined. Time stopped and Sarah's heart beat a bit faster. "Nothing will come between us." Mose promised. "You'll see."

Sarah looked completely over her illness after eating, but he could sense her nervousness. Mose knew Sarah had never been in an automobile, much less on a train. The black machine had to appear imposing and impossibly large to her. She might be frightened and rethinking the wisdom of going to Florida inside such a massive contraption. At least the *kinder* had experienced the train ride up to Lancaster County and seemed calm and ready for travel.

He was glad the tiny wedding party had piled into Eric's old hay wagon and the few well-wishers had been able to wave them off just blocks from the train station.

"How much time do we have, Mose?" Sarah's white-knuckled grasp on her suitcase showed she was frightened.

"We'll be boarding in a few minutes. You have time to say your goodbyes." He held Beatrice tight by one hand. Mercy was cradled in a warm blanket in his other arm. He watched as Sarah wrapped her arms first around Marta and then Eric. She clung to her brother for a moment, her tears flowing freely. He saw her whisper something to Marta, which made them both laugh.

"*Ya*, we will be coming to see you. Maybe in the fall, I think. When life has settled down after harvest." Marta grabbed Sarah close once more. Eric joined the hug and the three stood as one, whispering words of love to each other.

Mose shifted the baby to his shoulder. "I hate to tell you, but the train will be leaving soon. We should get settled."

Sarah broke away and scooped Mercy out of Mose's arms, allowing Beatrice to grab hold of her skirt. The two men hugged. "*Gott* be with you and keep you. Make my sister happy and bring her peace or I'll come find you," Eric said with a smile.

Mose's big palm slapped Eric on the back. "May *Gott* bring a *bobbel* into your household. May he prosper you and bring you joy."

Marta and Sarah laughed as the two grown men shed tears, their own eyes red and glistening.

Mose set down his case, then added Sarah's smaller valise, which weighed next to nothing in his hand.

Eric gave one last hug to his sister and then looked straight into her eyes. "We are brother and sister. We will always be connected by blood. If you need me, you know where I am. You are a wonderful sister. I was lucky to have you close by my side."

Sarah's face grew red, fresh tears slipping down her cheeks. "You are my blessed brother."

Beatrice pulled at Sarah's skirt. "Hurry, Sarah. We don't want to miss the train."

Mose saw Sarah smile sweetly at his daughter. "Yes, *liebling*. Our new life awaits us."

"I'm tired, *Daed*. Hold me," Beatrice whined, reaching her arms out to Mose for comfort.

"Would you hold Mercy while I see to Beatrice?" Mose offered the baby up to Sarah.

"The poor *liebling* is one tired little girl." Sarah took Mercy and cuddled the baby's small, warm body close to her own quick-beating heart and breathed in the sweet smell of her neck. The child stirred and Sarah adjusted her blanket, covering her cold legs. Sarah cooed in the baby's ear, comforting her with a rhythmic backrub until the child slept. She'd been taking care of Mose's *kinder* only a short time but already the weight of the baby in her arms seemed perfectly normal, as if she'd been the child's mother since birth.

Mose shifted an already sleeping Beatrice to his shoulder. "I think we board the train down this way."

Sarah hurried past a young *Englisch* couple and saw them exchange a look. She'd seen that glance before. She was too tired to give it more than a passing thought. Moving about in the *Englisch* world always brought out the worst in her. She hated feeling odd, like she was a freak show put on just for them. Their clothes were odd to her, too. She gave a disapproving glare to the woman's short denim skirt that showed off more of her legs than Sarah deemed respectful. Had Mose averted his eyes as this woman passed, or had he admired the beauty of her youthful body?

With nervous fingers she set her *kapp* on straight and determined to ignore the looks and laughter coming from the *Englisch* couple. She patted Mercy on the back, her walk brisk, her gaze on Mose's strong back just inches away.

Mose slowed, ushering her toward a door on the side of the train. The immense size of the metal monster gave her pause and she stopped for a second, her fear so great she considered running in the opposite direction. Then she stepped up into the train, and her fear gave way to determination. She would make a fresh start with Mose and the *kinder*. No matter what.

They switched trains in Philadelphia taking one heading south. To their delight, both *kinder* fell asleep before lunch. An hour later Mose opened one eye and watched as Beatrice tried to climb over his body without waking him. "Where do you think you're going, young lady?"

"I'm going with Sarah and Mercy," she said in a sleepy voice, her small fists rubbing sleep from her eyes.

The seat next to him was empty and the diaper bag gone. "I have a feeling your sister needed a change of clothes and a fresh diaper. Sarah will be right back, if you wait just a moment."

Beatrice bounced up and down on the empty seat. She frowned at him. "I have to go to the bathroom." She began to grimace, a look of strain on her face. Mose lost no time grabbing her up and hurrying her down to the nearest ladies' room. He knocked once and then knocked again. Beatrice's squirms became wild and insistent.

Mose knocked again on the bathroom door. "Sarah. I know you're busy in there with Mercy, but Beatrice seems to be in a real hurry. Do you think you could…?"

The door slid open just a crack and a clear-eyed Sarah

greeted him with a shy smile. "Come in, Beatrice," she said, but only opened the door wide enough for the child to slip through. Mercy smiled at her father, her naked little body squirming in Sarah's arms. "We had a bit of a wet diaper situation and her bottle didn't stay down, but she seems fine now."

"Why don't I wait here for Beatrice? You can send her out to me when she's finished."

It struck Mose how formal they still were with each other. Almost strangers…but then, they *were* strangers…married strangers. Time would take care of the formality between them over the *kinder*, but what about their relationship? Hadn't he noticed signs of genuine regard from Sarah already? They were growing closer and one day might fall in love.

Sarah was a spirited woman, the type of person he could be drawn to in a powerful way, like he had been with Greta. Would Sarah ever get over her guilt, the love she felt for her dead husband? He wanted to care for this woman standing just inches away. She deserved love. Would *Gott* bless their marriage? *Gott's* will be done.

Chapter Seven

Sarah stood behind Mose as he approached the dining car and pulled open the heavy door. *Englisch* filled the plush car. Their lively chatter and robust laughter engulfed the narrow hall where she waited. Her experience with mealtime had always been one of quiet conversation and hadn't prepared her for such loud volume or casual interaction.

Glancing around, all the booths looked full. There was only one empty booth located at the back of the car. The thought of walking past more staring, inquisitive eyes didn't appeal to Sarah, but she had two hungry *kinder* to feed. Mercy wailed for her bottle and almost wiggled off Sarah's hip. She resigned herself and endured the curious glances. Head down, she moved forward.

Mercy squirmed hard and Sarah almost dropped her. She had to get used to the small child's strength. She clasped her hands behind the little girl's back and held on. She'd get the hang of carrying an energetic baby. It would take just a short time.

Mose led the way down the narrow corridor between

the tables. Sarah watched as, like Beatrice, he greeted each person who turned his way. His demeanor was calm and at ease. Sarah envied him. She wished she could accept the stares as easily, but he had more exposure to the *Englisch*. Perhaps time in a less strict community would teach her to be less formal, too.

Beatrice claimed the bench seat nearest the window and pressed her nose against the huge glass pane. Mose scooted in beside her. Sarah slid into the bench seat across from him, placing Mercy on her lap.

"What would you like to eat, Beatrice?" Mose moved aside the crayons lying on a colorful sheet of paper and glanced through the small children's menu placed on the table. "They have burgers, hot dogs and pancakes."

"Pancakes!" The child's voice rang loudly through the dining car. Several people close by laughed at her excited response.

"Pancakes, it is. And you, Mercy? What does *Daed's* little girl want?" The look of love sparkled in his blue eyes as he gazed at his younger daughter and spoke louder.

Mercy continued to play with the rag doll in her hands, her head down, her blond curls short and shiny. Had she not heard her *daed's* question? Sarah touched the child's shoulder and watched as she turned her head and glanced up, her eyes questioning. "Would you like pancakes, too?" Sarah asked with a grin.

Mercy smiled at her and went back to playing with her doll. Sarah looked at Mose. His forehead creased in a troubled expression.

"Does she talk at all, Mose?" Sarah waited for him to say something positive about her limited vocabulary and attention span.

He laid the menu down and sighed. "*Nee*, she doesn't talk, but my mother says that's nothing to worry about. Her words will come. Some *bobbel* are just late bloomers, and Mercy seems to be one of them."

Their conversation was interrupted by a tall, lean, uniformed waiter carrying a tray of short glasses filled with ice water. He looked at them with obvious curiosity and lifted his pad, ready to take their order. "What can I get you folks?"

"My *frau* and I just sat down, but I think we're ready to order." The word *frau* slipped off Mose's tongue with ease, as if he'd been calling her his wife for years. A knot formed in Sarah's throat. *Frau*…she liked the sound of it.

Sarah ordered dry toast, hoping to squelch the remaining effects of the virus she'd been dealing with. She sipped from the glass of cold water in front of her.

Mose ordered fried chicken and mashed potatoes, and confessed with a little boy's grin, "I'd eat it every day of my life if I could. No sense changing habits now." He smiled, his deep dimple showed, making him look younger than she knew him to be. For the first time she realized how handsome he was. Heat flushed her face and her heart fluttered.

The sudden sound of a loaded tray of food hitting the floor startled them. Beatrice began to cry. Mose collected her in his arms and patted the child's back. "It's okay. Someone just dropped some plates. All is well, my rose."

Sarah looked at Mercy and was amazed to find the child fast asleep, her breathing soft and regular. Her finger caressed the lovely child's velvety cheek and watched as she stirred. Fear clenched Sarah's stomach. Mercy should have been awakened by all the noise.

She glanced over at Mose as he shoveled one of Mercy's crackers into his mouth. She started to say something about Mercy's lack of reaction, but decided she'd best bring up her concerns when Beatrice wasn't around to hear.

Sarah realized there had been one other time Mercy had failed to react to loud noises on the train. How many times had the child's lack of reaction gone unnoticed? *Gott, don't let this child be deaf.* Could it be possible the child had hearing problems? How should she approach her concerns with Mose without sounding like an inexperienced mother?

"You look very serious." Mose wiped his mouth with the bright red cloth napkin.

"I'm new at being a mother and worry over everything. We'll talk about it when the *kinder* are asleep."

Hour after hour the train rolled on. Beatrice fought her nap with the stubbornness and energy only a four-year-old could maintain. Mose walked the child to the end of the corridor and spoke to her firmly, but the talk did nothing to dispel the sour mood, or the loud crying that erupted from her.

"Any suggestions," Mose asked after a half hour of the child's wailing. A deep frown revealed how upset he was. Being a single parent had to have been hard on him. He had been very fortunate to have his mother's help.

"Perhaps she's too old for naps now," Sarah suggested. She rubbed Beatrice's back and got a bad tempered kick in the leg from the child for her efforts.

"Beatrice Fischer. You will be kind to your *mamm*. There is no need for violence." Mose's tone was quiet, but firm with frustration. Several people turned to stare at Beatrice.

"I will *not* go to sleep. I'm not tired and I want my real *mamm* to pat my back, but she's with *Gott. Grandmammi* Ulla says I'm not to ask for her, but I want her." Fresh tears began to pour down her already mottled face. "I wish I was with her. I hate you," Beatrice shouted, then twisted around and buried her face in her small pillow, sobbing in earnest.

Mose began to rise but Sarah stopped him. "*Nee*, please don't scold her again. What she says is true. I'm not her real mother. She's confused by her feelings. She needs time to adjust. She's just tired and cranky from the long train ride. She'll be asleep any moment now and everything will be okay."

Beatrice curled herself into a small ball on the train's bench seat, snuggled close to her sister and together the two girls hugged. Mose watched Sarah's expression and saw love sparkle in her eyes as she soothed his eldest daughter. *Kinder* could be so hurtful without realizing the gravity of their cruel words.

Beatrice finally ran out of steam and grew quiet. He reached over and took Sarah's small, soft hand in his and smiled, wishing this emotionally frail woman knew what a gift she was to him. A mother for his *kinder*, someone who'd love them no matter what. To him she was lovely and priceless. He squeezed her fingers and smiled. "I'm sorry. I know her words must have hurt."

"She'll come around. You'll see." Sarah squeezed his hand. "There are times I'd like to stamp my foot and cry myself," she confessed.

"You must be tired." Mose hadn't missed Sarah's

yawn or the way she pulled her hand away and tucked it under the fullness of her skirt. He had to remember she was still a widow grieving for her dead husband. Sarah had only been mourning Joseph for six months. Not nearly long enough to welcome him into her heart. What a fool he was.

"I didn't know you worked in the school back in Lancaster." He lightened the mood with his chatter and watched her facial expression relax.

"Yes, I did, but only for a short while. We had an abundance of trainable girls, and I took my turn when it came. Naturally I failed miserably as a teacher. I just wasn't the right material for such a job. I turned to quilt-making instead. I love to sew."

"My wife is—" He stopped himself, and his smile disappeared.

"Please, go on. I want you to feel free to talk about your wife." Sarah's smile looked genuine.

"*Danke.* I appreciate your understanding. Sometimes her name just slips out. It's almost as if she's still alive in Florida and waiting for me to come home."

"I understand. I often wake and think Joseph is out in the fields...until I remember he's dead."

"His death was so sudden. There was no warning, no illness to give you time to prepare." Mose lifted his hat and ran his fingers through his curls.

"And so final. I still find it hard to believe he's dead, even though I know he is. There was no body to see. Joseph was always careful with the gas lights. I was the one he said would burn the house down some day with my carelessness." One lone tear slid down her cheek.

He leaned toward her. "You're a good woman, Sarah Fischer. Without you I'd be a lonely man heading back to an empty home. I don't believe for a moment you caused Joseph's death."

Moments later, the aroma of coffee moved closer to their table. A wave of nausea washed over Sarah. She fought hard to hold down her meal but knew she had to make a run to the bathroom or throw up on one of the sleeping *kinder.* "I'll be right back." She sailed past Mose and quickly maneuvered around arriving diners.

The door to the bathroom was unlocked. She burst in, her hand to her mouth, frantically looking for an open toilet door. She got as far as the row of shiny sinks and lost all hope.

A female voice said, "Oh, you poor girl. Let me get a cold compress for your neck. That always helped me when I was pregnant."

Sarah looked into the mirror and watched as a stout *Englisch* woman of about sixty wet down the fluffy white washcloth she'd jerked from her makeup bag. "I'm fine, really. I'm not pregnant. I'm fine."

"Nonsense. You're not fine at all. Let me at least put the cloth on your neck. It's a trick my dear ol' mama taught me as a child." The older woman's gaze locked with Sarah's in the mirror. She approached and gently laid the cold cloth across Sarah's heated neck. Relief was instantaneous and much needed. A few moments of deep breathing and Sarah began to feel better.

"How far along are you?" the woman asked as she washed her hands.

Sarah froze. *She thinks I'm pregnant?* What foolishness. There was no way she could be pregnant. Joseph died almost six months ago. She would have known before this if she was pregnant. *Wouldn't she?*

The woman sat down on a short bench against the wall and continued to smile at Sarah. "I assume this baby is a wanted child."

For the first time, Sarah allowed herself to think about what it would mean to be carrying Joseph's child. She'd have a part of him she could treasure forever. Joy shot through her and she began to count her skipped periods, the ones she'd thought stress had caused her to miss. It had been over five months since her last one. She lifted her head and smiled back at the woman through the mirror. "If I am pregnant, he or she would be a gift from *Gott*."

"I have three gifts from God and one is driving me nuts right now, but he's still my little boy at thirty-nine."

Sarah moved to a clean sink, and then wiped her pale face.

How would she explain to Mose she might have to see a midwife? Her mind had been so preoccupied with Joseph's loss, the missed cycles hadn't worried her. Dealing with her father's demands about selling the farm after Joseph's death had kept her out of sorts and in a flux of grief.

What kind of reaction would she get from Mose when she told him about the possibility of a *bobbel*? She knew he was a good man, but could she ask him to raise another man's child? A pregnancy might be more than he bargained for.

The *Englisch* woman smiled at Sarah before they left the bathroom. "Good luck with that new baby."

"Danke," Sarah murmured and followed her out the door.

Sarah slid into the bench next to a still sleeping Mercy and sipped her water. "I'm sorry I took so long."

The *Englisch* woman walked over to Mose and Sarah. "You have lovely children, ma'am." The woman continued to walk down the narrow aisle. "I'm sure this next child will be just as darling as the other two."

"Stomach problems again?" Mose asked. "You're as white as a sheet."

Sarah felt in a state of shock. She nodded, not trusting herself to speak. *Could I be pregnant?*

Chapter Eight

Mose glanced up from the checker board, his gaze resting on Sarah's face. "We're almost in Tampa. You should hurry. You might not have time to make that last move you're so busy contemplating." He grinned. She scowled back but then broke out into a wide smile, her fingers poised. Alone on the board full of black checkers, his last red king sat ready to be served up.

Her teasing expression made her face appear young and spirited. She wore an impish grin of victory. "I have time for this." She moved her black checker toward his lone red king and snatched it off the board.

"Beginner's luck," Mose taunted, laughing at the cross expression stealing her smile.

Sarah's huff confirmed his suspicions. He had a competitive wife.

"We'll see if its beginner's luck next time we play." She straightened the ribbons on her *kapp*, then busied herself with wiping drool from Mercy's neck.

He loved that he'd married a feisty woman, and looked forward to their next checker game. He would only throw a game once. He was competitive, too.

The train's arrival in Tampa was announced over the intercom. The man's voice carried a heavy Southern accent. "Please remain seated while the train comes to a complete stop."

"We're finally home," Beatrice declared with a deep sigh.

Moments later Sarah held on to Beatrice and Mercy as the train lurched to a stop and people stood and gathered their belongings.

After grabbing the bag of small toys, she scooped up Mercy, and Mose inched his way off the train with Beatrice hanging off his back, the child's thin arms locked around his sunburned neck. Her head bobbed as his long legs ate up the distance to the outer doors. "Let's go, my little dumpling." He laughed as he stepped off the train, turning to take Sarah's hand as she stepped into the sweltering afternoon heat. *"Danke,"* she said.

Burdened with *kinder* and the carry-on bag, they made their way across the parking lot toward a small bus stop. Mose pulled out his cell phone from his pants, checked that it still had power and punched in numbers. "I'm calling my brother to let him know we've arrived. He should be here already," he told Sarah.

"Your community allows the use of phones for everyday use?" Sarah watched him, amazement on her face as he spoke into the quickly dying phone, then ended his conversation.

Mose smiled. "Our phones are mostly for work. We get a lot of business calls from out of state. Customers have to be able to communicate with us. Without their furniture orders we'd quickly go out of business in this difficult economy."

"I'm just not used to having one, that's all. We always had to use the phone box across the road for emergencies."

"My brother, Kurt, said they're at the back of the parking lot under a tree."

He watched relief spread across Sarah's face as she glanced over at the big buses parked in rows on the glistening tar-covered parking lot. Had she thought they would be their mode of transportation to Sarasota? She was probably unprepared for a bus ride.

As they waited, loving family reunions erupted all around them. Smiling faces dotted the small bus walkway. Mingled among them were Amish and Mennonites alike, most dressed in plain clothes and sensible shoes. Seeing so many Amish in one place, Mose wondered if they reminded Sarah of the community and the people she'd left behind. He pushed away those thoughts and glanced around. He hoped she liked what she saw of Tampa. Palm trees grew everywhere and shops of every kind lined the wide streets. They'd arrived before the gray gloom of night could steal the day's last glorious rays of sunshine. The tall, swaying palm trees gave the town a tropical feel. He hoped she'd find Sarasota just as beautiful as Tampa.

Mose swung Beatrice onto his shoulders and caught Sarah's attention with the wave of his hand. "I don't want you to be concerned about meeting Kurt. I spoke with him early this morning. He knows all about our marriage and is very happy for us. He knew Joseph, too. We all grew up together in Lancaster, as boys. When we heard about Joseph's coming marriage, we both decided to go back up and help build the farmhouse. We wanted only the best for Joseph and his new bride."

"*Danke* for all your work. So much was going on

during that time. I failed miserably at giving a proper thanks to all the workers who came to do the hard work. You and Kurt must have thought me terrible."

"*Nee.* I saw you at a distance one day and thought you lovely and Joseph a lucky man."

Sarah blushed at his compliment. She clutched Mercy to her chest and looked away.

Mose leaned down and grabbed Sarah's free hand, leading her away from the buses. Mose rubbed her wrist with his thumb and she smiled, accepting his touch.

Walking along with Sarah, a sudden breeze cooled his neck.

"What did you tell your *bruder* about our circumstances? Does he know I was going to be shunned? That you were there for me when I needed you most?"

"I told him I found you to be a wonderful woman who makes me happy. That's all he needs to know."

Sarah sighed deeply. Mose knew she probably dreaded meeting his family, but hoped for the best. *Will they accept her after all the rumors floating between Lancaster and here?* He longed for a start fresh for her in Pinecraft, the tiny Amish community he lived in just outside of Sarasota. *Gott* had provided a haven for her. There were a lot of things she didn't know about his family, but he knew them to be generous with their love.

Just feet away, a shiny black van with the sign Fischer's Transport came into view. Sarah's brows lifted. She tugged at Mose's hand, her questioning gaze seeking his. "Who owns the van?"

Beatrice broke free of her father's grip and ran toward the front passenger door, her small fists pounding on the metal as she yelled, "Unlock the door, *Aenti* Linda. We're finally home."

Mose waved at someone inside and placed his hand lightly on Sarah's back, directing her closer to the back passenger door. "My *bruder* does."

"I'm surprised he doesn't drive a horse-drawn wagon." Sarah knew her words came out sounding judgmental. She hadn't meant to be rigid. The idea of riding in the back of this huge vehicle, instead of an Amish wagon, left her breathless with anticipation.

"Kurt usually brings the mini bus, but tonight you get a special treat and get to ride in his new touring van."

Sarah wasn't so sure riding in the back of a van was a special treat, but she would tolerate anything to get a chance to settle the *kinder* down and get some rest. They walked up to the driver's door and she held her breath. *Gott, let them like me.*

"Hoe gaat het, bruder?" Mose greeted his lanky younger brother with a bear hug and several warmhearted back slaps. He grinned at his sibling's attempt at growing a beard since his recent marriage, the beard unkempt and scraggly. Reddish-blond hairs jutted in all directions. "I see you're having some problems here." Mose jerked the straggly beard and laughed. "I hope your marriage is going better than this mess."

"Not everyone can jut out a forest of hair in weeks, *bruder*." Kurt laughed.

Enjoying his brother's discomfort, Mose grinned over at his sister-in-law, Linda. Beatrice had already managed to connect herself to the thin woman, her blond head snuggled against her chest.

Mose brushed aside a momentary pang of concern for Linda. Pregnant with her first child, she didn't look a day over seventeen, even though he knew her to be close to Sarah's age. She oozed healthy confidence and looked forward to the birth of her first child. Not everyone had complications. *But Greta had. Gott, let all will go well for this baby.*

"You're looking very rosy-cheeked and happy," Mose teased. "Pregnancy seems to suit you. It's given you that motherly glow everyone talks about."

He watched as Linda glanced over at Sarah and a smile lit her face. Not prepared to explain anything about Sarah and their marriage, he pretended to pat Linda's tiny, protruding tummy.

Kurt seemed happy now that he had married his childhood sweetheart. Mose grinned. He would pray for an easy birth for Linda and leave their fate in *Gott's* capable hands.

Standing behind him, Sarah tried to hide herself. He reached around and urged his new wife forward to introduce her. "This is Sarah, my *frau.*"

Sarah had never been a shy person, but today she felt dimwitted and backward. She had dreaded meeting Mose's family and worried they might reject her. Only *Gott* knew what Kurt must think of her, marrying his *bruder* so soon after Joseph's death. Amish custom in her Old Order community required a two-year waiting period to remarry and, even then, people would talk about the short interval. She moved forward and did her best to smile at him in a friendly manner.

Kurt extended his hand. Sarah took it and he squeezed her fingers in a firm grip. She was surprised at the *Englisch* gesture coming from an Amish man. Back in Lancaster, hand-shaking was often avoided.

She had to keep reminding herself she didn't live under harsh rules anymore. This new community would allow her freedoms she'd always longed for. *Everything will be okay, please Gott.*

Kurt looked nothing like Mose with the exception of his piercing blue eyes. He had a slight but muscular build, with a thick mass of sandy red hair. His skin color, which should have been pale and freckled, looked tan and glowed from the warm days in Florida's sunshine.

Sarah finally allowed her gaze to move to her new sister-in-law and her knees almost buckled with relief. Linda Troyer stood at Kurt's side. She was an old friend Sarah had known since childhood. They'd gone to school together, and years later, had taught the younger *kinder* during the same semesters. Linda smiled at her, draining all the stress and fear from Sarah's body.

"Linda Troyer! I can't believe my eyes. I knew you'd moved to Florida, but I didn't know you knew Mose's family."

"Kurt and I got married last fall, just a few months after my family moved down here. My last name's Fischer now, like yours." The two women hugged tightly, their reunion as warm as the brothers had been. Their happy tears mingling as they kissed each other's cheeks and laughed.

"I forgot. You did tell me you'd met a man named Fischer during *rumspringa* a couple of years ago. I guess I was too wrapped up in my own courting and coming marriage to Joseph to remember everything. Forgive me."

Linda grabbed Sarah's hand. "I don't know how you forgot. I must have mentioned Kurt's name a million times. I bored you with details for weeks. Remember, you even threw a going-away party when my family decided to leave for Florida. Your dad got so mad at me for dancing like a heathen in your front yard. Don't you remember him running me off and calling me an ugly name?" Linda laughed as she drew Sarah close for another hug, her fingers pinching Mercy's chubby cheeks before she leaned away. "Those were the good ole days. I've missed you."

Sarah grinned. "I probably missed you more. I am so thrilled that you're living in Florida."

"Not just Florida. We live in Sarasota, at Pinecraft. We're going to have the best time picking out a new home for you that's close to ours. You won't mind, will you, Mose?"

Both women turned toward the two silent men standing next to the van.

Strong emotions flitted across Mose's face, his brow furrowed, but his words came out friendly and light. "Wherever you want to live is fine with me. As long as it's near the schoolhouse." His smile seemed genuine, but there was still something in his expression, something she couldn't define that troubled her.

Chapter Nine

"You're being awfully quiet for a guy who's got a lot of explaining to do." Kurt lifted the girls' bag of toys and threw it over his shoulder.

Not sure what to say, Mose slowed his pace. He shifted the suitcase he was carrying from one hand to the other and repositioned the bulging dirty clothes bag slipping out from under his arm. Mose cleared his throat. "I really don't know where to start."

"Start at the beginning. What made you propose to Sarah, and why does she look so ill?"

"We really don't have the time to dig into all this right now. The van's just a few more rows over and the women will be wondering what happened to us. We're supposed to be picking up the remaining luggage from the train, remember? Not having a friendly chit-chat like two old women."

Kurt stopped in his tracks and gave Mose a piercing look that spoke volumes. He seemed determined to get the facts, one way or another.

"Do it now, or do it later, but tell me you will."

"All right. Sarah was in a deep depression over Joseph's passing. She needed help. We got to know each other while she cared for the girls. I offered to marry her to get her out of a bind."

"A bind? Marriage is an awful lot of help, Mose. I know you're a kind man, but people don't up and marry a widow of less than six months just because she's in a bind. Not even when they were best friends with the widow's dead husband. There has to be more to this story than you're telling me."

"I didn't marry her just to help her out. I need help, too. She had to leave Lancaster and the girls were desperate for a mother. They fell in love with her while I helped rebuild the burned-out barn. Sarah's a very loving woman and so good with the *kinder*. Her situation came up suddenly and we married out of convenience, nothing more. We have a clear understanding. Now, can you stop making more of this than there is, and let's get going? We can talk later. These bags are heavy and it's getting late."

Mose took off, his leather soles smacking against the parking lot pavement. He had enough on his mind without trying to satisfy his younger brother that he hadn't completely lost his mind. He knew he hadn't lost contact with reality and needed time to think, to talk to Sarah. This would all work out. He just prayed to *Gott* the rest of the family wasn't going to be this inquisitive.

Sarah looked inside the big van, comparing it to the small Amish wagons she was so used to. This vehicle was amazing, plush and definitely not plain. Three rows of soft leather seats lined the back, enough room for at least eight people. The space amazed her beyond words. She stepped in, the carpet under her feet like walking on marshmallows. Weak as a kitten, she longed for a nap. A sigh of relief escaped her as she bent forward and lifted Mercy's body into a child's car seat. A few minutes of fiddling had the baby secure in the strange contraption. Jerking on each strap, she made sure everything snapped into the right slots and flopped down next to Mercy for a moment of rest.

Linda slid Beatrice into the child seat at the front of the van with experienced ease, then gave her a box of animal cookies to quiet her.

Linda patted the seat next to her and motioned Sarah deeper into the van. Both women slid into the third row. Linda grinned. "It's really wonderful to see you, Sarah. I've been wondering how you were doing. I started to write when we first moved away, but figured your *daed* would just throw my letters away."

They laughed. Sarah enjoyed the moment of relaxation. "You know, he probably would have thrown them away." Sarah grinned and hugged her friend. "You have to no idea how wonderful it was to see you standing there next to Kurt. Recognizing your smiling face was such a surprise and a blessing." Sarah took Linda's hand and squeezed. "I've missed our friendship so much."

Linda laid her hand on her protruding stomach and rubbed lovingly. "Did you notice I'm pregnant? I told Mose to tell you when he got to Lancaster, but knowing him, he probably didn't."

"Sarah patted her friend's hand and squeezed it with joy. "I'm so happy for you and Kurt. Having a *bobbel* is such a blessing from *Gott*. You must be so excited."

"I am, but it's Kurt who's behaving like a fool. He's thrilled over the prospect of being a father."

Sarah listened as Linda laughed and continued to

ramble on. But in the back of her mind, the words of the woman on the train came back to haunt her. *Could I be pregnant, too?* Was it possible all the nausea and lethargy she'd been experiencing were from an unexpected pregnancy? How could she possibly be pregnant and not know it? *Wouldn't I have suspected something by now?*

"Just listen to me. I'm rattling on about my life and I haven't asked you if you're doing okay." Linda's expression became somber. "I was so sorry to hear about Joseph's death. I can't imagine what you've been going through."

Sarah felt a warm tear slide down her face. "It was all so sudden. Joseph and I were so happy. Life was perfect for the first time in my life...and then he was gone and everyone kept saying his death was *Gott's* will. I was told not to talk about him, to forget him. They expected me to act as if he never existed." Sarah wanted to share how she'd blamed herself for his death. Linda deserved to understand why she'd married Mose so soon after Joseph's death. A quick remarriage was completely out of line with their teachings. *She'll be wondering, thinking I've made a big mistake.*

What would Mose's people think when they heard she had been threatened with being unchurched for helping the neighbor boys leave their abusive father? Her heart ached with regret, but not for helping the boys. She hoped her old friend would understand that her motives had been pure, but what about the other family members? Beads of sweat dampened her forehead.

"You're so pale. Have you been eating well and drinking enough water?" Linda handed Sarah a lacy handkerchief and watched her as she mopped her face.

"I'm fine, really." Sarah reassured her. "I've just been sick to my stomach lately. Probably just a bug."

"When did these stomach problems start?"

"A while back. Nothing big, just off-and-on nausea and I'm tired all the time. But that could be from all the stress and chasing after the girls." Sarah leaned over to cover Mercy's bare legs with a lightweight blanket. She smiled as the tiny girl puckered up, as if she was nursing on a bottle.

Linda's hands pressed into her growing waistline. "Have you seen anyone about the stomach problems?"

Sarah watched for Mose and Kurt. "*Nee*, I thought about it, but I've been so busy that I put it off. I'm sure I'll be fine in a day or two." Sarah fiddled with the dangling ribbon on her *kapp* as she turned back to Linda. "You'll get a good laugh from this. A lady on the train saw me throw up and assumed I was pregnant. Can you believe it?" Sarah held her breath as she waited for Linda to laugh, to reassure her she had nothing to worry about.

"Are you?"

Sarah hadn't expected her serious question. Linda wasn't laughing. "I don't see how. It's been six months since Joseph died."

"Pregnancy can sneak up on you. One morning I smelled coffee brewing and threw up in front of Kurt's *mamm*. She knew right off I was pregnant."

Sarah flashed back to her problems with the smell of food and began to tremble. "I've been having to eat crackers to calm my stomach and…"

"What, Sarah?"

"My breasts are tender. They have been for weeks. I thought it was from my period being late…it's been months. I've been so wrapped up in Joseph's death. I thought it was just the stress keeping it away."

"I think we'd better get a test."

"What do you mean, a test?" Sarah asked.

"The *Englisch* have pregnancy tests. They cost a few dollars and within minutes you know if you're pregnant or not. I took one, just to be sure. It was positive."

"Mose might not approve of such tests."

"Are you kidding? He's the one who picked one up for me. You aren't in Lancaster anymore, Sarah."

Sarah began to cry. She was so confused and torn. She'd know for sure if she was pregnant and then how would she feel? Had *Gott* blessed her with a baby from Joseph? How would Mose react? He hadn't bargained on raising another man's child in the agreement they shared.

"I didn't mean to bring up Joseph and make you cry." Linda leaned forward and smoothed a tear from Sarah's cheek. "We'll get a pregnancy test in a bit and you'll take it. No more guessing and worrying. You hear?"

Always a take-charge kind of person, Linda leaned back into the soft seat of the van. Her gaze cut back to Sarah. "How did you and Mose end up married, anyway? I know you, Sarah. There's no way you'd marry again so soon after Joseph's death. Not unless something was seriously wrong. What happened? How could you have fallen in love with Mose so soon?"

The sound of the men approaching stopped Sarah's response, but she knew there'd be time for explanations later and prayed Linda would understand.

Linda greeted the men loading suitcases into the back of the van as if they'd been talking about the weather.

"Listen to them huffing and puffing, Sarah. You'd think they'd been carrying luggage for a family of six."

"These bags are heavy. Sarah must have packed everything she owns in here," Kurt teased.

Mose smiled through the window at Sarah and waved, his expression friendly and calm. She put on a brave face, smiling and pretending everything was fine. If he did see her tears he'd think it was just her nervousness about her first van ride, not to mention her concerns about meeting his family. She willed her stomach to calm down.

"Let's hit the road before it gets dark. I want Sarah to be able to see some of Tampa's sights before we head down to Sarasota." Kurt slipped into the driver's seat and waited for Mose to slide in and shut his door.

Mose looked back at Sarah. She grinned, silently reassuring him she was fine. *But I'm not fine.* Her mind raced like a runaway train. Kurt started the big van's motor and Sarah sucked in her breath.

"Remember, this is Sarah's first automobile ride," Mose reminded Kurt. "You don't want to scare her to death with some of your wild driving."

"As if I would," Kurt teased and gunned the powerful motor seconds before the van roared off down the road.

Sarah tucked her shaking hands under her legs and closed her eyes. It was going to be a long ride to Sarasota.

Florida was more beautiful than Sarah had imagined. Palm trees lined every street and the sky looked bluer than any sky she'd ever seen. Highway 275 quickly turned into HI 19 and the impressive Sunshine Skyway Bridge came into view, amazing Sarah with its massive size and length that stretched out over the bay. She was fascinated and terrified at the same time.

I can do this. She'd been through so many impossibly hard things the past few months. She looked back at Linda. Her friend seemed perfectly calm, as did everyone in the van. Digging her toes into the soles of her plain black shoes, she closed her eyes and prayed. *Give me strength to get through this trip across what looks like a death bridge.*

Kurt spoke, "What's wrong, Sarah?" His tone was playful but without mercy. She opened her eyes and met his gaze in the van's mirror. "You're not scared of heights, are you? It's either the bridge or walk."

Mose turned toward Kurt and sliced him a cutting look. Anger built inside Sarah, a typical example of her shifting moods of late. She would not have her husband pitying her over something as silly as a fear of heights. "Would you like me to sit in the back with you while we cross?" Mose offered.

Sarah looked back to the bridge and glared at Mose. He probably had no idea he'd just insulted her. "*Danke*, but I'm fine." Sarah pulled at the strings of her prayer *kapp*. She squared her shoulders in determination. "I'm sure thousands of people go across this bridge every day. I'm fine."

The awkward moment evaporated when Beatrice woke from a sound sleep and chimed, "I'm hungry. Aren't we there yet?"

Chapter Ten

Before leaving Lapp's restaurant, located a few miles from the edge of Sarasota and the tiny town of Pinecraft, Sarah watched as Mose paid their bill and shifted Beatrice in his arms as he slipped the change into his pocket.

Sarah's hands shook as she placed Mercy's empty formula bottle on top of the restaurant counter. She used a clean napkin to wipe the milk ring from Mercy's lips and smiled when Mose glanced her way.

"I want cookies," Beatrice demanded. Determined to grab the plate of plastic-wrapped chocolate chip cookies on the counter, she began to squirm in her father's arms, her arm stretching out.

"You ate enough food for two." Mose patted his daughter's stomach. "No cookies for you this time, young one." Her golden ringlets danced as she shook her head in disagreement. They headed out the door, following after Kurt and Linda.

Dusk had fallen and Sarah marveled at the glorious sunset. She drew in a long breath, taking in the smell of the sea. She kissed Mercy on the crown of her head and followed close behind Mose.

"Why don't Sarah and I go over to the pharmacy across the street? I need to pick up a few things before we go home." Linda told the lie with a big grin.

Kurt smiled down at his petite wife, oblivious to the prearranged plan. "Sure. You ladies take your time. Mose and I will strap the kids in and enjoy the last of the sunset."

Sarah was surprised at how normal Linda's voice had sounded as she'd lied and how easily she'd manipulated her husband.

Mose looked Sarah's way and dug into his pant pocket. "You might need some money." She held out her hand and he slipped two twenty-dollar bills onto her palm. "Enjoy." He smiled.

Sarah pulled on her prayer *kapp* ribbon. "I will. *Danke*." She waited until he turned toward the van before she picked up her long skirt and ran, finally catching up to Linda just as she opened the store's glass door.

"You could have waited for me," Sarah scolded, and then became speechless as she took in the big, bright store with shelves full of things she'd never laid eyes on before. *What do the Englisch need with all these things?*

"Over here." Linda grabbed Sarah's wrist. "I see makeup. The tests should be somewhere close to that section."

"Where are the tests?" Sarah glanced around. "I don't see them." These mood swings concerned her. She hadn't meant to bark at Linda.

"Don't snap, *liebling*. You're stressed out. It won't take a moment to find them, and then we'll know for sure if you're with child." Linda's head twisted back and forth as she looked up and down the aisles.

Sarah tapped her on the shoulder. "Shh. Someone might overhear you."

"And who would hear?" Linda snapped back. "Kurt and Mose are in the car." She led Sarah in a different direction, then pointed to a brightly lit ceiling sign. "The pharmacist can tell us where the tests are located. Come on. Time's wasting."

Linda rushed off and Sarah struggled to keep up. A large-boned woman with kind eyes and a friendly smile spoke to Linda in a quiet voice from behind the shiny counter. Linda handed the woman money and Sarah heard Linda say, *"Danke."*

The lady smiled. "Good luck. Hope you get the answer you want."

Sarah backed up as if the package Linda carried would jump out and bite her like a snake.

"Come on. This way." Linda grabbed Sarah's wrist as she flew past.

A shiver rippled through Sarah as she rushed forward, her feet heavy.

Linda pulled the box out of the flimsy bag and extended it toward Sarah. "Read the back carefully and then pray before you…ah…you know. The lady said this test is a good one and only takes about thirty seconds to show results."

"But…"

"You need to know, Sarah. This is no time to be stubborn. Take the test, find out if you are carrying Joseph's baby or not. You have to get on with your life. Mose deserves more than a nervous woman for a wife."

Linda's simple words reached her. The package in

her hands felt light as a feather. This test kit would tell her all she needed to know. She had to take it. Heading toward the door marked Women, Sarah turned back. "I know you're right. I'll be out in a minute."

Moments later she held the plastic device out in front of her, waiting for something to happen. Sarah picked up the box off the edge of the sink and reread the instructions just to be sure she'd done everything right. Time seemed to stand still. The music playing overhead grew silent. A line formed. She was pregnant. She didn't realize she was crying until tears began to hit the box in her hand.

With a shove to the door she exited the bathroom and smiled at Linda, their secret a strong bond between the two women. She gushed, "I'm pregnant."

"How far along do you think you are?" Linda called out as they'd darted across the street.

"I have to be at least six months. How can it be? Why didn't I know, Linda? Am I simple-minded?"

Stopping, she hugged Sarah. "*Nee.* It's your first pregnancy, silly. You were in a state of shock after Joseph died. It's no wonder you didn't notice the changes in your body. You'll have to go see the *Englisch* doctor for a sonogram." Linda turned toward the parked van. "You didn't take care of yourself or see a doctor. Something could be wrong and you wouldn't know it.

Sarah digested Linda's words. She would have to see a proper doctor. She owed it to the baby and to Joseph. "I will go as soon as I tell Mose."

"Don't take too long, Sarah."

"I promise I won't."

Moments later Sarah and Linda entered the van and settled down for the short drive to Mose's mother's house. Nervous that Linda might blurt out something, Sarah pulled at her prayer *kapp* ribbons. A sign on the side of the highway declared Sarasota was just three miles ahead.

Mose turned on an overhead light and glanced back at her and then the girls. "Everything good back there?" His tone was calm but his face appeared tense, his brow furrowed. Was he having second thoughts? Did he regret marrying her? Was he concerned how his family would react to her now that they were almost there?

"Everyone's good," Linda chimed in, grinning.

The light went out and Sarah breathed in. She had to stop holding her breath.

"I'm hungry," Beatrice spoke in the darkness, drawing Sarah's attention.

"I'll find you a snack," Sarah said, rummaging through the diaper bag. Her fingers hit the pregnancy test tucked deep at the bottom of the bag and she froze. Had Mose seen the box when he'd grabbed Mercy's bottle moments before they'd driven off?

She found the plastic container of cheese crackers and handed several to Beatrice. "These ought to tide you over until we get to your *grandmammi* Theda's house, sweetheart." She closed her eyes and prayed, determined in her heart to be a good wife and mother.

She'd dozed off, and then someone said, "Sarah. It's time to wake up."

Sarah blinked and looked directly into kind blue eyes. It was Mose. Reality rushed in and she struggled to wake up completely. "I'm sorry. I must have dozed off." She blinked and looked around. It was growing dark outside, the small van light shining overhead. Her prayer *kapp* lay in her hand. With care she searched for her pins and put the wrinkled covering back on her head.

"It's been a long and tiring trip. I'm not surprised you nodded off."

Her body felt sore from sitting still for so long. She struggled to step out of the van. Mose offered his hand and she grasped it, noticing the roughness of his warm palms. "Where are we?" She looked into the creeping darkness shrouding the last rays of sunlight. Rows of wood-framed white houses lined the short street, the van parked in a long gravel driveway. The flat yard, filled with sand, grass and palm trees, was illuminated by a tall black gas lantern positioned at the front of the box-shaped white house trimmed with black storm shutters.

"This is my mother and father's home. We'll be staying with them for a few days. Just until we can move into a home of our own," he reassured her.

"Yes. You did tell me that on the train." She shook out her skirt and fussed with her *kapp*, making sure it was pinned in the right places.

Mose held her arm for support until she started moving toward the door. Thick grass underfoot made walking difficult. She almost fell. Mose grabbed her around the waist, stabilized her and then took his arm away from her midsection. "You okay now?"

It had been a long time since she'd been held so close. His hand felt natural. It was as if he belonged with her. She pushed the thought away. Mose was in love with his dead wife. They had an arrangement. Nothing more. She stepped on the wide porch step. The wood creaked underfoot. A line of white rockers with colorful cushions welcomed her. A bright electric bulb attached to the door frame washed the big porch in artificial daylight.

The front door flew open and Beatrice came racing out. A smaller, dark-haired girl followed close behind.

"Where are you going, young lady?" Mose asked and grabbed his daughter by the sleeve.

"To *Grandmammi* Ulla's. She has candy for me." A layer of thick chocolate candy smeared a dark circle around Beatrice's mouth.

"I think asking permission to go out is in order, don't you?" Mose used the palm of his hand to turn and lead Beatrice back into the house. Her little friend followed meekly behind.

Beatrice's outburst of tears came instantly. Mose moved through a small group of welcoming people and headed to the back of the house. A dining-room table burdened with food blocked his path. Plain men and women sat at the table together, something Sarah had never seen before. Old Order Amish folk ate separately, the men always first while the women were busy feeding the *kinder*.

Beatrice tried to run off, but Mose caught her by the collar of her dress. "I think some time in the back bedroom is the answer to all this commotion."

An older woman, her gray hair wrapped in a tight bun and covered with a perfectly positioned prayer *kapp*, lifted her portly body to her feet. Her blue eyes flashed fire. "You've upset her now. It will take me hours to calm her down. Why don't you let me take care of this and you find yourself a spot at the table?"

Sarah stood just inside the great room's door watching the scene play out across the room. "I could..." she began, only to be cut off by Mose.

"*Danke*, Sarah, but I think I can manage this young rebel without anyone's help."

The woman turned in Sarah's direction and glared at her with a hard stare that twisted her features. "Who is this woman and why is she here, Mose?"

"This is none of your concern, Ulla. As Greta's mother, I'm sure you only want what's best for Beatrice and meant no harm, but babying the *kinder* only makes her moods worse."

Mose turned toward Sarah, Beatrice still in tow. He motioned for Sarah to join him and then put his arm around her waist as they walked toward the dining-room table at the back of the room. "*Mamm*, *Daed*, let me introduce you to someone very special. This is Sarah, my new *frau*. We met in Lancaster and married there. I hope you will make her feel *willkummed* in your *haus*."

Sarah didn't know what to do or say. She stood stone still next to Mose, watching the tiny woman who birthed Mose smile at her in bemusement from across the table. *How could such a small woman have given birth to someone as large as Mose?* His *mamm* looked to be in her late sixties. Even dressed in Amish clothes, she looked more *Englisch* than plain because of her wild shock of red hair. Thick locks pushed at her prayer *kapp* from every angle and left it tilted in disarray.

His father, an older version of Mose, wore his blunt cut, blondish-gray hair to his ears. His beard reached his shirt front. Impressive gray streaks blended in with wiry red and blond strands, making him look distinguished.

She waited for their reaction to Mose's declaration. *Let this go well.* Linda came over and put her arm around Sarah's shoulders in a show of solidarity.

Mose's mother looked at her husband in confusion,

as if someone had just said the moon was made of green cheese. His father, clear-eyed and alert, was the first to come to grips with Mose's words. "*Willkumm*! Congratulations, my son and new daughter. This is *gut* news. It's time you found a woman, Mose. Come, Sarah. Sit with us, and eat. You have to be tired from your long journey."

The look on Mose's father's face told her he knew who she was. He'd grown up with Bishop Miller. Mose had told her they were still friends. He must have heard everything by now. News traveled fast in their world. He restrained himself as he spoke words of welcome he might not feel. "I'm sure you will make my son very happy. *Bitte*, sit. Its humble food we offer, but I'm sure you're used to eating this plain way."

Several people rose from the table and took their plates to the front of the house, making room for them at the long table. Sarah and Linda chose a spot next to each other. Sarah's stomach roiled, the meal's aroma so strong she thought she might be ill. "*Danke* for your warm *willkumm*." She struggled to smile. "I'm sure my arrival has come as quite a surprise to you all."

A loud voice rang out in the great room. "I will not be hushed. Mose had no right. No right. Greta is barely cold in the grave and he marries this woman. I will not have it, do you hear." The front door slammed shut. Silence screamed through the house.

Sarah looked around for Greta's mother, the silver-haired woman who'd made such a fuss just moments before. She and the beautiful young woman standing next to her had disappeared from the gathering.

Linda reached for a bowl of buttery potatoes placed in front of Sarah, and whispered in her ear. "That was

Greta's mother. She's upset. Time will heal her pain and anger."

Sarah's stomach churned. She took the bowl of potatoes and quickly passed them to the man on her right. The smell of them was more than she could manage. Reaching out, she grabbed a hot roll and stuffed it in her mouth and chewed fast. *Please, Gott. Don't let me get sick. Please.* She glanced up and saw Mose's mother looking at her, her brow knitted with a questioning glance. Mose had sisters and brothers. The older woman had been pregnant many times. Did she know already, just by the look on Sarah's face, that she was pregnant?

When the meal was over and Theda and her two teenage granddaughters had cleared the dishes away, the men made themselves comfortable on a well-stuffed couch in the great room. Linda led the way to the back bathroom.

Beatrice, excited by the promise of bubbles in her bathwater, undressed herself with lightning speed. Sarah undressed Mercy and slipped the toddler into the warm, sudsy water next to her older sister. "The bubbles tickle me," Beatrice insisted, splashing water toward her little sister, who cried the moment the water touched her warm body.

"That wasn't very nice," Sarah scolded and felt disappointed when the girl didn't seem the least bit ashamed of her actions. She had splashed Mercy in the face intentionally. Sarah knew the child needed discipline, but wasn't sure what to do. She handed Mercy over to Linda and took a seat nearer Beatrice. In her most authoritative voice, she said. "I think it best you wash and get out, Beatrice."

Beatrice ignored her directions and dived under the water, coming up as slick as a seal. Sarah took the washcloth Linda handed her and began to apply soap to the soft rag. Hitting all the important spots, she cleaned Beatrice as the child wiggled and squirmed to get away. With a fluffy white towel she'd pulled from the rail, she wrapped it around Beatrice and pulled the resisting child from the tub. As soon as Beatrice's feet hit the bathroom rug she tried to get away from Sarah's grasp and run. Sarah held her by the arm.

"Perhaps tomorrow, after you've thought about how you scared Mercy, you can have a longer bath. But for tonight, it's bedtime for you."

Sobbing, Beatrice slapped at Sarah's hands but finally put up with being dried as a shiver hit her.

"Sounds like someone needs an early night." Mose stood in the bathroom door, his hand braced against the wood framework. He smiled at Sarah, but his brows lowered as he glanced over at Beatrice. "We've talked about this before, young daughter. Your sister does not like water splashed in her face."

Beatrice shrugged but seemed to know better than to talk back to her father. "I'm sorry, *Daed*. I was just having fun."

"I don't think Mercy was having fun. Do you?"

"Nee."

"Tell your sister you're sorry." Mose waited.

"I'm sorry, Mercy." Beatrice's frown told Sarah this spoiled little girl would need a lot of love and training in order to set her on a straight path.

Mose glanced at Sarah. "I guess we've let her get away with too much. It was hard to know when to discipline and when to overlook her behavior."

Sarah thought of Greta and how much this child must miss her mother. Any child would act out after the loss of her mother. She thought back to her own behavior after her mother had left, and sighed. "Time and lots of love will work all this out."

"I hope you're right." Mose smiled at Sarah.

Mose was a sweet and understanding man. Sarah only hoped she could someday give him what he deserved. A wife's love.

Chapter Eleven

Mose drained the last drops of his second mug of coffee and reached for the pot.

"Too much of that will put your nerves on edge."

Mose poured a half cup and flashed his mother a welcoming smile. *"Guder mariye, Mamm."*

She scuffed toward the deep farm sink. A black apron already draped her light pink day dress. Her swollen feet were stuffed into the same fluffy blue house shoes she wore every morning, the bright shade of blue a secret passion of hers. After grabbing a white cup from the open shelf overhead, she pulled out a wooden chair and joined him at the small kitchen table littered with egg-smeared breakfast dishes.

Sunlight streamed in through the small window at the sink, filling the once dim room with the bright yellow glow of early morning. For as long as he could remember, his mother had risen with the sun and gone to bed with the chickens. "I know I drink too much coffee. I have a lot to do today and not a lot of time to do it in. I need the energy." Mose poured her a cup of the dark brew. He murmured a laugh when she scooped out three heaping teaspoons of sugar and made a terrible racket stirring the coffee, erasing the evidence of her sweet tooth.

Mose patted her wrinkled hand and met her gaze. She'd done her best to pin down her prayer *kapp* but a froth of ginger curls, brought on by high humidity, had left her disheveled. He noticed deeper lines and wrinkles on her face and made a mental note to spend more time with her now that he was home. She was getting older and he wanted her to know how much she meant to him. "Everyone still sleeping?"

"All but your *daed*. He woke up with the roosters. He had an early job over at the big house he bought last week."

"I didn't know he was interested in enlarging the community." Mose downed the last of his coffee and added his heavy mug to the pile of dishes in front of him.

"He's been talking about expanding for months and is excited about this last *haus* purchase now that you've remarried. You'll be needing a new place to live. He's decided to fix it up real nice for you and Sarah."

Mose watched his mother draw circles on the wooden table, a sign she wanted to talk. She probably needed to ask a few questions. Questions he had no interest in answering. "He doesn't have to do that, *Mamm*. The *kinder* have loved living here the last year, but Sarah and I can start out our marriage at my *haus* for a while. I'm sure the girls will feel more at ease in familiar surroundings."

She looked at him, her brows furrowing. "Do you really think your new wife will want to live with all of Greta's things around her, reminding her you had a beloved wife who died and left everything behind for her to dust?"

Mose heard his mother's common sense. "I hadn't thought—"

"*Ach*, a man wouldn't, would he? But a woman would, and I can tell you, I'd have a problem with it. Let your *daed* do what he can to make you and Sarah comfortable in this new place. He wants to help, to feel useful in his old age. You can pay us rent until you find a different place if this house doesn't suit Sarah. Or is your pride the issue?" Her ginger eyebrow went up in an arch. She knew how to push his buttons.

"*Nee*, it's not pride. I just didn't think how living around Greta's things would make Sarah feel. She deserves her own home, things that make her happy."

"She does." His mother busied her fingers tidying her *kapp*. "I'm not sure what's going on between you and Sarah, but I know you. I trust your wisdom. She's only been a widow for six months. I can't see how she'd be over Joseph's death so soon, not the way I hear those two were in love. You showed no interest in getting a new *frau* before you left. All this leaves a *mamm* to wonder what's going on. There's been rumors floating around and people talking. Some say Sarah was to be shunned before you married her. I was wondering if it's true."

"Ignore the rumors. You know how people are. They have too much empty time on their hands. Do you really think I'd have married Joseph's widow if there hadn't been a good reason? Sarah and I need each other, so we got married. It's as simple as that. Joseph would have done anything for me, and I'm just making sure his widow is well cared for. You know better than I that love can grow from friendship. You and *Daed* married after knowing each other just two weeks."

"Now, let's not go throwing stones in my direction,"

his mother said with a frown. She snatched up his dishes and started to stand.

"*Mamm*, my girls needed a *mamm*. Sarah needed a husband. If she was good enough for Joseph, she's good enough for me. We struck a deal. She makes me happy and I think she's happy, too. Time will tell if we can make a strong marriage out of this friendship. I trust *Gott* to direct us, and as long as the girls are happy and well cared for…that's all I need."

Placing her son's dishes in the sink, she turned on the faucet and ran water. Sloshing the dishes around, she turned toward him, a playful glint in her blue eyes. "You know I never meddle. Do what's best. I didn't mean to sound critical of your choices."

Mose smiled at his petite *mamm*, but then got serious. "I do have something I need to talk to you about, and I don't want you to start to worry." He watched her cheerful smile disappear.

"You sound so serious. Is it Sarah?" She sat back down, her damp hands flat on the table.

Mose shrugged. "No, Sarah's fine, but she did notice Mercy has difficulty hearing. We're taking her to the pediatrician. I called their office a minute ago. We have an appointment this afternoon." He patted her hand. "I don't want you to worry. Sarah said this could be nothing more than built-up ear wax, but we need to be sure. Please don't mention any of this to anyone."

"If you mean to Ulla, of course I won't. She's already upset with you for bringing home a wife. What do you think I am, a trouble-making gossip?"

Mose laughed out loud. Gossip was the Amish woman's television. "Of course I don't. It's just better to know what we're dealing with before we mention to family that Mercy might be deaf."

"Oh, dear. You think it could be that bad? But if she is, we must know this is *Gott's* will for her life." She reached out for his hand, her fingers digging into his skin.

Mose unplugged his charging cell phone from the electrical outlet and turned back to his mother. "As soon as we find out what's up, I'll call you from the doctor's office. I'm leaving my phone on the table so you won't worry any longer than you have to."

His mother's face paled. She took the phone and slid it into her apron pocket.

Mose had no memory of ever being in a doctor's office. Greta always took the girls to their medical appointments. He wasn't sure what he'd expected, but it certainly wasn't this big, modern office, or the crowd of people peppered around the room. Comfortable-looking chairs lined walls painted a pleasant tan color. Pictures of *Englisch* children's favorite cartoon characters were everywhere.

Glancing about, he was surprised to see several plain people clustered together in the corner of the room, just on the edge of *Englisch* mothers, their children in tow or playing nearby with simple toys.

He motioned for Sarah to sit in one of the chairs nearest the door and watched as she made herself comfortable.

He walked to the opened window at the left of the room and waited for the young woman typing on a computer to look up.

"May I help you?" She spoke loudly when she finally

acknowledged him. No doubt trying to be heard over the crying babies and chattering mothers.

"My name is Mose Fischer, and this is Mercy Fischer. We have an appointment with Doctor Hillsborough at ten o'clock." He kissed his daughter on the top of her *kapp* and returned the woman's half smile.

All business, the young woman continued to type, her fingers dancing across the keyboard. She glanced at him. "Doctor's running a bit late. Just have a seat, and I'll let you know when you're next."

"Danke." He sat next to Sarah, who seemed mesmerized by all the colorful art around her. "Your first time in a doctor's office, too?"

She smiled, a dimple he'd never noticed before making her look young and very attractive. He watched as she began to rummage through her big bag and brought out a faceless doll for Mercy. Knowing her background and Adolph's rigid ways, he doubted she'd ever set foot in a doctor's office, much less a pediatrician's office, no matter how sick she'd been.

"Yes, my first time. You?"

"I'm sure I must have gone to the doctor at one time or another when I was young. I just don't remember, so it's like the first time."

Mercy reached for the bottle in his hand and began to suckle. She seemed so calm and healthy. How could anything be wrong with her? "Do you think we've made a mistake?" Mose asked. "She looks fine."

Sarah leaned back in her chair and pondered his question. "Right or wrong, we have to know. She deserves to be checked. If it's not her hearing slowing down her speech, we have to find out what is wrong.

She should be saying words by now, making sounds. She's too quiet."

Mose saw her concern and felt foolish for asking his question. Sarah was a good mother, kind and attentive. He and the girls were blessed to have her. *Gott* had filled an empty spot in his heart. Every day he grew more grateful to have Sarah in his life. "I know you're right. I guess I'm just nervous."

She looked at him. Worry etched her face with lines. "I'm concerned, too. Let's try to stay calm until the doctor tells us something concrete. *Gott* has a plan for her life, and I'm praying it doesn't involve deafness."

"Mercy Fischer."

Mose grabbed Sarah's hand and together they walked behind the woman holding Mercy's chart.

Down to just a cloth diaper, Mercy squirmed in her father's arms, her face red from crying throughout the extensive medical examination given by the pediatrician.

Standing next to Mose, Sarah brushed back the sweaty fair hair from the child's forehead and glanced into her husband's face. To a stranger his expression may have appeared calm, but she noticed the slight tick of nerves twitching his bottom lip. She knew he was as nervous as she felt. Would the *Englisch* doctor's diagnosis be grim?

"I have a good idea what's going on." Dr. Hillsborough finally spoke. She looked at Sarah and Mose and smiled. She grabbed her prescription pad off her desk and began to write. "I'm pretty sure Mercy has had several serious ear infections, which is very common in children her age. It looks like fluid's now trapped behind her eardrums, keeping her from hearing little more than muffled sounds. This much fluid could cause uncomfortable pressure. Has she run a temperature recently, or seemed unusually cranky?"

Mose hung his head. "She seemed hot and cried a lot on the train a few weeks ago, while on our way to Lancaster. I thought I'd just dressed her too warm and didn't pay much attention to her crankiness. She's cried a lot since her mother died and she's been teething recently."

"You shouldn't feel guilty, Mr. Fischer. Ear infections can easily crop up and get out of hand fast, even under the best of conditions. Babies are often cranky, and we assume it's their teeth breaking through or a sour stomach. Let's just make sure she takes a full ten days of the antibiotic I'm prescribing, and then we'll have her in for a myringotomy. I'll insert drainage tubes, so this buildup of fluids doesn't happen again. The procedure is simple and then the tubes can alleviate any pressure pain she's experiencing." She tossed her pad on her crowded desk and turned to take Sarah's hand. "Stop looking so concerned, Mrs. Fischer. Children are very resilient. They bounce back faster than we adults do."

"You're positive surgery is necessary?" Mose's arms tightening around Mercy's thin body.

"I do this procedure almost every day. It's not a serious operation, I promise you. She'll only be in the hospital for a few hours at most and then go home. Simple infections have been known to become very serious if ignored over a period of time. It's good that you noticed the problem so fast, Mrs. Fischer, and brought her in. Children have gone deaf from ear infections left untreated."

Sarah leaned in. "Is it possible the medication can work out her problems and the surgery not be needed?"

"Sadly, no. The tubes in Mercy's ears are very tiny, and she's probably going to have problems until they grow a bit larger. I suggest we start her on the medication today and go from there. We'll schedule the operation while you're in the office…for two weeks from now. I'll recheck her the day we do the surgery. Does that plan work for both of you?"

Mose and Sarah nodded their head in unison. Sarah spoke up. "She will be able to hear clearly again?"

"Oh, yes. She'll be catching up with her sister's chatter in no time. I know this has been a trying time for you and your husband, but now you can relax. You're doing your very best for her."

Sarah was relieved when they walked out of the doctor's office, into the warm breeze. She glanced over at Mose, saw the grin on his face and knew he was as thrilled with the doctor's diagnosis as she was. There was only the surgery to get through and Mercy's hearing would be restored. She lifted her face toward the morning sun and enjoyed its warmth. *Thank you, Lord. You are ever faithful.*

That evening Mose ate his meal, but didn't taste the food. His mind stayed on Mercy and the upcoming surgery in a few weeks. Sarah had given the baby her first spoonful of antibiotic and he prayed *Gott* would protect the child sitting next to him.

Mose leaned over, cutting Beatrice's chicken, and reminded his daughter to use her napkin. He smiled at Mercy. The child banged her spoon at him, her grin growing into a drooling river of squished peas.

"Today we took Mercy to see the doctor," Mose said, picking a quiet moment at the table to speak.

Otto's fork full of cottage fries froze halfway to his mouth.

Theda leaned forward. "You told me on the phone she'd be fine, but what else did you learn?"

Mose looked into his mother's eyes. "Mercy has an infection in her middle ear. She'll need to have tubes inserted to help drain the fluid."

Otto finished his bite of potatoes. "Has this infection you speak of...has it damaged her hearing?"

Mose pushed his peas around the plate. "Yes, her hearing was affected, but the doctor feels the surgery will fix the problem."

"Is the doctor sure?" Theda's gaze was glued to Mercy.

"We will ask for *Gott's* will. He loves her more than we do." Mose looked over at his *mamm* and then to Sarah and forced a smile.

"Yes," Otto agreed. "When is this surgery to happen?"

"Soon. Two weeks," Mose said, looking at his father.

"*Gott* has a plan for Mercy. We must not question why this happened." Otto continued to eat. The conversation had ended as far as his *daed* was concerned, but Mose's brows pinched with concern. He'd believed in *Gott's* will for Greta, and she had died in his arms.

Would *Gott* protect Mercy? He wasn't so sure. Mose looked at his food on his plate, his appetite gone. His thoughts swirled. Could he live with another loss?

Sarah reached across the table and grasped his hand, her eyes conveying her love for his youngest child. "She will be fine, Mose. We have to believe *Gott* knows what He's doing."

Chapter Twelve

The shiny black car Mose had borrowed from his brother to run errands that morning seemed quiet without Beatrice's constant stream of questions and comments coming from the backseat. They'd dropped the girls off at their *Grandmammi* Ulla's house, and then gone for a ride through Sarasota, giving Sarah some much-needed rest and relaxation.

The sway of the automobile soothed her, as Mose drove through the streets lined in plain white houses and tidy lawns. She fought the urge to close her eyes and sleep. Florida, with its sunny beaches and tall palm trees, was so different from the rolling Lancaster farmland she was used to.

This morning she'd been glad to discover the town of Pinecraft was bigger than she'd first thought a week before. Small, brightly painted storefronts, with unique names, offered homemade goods and hot Amish meals to the constant flow of tourists invading the town in staggering numbers during the winter months. Pushing aside the damp hair that escaped her *kapp*, Sarah welcomed the cool breeze blowing in through the car window. It had rained in the early morning hours, just long enough to make the hot Florida air feel drenched with humidity.

"*Daed* said the *haus* will be ready later today. I want you to see it before I tell him we'll take it." Traffic was brisk but Mose flashed a quick smile Sarah's way.

A small scar next to Mose's mouth came into view. She'd never noticed it before, but then, there were a lot of things about Mose she didn't know. Things she needed to know if she was going to be a good wife to him.

"That's *gut*," she said. "The girls no longer have a place to call home. They're desperate for order in their lives. Things have been so hectic this past week and Beatrice is having a hard time."

"If you mean she's behaving badly, I agree." Mose drove slowly down the street just blocks from his parents' home. Every house in the neighborhood of central Pinecraft looked exactly the same. Square, white and set back from the road. Mose turned into one of the long driveways and slowed to a stop at the edge of the wide, wooden porch painted a glossy white. He jerked the keys out of the car's ignition and turned back to her.

"You sound like my *mamm*. Always making excuses for Beatrice. The time has come to get that young lady under control. I won't have her treating Mercy badly, and the way she talks to you is completely out of line." Mose reached over and touched Sarah's hand, spreading a warm tingling sensation he'd come to enjoy. "I'm glad she has you, Sarah. You're a kind woman and wonderful *mamm*."

"She doesn't see me as her *mamm* yet. I'm just someone who takes time away from you. Give her grace until she's adjusted."

Otto Fischer walked out of the house and waved, beckoning them to get out of the car. Cream-colored paint dotted the navy overalls that covered his shirt and pants. His gray hair stood in spikes, as if he'd been running his fingers through the thick mop.

"Looks like *daed's* ready to get this *haus* inspection over with."

"I've noticed your *daed's* not a man to waste time." Sarah gazed around the front yard as she stepped out onto sparse, crispy grass that begged for a soaking from the cracked hose on the ground.

"You two took long enough." Otto's smile took the bite out of his words.

"*Guder mariye* to you, too, *Daed*." Mose stepped aside and insisted Sarah go into the house first. "We had to take the *kinder* over to Ulla's, and she had much to say to me before I left."

"How many times did she mention she hasn't seen the girls in a while? She called last night and you'd have thought it had been a year since their last visit to her *haus*. *Guder mariye*, Sarah. Did you sleep well?"

"I did, *danke*." Sarah glanced around the large open room they'd stepped into, taking in the dark wood floors and creamy walls. She hurried over to the gleaming kitchen in the corner, drawn like a bug to a light. She touched the island's stone counter with her fingertips and marveled at the swirl of colors within the large slab of smooth granite. Making bread here would be a joy.

She took a slow turn and tried to take everything in. She'd never seen a house as big as this. Linda had told her these large, newly built homes existed on the fringe of the small Amish community of Pinecraft, but to live in one herself? Sarah was used to small, closed-in rooms. This large area glowed with early morning sunshine. She'd never seen such fancy fixtures or appliances. How would she learn to cook on this gleaming stove with five burners? The house had to use electricity. She looked up and saw the light fixture and knew these were not oil lights. Perhaps a gas generator fueled the electricity? She turned to face Mose. This was an *Englisch* house he'd brought her to. What was he thinking?

"I'll leave you two to have a look round. I'll be back inside later. I've still got to fix that sliding patio door. The thing keeps sticking." Otto shifted the paint bucket and plastic sheeting he held in his hands. He scrubbed one paint-spattered hand down his overalls before opening the front door and letting it bang behind him.

Mose turned to Sarah. "So, is the *haus gut* enough, or do you want to look at a few more? *Daed* can rent this one to someone else. We won't hurt his feelings."

The grin on his face told her he liked the house. Would he understand if she didn't want to live here? She wanted to please him, not be picky and difficult, but would she ever feel at home in this modern palace? "There seems to be plenty of room."

"I hear a but on the end of that sentence." Mose moved closer and took her right hand. His thumb rubbed her palm in a swirl of rough skin against soft. His gaze flirted with hers until she looked away, a shy smile on her lips, the room suddenly uncomfortably warm. She pulled her hand away and turned toward the window above the deep sink. Somehow Mose had gotten under her skin, made her feel things she hadn't felt since Joseph was alive. The emotions swirling in her stomach scared her. Clearing her voice, she spoke, hoping she wouldn't sound as shaky as her legs felt. "*Nee…nee.* I like the house. It's just more modern than I'm used to, that's all. And so large."

"We can look at other houses."

She turned back to Mose and silently chastised herself. Mose's father had gone to a lot of trouble to make this house nice for them. The least she could do was make a fair assessment before coming to a decision. "Please." She forced a smile and prayed *Gott* would speak to her about what to say and do. Often she handled things wrong and she so desperately wanted to get this right. "Let's look through the rest of the house and see if we can make a home here. I'm just surprised by the extras. I'm not used to such grand living. Pinecraft is so different from Lancaster. I hope you understand."

His grin was back, his gaze warm. He took her by the arm and playfully propelled her forward. "Let's go take a look."

Sarah smiled and let him guide her down a long hall lined with closed doors. She enjoyed his lighthearted manner and thanked *Gott* she'd found him. Joseph had been easygoing and had often made her laugh, too. Her heart ached as soon as she thought of Joseph. She touched her stomach with the flat of her hand and felt the bump, their child growing deep inside. She had to tell Mose about the baby. There was no use putting it off. The truth had to come out.

"Look at this bedroom. It's perfect for the girls."

Sarah realized she still stood in the hallway, her hand on her stomach, reeling with new, raw emotions. She was going to be the mother. The thought was so wonderful she had to fight not to cry.

"I'm coming," Sarah called and entered the soft pink room. She whirled around, her long skirt fluttering about her ankles. The room had big windows and a closet large enough to hold all their clothes and then some. "What a terrible waste of space." Shelves filled one side and two clothes bars filled the other. "Do the *Englisch* really have this many clothes?"

"I can't speak from experience but since this house was once owned by *Englisch*, I have a feeling they do." He walked a few feet and opened a pair of double doors at the end of the hallway.

Sarah gasped as she took in the sheer size of the light tan room. Large windows and a sliding glass door allowed light to flood inside.

"It's not that big." Mose's laughter mingled with his words.

"Maybe not to you, but to me it's the size of a barn." Sarah tried to imagine a bed and dresser swallowed up in the expansive room. "What will we fill the room with?"

"The new king-size bed I finished just before I left for Lancaster. It's been waiting in the barn for someone to buy." Mose grinned and disappeared through a door at the back of the room.

She'd never seen a king-size bed, but couldn't wait to see it. Several pieces of furniture in his *mamm's* house showed his fine workmanship and she grew excited.

She walked into the master closet and shook her head in disgust. Again, what a waste of space. She owned a handful of dresses and two pairs of shoes. She had no clue how many clothes Mose owned, but they'd never fill this large walk-in closet.

"The bathroom's nice." Mose's voice echoed, bouncing off the walls.

Sarah moved toward the door he'd disappeared through and paused. Two sinks, a toilet and bathtub gleamed in the bright overhead lighting. Stepping in farther, Sarah saw her own reflection in the massive mirror over the sinks. She had no idea her hair was so bright red, or that she'd put on so much weight. What made Mose look at her as though she was a plate of iced cookies? She turned on her heel and scurried back to the kitchen.

"You don't like it, do you?" Mose's disappointment was palpable.

"I do like it. It's just not what I'm used to," she murmured.

"We don't have to take it, Sarah. Like I said, *Daed* can easily rent it out to someone else." He stood just inside the kitchen, his shoulder resting against a smooth wall.

"You like it, don't you?" Sarah knew his answer before he spoke. She was able to read his expressions.

"I can see the *kinder* running and playing without bumping into walls." He grinned, adding, "We'd have lots of room for a couple more *bobbels* here."

Sarah's tongue glued to the top of her mouth. She forced herself to look up. His smile was infectious and she returned a trembling, shy grin. They were alone. Nothing held her back from telling him her secret. She trusted him. Wanted him to know. Longed for him to be happy for them. Sarah took in a breath. "I need to talk to you about something wonderful, and I want you to hear me out before you speak."

Mose frowned at her, his concern adding wrinkles to his forehead. "Did I upset you with the suggestion there could be more children growing up in this home?" He reached out to her.

Sarah grasped his hand in hers and smiled, strong feeling for this vibrant man building in her heart. "No, not at all. It's just the opposite. I'm having a *bobbel*, Mose. I wanted to share the news with you."

Mose pulled her into his arms and crushed her to his chest as he murmured, "I already know."

Sarah leaned away. Mose's smile of joy left her breathless. "You already knew?"

"Of course I knew, silly. I'm the father of two. I know when a woman is carrying a child. I've known since I met you."

"But why didn't you say something? Why would you marry me if you knew I was pregnant?" Sarah's mind reeled, memories flashing like a slide show. She'd never known anyone as generous a Mose Fischer. He'd known all along and had never said a word, never questioned her.

"I first married you because I loved Joseph like a *bruder*. We grew up together, shared our hopes and dreams. I found his wife in need of me, and I found her fascinating. I needed a mother for my *kinder*. There was never a question of what should be done. It made perfect sense to do the right thing. Who else would love Joseph's child as much as me? I'll make a good father for him or her. I promise you."

He pulled her closer as tears began to flow down her face. Tenderly he held her in his arms, patting her as she clung to the front of his shirt. Grief flowed out of her, and in its place came relief and gratitude. Weak with emotion, she leaned against his chest and took in gulping sobs of air laced with joy.

Joseph was gone, but Mose was here now.

"Have you seen a midwife yet?" His warm breath stirred her hair as he spoke softly in her ear.

"Not yet," Sarah admitted, her head still pressed against his chest. She liked the feel of his arms around her, the way he tenderly kissed her cheek. "I just recently found out. But Linda says I must go to the *Englisch* doctor for a sonogram, to make sure the *bobbel* is okay."

"We'll get an appointment for you." Mose rubbed her back, making her warm and breathless in the cool, air-conditioned house.

Sarah was thrilled and relieved that she wasn't alone anymore. But did she truly deserve this happiness? She wasn't so sure.

A few hours later, Mose and Otto lifted out the heavy sliding glass door and together leaned it against the patio wall.

"I just need to take these old runners out and put in some new ones." Otto glanced Mose's way. He grunted as he squatted, his old knees cracking like popcorn. It took only a moment to remove the old tracks, stuff the plastic packaging into his overall pocket and slip the new tracks in place. "I'm glad you two decided to take this place." Otto checked the rollers and grinned in satisfaction. "I have a good feeling about this *haus*. It may be a bit fancy, but it will make a great home for the *kinder* to grow in."

"Sarah's finally okay with the *haus*. At first she was concerned what people might say, it being so different than the tract homes close by."

Otto's brows arched. "How are you two doing? Rumor has it the girl's got a temper. She use it on you yet?"

Mose frowned in frustration. He dreaded the talk he knew he had to have with his father.

Together the two men replaced the door in its railing. Mose stretched out his back. "That door was heavy. Let's rest." He pointed to the wooden steps that led down into the shaded yard and sat on the first step. His father sat one step down.

Mose prayed to *Gott* as he looked at his scuffed steel-toed boots and tried to gather the right words to say. "I don't know what temper you're referring to, *Daed*. Sarah's never flared up at me, but that's not saying she won't, or that she doesn't have a temper. Most women do, including *Mamm*." He and his father shared a secret grin. "Sarah and I are getting along fine and the *kinder* seem happy, which makes me happy. I've got nothing to grumble about, except certain family members who keep poking their nose where it doesn't belong. Especially Ulla. You know what she's like. You're her bishop. Maybe you could help keep her in line and out of my personal life."

"I have talked with her, Mose...but you must talk to her, too." Otto swatted at a mosquito. "Ulla thinks you've replaced Greta too soon. She's hurting. *Gott* made women tenderhearted. She needs time to heal. It's the other rumors causing all the family to chatter. Ever since you brought Sarah home there's been speculation flying back and forth between Pinecraft and Lancaster County. Mostly about her behavior back home. Even your *mamm's* guilty of adding to the drama. She thinks Sarah's pregnant."

Mose rubbed his hand across his damp forehead. "Sarah *is* pregnant."

"Then why in the world would you…" Otto's sandy brows furrowed in astonishment as he looked up at his son.

"Marry her? Is that what you're asking? Why would I marry Sarah and raise Joseph's baby as my own?"

"How can it be Joseph's *kinder*, Mose? Do the math. He's been dead for six months. She's feeding you a lie and you're believing her. Ralf Miller warned me Sarah would bring trouble to our community. I'm beginning to believe him." Otto stood up, his face flushed with anger.

"Lower your voice, *Daed*. Sarah's just inside the *haus*. She might hear your foolishness."

Otto sat back down on the step with a thump. "Then tell me. How do you know for sure this baby is Joseph's?"

"Because I trust Sarah. I've never caught her in a lie. She's an honorable woman. She didn't suspect she might be pregnant before Joseph died, and later blamed her weakness and bad stomach on grief, but I knew better. She's had a test and it was positive."

"*Gott* bless her. Poor woman." Otto wiped sweat from his upper lip. "Joseph died in such a tragic way. I can see how she could have missed the signs."

"Life's caught up with her. The *bobbel* will be due in a few months, maybe less. Sarah will have an appointment for a sonogram in a couple of days. When we tell the family, they'd better be kind to her, *Daed*. I won't have her upset over their unwarranted suspicions. She's been through enough."

Otto's shoulders visibly slumped. "Pregnant. Who would have guessed? I'll talk to the family and church elders. They'll be good to her and the *kinder* or they'll answer to me. What a blessing this child would have been to Joseph's *mamm* and *daed*." Otto met Mose's gaze. "I'm sorry I didn't trust you. I should have known there would be more to her story."

Mose put his hand on his father's bony shoulder. "Sarah and I are going to break the news about the baby at Mercy's birthday gathering tomorrow night. Maybe once everyone knows the facts, they'll shut their mouths."

"Don't count on it, especially when it comes to Ulla." Otto smirked. "She likes to talk."

Sarah slid open the glass door and stepped out onto the wooden deck behind them. "The door opens so easy now. You two did a fine job."

"That we did." Otto stood and wiped his brow.

Mose patted the wooden step his father had just vacated. "Come, join me. You haven't seen the back yard yet."

Sarah hurried over, gathered up her full skirt and eased down on the wooden plank. She scooted close to Mose as Otto stepped past her with a smile.

"It's lovely out here. Just look at that palm tree." She pointed to a tall, well-trimmed tree in the corner of the fenced yard. "It has to be twenty-feet tall. The *kinder* are going to enjoy playing in the shade in the afternoon." Sarah's eyes were bright with excitement.

"I can see the two of them digging in that flower bed. Beatrice loves to eat dirt. We'll have to watch her closely." Mose laughed and grabbed her hand, his thumb rubbing the top of her knuckles, his heart full of joy. Sarah had become his friend, and now other emotions flooded his mind. He longed to pull her close, touch her hair, where a soft curl danced in the wind.

Sarah laughed with him. "This is going to make a wonderful home for us, Mose. You, me and the *kinder*."

Mose glanced at his father and smiled. Everything seemed to be falling into place. He hadn't felt this worry-free since before Greta had died, and the feeling was wonderful. Thunder rumbled overhead, the fast approaching cluster of dark clouds threatening a storm soon to come.

Chapter Thirteen

Linda honked from outside, the golf cart motor revving as the front door opened. Sarah gave her impatient friend a wave. She grabbed her satchel and turned to Mose's mother.

The old rocking chair groaned with Theda's every movement. Her fingers knew when to pull and tug on the thick yarn as she crocheted a pink blanket for Beatrice.

"I won't be long. Linda and I are just going to Mose's shop to pick out some furniture for the new *haus*." Sarah rubbed her hand across her slightly protruding stomach, the baby's movements growing stronger as each day passed. "The girls should sleep for at least another hour."

"Don't worry about those two. Do your shopping and have a nice time. And tell that girl I said not to drive so fast in that fancy cart." Theda sounded firm but softened her words with a generous smile.

Pausing at the opened door, Sarah straightened her *kapp* and reinforced several pins to make sure the lightweight prayer covering was firmly held down. The brisk Florida winds often caught her unaware.

"Is there anything I can get you while I'm out? We're going to the market for a few things for the party tonight."

"*Nee.* Everyone's bringing a dish. There'll be enough food. Go. Enjoy yourself. You spend too much time in the house worrying about those girls."

Sarah hurried out the door, her blue dress flying behind her as she ran across the grass to the light blue golf cart. She plopped on the passenger seat. The new cart's seat cushions were made of the softest leather. She allowed her fingers to knead into the soft hide before buckling her seat belt, and then fiddled with the dangling white leather canopy that embellished the fancy cart. "Another *Englisch* contraption, Linda? Does no one use a buggy in Pinecraft?"

"Not really. There's one parked at the restaurant on the edge of town, but it's just for show. Kurt took the van this morning, so it was the old tandem bicycle or this. What would you have grabbed?"

Her question was accompanied by a mischievous grin. Linda's dress, the palest pink, matched her flushed cheeks to perfection. Sarah noticed her white *kapp* sat sideways on a twisted bun of dark hair positioned at the back of her head. Her sister-in-law looked surprisingly spry for a very pregnant woman due to have her first baby soon.

"*Ya*, I think the golf cart." Sarah had no idea what kind of driver Linda might be. A shiver of excitement tingled down her spine. She'd longed for change and now she had it. "I shouldn't be enjoying all these new experiences so much. *Gott's* going to get angry at my growing *Englisch* ways."

With her petite hands on the steering wheel, Linda looked at Sarah and made a silly monkey face. "Don't be ridiculous. You're no longer Old Order Amish or under your father's thumb. *Gott* just wants us to love Him. He doesn't worry Himself with how we get to and fro. Besides, the cart only goes 25 miles an hour and that's only if the wind's blowing at your back." Linda hit the gas pedal, glanced behind them and backed out of the drive. The street was quiet, not a car in sight, which wasn't unusual that early in the morning. "I won't be able to drive much longer. I'm going to enjoy my time behind this wheel while I can." The cart sped down the tree-lined street, going full out. Loose strands of Sarah's long hair whipped her in the face. She leaned back, grabbed the metal frame of the canopy and held on with a death grip.

The old barn smelled of freshly cut wood, stain and the heavy cologne of Mose's last *Englisch* customer.

He wiped a tack cloth over the dusty spindle he'd just cut, admiring the shape and feel of the wood in his hand as much as he had as a boy, when the dream of owning his own furniture business began to form and then consume him.

His father had expected him to become a farmer, like him and his father before him. But Mose had stood his ground, only working on the family farm during harvest, when everyone was expected to pitch in before the weather changed and ruined the crops with frost back in Lancaster County.

The family exodus to Florida had been his dream's

saving grace. He'd bought the old barn with his own hard-earned savings, and soon orders for oak furniture were coming in faster than he could fill them. He'd been forced to hire help, and even with the economy's downturn, he'd found himself dedicating more and more time to furniture-making.

Mose dusted off his pants and ran his fingers through his sweaty hair. He never wore a hat while he worked, but he reached for it now. His growling stomach reminded him he had a roast beef sandwich waiting for him in the cooler up front. Placing the straw hat on the back of his head, he made a move for his office, his mouth watering.

"Another order for that bishop bench came in," Samuel Yoder called over to Mose as he weaved through the sales floor littered with furniture waiting for pickup or delivery.

"*Gut.* You can work late tonight making the seat since you're so good at it."

Short, blond and full of energy, the young new hire gave his boss a grin. His apprenticeship was going well, and he'd soon be working in the back next to Mose. Another man would have to be hired. Someone who would learn like Samuel, by trial and error. They would soon need another hand to fill orders. Mose had learned from the beginning, you got more work out of a happy employee.

"I'm eating early," Mose called over his shoulder. "Sarah made roast beef last night and the leftovers are calling to me. I'll be in the office if you need me."

Samuel sent an envious smile Mose's way and playfully flipped the dust cloth at him as he dusted the table tops around the showroom. "Someday I'll find myself a wife and have a fine sandwich waiting for me, too."

Mose laughed and went into his office just off the main door, his thoughts on Sarah, until Greta's face pushed its way into his mind. His smile faded. He'd begun to miss Greta in a different way since he'd married Sarah. Thoughts of his dead wife came less and less often. He tried to remember how her voice sounded, but Sarah's voice filled the void in his mind. Was it possible to love two women at once?

The bell over the sales door rang out. A strong gust of wind blew in, disheveling papers on his desk. Mose looked up and saw Linda hurry in with Sarah close behind, both women's dresses spotted with fat drops of rain. They busied themselves righting their *kapps*. Sarah waved at Samuel and greeted him. "How are you this fine morning?"

Samuel blushed a fire-engine red as he always did when he saw Sarah. He smiled and dipped his head. "*Guder mariye*, Mrs. Fischer."

Sarah looked young and happy, her pregnancy beginning to show under her loose-fitting dress. Joseph would never see the glow of pregnancy on her face or watch her body blossom with child. Mose pushed away the grief he felt for his friend and forced a smile of welcome on his face. His heartbeat quickened as he walked toward Sarah. "You ladies picked a fine time to be out. It's about to storm from the looks of it."

Sarah whirled at the sound of his voice and rushed over to him. "Mose, the cart ride was wonderful. I felt like a child again, the rain hitting me in the face and the golf cart sliding on the pavement."

He stood and pulled his handkerchief from his pocket

and gently wiped her face dry as her eyes shined at him. He fought the urge to kiss her, his feelings for her becoming more obvious to him every day.

"I'm sorry I dampened your handkerchief."

"Silly girl. That's why I carry the rag. To help beautiful damsels in distress." He heard the flirting in the tone of his voice, like he might have done at nineteen when he'd first met Greta. He cleared his throat and sat back on his leather chair, his thoughts scrambled with joy and sorrow. Greta was his past. Sarah his future. He got up and walked around the old wooden desk that had been his *grossdaadi's* pride and joy. "You've come to pick out furniture?"

Linda stumbled into the room, using the hem of her skirt to wipe away the last of the rain drops from her face. "We have. I hope now's a good time."

"It is. Business has been slow all morning, but Samuel tells me he sold another bench earlier."

Samuel grinned, still busy dusting furniture. "I put all the pieces you mentioned in the corner."

Mose took Sarah's elbow, leading her through a maze of dining-room tables and chairs.

Linda followed and then stopped to touch a rocking chair with a padded seat. "We'll both need one of these soon, Sarah."

Mose watched a happy expression soften Sarah's face. Her hand went to her protruding stomach. "We will, but for today its dining-room furniture that brings me." A warm glow coursed through his body. He'd felt the same draw to Greta while she had been pregnant. The urge to protect and provide. To love.

The king-size bed he'd told her about came into view

and he slowed. "That's the bed I mentioned. Do you think it's going to fit the room okay?"

Sarah glanced toward the bed and then turned to Linda. The women exchanged looks he couldn't read. Neither of them spoke for a moment. Linda finally said, "It's lovely. Did you make the frame?"

"I did. Just finished the project this morning with a mattress set. I'm having it sent over to the house this afternoon if it meets with your approval, *mein frau*."

Sarah's skin grew pink. "I love it. It will make a fine bed for us. *Danke*."

Mose nodded. "*Gut*, I'm glad you like it." In Lancaster he'd felt sure this arranged marriage would work as just a convenience. But now? His heart had become engaged. These new feelings for Sarah made him uncomfortable, as though he was being unfaithful to his dead wife, but he was growing to care for Sarah. Very much.

"There's two sets of dining-room furniture to choose from over there." Mose gestured toward two large wood tables and matching chairs at the back of the showroom. His voice sounded perfectly normal, but he didn't feel normal. He felt like a fool torn between two women. One vibrantly alive. The other...dead.

Sarah and Linda moved toward the tables and examined the matching chairs, their voices low as they chatted and compared styles and colors. Sarah let her hand slide across the smooth surface of the light oak top. "I like this one." The oblong table with simple lines also appealed to him.

Mose motioned to Samuel. "Make sure that dining-room set goes on the truck, too."

"Will do."

"I have to get back to work, Sarah. I can hear my phone ringing." Mose hurried away, leaving the two women to look around the big store on their own. As he grabbed the phone, he threw his hat on his desk and plopped down in his chair, his thoughts on Sarah and the pending birth of the *bobbel*, rather than the customer talking in his ear.

The rain shower passed. Linda chatted as she drove the cart, her thoughts about the furniture they'd seen bubbling out. Sarah couldn't shake the feeling something had been wrong when they'd met up with Mose. He'd seemed quiet and distracted before they left. "Do you think Mose was acting himself?"

"What?"

"Mose. Did he seem tense to you. Withdrawn?"

"*Nee*, just busy. Why?" Linda frowned over at Sarah as she drove down the main road to Pinecraft.

"I just thought he wasn't himself."

"Maybe something's up at work. Or he's just behaving like a man. Kurt's always acting strange. Men, they're different. Kind of weird and romantic at the strangest times."

Had she imagined his mood? He might have just been hungry or tired. "Do you think we could stop by a clothing store? Beatrice needs a few pairs of socks and that sweater she wears is terrible. I'll make her one for winter, but for now a store-bought one will have to do."

"I have a better idea. Why don't we go pack up the rest of her clothes and take them to the new house. We've got plenty of time before we have to be back." Linda did a quick turn down an unfamiliar street and pulled into the driveway of a simple white house.

Sarah realized this had to be the home Greta and Mose had shared. "I think I'll wait in the cart."

"Don't be silly. Mose won't mind you coming in. He's had the place locked up for almost a year. It's time Beatrice has all her things, and someone's got to bring the clothes over to the new *haus* anyway. It might as well be us."

Sarah slid out of the cart. "Do you have keys?"

"Sure. I used to babysit Beatrice when she was little, before the temper and your bad influence on her." Linda grinned. "She's become a little terror since Mercy was born."

"She got a new sister and lost her *mamm*. That's a lot for a four-year-old." Sarah understood the child's loss, but was being firm and consistent with her rules and affection.

Linda stuck the key in the lock. It turned with ease. The front door swung open to a dark house. "It smells dusty in here. Probably from being closed up for so long. Mose needs to think about selling this place or at least renting it out."

Sarah stepped in and looked around, her eyes slowly adjusting to the darkness. She bumped into an overstuffed chair and rubbed her shin. "No electricity?" She tried a switch and was surprised when the overhead light came on and a warm, inviting room was exposed.

Toys lay on the hardwood floors by a comfortable-looking overstuffed couch. Two glasses sat next to each other on the coffee table. The only time Mose had spoken of Greta at length, he'd said her labor had come on suddenly and had lasted for days. She'd hemorrhaged just hours after Mercy's birth and had passed away quietly. She remembered how sad Mose had sounded when he'd told her there had been nothing the doctors could do.

A shiver scurried down her back. No one had disturbed the house in a long time. The dust layer was thick. This had to be the way the house had looked a year ago when they'd left in a hurry for the hospital, their hearts joyful, and the *bobbel* finally coming. She backed up toward the door, feeling like an intruder. This had been Mose and Greta's home. She needed to leave.

"What are you doing here?"

Sarah whirled around, wishing the floor would open and swallow her. Mose stood at the doorway, his face pinched, a mask of pain. "I… We were…"

"Get out!" Mose's tone was harsh, almost whip-like.

Sarah brushed past him in a run, her legs jelly under her, her hand protectively holding her stomach.

What have I done?

Chapter Fourteen

"Please be still, Mercy," Sarah pleaded. "It's almost time for your party and you're not dressed." Bending farther over the bed, Sarah raked her fingers through her disheveled hair and poked wayward strands under her *kapp* and out of her eyes.

She made a grab for one of Mercy's chubby little legs. Wiggling like a worm, Mercy proved too fast and flipped over, her dimpled knees digging into the quilted bedcover. She quickly got away from Sarah, one shoe on, one shoe off. Mercy twisted into a sitting position and smiled a toothy grin.

"*Ach*, for a second pair of hands." Sarah groaned and reached for Mercy again.

Out of thin air, Mose's hand appeared and grabbed Mercy by the foot. He pulled her kicking and giggling toward Sarah. "She's in rare form today." He held the baby's foot while Sarah quickly tugged on the shoe.

"*Danke.*" Sarah slipped the soft cotton dress she'd made for Mercy over the baby's silky head. Two snaps up the back of the dress took forever to fasten. "Let me put your apron on and you'll be ready to meet the world one year older."

Mercy smiled at her and pulled her hand out of her mouth. "Ma…ma…ma," Mercy cooed and grabbed for Sarah's skirt with wet fingers.

"That's right," Sarah encouraged and slipped her white prayer *kapp* on her small head. "You practice your words. After tomorrow's surgery you'll be talking as well as your sister, I promise." She quickly tied the two white ribbons under the child's drool-soaked neck and lifted the baby into her arms.

Mose sat down on the edge of the bed and bent to remove his work shoes. "Put Mercy in her cot for a moment, please. We need to talk."

They hadn't spoken since Mose had ordered her out of his home that morning. Sarah tensed. His demeanor had alarmed her. She raked at her hair, trying to gather up the loose strands. All afternoon she'd replayed what had happened and had regretted her actions. She'd inadvertently crossed an invisible line. What he had to say couldn't be good. Sarah sat Mercy in her bed with one of her favorite cloth books and turned back.

Bent at the waist, Mose placed his elbows on his thighs and sighed deeply. Sarah looked down at his clenched, white-knuckled hands. "I'm sorry for the way I acted. What I said earlier was out of line. Please forgive me." Mose looked up, his eyes rimmed red, his face contorted with pain.

"You mustn't ask for my forgiveness. I should never have gone to your *haus* without permission. I knew it was wrong the moment I stepped through the door. I ask for *your* forgiveness, Mose. I never meant to hurt you." Sarah sat beside him, reaching to take his hand. Her insides trembled.

Mose turned to her. "You didn't hurt me." He patted her hand and kissed her knuckles. "You didn't hurt me at all. I hurt myself. Greta is dead. Life should go on, but I thought…I don't know what I thought." He dropped her hand and pushed his fist into the soft mattress. "I thought if I could keep the house the way it was the day she…perhaps Greta would come home again. I was crazy with pain. Out of my mind and not thinking clearly. That's no excuse for my behavior. I know she's never coming home. I have to face facts and get on with my life. The house needs to be emptied. Someone else will make it a home and bring it back to life with *kinder* running through the halls."

Sarah squeezed his hand in hers and sighed. She knew the depths of his pain and understood completely. She'd left Joseph's clothes at the foot of their bed for months, waiting for him, yet knowing he'd never wear them again. If someone had disturbed them she would have lashed out, too. Sarah wiped a tear from her cheek and blinked. They had this loss in common.

Mose's eyes darkened. Deep lines cut into his forehead. "I'm selling the house. I hadn't been back to our home since the day she died, and yesterday I sought clarity and closure. I needed to feel her presence one last time. I struggle with the fear that I might forget her, the way she smiled, the sound of her voice."

His revelation shook her. Mercy chose that moment to cry and broke the bond of trust building between them. Sarah moved to the cot and picked up the squirming baby. "You'll never forget her as long as you have your *kinder*, Mose. Greta lives on in them."

Mose reached for Mercy. Sarah placed the child in his arms. She watched as he snuggled his face in her neck and whispered, "I have you, *liebling*."

Sarah slipped out the door and hurried to the kitchen to help Theda finish the birthday meal. Father and daughter needed a moment together, and she needed time to remind herself she would have a baby soon. Her heart ached so deep in her chest it was almost painful. She worked on a fresh green salad, tearing lettuce leaves and slicing onions and tomatoes. Her child would never know the love of its *daed*, but it would have Mose, wonderful Mose, and for that she was grateful.

Explaining birthdays to a four-year-old became a battle royal minutes later. "Where is my cake?" Beatrice stamped her tiny foot against the kitchen tile. "Why does Mercy get a cake and not me?"

"It's her first birthday. A time to rejoice with her. You'll get a cake soon. Your birthday is just a few weeks away. That will be your special day."

"Mercy never had a special day before." Beatrice poked her finger toward the cake for a taste.

Sarah brushed her hand away just before the child's finger reached the edge of the swirled buttercream frosting. "You could end up on the naughty step if you keep acting like this, Beatrice. Mercy is the birthday girl today. Next time you'll be the birthday princess."

"I don't want Mercy to have a birthday. *Mamm* went to heaven because of Mercy. I heard my *groossmammi* say so. I want my *mamm*. Not Mercy." Tears poured down the child's face. Beyond control, Beatrice stormed into the bedroom and slapped her sister.

Sarah rushed into the room as Mercy cried out, and saw the deep red handprint on her face. Without a word, Mose scooped Beatrice away. The unhappy child kicked and screamed for her *mamm* as they hurried out of the bedroom. Sarah's heart pounded in her ears as she lifted Mercy off the quilt on the floor and embraced her. She headed for the rocking chair and cuddled her. "It's all right, *liebling.* Your sister is just unhappy. She loves you. She's just missing your *mamm* and doesn't know who to blame." Sarah wept for Mose's motherless *kinder,* for Mose's loss and for her own baby to come.

When she returned to the kitchen, Theda moved around the wood island in the middle of the room, leaving the food she had been preparing. She wiped her hands on her apron, her forehead creased. "Don't upset yourself, Sarah. Mose will deal with Beatrice. He's good with her when she gets like this."

"I just feel so sad for the *kinder* and Mose. Life can be so cruel." Sarah brushed back the damp blond curls from Mercy's forehead and pushed out a deep sigh.

"Death always hits the *kinder* hardest, Sarah. Beatrice doesn't understand yet. She's too young, and it doesn't help that Ulla's bitterness is rubbing off on her. *Ach,* only *Gott* knows what that old woman has said to her. I blame her for this outburst, not Beatrice. It's time Otto had another long talk with Ulla. Maybe the threat of the ban will bring about change."

Sarah was glad for her caring mother-in-law. By marrying Mose, she'd gained Theda, Otto and the rest of the Fischers as her family. She was truly blessed.

Two long tables with benches on either side provided enough room for everyone to sit together in the dining room. Men at one table, women and *kinder* at the other. The afternoon drama seemed all but forgotten.

Mercy ate her food and grinned when Sarah placed a slice of birthday cake on her tray.

Beatrice sat with her father, away from the other *kinder*. His arm pulled her back when she tried to get down from the bench.

"You're deep in thought," Linda murmured close to Sarah's ear.

Sarah wished she had a private moment to talk to her friend. "I'm sorry. It's been a difficult afternoon."

Linda leaned closer. "I'll bet. Did Mose give you a hard time about going to the house? I thought he was going to bust a blood vessel when he kicked us out."

"He was very apologetic about the whole incident. He's still grieving."

Linda looked around, making sure no one was listening. "It's been a year, Sarah. You're more forgiving than I would be. I'd have Kurt's head on a platter if he'd spoken to me like that."

Sarah fed Mercy another bite of cake. "He's been through a lot. I think he just reached his breaking point and lost control."

"You're too kind. He doesn't deserve you, but I'm glad he's got you." Linda shrugged. "I guess I'm just mean-spirited. Why don't we go make sure everyone's got cake and get this mess cleared away? My feet are swollen, and I need to get home."

Sarah nodded and wiped Mercy down before putting her on her unsteady feet. The baby toddled away and headed for the toy box in the corner.

Generous slices of cake were cut, and Sarah began to hand them out to the ladies who'd been busy serving and were still eating. Ulla sat at the head of the table. She looked away as Sarah approached and sat a plate of cake in front of her. With a shove, Ulla pushed the plate away and got up from the bench.

Linda pulled Sarah into the kitchen. "Don't let that old woman get to you again. She's full of bitterness. She'll never forgive you for marrying Mose."

Sarah ran hot water into the sink and added home-made soap. She slid a stack of dirty dinner plates into the swirl of soapy bubbles.

Linda kept up with Sarah, each piece placed on the island behind them until the last dirty dish was finished. "I'll go get the silverware. Linda paused as she turned toward the door. *"Was tut Sie hier?"*

Sarah turned, her apron damp against her round stomach, wondering who Linda was talking to.

Ulla stood just inside the kitchen door, her burning gaze on Sarah. "I can't have what I need, Linda. You know that. *Gott* has taken my Greta away from me, and Mose has replaced her with *this* woman," she spat out in fury, her bony finger pointing in Sarah's direction. "I will never accept her as the *mamm* of my *enkelkinder. Nee.* I know the wrong she's done. She brings trouble. She will not be accepted in *die familye* as long as I breathe." Ulla hurried out of the room, her loud weeping permeating the house just before the front door slammed behind her.

Sarah took off her *kapp* and laid it on a wave of wrinkled fabric at her knees. She looked into the sky, through the palm tree next to the wooden steps and pushed a deep sigh through dry lips. Peeking out from palm tree fronds, the moon glowed golden and then disappeared.

Behind her the house grew dark, only a slice of light

cut across the porch from the nightlight in the front bathroom. Winds carrying the scent of jasmine picked up and blew hard, mussing the knot of hair at the back of her head. Somewhere nearby a frog croaked, disturbing the blessed silence calming her troubled soul.

The words in her *bruder's* recent letter came back to her. *We've had a few chilly days and I thought of you in sunny Florida.* A million miles away, Lancaster County shivered in the cold.

The screen door groaned and footfalls announced an intruder. Sarah turned and silently grumbled as she made out the shape of a man.

"Can I join you?" Otto murmured.

Sarah heard the creak of the white rocker as he sat behind her. She wanted to shout at him to go away, to leave her to her thoughts. Instead she said, *"Ya."* She'd had enough drama for one day.

Silence, interrupted by the steady squeaking of the rocking chair, fled.

The old German clock in the house chimed twice. She should be in bed sleeping. Moving day would come early and she needed her rest. The boards grew hard under her, and she resettled herself. She lay her hand on her stomach and enjoyed the *bobbel's* strong movements. The *kinder* lurched, restless, too.

"When Theda and I married, her *grossmammi* disapproved of me."

Sarah jumped at the sudden sound of his voice. She didn't know if he expected a response. She had none to give.

"She caused as much trouble as we'd let her." Otto stopped rocking. "My *daed's* advice made all the difference back then and still rings true today. 'Live your life to please *Gott* and no one else.' I still practice this advice and find it profitable today. I shared it with Mose and now you."

Sarah bowed her head. *"Danke."*

"There's nothing to thank me for, Sarah. We all need advice from time to time. I know Ulla is causing you grief, but she's just an angry old woman. The rest of the community is happy you're here. I see the difference in Mose, and so do they. He's opening up. Ready to go on with life since he found you. Sarah Fischer, you are an answer to prayer."

"But I thought…"

Otto began to rock again. "Then you thought wrong."

Sarah slipped on her shoes and stood. "I'd best go to bed."

"*Ya*, you best had. The sun will be up in a few hours and moving day is fast approaching."

Sarah looked at the moon one last time. A cluster of billowing clouds hid the golden globe. "Good night," she whispered. She opened the door and stepped into the house.

"Sleep well."

Sarah sighed. "I will."

Chapter Fifteen

Dressed in an old, soft dress she'd often slept in, with a medium-sized box tucked between her legs, Sarah concentrated on the task at hand. She folded a plain slip of Beatrice's and tucked it down the side of the bulging container before fighting a roll of sticky tape to finally seal the box.

Mose walked into the bedroom, his light blond hair darkened and mussed by the shower he'd just taken. A towel draped around his neck and his pajama top was damp from the water dripping from his hair.

"Can I help you finish packing? It's late." Mose rubbed his head dry and threw the towel in the dirty clothes basket, still damp.

Sarah watched the wet towel flop on dry clothes. Joseph had always hung his towel on the shower pole and let it dry. The idea of wet clothes in her laundry basket annoyed her beyond reason. Perhaps she should say something, but she seemed to be nagging him a lot for little things that didn't really matter. Linda told her she did the same to Kurt. That they were just having pregnancy mood swings and had nothing to worry about. Sarah hoped her friend was right. She couldn't remember being so prim and proper with Joseph. She looked Mose's way. "*Danke*, but this is the last box. I think we're ready for the move tomorrow."

Mose padded over to Mercy's cot. "She looks so restful. Like nothing's wrong."

"*Ya.*"

"Linda's coming for both girls early in the morning, but I guess you already know that." Mose turned toward her, his hand raking through his wet beard.

The action reminded her of Joseph. Pain stabbed her heart but she pushed the memory away. "Linda said to have them ready at seven. Beatrice likes to sleep in. I have a feeling she'll be a handful unless she gets an early nap." Sarah took of sip of water from her glass, poked a vitamin pill into her mouth and swallowed. "Her offer to watch the *kinder* was a blessing. Try to imagine them underfoot during the move."

"A nightmare." Mose smiled. "I'm sorry for what Ulla said. She must be dealt with. *Daed* plans to see her tomorrow with several of her favorite deacons in tow. Her harsh attitude has to stop."

"She said what she saw as truth, Mose. We did marry fast. She's old and having a hard time dealing with her daughter's death. Plus, she's heard the rumors."

"You're more generous than I am," Mose said. "That woman doesn't deserve your kindness."

"I seem to take trouble wherever I go."

Mose looked over to Sarah, who was still sitting on the edge of the bed. "I was drawn to you from the moment I met you. Do you know that? Your kindness to my *kinder* convinced me you were the right woman for this family before your problems with your father began. Did I love you?" His eyes grew dark. "*Nee*, but I was fond of you. Now I treasure you. Things will get better, *frau*. You'll see. Sleep well." He got into bed and snapped off the lamp.

Sarah placed her hand on her stomach and felt her child kick. *Please be right. Let this marriage work. Help Mose to love me.*

Gray skies and a light drizzle didn't slow their moving day, or the flow of boxes, small pieces of furniture and lamps into the house.

Sarah opened the front door to let in workers loaded down with all manner of things. She handed them bottles of water and pointed out places to place unmarked boxes. Mose made it very clear at breakfast that she was to do no lifting or moving of furniture. None. Rebellious since the day she was born, Sarah shoved over boxes with her foot and kept the path clear. When no one was watching, she added an extra push when the front door fought the new refrigerator for space. She was pregnant, not sick.

Theda hurried up on the porch, her mitt-covered hands holding a covered bowl that smelled wonderful. "I see they found a job for you, too. I was put on lunch duty."

Sarah opened the screen door to let the short woman pass. "*Ach*. Whatever that is smells wonderful."

"*Danke*, Sarah. Look, it's really starting to rain now. We could have done without the showers but *Gott* knows what He's doing. His way is best."

"*Ya*," Sarah agreed and sniffed the bowl. "*Wunderbaar.*"

"I made Mose's favorite dish. I hope you like chicken and dumplings."

Sarah's mouth watered. "*Ya*, very much."

His arms full of folded quilts and blankets, Mose stumbled through the opened door and grinned at Sarah, rain dripping off his nose and beard. "We're almost finished. Just one more load of toys and Beatrice's wagon."

"You all have worked so hard." Sarah opened the door again, letting Otto in carrying Mercy's bed slats and headboard. "The cot will have to be wiped down before it can be set up. Mose better do it before tomorrow or you'll have two kids in bed with you," he chortled, dabbing at the rain on his face. "Kurt said the *kinder* are coming home tomorrow morning, early. They slept well, but Beatrice is running Linda ragged."

"*Ya*, we know. She called Mose this morning and complained about Beatrice's energy level." Sarah shared Otto's laugh and then got serious. "Don't forget, Mercy has her surgery in the morning. Please pray *Gott's* will for her life, Otto. Ulla graciously offered to care for Beatrice until the procedure is over." Sarah couldn't help but wonder how the conversation had gone between Ulla and Otto the night before, but didn't dare ask.

Otto and Mose dropped their burdens and hurried to the kitchen, the aroma of chicken and dumplings drawing them back. Sarah followed, the tower of boxes and furniture scattered around bothering her sense of rhythm and order.

Theda set the table with deep paper plates and napkins. Sarah helped her add plastic knives and forks, and then sat down next to Mose. A river of thick chicken broth, chunks of white meat and fluffy dumplings swallowed up their plates as Theda ladled out the steaming food.

"The meal looks *wunderbaar*, as usual." Otto dug in.

Sarah smiled, growing more and more comfortable with the Fischer family. In Lancaster only silence and hurtful looks had accompanied their meals. Thoughts of her father brought nothing but pain. Sarah pushed the memory away and began to eat.

Mose pulled out the plastic trash bag and tied a knot in it. "*Danke* for lunch, *Mamm*. I appreciate you taking some of the strain off Sarah."

Has she seen the doctor yet?"

"*Nee*, but she has an appointment."

"You go with her, Mose. She will want you there."

"I have…"

"*Ach*, you men are all alike. You have no idea what you'd do there. I know men take no interest in such things, but she will need you that day, son. Trust me."

Mose stopped throwing away paper napkins. "*Ya*. I think you could be right. Linda can't go with her. She has her own doctor's appointment. I'll offer to go and see what Sarah says."

"You're a good husband. Just like your *daed*." Theda threw an empty box his way. "You best hurry up or you'll be living in this mess for days."

"Do you think Sarah likes the *haus*? I mean, *really* likes it?" Mose set the stack of boxes down and pulled out a chair.

"I'm sure her past keeps her from enjoying a lot of life's pleasures, but she'll get over that in time. Be patient with her. Once the baby comes, all will be well between you and her."

"I'm praying you're right." Mose hugged his mother, wanting this kind of parental love and connection for his *kinder* with Sarah.

* * *

Handed over to the pediatric nurse, Mercy smiled as she was carried away. Mose wanted to call her back. He didn't completely trust doctors, and allowing one of them to cut into his daughter's eardrums shook him to the core.

"I think this is the waiting room." Sarah took a seat close to a big picture window and patted the comfortable-looking chair next to her.

Mose shook his head and began walking up and down the narrow path between chairs, too restless to do anything but pray and pace. *Gott, keep my daughter in your hands. Bring her through this surgery with healing and restoration.*

Sarah sat completely still, eyes closed, head, hands clenched in a prayerful pose.

"She'll be fine. It's not a complicated surgery. Just tubes inserted. We have nothing to worry about." Mose didn't completely believe the words he spoke. But he wanted to reassure Sarah, keep her from stressing.

Sarah opened her eyes. "You're not worried at all?" Her eyebrow arched, waiting for his reply.

Mose hung his head. He hadn't fooled her. Of course she knew he was worried. "*Ya*, I'm worried, but I always am when doctors are around."

"I hate hospitals. I have no reason to. I just do." Sarah shrugged her shoulders and picked up a magazine. She read the title splashed across the front, threw the limp book back on the table and murmured, "Hunting books! Who wants to see dead animals in a hospital waiting room?"

Mose smiled and walked over to the vending machine. He turned Sarah's way. "Would you like some chocolate?"

"It's not good for the baby, but *danke*."

He'd become infatuated with her. He longed to see her when he was at work, took joy in the sound of her voice and the way she moved. Mose grabbed the bag of chocolate peanuts from the dispensing tray and tore open the bag. He wished Sarah would pick a fight with him or debate the merits of growing hay versus barley. Anything to keep his mind off Mercy and what was going on.

"Beatrice was in a good mood today." He settled in the chair next to her and reached for the hunting book.

"*Ya*, she was. Did Ulla say anything about your dad's conversation with her?"

"*Nee*. She acted quiet, but very polite when I dropped Beatrice off. Something she hasn't been in a long time."

Mose put down the book and slipped the candy bag into his pocket. He tried to find a place for his hands, failed, and then gripped the chair arms in frustration. Moments later he looked at his pocket watch and sighed. Only twenty minutes had passed, but it felt like hours.

Sarah laughed, then snorted.

"What's so funny?" Mose knew what she was laughing at and he didn't like it one bit.

"You, you silly goose. Relax. Pray, but don't work yourself into a nervous fit." She smoothed her skirt and adjusted her prayer *kapp*.

Sarah didn't look any too calm to Mose, with her lopsided *kapp* and worry lines as deep as corn rows across her forehead. "Oh, and you're so calm? *Nee*, I think you're just as concerned as I am and poking fun to distract me."

Sarah turned toward Mose, the smile gone. "*Ya*, I was teasing but you need to remember *Gott* loves our Mercy, and all will be well. We have to believe."

Mose smiled, his lips dry. "I'm so glad you're here with me. You bless me, *mein frau*."

He felt strong emotions for Sarah. His heart raced when he thought of Sarah, saw her or smelled the fragrance of her soap. Could he be falling in love with this kind, thoughtful woman so quickly?

Two hours later Mose lifted Mercy from her car seat and handed the sleeping baby into Sarah's waiting arms. Small squares of cotton gauze covered Mercy's ears, but her cheeks weren't flushed and she'd smiled at them when she'd woken up in recovery earlier. A sense of calm came over Mose. Mercy was home, all was well with the *bobbel* and they were almost settled into their new home.

"You hungry?" Mose opened the refrigerator door and poked his head in. The leftover baked chicken looked good to him. Maybe a sandwich and warm potato salad would satisfy his hunger pangs.

"I am." Sarah washed her hands, pulled out a loaf of homemade bread and sliced off four perfectly carved servings. "Chicken or roast?"

"Chicken." Mose grabbed the plate of chicken and bowl of potato salad out of the refrigerator.

Working together, they prepared the meal and sat down to eat, both hesitating for prayer. Mose bowed his head and Sarah followed suit as they prayed silently.

Mose took a giant bite from his sandwich and Sarah watched as thick slices of chicken toppled down his clean shirt, covering the front with creamy smears of mayonnaise. She handed him a napkin and watched as he cleaned up the shirt and placed the chicken back on the bread slices.

"Do you want me to make you another sandwich?"

"I'll eat this one. If you knew some of the things I've eaten in my life, you probably wouldn't have married me."

Laughing together released some of the tension built up from the morning.

"You have plans for this afternoon?" Mose stuck the last of the sandwich in his mouth and popped in a pickle slice for good measure. "The doctor said Mercy would probably sleep the day away, and Beatrice isn't home for hours."

Sarah pondered the idea of free time without Beatrice underfoot. She grinned. "I think I'll put some order to my sewing room. I've been wanting to do that for days."

Mose returned her grin, a smear of mayonnaise on his face making him look more like a five-year-old child than a twenty-five-year-old adult. She grabbed a napkin and wiped his mouth like she might one of the girls. "I can't take you anywhere," she scolded and seemed to enjoy watching him flush. She gathered up the dishes, a smile on her face.

"I think I'll call *Daed* and let them know how the surgery went while you're busy."

"Make sure you call Ulla, too. She's bound to be concerned and won't rest easy until she hears Mercy is all right."

Mose left the room, reaching for the cell phone in his pocket, grinning from ear to ear as he headed for the bedroom where Mercy lay sleeping.

Chapter Sixteen

Boxes littered the small beige room with north-facing windows. Sarah had dreamed of a room such as this all her life. Somewhere to sew until her eyes grew tired and blurry.

She stood in the middle of a pile of boxes and turned slowly. She pictured a big cutting table in the corner, and a fixture on the wall to hold all her spools of thread. Not that she had that many right now, but she would. Soon.

She stepped, and stumbled over an oblong box, the weight of it almost knocking her over. She tried to lift it but the box fought back. She struggled to open it and groaned when she found heavy brads clamping the box shut. *What can this be?*

She read the label printed on the container and recognized the name of a professional sewing machine manufacturer, the brand so expensive she'd never dreamed of owning one. *Do I dare hope?* Her hands became claws. She tore at the cardboard box, ripping away bits and pieces of cardboard.

Frustration sent her scurrying around looking for a

screwdriver, box cutter…anything. She finally found a suitable tool in the least likely place. On the floor.

"Argh." She grabbed the large screwdriver and forced it under the heavily clamped cardboard flap. Five or six pokes and the flap gave way, sending Sarah flying forward so violently she had to grab the heavy box to steady herself.

With sore, trembling fingers she tore the last of the box away and reached in, removing the clear plastic zip bag with a medium-sized book inside and some kind of small tool kit. Peering back into the box, a white sewing machine waited for her release. Like giving birth, she pushed and pulled, willing the sewing machine to come out. The idea of using the sharp tool on the box again gave her pause. She might scratch the fine machine, and she loathed the idea. Her heart pounding with excitement, she took a long, deep breath and pulled hard. The heavy sewing machine skidded across the floor and landed inches from the doorway and Mose's booted feet.

Sarah glanced past his rain-dampened boots, wrinkled pants and shirt, to his smiling face. His generosity overwhelmed her. Tugged at her heartstrings. She didn't deserve such kindness.

"Need some help?" Mose squatted down in front of Sarah and her precious sewing machine.

"Looks like I do."

The next morning, the doctor's office was empty except for Mose and Sarah. He paced the length of the office, his hands stuffed deep into his pockets.

Sarah, determined to look calm, leafed through a modern *Englisch* magazine. She gazed at the faces of beautiful women and handsome men and wondered what their lives were really like. Were they as happy as their smiles implied? *Am I happy?* Her life certainly had taken a sudden turn for the better. She felt more content now that Mercy was on the mend and doing so well, and Mose seemed more and more attentive to her. *But do I dare love him?*

"Eight o'clock, right?" Mose looked at his pocket watch, a frown wrinkling his face.

"What? *Ya*, the appointment is for eight o'clock." Sarah held back a smile, afraid she'd offend him. Mose was one of the most impatient men she'd ever met, but she wouldn't rub his nose in it. Let him have his impatience. *Gott* knew she had enough flaws of her own.

"You filled out all the papers?" He flopped down next to her and pulled his long legs under the chair as far as they would go. He glanced at the woman sitting behind a short partition.

"She'll call us soon." Sarah smoothed out her collar and straightened her *kapp*. She caught Mose glancing over her shoulder and smiled to herself when he made a noise deep in his throat, almost like a cat hacking up hair balls.

"What?"

"Nothing." Mose stood and began to move about the room. The watch came out again. He snapped it shut, mumbling under his breath about punctuality and professionalism.

"Sarah Fischer?"

Mose turned on his heel. Sarah stood to her feet. Neither moved.

"Mr. and Mrs. Fischer?" Tall and lean, and dressed in white slacks and a pullover top covered in colorful zoo animals, the technician motioned them back and waited at the door as they passed into the back office. "Find a seat, Dad. Mom, please get on the table." The woman smiled at both of them.

Sarah looked at the metal table covered in paper in the middle of the room and fought the urge to run. A gown lay folded on the paper. *Would she have to get undressed in front of Mose?*

Preparing the machine, the technician scurried around, moving things on and off. "I'll let you change into the gown. Just leave the door open a crack when you're ready."

Sarah looked at Mose and then the exiting nurse. "I…"

Mose turned his back to her and faced the wall. He murmured, "I'll keep my back turned."

Sarah complied, her dress flying off and then her slip. They lay in a crumpled pile on the chair next to the table as she pulled on the gown, leaving the thin cotton open at the front but pulled tightly closed against her body. With difficulty, she sat on the edge of the table and covered her legs as much as the short gown would allow. She wiggled her toes, not sure what to do next. "All right," she murmured. "Open the door."

Mose did as he was directed and sat in the chair at the back of the room.

"Is this your first sonogram, Mrs. Fischer?" The technician hurried in and shut off the bright overhead light. The room was bathed in a gray glow. She sat down in a swivel chair and turned knobs and flicked levers on the strange machine next to the table.

Fascinated with what the technician was doing, Sarah almost forgot to answer. "*Ya.* My first."

The woman pushed buttons, opened a drawer and

took out a tube of some kind of cream. "If you'll lie back, we'll get started." She smiled reassuringly at Sarah and then glanced over at Mose. "You'll need to get closer, Dad, if you want to see the baby." She opened the gown just enough to see Sarah's stomach.

Sarah jumped when cold liquid hit her skin.

"Sorry, I should have warmed that with my hands." She began to rub an extension of the machine on Sarah's stomach. With her finger she pointed to a screen. "You'll both want to be looking here."

Sarah saw strange wavy images and movement. A sound filled the room, its rhythmic beat fast and steady.

"That's your baby's heartbeat."

"Oh…" Emotions she'd never felt overwhelmed her. The beat sounded strong, but fast. "Is it normal for the heart to beat so fast?"

"Sure. New moms always ask me that." She moved the apparatus around Sarah's stomach again and more images appeared. She pointed to the screen. "There's a hand and that's the baby's spine."

Sarah blinked, not sure what she was looking at, but determined to see her child's image.

"Look, Sarah. There's the face." Mose's words came from the end of the table.

The woman pointed and suddenly the image became clear. A face, with closed eyes, a tiny button nose and bowed mouth became clear. Then the face disappeared and Sarah felt deflated. She wanted to see it again but there was more to see. Slender legs squirmed and kicked, floating in and out of view, a tiny foot with five distinct toes flexed.

"Do you two want to know the sex of your child?"

"Nee," Sarah said. She longed to know, but knowing

would take away some of the thrill of birth, and she'd have none of that.

"Better turn your heads away then."

Sarah looked away, longing to look back.

"Okay, let's see if we can find the head again and take some measurements. Then we'll be through."

Sarah looked back at the screen and saw what looked like a head full of curly hair. The screen went blank, and Sarah drew in a deep breath, holding back tears of disappointment. She wanted to see more, much more.

"Looks like everything's fine." The technician wiped the jelly off Sarah's stomach with a paper towel. "Your about 30 weeks pregnant, even though the baby is a bit small. I'd put your due date around six weeks from now, give or take a day or two, but the doctor may change that a little when you see her. You have an appointment with her, right?"

"Ya." Mose cleared his throat.

"Good. You did really well for a first-timer, Mom. You can both rest easy. Your baby appears healthy."

"Danke," Sarah murmured, pulling the gown closed as she watched the woman leave. Mose gave her a hand up and she sat still for a moment, letting everything she had seen and heard sink in.

"Danke for letting me be here." Mose's emotion deepened his voice and moved her to tears.

Sarah held the gown closed with one hand and wiped a tear away with the other. *"Nee,* Mose. I should be thanking you for coming with me. This *Englisch* way of checking the baby had me afraid, but now I wish they could do it all over again."

A silly smile played on Mose's lips. *"Ya.* I wish that,

too." His look was different. Almost as though he was in a daze.

They had shared the wondrous moment together, but then Mose faced the wall once more. "Time to get dressed, I guess."

"Ya." Sarah dressed quickly and touched Mose's arm. "Okay. I'm ready."

Mose took her by the elbow and led her through the hall. They passed the technician and stopped as she called out to them.

"I almost forgot to give you these." She handed over a white office envelope and scurried away.

"What is this?" Sarah pulled out stiff pieces of paper. She looked down, right into the face of her child. "Mose. It's pictures of the *bobbel*."

Mose gave Sarah a hand up into the old furniture delivery truck. He waited until she'd buckled her seat belt and tucked her skirt under her legs before he shut the door. A quick maneuver around two golf carts vying for his vacated parking spot, and the truck merged onto Bahia Vista Street. The slow-moving traffic wove through the quaint town of Sarasota, sweltering in the late spring humidity.

Quiet and still, Sarah held on to the envelope of pictures, her fingers white-knuckled. "Hungry?" Mose asked as he shifted gears. The engine strained, making an unfamiliar noise. He shifted into third and sped up.

Sarah tucked the pictures in her white apron pocket and patted the spot. "Not really."

"I'll bet the baby could use some eggs and bacon with a side of cheese grits." He grinned at her, trying to keep the mood light. "He or she could use some meat on those tiny bones."

"You're right. I need to eat more. I just don't have much of an appetite lately."

Mose felt guilty. He'd used the baby as a reason for her to eat. Sarah looked thoughtful. Was she thinking it was her fault the baby was a bit undersized? He kept his voice easy and calm, knowing she was stressed. "How about Yoder's? We ate there when we first got into town. They always have great food and you can get another look at the only buggy you'll see around here for miles. Kind of a reminder of what you're missing."

Sarah smiled at his last remark. "I don't miss those hard seats, Mose Fischer. Not one bit."

Mose pulled into Yoder's parking lot five minutes later and parked between a seldom-seen shiny black BMW and a couple of beat-up tricycles so commonplace in Pinecraft and Sarasota. After opening Sarah's door, he offered her his hand and smiled when she took it and squeezed his fingers tight. Her pregnancy was obvious to anyone who looked her way now. She glowed in a way Greta never had, her hair shining in the bright sun, her complexion rosy and smooth. He felt a sharp pang of guilt at the thought. It was wrong to think such things. He marched up the driveway, Sarah at his side, his mood suddenly soured.

Sarah forced down toast and scrambled eggs, not even looking at the glass of orange juice she would normally down in one long gulp. The juice gave her heartburn now, and she avoided it like a poison. Linda often teased her the baby would have lots of hair because of her stomach issues. The scan of the baby proved her sister-in-law's theory correct.

"You're deep in thought. Something troubling you?" Mose scooped up a spoon full of grits and shoved it in his mouth as if he was eating orange ambrosia, her favorite desert.

"We need to talk, Mose." Sarah nibbled on her last slice of dry toast and washed it down with a sip of cold milk. "Seeing the baby on the scan made this pregnancy so real to me." She pushed back her glass and looked into his eyes. "I've finally awakened from my stupor. I have just over a month before the baby comes, and I haven't made diapers, much less gowns and bibs. Plus, we haven't mentioned the baby to Beatrice. She has to be told. There's no telling what kind of reaction we'll get from her."

"You're a worrier. Worriers get wrinkles. Didn't anyone ever warn you about that?"

Hormone levels sending her mood into overdrive, Sarah flung her triangle of toast on her plate and glared at him. "I'm trying to have a serious talk with you about important issues and you want to joke around. Seriously! Sometimes you are one of the most infuriating men I've ever had the misfortune to meet."

Mose looked across at her, his sparkling eyes holding her gaze as he sipped coffee from a big white mug. He sat the mug back on the table. "In time you'll realize nothing is going to change, no matter how much you fret. The baby will be born. It will have clothes to wear, even if we have to buy them from an *Englisch* store. And the girls will love the baby because that's what *kinder* do. They love *bobbels*."

With one quick swipe Sarah wiped her mouth, threw

the red cloth on her plate and stood. "I'm going to the bathroom, and while I'm gone I'd appreciate it if you'd pay the bill. I'd like to go home now."

"Sure. I can do that, or I can wait for you in the truck and take you to the fabric store for supplies. It sounds like you're going to need piles of material for all those diapers and outfits." Mose grinned as he walked to the front of the café.

Chapter Seventeen

The sunny, late-spring morning started off rough. Beatrice crawled out of bed grumpy and demanded she be allowed to wear her new church dress. Sarah's calm insistence finally prevailed and peace was restored. The sounds of two active *kinder* laughing and tearing through their playroom rang through the house and put a content smile on Sarah's face.

She flopped in an oversize chair in the great room for a moment of rest and put up her swollen feet on the matching ottoman. The breakfast dishes were washed and put away, and the last load of baby clothes gently agitated in the washer. A month of Florida living had calmed Sarah's troubled spirit. Life was calmer, more serene.

A shrill scream rang from the back of the house. Sarah sprang up and ran, her heart lodged in her throat. "What's happened?" At the door of the playroom she relaxed and chuckled as she took in the situation.

Beatrice lay sprawled on the carpeted floor on her stomach, her healthy little sister's chubby legs straddled across the middle of her back, a hand full of her curly hair wadded up in Mercy's tugging, pudgy fingers. Mercy jerked with all her might. Beatrice wiggled and tried to dump her sister off her back. Her legs pummeled the floor as she wailed, "Make her stop. Get her off me."

Sarah had known the day would come, when Mercy could hold her own and pay back her older sister for all the times she'd been pushed or forced to play with toys she didn't want.

"Mercy. You mustn't hurt your big sister." Sarah lifted the younger child off Beatrice's back and pulled the silky strands of golden hair from her fingers. "Beatrice won't want to play with you if you hurt her. You have to be kind to your big sister."

"Nee," Mercy shouted, using her new voice, her words still not crystal clear, but getting better every day. She grabbed her doll from Beatrice's hands and smiled. "Mine."

"Did you take her doll and give her yours?" With difficulty, her protruding stomach getting in her way, Sarah bent over Beatrice and gently combed her fingers through the child's snarled hair. Strands of pure gold went into the trash container, the remnants of the sister's fight over the doll.

"Yes, but she likes my doll. I wanted to play with her doll, but she yelled at me and pulled my hair."

"We've talked about you taking your little sister's toys before, right?"

Beatrice glared at Mercy playing across the room. "Yes, but…"

"You have to allow Mercy to have toys of her own, too. You like having your own special babies, don't you?"

"*Ya.*"

Sarah handed Beatrice her favorite doll and smiled as it was swallowed up in the older child's warm embrace. "You love your doll and sometimes you like to be the only one to play with it. Mercy loves her doll, too, and she doesn't want anyone else to play with it. Do you understand?"

Head down, Beatrice nodded.

"*Gut.* In a minute I'll talk with Mercy about not pulling your hair anymore."

Beatrice began to gather up the plastic dishes scattered at her feet. "I'll make pretend juice for Mercy and me. We can have a party."

Offered an opportunity to talk with Beatrice without her being too distracted, Sarah helped the child place tiny cups and saucers on the round table Mose had made for them just weeks before. He had agreed she'd be the best person to break the news to the *kinder* about the *bobbel.* She had waited and prayed for a time just like this. "How would you feel if you and Mercy got a real *bobbel* to play with?"

"Do we have to keep Mercy?" Beatrice pretended to pour tea into a tiny cup.

"Of course, silly girl. We would never send your sister away." Sarah pulled over a sturdy wooden stool and sat, waiting for more questions.

"If you have a baby, will you go to live with Jesus like my *mamm* did?" Tiny blond brows furrowed as she placed pretend cake on several little plates and handed one to Sarah.

"*Nee.* What happened to your *mamm* doesn't happen very often. Something went wrong and your *mamm* got very sick." Sarah was not sure what she should say about Greta dying. How much the child should be told. She prayed for wisdom and allowed *Gott's* love for this child to direct her. "A new baby is always a blessing, Beatrice. Like you and Mercy were when you were born."

"Mercy's mean. I don't like her sometimes." Beatrice knocked the dishes on the floor. The troubled child's shows of temper came less frequently now, but still had to be handled with care.

Sarah dropped to her knees in front of Beatrice and held her gaze. "Throwing down dishes doesn't solve anything. It only gets you in more trouble. Maybe together we can think of better ways to express your anger with Mercy, like telling her how it makes you feel when she makes you angry. You're her big sister."

"But I don't like being her big sister today." Beatrice looked at Sarah defiantly. Her lip puckered and tears rolled down her flushed cheeks.

"I know you don't like her right now, but remember when you two were on the swings yesterday? You had so much fun together. You laughed a lot, and it was fun to have a little sister then, right?"

Beatrice looked up through tear-soaked lashes, her eyes sparkling. "*Ya*, it was fun."

"Well, Mercy needs you to help her grow into a nice young lady. She's going to be a big sister, too, when the baby comes. Someone older, like you, has to help Mercy be a good big sister. Do you think that someone could be you?"

Sarah watched the play of emotions flit across the child's face. She finally smiled a dimpled grin. "I could teach Mercy to be nice to the baby when it comes. I'm the oldest, and she listens to me…sometimes."

"That's right. You're the big sister." Sarah took Beatrice's hand and placed it on her protruding stomach. The baby had been active all morning, and it seemed the perfect time to introduce the unborn child to Beatrice. "Did you feel the baby kick?"

Like it was planned, the baby kicked hard under Beatrice's hand, putting a glowing smile on the child's face and a sparkle in her blue eyes. "*Ya*, I felt him kick."

"I bet you did. You know, we have to think of a good name for the new baby. What do you think we should call her if she's a girl?"

Beatrice looked up, smiling, but serious. "It's a boy. I know it is. We have to call him Levi."

Shaken, Sarah tried to stay calm. Levi had been Joseph's *daed's* name, a name she had already considered for a boy. "Why Levi, Beatrice?"

"Because Jesus told me my brother would be named Levi and that he'd grow up to be a good man, like his *daed*."

Sarah pulled the little girl close and hugged her, tears swimming in her eyes. "Then Levi it will be, liebling."

After church the next day, Linda carried a tray of salt and pepper shakers over to the extra deep counter at the back of the church kitchen and put it down with a bang.

"That Sharon Lapp makes me so mad."

Used to Linda's rants, Sarah smiled her way. "What did she say?"

Linda slid onto a kitchen stool and braced her feet under the slats, her protruding stomach bullet shaped.

"It's not what she said. It's how she treats me. She acts like I should just sit in a chair and wait for the pains to start just because I'm overdue. It's not some kind of sin being two weeks late. The baby's just lazy like his *daed*." She laughed at the remark as if it was the funniest thing she'd ever heard. "And now she just told me I can't help with clean up. Who is she to tell me anything? I'm not bedridden, for goodness—" She broke off her words and let two women pass before she restarted her private rant with Sarah. "Besides, I feel great and have so much energy."

"I think she's right. You look ready to pop at any moment. Maybe Kurt should take you home and let you put your feet up. Church lasted a long time today with all the new preachers showing off. You're bound to be tired. I know I'm ready to get off my feet."

Linda's scalding glare wrinkled her forehead and put a twist to her lip as she spoke. "Your feet might be hurting you, but I feel fine and I'm not..." Eyes wide, Linda's expression turned from anger to opened mouth horror. "*Ach*! *Gott* help me, Sarah. I think my water just broke."

Sarah put down the pan she'd been drying and hurried over to Linda. "Are you sure?" Liquid dripped off Linda's shoe and onto the floor.

"*Ya*, I'm sure. I'm not prone to wetting myself on kitchen stools. What am I going to do? I'm soaked and everyone will know what's happening. Oh, mercy, even that know-it-all, Sharon Lapp."

Sarah thought for a moment, her legs trembling. "I'll go get Kurt and Mose. One of them can bring the truck around, and the other can carry you out the kitchen's back door. No one will see you. I'll make sure."

"Hurry. I feel like a fool sitting here in a puddle."

Sarah found Mose first, the last of his celery soup forgotten as soon as she whispered the frantic situation

in his ear. He motioned for Kurt to come over and within
seconds both men were at a full run, Mose headed out
the front of the church to pull the truck around back.
Kurt fumbled his way to the kitchen, knocking over a
chair as he hurried. Minutes later, Linda waved a frantic goodbye to Sarah as Mose peeled out of the church
parking lot and burned rubber down the farm road.

Thoughts of her own birth raced through her mind.
She'd been warned the pain could be overwhelming.
Plus, there were the added responsibilities to consider.
Was she ready to be the mother of a tiny *bobbel*? Jo-
seph's *bobbel*. What if the *kinder* resented it?

Would she be able to cope with three children and
still be a good wife to Mose?

Chapter Eighteen

The soft mallet tapped the last spindle into place, and then Mose twisted the chair to an upright position. The back fit snugly into the seat, all four legs flared in perfect alignment. He stood back and looked at the completed project, his hands testing for weak joints. His trained eye searched for flaws, anything that might require a minor adjustment, and saw none.

Otto Fischer breezed into the back workroom, his pants and shirt covered in mud splatter. "*Wie gehts*, Mose?"

"*Gut*. I can see you've been working hard." Mose smiled at his father. "Will you ever retire?" He put away tools and then downed a bottle of water as he listened to his father's ramblings.

"Not while there's still breath in my body. I'd rather slop pigs and dig trenches all day than spend all my time with Theda when those gossiping women are in my *haus*. They pretend to make quilts every week, but really they gather to talk." He used his hand to imitate a duck quacking. "You should see them leaning over that big quilt frame, their mouths working as hard as their thimbles." Otto grabbed an old wooden chair and sat, his legs sprawled out in front of him.

"*Mamm* would keep you busy doing little jobs around the *haus*. You'd never have time to be bored." Mose sat in the new chair, wiggling in the seat, still testing. "You get her off to her sister's in time?"

"*Ya*. But she took too many suitcases, as usual, and the train was late."

"Maybe she plans to be gone a while."

"*Ach*, she says three, but I can count on four or five days of peace." Otto smirked, his lip curling into a happy arch. "You know how your mother is. Once she gets to Ohio and sees her sister, she'll stick like glue for a while."

"Come eat with us if you find yourself hungry. Sarah's a *gut* cook."

"That she is. Still, I might go to Lapp's every night. I can eat all the things your *mamm* won't let me have. They make good apple strudel." He grinned like a naughty child.

The big room darkened. Mose flipped on the overhead light and jerked back the curtain. Gray clouds billowed overhead. A sudden gust of wind blew a trash can lid across the parking lot. The plastic orb slammed into the fence. "Looks like a storm's brewing. You heard a weather forecast today?"

Otto came and stood next to Mose. "*Nee*, but it got nasty out there fast. Maybe there's something blowing in we don't know about."

Fat splats of rain hit the window. Mose dropped the curtain and turned on a small, dusty radio on the shelf next to him, his finger twisting the knob until he found the weather station.

Both men listened silently. The voice reported a mild tropical depression just off the west coast of Florida. Heavy rain and moderate winds were headed inland, moving toward the Tampa Bay area. Mose breathed a sigh of relief when the man reported the weather bureau didn't expect the depression to grow into a hurricane this late in the season. He flipped off the radio and grabbed his cup. "You want some stale coffee?"

"*Nee*. I should get back to the house and make sure all the windows are shut. I just came by to pick up that footrest you made your *mamm*."

"Sure. It's up front."

The two men walked to the front of the store. "*Guder mariye*, Austin. How are you?" Otto greeted the young salesman now that he wasn't busy with a customer.

"*Gut*, Mr. Fischer. It's been busy, but the rain's run off all our customers."

Otto looked out at the sheets of rain blowing and pulled his hat down around his ears. "This one's going to be a soaker. I think I'll pick up that footrest another time, Mose. Just don't sell it out from under me. Oh, *ya*. I almost forgot. Linda had a seven-pound baby girl last night."

Mose breathed a sigh of relief and grinned. "All went well?"

"*Ya*, no bumps in the road."

"Kurt has to be thrilled." Mose said.

"He is, but he wanted a boy, but don't tell Sarah that bit of information. You know how women are. She'll tell Linda and it could get ugly at Kurt's house." Otto smiled playfully and gave his son a generous smack on the back, then waved to Austin as he headed out the door. "Keep dry," he called over his shoulder and faced the onslaught.

His bike was parked next to the door. Otto kept to the sidewalk. His clothes were soaked to his skin before he rode away.

"*Mei bruder* puts on roofs. I know he got sent home today," Austin murmured, watching Otto struggle to pcddle down the wet street.

"*Ach*, you might as well go, too. I won't dock your pay. No one's coming out in this weather. I'll watch for stragglers for a while. You go before you can't ride your bike home."

Books and toys were strewn all over the playroom. With both girls napping, Sarah dropped to the carpeted floor and began to clear up while she could. Dolls went into the tiny cot Mose had made before she had become his wife. Greta must have been so pleased when he'd walked it through the door. *Kinder's* books were stacked on the low bookshelf, something else he'd built early on. All around her were reminders of Mose and Greta's family. Sarah's family now. She wished she'd met the woman. Everyone had only good things to say about her.

The back door slammed shut and Sarah shuddered. The sudden noise scared her. She hated storms. She had Adolph to blame for that. She remembered the day he'd put her outside for not doing a chore while one had raged overhead. Only a child, she had begged to come in, but her cries had fallen on deaf ears. She'd hidden in the chicken coop, holding her favorite hen to her breast as she'd sobbed and lightning had flashed overhead. She'd screamed every time thunder crashed around her. Pushing the memories away, the tear trailing down her cheek, she grabbed the last toy and put the fat teddy bear on Beatrice's rocker.

Sarah closed the window over the kitchen sink and wiped down the kitchen counters, even though she'd already cleaned them an hour ago. She needed something to do.

The doorbell rang and her hand stilled. It rang again. *Who is out in a downpour like this?* A peek out the front window showed a man in a police officer's uniform wiping rain off his glasses. He stood with another man, this one in a suit and plastic raincoat. He leaned a wet umbrella against the doorframe and waited. Both men looked very official.

Leaving the security latch on, Sarah opened the door a crack. *"Ya?"*

The police officer leaned in to be heard over the heavy rain, his face inches from the door. "Are you Sarah Nolt Fischer?"

She began to tremble. Her legs threatened to collapse from under her. *"Ya,* that's me. Can I help you?" She opened the door a bit more and looked at the badge the man thrust at her. "I'm Officer Luis Cantu from the city of Sarasota. This is Frank Parsons, our liaison officer." Rain dripped off his nose as his head nodded at Sarah through the cracked door. "Can we come in?"

Sarah pulled on her prayer *kapp* ribbon. *"Ya,* come in out of the rain." She unlocked the door and stepped back.

Both men glanced around as they stepped in and wiped their wet feet on the door mat. "I need to talk to you about your late husband, Joseph Nolt. Can we sit down?"

"This way." Sarah showed them to the great room

and motioned toward the couch. She sat in a matching chair across the room, and placed her trembling hands in her lap.

The man in the dark navy suit pulled off his raincoat and sat on the edge of the couch. He took a small black notebook out of his breast pocket and flipped through several pages.

Sarah's heart beat so loudly she couldn't hear the rain anymore. She forced her mind to focus, pushing every thought aside until he spoke.

"Are you aware the death of your husband was not an accident?"

Sarah forced herself to breath in. "*Nee.* They told me he died of…the smoke." She held back a sob with her hand.

"Mrs. Fischer, is there anyone I can call for you? Your new husband, a friend?"

Her fingers nervously pulled at the ribbon on her *kapp.* "Why? Am I in trouble?" A cramp began in the lower part of her back and traveled to her stomach, tearing at her insides. Linda told her to think of the pain as prelabor, her bones moving over to prepare for the baby's birth. The pain was normal. Nothing to worry about.

"No, but since you're pregnant, I thought you might like someone with you. This conversation could be upsetting." His brown eyes looked her up and down, assessing.

Sarah glanced at the clock on the wall. "Mose will be here soon. He usually eats lunch at home."

The man sat back. "Good. We can wait for him."

"*Nee*, tell me what you have to say. This is my business. I was married to Joseph. I have a right to know everything about his death."

He glanced back at his notebook and gave the police officer a quick glance. "Okay." The man cleared his throat. "Your husband did die from smoke inhalation, but he also had blunt force trauma to his head."

"No one told me." Sarah shuddered. "Is this why you came? To tell me this?"

"Not just that. I just thought you'd want to know all the details. That's why I wanted your new husband with you."

Her hand pressed against the pain in her back. "Go on. Tell me the rest."

"The reports from the Lancaster County sheriff's office shows a Benjamin Hochstetler Sr. confessed to the killing of your husband several days ago. I believe you knew the man. Am I right?"

"*Ya.* He was our neighbor, but what do you mean he confessed to killing Joseph? I thought…" Sarah looked away, ashamed to look him in the eyes. Was it true? Had Benjamin Hochstetler killed Joseph?

"Some new facts have surfaced and the community's bishop, Ralf Miller, asked that we contact you now that we've put all the pieces of the puzzle together. He said you'd be interested in what we've learned."

Sarah's mind reeled. Her throat seemed to constrict as she asked, "What is this additional news? I want to know everything."

"Hochstetler was arrested for drunk and disorderly conduct. During questioning he began to talk about his children, how much he hated Joseph Nolt for interfering in his personal business." The police officer flipped the page he'd been referring to and continued. "We put his ramblings down to the drink and he bailed himself out the next morning, still rambling about the loss of his two sons, Lukas and Benjamin Jr." He looked up. "You knew the boys?"

Sarah sighed. "I knew them. They are *gut* boys." Wind-driven rain lashed the windows. Lightning struck somewhere close and thunder rumbled, shaking the house and Sarah. Overhead lights flickered. She longed for a glass of water but didn't think her legs would hold her if she tried to walk to the kitchen.

"When the forensics team got through with the barn, they had noted there was no sign of your cow, Mrs. Fischer. You did say a cow had been in the barn the night your husband died?"

"*Ya*. I thought Lovey died in the fire, too. Are you saying you've found her after all these months?" *Stop asking questions. Shut up. Listen.*

"They did. She was grazing in a nearby field owned by Hochstetler."

"I see." A terrible trembling began to shake her entire body. She fought for control.

Another page turned. The man cleared his voice. "Two days ago the body of Benjamin Hochstetler was found hanging by a rope. He'd killed himself some time during the night. He'd mailed a letter to his lawyer confessing to killing your husband in a struggle. He said he'd come to steal the cow and your husband had caught him. He wrote that during the struggle, he pushed Joseph Nolt, and his head hit a concrete block. Sure that he was dead, Hochstetler set a fire in the barn, hoping to hide any evidence that might connect him to the crime. He ran back to his farm, hid the cow in the barn and went to bed, burning the clothes he'd worn the next day."

"But I heard Joseph's cry for help. I tried to get him out, but the fire…my hands, they were burned. After a moment he stopped screaming and I must have fainted. Someone called the fire department and they found me lying in the dirt just outside the barn. They discovered Joseph's remains later that morning. How can Benjamin Hochstetler's story be true if Joseph called out to me?" Sarah searched the man's eyes for clarity.

"We believe your husband didn't die from the fall. He must have been knocked out and woke, unable to make his way out of the barn. The fire was too hot from the accelerant used and spread fast. It stopped him like it stopped you."

Sarah nodded, tears streaming down her face. "If only… Did he suffer, you think?"

"No, the smoke probably got him before the fire did. I'm sorry for your loss, Mrs. Fischer. You have my condolences. I hope knowing the truth will help you put away this nightmare so you can go on with your new life."

Sarah needed to have time to think about what she'd just learned. She stood to her feet and then fell back against the chair, the sound of rain and her name being called swirled in the black fog enveloping her.

Chapter Nineteen

Mose unfolded his napkin, wiped food off Mercy's mouth and sat her on the quilt next to Beatrice. "You share those toys. If I see you taking anything from your little sister's hands, it's early to bed for you."

"Sarah told me I'm a big sister now. I have to be good."

"Yes, you do. Now play with your doll and I'll read you a book in a moment." He looked over at the couch, his gaze on Sarah. She leafed through a magazine on child rearing. She seemed okay now, looked normal enough. No pale skin, or grimace. Nothing to indicate something was physically wrong. *So why am I still so worried?*

Coming home and finding an ambulance in his drive had shaken him. He had thought one of the *kinder* had been hurt, but it was Sarah the two medics were leaning over when he rushed in the door. They explained she'd passed out for a few seconds but checked out fine. Nothing to warrant a trip to the hospital.

She'd been alert when he'd asked her how she felt. While the medic took her blood pressure again she'd reassured him everything was fine. "I heard about the Hochstetler man killing Joseph and later himself. I think I hyperventilated. That's all. Nothing more to worry about."

Now he watched her and prayed. "Can I get you anything? Maybe a cold drink?"

"*Nee*, I'm good. You sure you don't want me to clear the dinner table, Mose? I'm perfectly fine. Really. You're treating me like I'm sick, and I'm not."

"You sit there and relax. I'm good at clearing up, and Beatrice can help me throw away the paper plates, right?"

"But I'm playing."

"It's bath and bed for you. That mouth of yours is getting you into a lot of trouble lately." Mose scowled at his oldest child, his temper already fired up by the policeman he'd almost thrown out of the house. He wiped down the table and counters. "Those police officers should have made sure you had someone with you before they broke the news about Joseph and what happened to Hochstetler. They could see you're pregnant. No wonder you fainted at their feet."

"You're cleaning the color off that countertop."

A grin tipped his lips and he took a final slow swipe. "I'm in a hurry to get the kids to bed. Mercy's tired." On cue, Mercy yawned, her mouth opening wide. He grinned. "See, I told you."

"I can bathe both of them while you finish."

"You're eight months pregnant, Sarah, and stressed out. You've had a shock, need to rest." He loved her spirited personality, but sometimes he wished she was less argumentative...*like Greta?*

Something hit the house with a thump. He turned on

the back porch light and groaned. The deck was soaked, the wooden lounge chair he'd made for Sarah blown up against the house. Sarah's newly seeded flower pots were full of rain and overflowing in muddy streams. "Noah, where's that Ark? Looks like we might need it tonight." Mose turned off the outside light and turned to an empty room. Sarah and the girls were nowhere to be seen. *Stubborn woman.* He headed down the hallway.

Warm water gushed into the tub. Sarah tipped in a capful of pink liquid soap and swished her hand back and forth, enjoying the feel of frothy bubbles creeping up her arm. The heady fragrance of strawberries rose with the steam.

Two fluffy towels sat on a stool next to her, along with a soft plastic frog with bulging eyes. Water in her face scared Mercy, and the frog was a great distraction when it came time to rinse the girl's hair.

"Can I sit up front this time?" Beatrice stripped down, her clothes thrown in an untidy pile on the floor instead of in the laundry basket. Sarah gave her nod and the five-year-old jumped in, splashing water on the tile floor with her tidal wave. Soaked, Mercy screamed and wiggled out of Sarah's arms. She slipped on the wet floor and almost joined her older sister in the foamy water with her dress and diaper still on.

"I usually take their clothes off before bathing them." Mose leaned against the bathroom door, his hands in his pockets. "You need some help?"

"*Nee.* I'm fine." Sarah unsnapped Mercy's dress and threw the cotton frock in the basket. Carefully she unpinned her dry diaper and lifted the lightweight child into the bubbles. *There'll be two babies in diapers soon.* A knife-sharp pain pierced her back and Sarah paused before she straightened, waiting for the contraction to pass.

"What's wrong?" Mose stepped forward.

"Just one of those pains Linda warned me about. I get them once in a while. There's nothing to worry about."

"You should have waited for me to do this. I wanted you to rest. You know you're tired."

"*Ya*. But this is my job and I'm fine."

"You're stubborn. You know that?"

Mercy's squirmed and Sarah let go of her arm. "*Ya*. I've always been."

Mose laughed. "What smells so good?"

Sarah shifted to a more comfortable position, her hand reaching for her back when another pain slammed her. She took in a deep breath, held it and then slowly pushed the air out.

Beatrice piped up. "It's me that smells good. My bubble-bath soap makes me smell good enough to eat. Sarah told me." She twisted around to grin at him and almost knocked her sister over with her sudden movement. "I need my bathtub toys," she sang out in a high-pitched tone.

"Use your indoor voice, please." Sarah steadied Mercy. With gentle pressure she began to scrub Mercy's neck and back with a washcloth. She wished she wasn't so tired. "No toys tonight. I'm tired and want an early night. You can have an extra-long bath tomorrow night with lots of toys. I promise."

Beatrice glared at Sarah and silently began to wash herself. Encouraged by the child's cooperation, Sarah decided against washing their hair and grabbed the towels. She dangled one in the air. "Who's ready to get out first?"

Mercy grabbed the edge of the white towel. "Mine."

Mose watched Sarah handle the child with ease, the big towel swallowing up Mercy as Sarah patted her dry. "I have good news for you."

Preoccupied, Sarah murmured, "*Ya*, what is it?"

"*Mamm* called today. Linda and the baby had their doctor's appointment and both checked out fine. The baby weights nine pounds already and is starting to look like Kurt, or so *Mamm* says."

Sarah looked over at Mose and smiled. "I'm so happy for them. It went well for her? No problems with her labor?"

Mose smiled back. "*Daed* said there were no bumps in the road."

Sarah went back to drying Mercy. "Didn't Kurt want a son?"

Mose grinned at her, ignoring her question. "I think I'll go check the water levels in the yard again. Be right back."

Under the streetlight, windblown rain pelted down at an angle. *When will this rain stop?* Mose dropped the blind slat and put his empty glass in the sink. He padded barefoot through the dining room, flipped on the light in the hallway and pushed open the girls' partially closed door. Both slept soundly, Beatrice sprawled out on her stomach, her head in the middle of her pillow. Mercy lay curled on her side. He covered the baby's bare legs with the light blanket bunched at her feet and touched one blond corkscrew curl before he wandered down the hall to his own bed. It had been a long, stress-filled day. He looked forward to some sleep and a hot meal in the morning.

Sarah had left the bedside lamp on. She lay sleeping in a fetal position at the edge of the mattress, her hand partially covering her face, her long hair in a thick plait on her pillow.

He sat on the edge of the bed across from her, listening to the rain. All he could hear was the downpour and the steady beat of his own heart. Sarah moved. His hand searched for the lamp switch and twisted it back on. He looked across the bed. She lay on her back, her body rigid, as taut as a bow. "Sarah? Are you awake?"

"*Ya*. The thunder woke me."

"I love thunderstorms. *Daed* and I used to stand on the porch and watch the sky light up. *Mamm* always fussed at the door until we came back in." He waited for a laugh, some kind of reaction, but got none. "Am I keeping you awake?" He wanted to make sure she was okay after her difficult day.

"I can't sleep with the storm overhead."

Mose liked the way the soft artificial light made her skin seem to glow. "I'm sorry I was late for lunch today. I had to drive home slow. The streets were flooded past the sidewalks. I wish I had been here with you when the officers brought the news about Joseph's killer."

Sarah looked at him, her eyes intense and bright. "I had to hear what they had to say. Hearing it was hard, but knowing the truth makes a difference."

"Months ago you blamed yourself for Joseph's death. Do you have peace now?"

Her bottom lip quivered. "For so long I've believed I caused the fire. That he died because of my carelessness. I've punished myself because of it. When I heard the truth, I was relieved and horribly angry. I wished his killer dead, Mose. I wished Benjamin Hochstetler would die, and then I learned he had. He'd killed himself." A sob escaped her. Her shoulders started heaving in great, gulping sobs.

Mose scooped her in his arms. She burrowed close, her tears dampening his shoulder. "Don't cry, Sarah." He rubbed her back, the baby kicking at the pressure of his body so close. "*Gott* understands why you were angry. He made us all fallible, with good and bad thoughts. You didn't cause the man's death. He killed himself, probably because his shame was more than he could live with."

"I thought for so long that Joseph had died because of something I didn't do. All those months I grieved, and this man knew the truth and said nothing."

"Be angry, but forgive. For yourself and the baby," Mose murmured softly. "Hatred does horrible things to a person's mind. It burns a hole in your soul. Don't let him steal your peace."

Sarah took in a shuddering breath, her body beginning to relax. Minutes ticked by and as she spoke she pulled away. "*Danke*, Mose. I needed to talk. You are so kind to me, mean so much to me."

The loss of her embrace overwhelmed him as she laid back down on the bed. His eyes watered with unshed tears. She needed comfort but still didn't trust him to understand.

"I think I can sleep now. *Gut* night." She turned onto her side, away from him.

Mose watched the rise and fall of her back become regular and deep. He stood up and got ready for bed.

Something was wrong. Sarah woke with a start. Pain tore at her, her stomach growing hard. Had she wet the bed? Her gown clung to her body, cold and damp. Pain ripped through her back and circled around to the lower part of her stomach. She sucked in a breath, waiting for the heavy cramps to ease. She flipped on the lamp and lifted the light sheet across her legs. Pink fluid circled the sheet and soaked her gown. *Did my water break?* Another pain hit, this one more intense, forcing her to moan. She took in a breath and pushed it out. *Is this labor? I'm not due for days.* Panic grabbed at her throat, made it hard to swallow. She called out to Mose, but her voice was a whisper. She inched across the bed, waiting for each pain to pass. Finally, she could touch his shoulder. She shoved with all her might. Mose murmured something low, unintelligible. She shoved again, over and over until he stirred and turned her way, his eyes opening.

"You all right?"

"I think my labor started." She cradled her stomach as it tightened, prepared for the next round of pulsing pain.

Mose shot out of bed, grabbed his work pants from the closet and pulled them over his pajama bottoms. "I'll be right back." He grabbed his cell phone and dialed his father's number. On the fourth ring he picked up.

"Otto Fischer here."

Mose opened the blinds in the kitchen and looked outside. The storm had calmed, but hours of heavy rain had completely flooded the street. Water lapped at the sidewalk in his yard. "*Daed*, its Sarah. She's in labor. Our roads are too flooded to drive. I can't get her to the midwife. Do you think you and *mamm* could walk over here? I need help fast."

"Mose. Remember, your *mamm's* not here. She left for her sister's yesterday."

"*Ach.* I forgot. I've got the girls asleep and no way to get Sarah help. What can I do?"

"Did you call the hospital, or fire department? Maybe a fire truck can make it through the water."

"I'll call, but I don't think there's time for them to get here. Her water's already broke and I don't have a clue what to do next."

Otto cleared his voice. "I've got a suggestion but you're probably not going to like it."

"I'm desperate. Tell me."

"I can get Ulla."

Mose looked at his cell phone, wondering if his father had lost his mind. "Are you serious? Ulla'd never come, and I don't think Sarah would let her anywhere near her, or the baby."

"Ulla was a midwife for over twenty years. I think you better reconsider your situation before you throw stones."

Mose looked toward the only light on in the house and sucked in his breath. "Okay, ask her if she'll come, and, *Daed*, please be careful. It's bad out there."

"I'll do my best. You call the fire department, quick."

Mose stood looking at his phone. He tore the fire department calendar out of the kitchen drawer and started pushing numbers as he ran to the back of the house. *Gott, don't let her die. I love her. Please don't let her die.*

Sarah watched from a chair as Ulla and her daughter, Molly, worked as one. It was if they knew what the other wanted before being asked. The bed was stripped, remade and a plastic sheet tucked under the bedding. Silently the soiled gown was pulled over Sarah's head and a fresh gown replaced it. She was helped back into bed without a single word being spoken. A fresh wave of pain hit and Sarah lay still, enduring what must happen to deliver her baby.

"Are you in pain?" Ulla placed her hand on Sarah's stomach, allowing a professional smile to crease her lips up at the ends.

"*Ya*, I was." Sarah watched as the older woman began to press her wrinkled hands into her softening stomach.

Ulla looked up, her expression changed, her forehead creased. "Molly."

The young woman stood, abandoning the chair she'd sat in. *"Ya?"*

Ulla's fingers continued to probe, her features pinched. "The baby has twisted. We must turn it before it reaches the birth canal. Put your hands here and push gently when I tell you."

"Ya." Molly followed her mother's instructions, pushing, and then waiting as Sarah's stomach hardened with a contraction.

"Breathe slow and easy. This will hurt but we must do what we can to make this baby come head first," Ulla told Sarah.

Sarah nodded, terrified but understanding.

The woman's blue-eyed gaze held Sarah's as they pushed and then waited for her contractions to pass.

Excruciating pain tore at Sarah's insides. She stifled a scream. Tremors hit her. She bit on the blanket, her teeth chattering. She wanted Joseph in that moment and then Mose's face filled her mind.

"There." Ulla straightened, waiting at the foot of the bed with Molly by her side.

Pains came at regular intervals, stealing Sara's breath, and then increased until there was only pain. The urge to push overwhelmed her. "I need to push." Sarah waited for Ulla's nod.

"Another moment, Sarah. I have to check the cord's placement first." Ulla finally grunted, "*Ya.* Now."

With all her might Sarah pushed, her face heating, sweat pouring off her.

"Again," Ulla instructed.

A wave of hot misery hit her and she pushed again. She felt movement and looked down. Ulla lifted her silent baby in the air and swung it by its blue feet. Sarah's heart pounded in her throat. *What is she doing?* A lusty cry filled the room and the baby began to squirm, his arms and legs flailing in the air, his skin turning a bright, healthy pink.

"A healthy-looking son with ten fingers and toes, thanks to his brave *mamm.*" The smile was back but wider. Ulla laid the baby on Sarah's stomach. She cut the cord and accepted the baby blanket held out by Molly. Seconds later she handed off the swaddled baby.

Her gaze on the child's face, Molly lay him on his mother's chest and smiled at Sarah as she stepped back. "He is so beautiful."

Sarah looked at her wailing son, his blond curls, and began to weep.

Mose tiptoed into the dim room, trying hard not to make a sound. Sarah lay in the bed, probably asleep after her ordeal, a tiny bundle in the crook of her arm.

"Mose?" Sarah turned his way, a smile gentle on her lips.

He walked to the bed and sat on the edge. *"Ya."* Sarah looked tired but good to his eyes. Her bright hair fanned out against the pillow, lose from its braid and damp at the crown.

She put out her hand and he took it, eager to touch her. The baby stirred, making a mewing sound and she was alert, checking him with her glance.

"Beatrice tells me she's named him Levi. Any chance she's telling the truth?"

"We girls heard from *Gott*. He will be Levi Nolt Fischer."

"And Levi's mother? How is she?" Mose squeezed her hand, longing to take her in his arms and kiss her cheek but afraid to move her.

"Levi's mother is fine." The bags under his eyes told her what kind of night he'd had.

"It was a fast birth." Mose had been through two lengthy births with Greta and was amazed how quickly Levi had been born.

"Ya. Levi wasted no time. He's small but healthy. Ulla said his tiny size helped speed things up." Sarah kept her voice low.

"Did she treat you well, she and Molly?" He moved closer, touching the baby's wispy blond hair.

Sarah nodded. "She and Molly were *wunderbaar*, Mose. They showed me every courtesy and were kind and professional. Not a word from the past. It was as if none of the ugliness happened."

"Gut, I guess *Daed* threatening her with being un-churched worked, plus, she's really not a bad person.

Just missing her daughter. I owe her a debt of gratitude for getting you and the *bobbel* through this."

"It can't have been easy for her." Sarah looked over at Levi and one side of the baby's lip lifted, almost into a smile. "You see, he likes her, so we must try harder for his sake."

"She wouldn't let me come in." Mose looked like Beatrice when she sulked, his mouth twisted in a grimace. "I wanted to be with you, but she kept me out."

"She's old-fashioned. In her day men drank coffee and slapped each other's backs while we women did all the hard work."

"*Ya*, well. I don't like to be ordered about in my own home. If I want to see you, then I should be allowed. You are my *frau*."

"We'll talk to her about that before the next *bobbel* comes, okay?" Sarah's smile spoke words she was afraid to say aloud. "If you want a child with me?" Sarah held her breath, her heart pounded in her chest. Their arrangement had been a simple one. No required affection, no love expected. Perhaps he didn't feel the way she did now. Maybe he didn't return her love?

Mose grinned down at Sarah and then his new son, love shining bright in his eyes as he gently pressed his lips to hers. "I've always thought six *kinder* would be enough to take care of me in my old age. What do you think, *frau*?"

Sarah looked into her husband's eyes and saw love there in the sparkle of his gaze and more.

So much more.

"*Ya*, I think six is a perfect number."

Epilogue

Sarah's fingers entwined with Mose's free hand. A smiling Mercy giggled, her feet dangling out of the canvas carrier looped around her *daed's* shoulders. Her blond curls bounced with each step he took down to the sun-bleached beach, the late-summer sun hanging low in the sky. Beatrice's tiny hand was engulfed in her father's other hand, her complaints of wet sand squishing between her toes ignored.

Levi lay nestled against Sarah, the chubby boy's shoulder sling protecting him from the setting sun and gentle, late-day breezes. "I've never seen the sky so blue," Sarah said, grinning over at Mose.

"I see beautiful sky blue every time I look into your eyes, *mein frau*," Mose murmured. She knew he didn't approve of public displays of affection, but today he seemed unable to resist and kissed her gently on the cheek.

"Hey, did you kiss my *daed*?" Beatrice squinted one eye as she regarded first her father and then Sarah suspiciously.

"*Nee, liebling.* He kissed me. What do you think of that?"

"I think it's funny, that's what I think. I need a kiss, too." Beatrice puckered up and noisily kissed her *daed* on his arm. "Yuck! Your hair tickles." She scrubbed at her mouth with the back of her hand and started to spit until she caught Sarah's warning glance.

"His beard tickles, too." Sarah turned to Mose and smiled.

Amusement sparkled in Beatrice's eyes as she smiled at her new *mamm*. "If you don't like him kissing you, tell him to stop. That's what I'd do if Danny Lapp tried to kiss me."

Mose woke from his quiet bliss, his tone the typical Amish father's bark. "You're too young to worry about boys, Beatrice Fischer. If that Lapp boy comes near you I better hear about it. You hear?"

"Yes. But, you kissed *Mamm*," Beatrice whined. Joy rushed through Sarah. *She finally called me mamm.*

Sarah gave Mose her best "I love you" smile and grinned as his eyes sparkled back at her. "Yes, I kissed your *mamm's* cheek, but we're married and it's allowed." He squeezed Sarah's hand. "When you get married, you can kiss your husband, too, but not a minute before."

"Okay." Beatrice began to skip, obviously less impressed with the subject of their conversation than Mose. Her feet kicked up sand. She yanked at her father's grasp, pulling him toward the incoming wave. "Can I go walk in the water? Please!"

Mose turned toward Sarah. He waited for her sign of approval. Sarah nodded and Mose released Beatrice to the churning surf with a firm warning. "Stay close to us. No rushing into the deep water like the last time."

Sarah spread out the full-size quilt she'd carried across her arm and sat down, her gaze on Beatrice. "Did you hear her call me *mamm*, Mose? I thought my heart would burst."

"She asked my permission last night while you were busy with Levi's bath. I told her she could make up her own mind, and I guess she did. I'm happy for you, Sarah. I know it means a lot." He pulled her close for a quick hug and then pulled Mercy's carrier off his back and placed the squirming child down beside him. Sarah kissed her on her blond head and handed the restless little one a bucket of sea shells to play with.

Mose's hands were gentle as he pushed a strand of hair blowing in Sarah's eyes. *"Danke,"* she said as she laid Levi in the shade created by Mose's broad back and changed the *bobbel's* wet diaper while watching Beatrice's silly antics in the inch-deep water.

"I thought it would never happen." Sarah laughed with surprise as Beatrice chased a flock of squawking seagulls up a small bank of sand. "She's come a long way since Levi's birth. I think seeing our love grow has given her a measure of peace, something she'd lost."

Quiet for a moment, Mose laughed, his gaze on Sarah as she frantically dug sand out of Mercy's mouth. She groaned. "You can't turn your back on Mercy for a second. This little *liebling* will eat anything, just like her sister."

Beatrice ran over and rushed round them, her little legs not still for a moment, her singsong voice raised to the heavens, declaring, "I love *Mamm* and *Daed*, Mercy, Levi, my *grandmammi* Ulla, *Poppy* Otto, *Grandmammi* Theda, *Aenti* Molly and the sand and trees. Did I forget anyone, *Mamm*?"

Sarah leaned against Mose, his arm around her shoulder. "No. I think you remembered everyone." *We're a real family at last*, she thought. Contentment put a smile on her face as she elbowed Mose and added, "Except...maybe Danny Lapp."

An elderly *Englisch* couple strolled past, both casually dressed, the wrinkled old man's arm linked with his gray-haired beauty in cutoff jeans and a summer blouse. "Beautiful family you have there," he said.

Mose nodded his thanks, pulling his straw hat off as a smile spread across his face. "*Gott* has richly blessed me with *mein frau* and *kinder*."

"I don't know what I'd do without mine," the old man said and waved as they continued down the shoreline.

Beatrice stopped her running long enough to ask, "Who was that?"

Sarah answered, "No one we know, *bobbel*. Just a passing couple who knows true joy when they see it."

* * * * *

HIDDEN IN PLAIN VIEW

Diane Burke

This book is dedicated to the family and friends who offered nothing but love and open arms to both my son and me during our long-overdue reunion. I also wish to thank Rachel Burkot, my new editor, for jumping in midstream and doing a phenomenal job of helping me make this book the best it could be.

Don't be afraid, for I am with you.
Don't be discouraged, for I am your God.
I will strengthen you and help you.
I will hold you up with my victorious right hand.
—*Isaiah* 41:10

Prologue

Mount Hope, Lancaster County, PA

Sarah Lapp wasn't thinking about guns or violence or murder on this unseasonably warm fall day. She was thinking about getting her basket of apples and cheese to the schoolhouse.

Pedaling her bicycle down the dirt road, she spotted the silhouettes of her in-laws, Rebecca and Jacob, standing close together in the distant field.

Sarah knew when she'd married their son, Peter, that she had been fortunate to have married her best friend.

But sometimes…

She glanced at them again.

Sometimes she couldn't help but wonder what true love felt like.

Chiding herself for her foolish notions, she turned her attention back to the road. A sense of unease taunted her as she approached the school. The children should be out in the yard on their first break of the day, but the ball field was empty.

She hit the kickstand on her bike and looked around the yard.

Peter's horse and wagon were tethered to the rail, a water bucket beside them. Children's bicycles haphazardly dotted the lawn. The bats for the morning ball game rested against the bottom of the steps.

Everything appeared normal.

But it didn't *feel* normal.

Sarah climbed the steps and moved cautiously across the small landing, noting the open windows and the curtains fluttering in the breeze.

Silence.

Her pulse pounded. *When was a room full of children ever silent?*

She'd barely turned the knob when the door was pulled wide with such force that Sarah was propelled forward and sprawled across the floor.

Peter started in her direction.

"Stop right there, Peter, unless you want to see your wife hurt." The speaker was John Zook, a cousin who had recently returned to the Amish way of life. He pulled Sarah roughly to her feet.

"John?" Sarah gasped when she saw a gun peeking out from the folds of the carpentry apron tied around his waist.

Immediately Peter and the teacher, Hannah, gathered the children together and took a protective stance in front of them, shielding their view of the room.

Sarah stood alone in the middle of the room and faced the gunman. She saw fear in his hooded eyes—fear and something else. Something hard and cold.

"John, why are you doing this terrible thing?" she asked.

"Is he out there? Did you see him?"

"Who, John? Who do you think is out there?" Sarah tried to understand what was frightening him.

"What do you want?" Peter's voice commanded from the back of the room.

"I want you to shut up," John snapped in return.

Sarah glanced at the children and marveled at how well behaved and silent they were. John had made sure the adults had seen his weapon, but Sarah was fairly certain the children had not. They seemed more confused and curious than frightened.

John lifted the curtain. "He's out there. I know it."

"John, I did not pass anyone on the road. It was just me." Sarah kept her voice calm and friendly. "We will help you if you will tell us what it is that frightens you so."

When John looked at them, Sarah was taken aback by the absolute terror she saw in his eyes. "He's going to kill me," he whispered. "There will be no place I can hide."

Peter, his patience running thin, yelled at the man. "You are starting to scare the children. I am going to let them out the back door and send them home."

"Nobody moves," John ordered.

Feeling the tension escalate, Sarah tried to find words to defuse the situation. "Peter is right. Whatever's wrong, we will help you. But you must let the children leave."

John shot a furtive glance at the group huddled in the corner and then nodded. "All right. Get them out of here, but make it quick."

Peter ushered the children outside, with whispers to each child to run straight home. When the teacher came up behind the last child, Peter ignored her protests and shoved her to safety, too.

John shoved a felt pouch at Sarah. "Hide this and don't give it to anyone but me. Understand?"

The heavy and cumbersome bag felt like rocks or marbles were nestled inside. She used several straight pins to bind it to her waistband.

Suddenly the sound of boots pounding against the wooden steps filled the air.

"Shut up. Don't make a sound!" John ordered. With trembling hands, he aimed his gun and waited for the door to open. But it didn't.

Instead, bullets slammed *through* the door.

"Sarah, get down!" Peter yelled from across the room.

Pieces of wood from the walls and desks, as well as chunks of chalkboard, splintered as each bullet reached a target.

John Zook grabbed his shoulder. Then doubled over and clutched his stomach, groaning in pain.

The door banged open and slammed against the wall. A stranger entered, this one much taller, with darkness in his eyes that cemented Sarah's feet to the floor in fear.

"Hello, John. Didn't expect to see me, did you?"

The slighter man's body shook. "I was gonna call and let you know where I was, Jimmy. Just as soon as I found a safe place for us to hide out."

"Is that so? Well, I saved you the trouble. Give me my diamonds."

Diamonds?

Instantly, Sarah's fingers flew to the pouch hidden in the folds of her skirt.

"You've got until the count of three. One."

"I don't have them. I have to go get them."

"Two."

"I don't have them!" John's voice came out in an almost hysterical pitch.

"Please, Jimmy, honest." John pulled Sarah in front of him. "She has them. I gave them to her."

Sarah looked into the stranger's face, and evil looked back.

"Three."

The sudden burst of gunfire shook Sarah to her core.

A small, round hole appeared in John's forehead. His expression registered surprise and his hand, which had been painfully gripping Sarah's arm, opened. He fell to the floor.

The loud, piercing sound of a metal triangle rent the air. The children had reached their homes. Help was on the way.

The shooter leered at Sarah. "Let's take a look and see what you're hiding in that skirt, shall we?"

"No!" Peter yelled, and ran toward her.

The intruder fired.

Her husband's body jerked not once but twice as he grabbed his chest and collapsed in a heap on the floor.

"Peter!"

Sarah's heart refused to accept what her mind knew was fact. Peter was dead.

Before she could drop to his side, something slammed into the left side of her head. Another blow to her arm. To her back. Pain seized her breath. Weakened her knees. Crumpled her to the floor.

She stretched her right arm out toward Peter, their fingers almost touching as she slid into blessed oblivion.

Chapter One

Where am I?

Sarah Lapp lay on a bed with raised metal rails. She noted a darkened television screen bracketed to the opposite wall. A nightstand and recliner beside the bed.

I'm in a hospital.

She tried to sit up but couldn't. She was hooked up to machines. Lots of them. Fear pumped her heart into overdrive.

Why am I here?

Again she tried to move, but her body screamed in protest.

Burning pain. Throbbing pain.

Searing the skin on her back. Pulsing through her arm and gathering behind her eyes.

She tried to raise her left arm to touch her forehead but it felt heavy, weighted down, lost in its own gnawing sea of hurt. She glanced down and saw it bandaged and held against her chest by a blue cloth sling.

I've injured my arm. But how? Why can't I remember? And why do I feel so scared?

She took a deep breath.

Don't panic. Take your time. Think.

Once more she inhaled, held it for a second, and forced herself to ever so slowly release it. Repeating the process a couple more times helped her regain a sense of calm.

Okay. She could do this.

She opened her eyes and stared into the darkness.

"Sarah?"

Sarah? Is that my name?

Why can't I remember?

Her heart almost leaped from her chest when one of the shadows moved.

The man had been leaning against the wall. She hadn't seen him standing in the shadows until he stepped forward. He obviously wasn't a doctor. His garb seemed familiar yet somehow different. He wore black boots, brown pants held up with suspenders and a white shirt with the sleeves rolled to his elbows. He carried a straw hat.

"I thought I heard you stirring." He approached her bed and leaned on the side rail. She found the deep timbre of his voice soothing.

The faint glow from the overhead night-light illuminated his features. She stared at his clean-shaven face, the square jaw, the tanned skin, his intense brown eyes. She searched for some form of recognition but found none.

"I'm glad you're awake." He smiled down at her.

She tried to speak but could only make hoarse, croaking sounds.

"Here, let me get you something to drink." He pushed a button, which raised the head of her bed. He lifted a cup and held it to her lips. There was something inti-

mate and kind in the gesture, and although she didn't
recognize this man, she welcomed his presence.

Gratefully, she took a sip, enjoying the soothing cool-
ness of the liquid as it slid over her parched lips and
trickled down her throat. When he moved the cup away,
she tried again.

"Who...who are you?"

His large hand gently cupped her fingers. She found
the warmth of his touch comforting. His brown shaggy
hair brushed the collar of his shirt. Tiny lines crinkled
the skin at the sides of his eyes.

"My name is Samuel, and I'm here to help you."

Her throat felt like someone had shredded her vocal
cords. Her mouth was so dry that even after the sip of
water, she couldn't gather enough saliva for a good spit.
When she did speak, her voice reflected the strain in a
hoarse, barely audible whisper.

"Where... What..." She struggled to force the words
out.

"You're in a hospital. You've been shot."

Shot!

No wonder she had felt so afraid when he'd moved
out of the shadows. She might not remember the incident, but some inner instinct was still keeping her alert
and wary of danger.

"Can you tell me what you remember?" There was
kindness in his eyes and an intensity that she couldn't
identify.

She shook her head.

"Do you remember being in the schoolhouse when
the gunman entered? Did you get a good look at him?"

Schoolhouse? Gunman?

Her stomach lurched, and she thought she was going

to be sick. Slowly, she moved her head back and forth again.

"How about before the shooting? Your husband was inside the building constructing bookshelves. Do you remember bringing a basket of treats for the children?"

His words caused a riotous tumble of questions in her mind. She had a husband? Who was he? *Where* was he? She tried to focus her thoughts. This man just told her she'd been shot inside a school. Had anyone else been hurt? Hopefully, none of the children.

"Hus…husband?"

"Sarah. There's no easy way to tell you. Your husband was killed in the shooting."

The room started to spin. Sarah squeezed her eyes shut.

"I'm so sorry. I wish there had been an easier way to break the news." His deep, masculine voice bathed her senses with sympathy and helped her remain calm. "I hate to have to question you right now, but time is of the essence." The feel of his breath on her cheek told her he had stepped closer. "I need you to tell me what you remember—what you saw that day, before things other people tell you cloud your memories."

A lone tear escaped and coursed its way down her cheek at the irony of it all.

"Can you tell me anything about that day?" he prodded. "Sometimes the slightest detail that you might think is unimportant can turn into a lead. If you didn't see the shooter's face, can you remember his height? The color of his skin? What he wore? Anything he might have said?"

He paused, giving her time to collect her thoughts, but only moments later the questions came again.

"If you don't remember seeing anything, use your other senses. Did you hear anything? Smell anything?"

She opened her eyes and stared into his. "I told you." She choked back a sob. "I can't…can't remember. I can't remember anything at all."

His wrinkled brow and deep frown let her know this wasn't what he had expected.

"Maybe you should rest now. I'll be back, and we can talk more later."

Sarah watched him cross to the door. Once he was gone, she stared at her hand and wondered why the touch of a stranger had made her feel so safe.

Sam stood in the corridor and tried to collect his thoughts.

Sarah.

He hadn't expected to be so touched by her unfortunate circumstances. He had a policy to never let emotions play a part when he was undercover or protecting a witness. Sarah Lapp was a job, nothing more, and he had no business feeling anything for her one way or the other.

But he had to admit there was something about her. He'd been moved by the vulnerability he saw in her face, the fear he read in her eyes. She was terrified. Yet she had stayed calm, processing everything he had to tell her with quiet grace.

She'd been visibly upset when Sam had told her about the shooting. She'd seemed shocked when he informed her that her husband had been killed. But learning that she had had a husband at all seemed to affect her the most.

He hadn't had an opportunity yet to talk with Sarah's

doctors about the full extent of her injuries. Was she really suffering from memory loss, and if so, was it a temporary setback or a permanent situation?

Sam often relied heavily on his gut. His instincts this time were warning him that he had just stepped into a much more complicated situation than he had first thought.

He needed to talk with the doctor.

When he glanced down the hall, he saw Dr. Clark, as well as several members of the police force, including his superior, with three Amish men in tow. Dr. Clark ushered the entire group into a nearby conference room and gestured for Sam to join them.

Once inside, Sam crossed the room and leaned against the far wall. He saw the men shoot furtive glances his way and knew they were confused by his Amish clothing.

He didn't blame them. He was disconcerted by it, too. He hadn't donned this type of clothing for fifteen years. Yet his fingers never hesitated when he fastened the suspenders. The straw hat had rested upon his head like it was meant to be there.

Jacob Lapp, identifying himself as the bishop of their community and acting as spokesperson for their group, addressed Captain Rogers.

"We do not understand, sir. Why have you brought us here?"

"Please, gentlemen, have a seat." Captain Rogers gestured toward the chairs around the table. "Dr. Clark wants to update you on Sarah's condition."

They pulled out chairs and sat down.

Dr. Clark spoke from his position at the head of the table. "Sarah is in a very fragile state. She was shot twice in the back, once in the arm and once in the head. She has a long road to recovery, but I believe she *will* recover. To complicate matters, she is suffering from amnesia."

"Will her memory return?" Jacob asked.

"I'm afraid I honestly don't know. Only time will tell."

The man on Jacob's left spoke. "Excuse me, sir. My name is Benjamin Miller. I do not understand this thing you call amnesia. I had a neighbor who got kicked in the head by his mule. He forgot what happened with his mule, but he didn't forget everything else. He still remembered who he was, who his family was. Why can't Sarah?"

The doctor smiled. "It is common for a person not to remember a traumatic event but to remember everything else. What is less common, but still occurs, is a deeper memory loss. Some people forget everything— like Sarah."

"When she gets better, she will remember again, *ya?*" Jacob twirled his black felt hat in circles on the table.

"I hope that once she returns home, familiar surroundings will help, but I cannot promise anything," the doctor replied.

The men looked at each other and nodded.

"There is something else. Sarah is sixteen weeks pregnant."

Sam felt like someone had suddenly punched him in the gut. Wow, this woman couldn't catch a break. As if amnesia, gunshot wounds and widowhood wasn't enough for her to handle. He raised an eyebrow, but steeled himself to show no other reaction to the news.

The doctor waited for the men at the table to digest the information before he locked eyes with Jacob. "Mrs. Lapp has informed me that Sarah has had two prior miscarriages."

Jacob nodded but remained silent. The information regarding this pregnancy seemed to weigh heavily upon him.

"I'm sorry to inform you, Mr. Lapp, that even though she has made it into her second trimester, she still might lose the child. She has experienced severe trauma to her body, and currently she is under emotional stress as well."

"With my son gone, this will be our only grandchild." Jacob's eyes clouded over. "What can we do to help?"

"You can allow me to protect her." Sam pushed away from the wall and approached the table.

The bishop's expression revealed his confusion. "Protect Sarah? I don't understand, sir. The man who hurt Sarah is gone, *ya?* She is safe now." Jacob looked directly at Sam. "Excuse me, sir. We do not recognize you. What community do you call home?"

Captain Rogers nodded permission for Sam to answer the questions.

"My name is Detective Samuel King. Standing to my left is my partner, Detective Masterson. To his right is Special Agent Lopez from the FBI. We believe Sarah is in grave danger."

"From whom?" Benjamin spoke up, gesturing with his arm to the men sitting on either side of him. "Her family? Her friends?"

Sam addressed his words to Bishop Lapp. "Since I was raised Amish, Captain Rogers thought it might be easier for me to blend in with your community as Sarah's protective detail."

All three men gasped, then turned and whispered in their native Pennsylvania German dialect commonly known as Pennsylvania Dutch.

Sam understood not only the words, but also the emotions and objections the men were expressing. The Amish do not care for law enforcement and try to keep themselves separate from the *Englisch* way of life.

"With respect, sir," Jacob said, "although grateful, we do not feel we need your protection, and neither does Sarah."

Sam sighed heavily. "You are wrong." When he had their full attention, he said, "If you do not allow us to help, Sarah will be dead before this week is over, as well as her unborn child and many of the kids who were inside that schoolhouse when the shooting occurred."

Samuel noted the sudden pallor in Jacob's face. He recognized bewilderment in the other men's eyes and glimpsed hesitation in their body language, but they continued to listen.

Sam pulled out a chair and faced the men. He explained about the diamond heist and the murders of the other thieves, which led to the shoot-out in the school.

Matthew Kauffman, the third Amish man in the group, spoke up for the first time. "If you were once Amish, then you know that we cannot allow police to move into our homes. It is not our way."

"I understand your dilemma," Sam responded. "I assure you that although I left my Amish roots behind, I never abandoned my respect for the Amish ways."

"You do not speak like us," Benjamin insisted. "You sound like an *Englischer.*"

Sam slipped easily into the lilt of the Pennsylvania Dutch dialect. "Many years of living with the *Englisch,* and you can start to sound like one, ain't so?"

"Why did you leave your home, sir?" Benjamin asked.

Sam took a moment to decide just how much he was willing to share with these men.

"In my youth, I witnessed too many things for a young boy to see. I witnessed theft of Amish goods that went unpunished. I witnessed bullying and cruelty against the Amish people, yet I could not raise my hand to retaliate."

The men nodded.

"I witnessed worse. I witnessed drunken teens race their car into my father's buggy just for the fun of it. My parents did not survive their prank."

Several heartbeats of silence filled the room as everyone present absorbed what he'd said.

"The Amish forgive." Sam shrugged. "I could not. So I left."

"It is difficult sometimes to forgive, to not seek vengeance and to move on with life." Jacob's quiet voice held empathy. His eyes seemed to understand that Sam's emotional wounds had not healed and still cut deep. "I understand how hard it can be. I just lost my only son. But…" He looked Sam straight in the eye. "It is not our place to judge." When he spoke, his voice was soft and sad. "Judgment belongs only to God, *ya?*"

"And vengeance belongs to the Lord, not us," Benjamin Miller added.

"I am not talking about vengeance," Sam said, defending himself. "I am talking about justice."

Jacob scrutinized Sam as if he were trying to determine his character from his words. "How do you know whether what you call justice, Detective King, is what God would call vengeance? Is it not best to leave these matters in God's hands?"

A sad ghost of a smile twisted Sam's lips. "I believe God intended for us to love one another, to help one another. I believe He expects us to protect those who cannot protect themselves. Children. Unborn babies. An innocent woman who doesn't even know the gravity of her loss yet. Isn't that God's will?"

Jacob remained silent and pensive.

Sam had to work hard to control his emotions. There was no place in police work, particularly undercover police work, to let emotions control your actions or thoughts. But he understood these people. He'd been one of them. He knew they were pacifists who refused to fight back. If a gunman walked up and shot them dead on the street, they'd believe it was God's will.

How was he going to make them understand the danger they were in? Or worse, defend against that danger? Jacob was their bishop. He was the one he had to win over. Sam knew the only hope he had of convincing Lapp to go along with the plan was to drive home the pain the man was still feeling from his loss. He challenged him with a hard stare.

"Are you willing to accept responsibility for the deaths of your loved ones, Bishop? Your neighbors' loved ones? To never see your grandchild? To attend the funerals of your neighbors' children? Because you will be killing them just as if you held the gun and shot them yourself."

Sam's voice had a hardened edge, but he made no apologies for his harshness. He had to make these men understand the seriousness of the situation if he stood any chance of saving their lives.

"Please, sir, listen to me," he continued. "A stranger entered your Amish schoolhouse on a beautiful, peaceful spring afternoon. He cared only about diamonds, not about God or the sanctity of life." Sam placed his forearms on the table and leaned closer. "This isn't his first crime. We suspect him of many other crimes, but have been unable to bring him to justice.

"No one who would be able to describe him has lived to talk about it—except Sarah. Don't be fooled. He will return. He will find a way to walk freely among you. He is not above using your children—perhaps killing your children—to accomplish his goals. You will never sense the danger until it is too late."

The three men shot concerned glances at one another.

"Please," Sam pleaded. "Even *with* your help, we cannot promise that he won't succeed. We are chasing a shadow."

Sam paused, letting the men absorb his words. He gestured toward the other law-enforcement officers in the room.

"We are not asking you to take up arms or fight back. But we cannot protect you from the outside alone. If we stand any chance of stopping this man, then we must be close. We must be on the inside. We are asking for your help."

Jacob's head bent, and his lips moved in silent prayer. After a few moments of silence, he wiped a tear from his cheek and turned to the other Amish men.

"How can we not help?" he asked. "This is our Sarah. Hasn't she been hurt enough? These are our children he speaks of. Is it not our duty as parents to protect them?

And what of the innocent child Sarah carries? Must we not protect that child, too?"

"Jacob, you know if this horrible thing he speaks of happens, then it is the will of God." Benjamin's voice was insistent. "We must accept the will of God."

Jacob nodded slowly. "*Ya,* Benjamin, you are right. We must accept the will of God." After a moment, he made eye contact with Benjamin. "Your Mary was in that classroom…and your Daniel and William." Jacob glanced from him to the other man. "Matthew, your children, Emma, Joseph, John, Amos…they were there that terrible day, too." His eyes implored both men. "Are we so eager to let the wolf snatch them away that we stand aside and open the door?"

Benjamin blanched as the realization of what was at stake finally hit him. Visibly shaken, he lowered his head, his voice almost a whisper. "But if it is God's will…"

"I agree. We must accept God's will." Jacob leaned forward and placed his hand on his friend's shoulder. "But I have to ask you, Benjamin, how many detectives do we know who used to be Amish? Maybe sending Samuel to us *is* the will of God."

The men exchanged looks, whispered together in hushed tones and then nodded their heads.

This time, Jacob looked directly at the police captain. "We will agree to this. But please, sir, find the man you seek quickly. We cannot endure this situation for long."

The captain stood and thanked the men for their co-operation. "We will be placing undercover officers in your town. They will deliver your mail, pick up your milk and serve in your local shops and restaurants.

But only one will actually enter your home—Detective Samuel King."

Sam hadn't been back on Amish soil for more than a decade. He'd have to keep his emotions in check, his mind clear and his thoughts logical. A woman's life, and that of her unborn child, were at stake. The gravity of the situation weighed heavily on his shoulders, and he prayed he'd be up to the challenge.

Chapter Two

Sarah stared out the window. It had been one week since the shootings, two days since she'd awakened in this hospital room and they still hadn't caught the shooter.

She watched the people below in the parking lot.

Was he out there? Waiting? Plotting? Biding his time like a poisonous snake in the grass, coiled and ready to strike?

Would he come back for her? And if he did, this time…

Sarah didn't have to remember the past to know that she had no desire to die in the present.

She studied the men passing beneath her window. Did any of them look up in her direction? Was the killer watching her even now?

Fear shuddered through her.

How could she protect herself when she didn't even know what the man who posed a threat looked like? How could she help the police catch him before he could hurt more people if her mind continued to be nothing more than a blank slate?

Her mother-in-law, Rebecca, and the doctor had filled her in on what they knew of the details of that day.

The story they had told her was tragic. But she had no emotional connection to that schoolroom, or to the children who had fled out the back door and summoned help, or, even worse, to the man who had once shared her life and was now dead and buried.

She knew people expected an emotional response from her—tears, at least—but she felt nothing.

Surprise? Yes.

Empathy? Of course.

Pain? Grief?

No. They were the emotions she saw every time she looked at the sadness etched in Rebecca's face. She had lost a son.

Sarah had lost a stranger.

Earlier Rebecca had told Sarah that she'd been raised *Englisch* until the age of eight. Try as she might, she couldn't find any memory of those childhood years.

Following her mother's death, she'd been adopted by her Amish grandmother, who had also passed on years ago. Then she'd come to live with Jacob and Rebecca, embraced the Amish faith and married their son. Sarah found it more difficult to come to terms with the person she was supposed to be than to try to summon grief she couldn't feel.

She was a pregnant Amish widow recovering from multiple gunshot wounds and suffering from amnesia. That was her reality. That was the only world to which she could relate.

She couldn't conjure up the slightest recollection of Peter Lapp. Had he been of average build? Or was he tall? Had he had blond hair like his mother? Or maybe brown?

Rebecca had told her they'd been married five years and were happy together.

Had they been happy together? Were they still as much in love on the day of his death as they'd been the day they married? She hoped so. But can true love be forgotten as easily as a breath of air on a spring day? If they'd been soul mates, shouldn't she feel *something?* Have some sense of loss deep in her being, even if she couldn't remember the features of his face or the color of his hair?

Rebecca had also told her that she'd had two prior miscarriages. Had Sarah told her husband about this pregnancy? Were they happy about this blessing or anxious and fearful that it, too, would fail?

A surge of emotion stole her breath away. It wasn't grief. It was anger.

She wanted to be able to grieve for her husband. She wanted to be able to miss him, to shed tears for *him.* Instead, all she felt was guilt for not remembering the man. Not the sound of his voice. Not the feel of his touch. Not even the memory of his face. What kind of wife was she that a man who had shared her life was nothing more to her now than a story on someone else's lips?

She was no longer a complete human being. She was nothing more than an empty void and had nothing within to draw upon. No feelings for her dead husband. No feelings for an unborn child she hadn't even known she carried. No memories of what kind of person she had been. She was broken, damaged goods and of no use to anyone.

Please, God, help me. Please let me climb out of this dark and frightening place.

In the stillness of her empty room, the tears finally came.

Sam stood up from the chair outside Sarah's door and stretched his legs. Hours had passed since Rebecca had left with Jacob. He hadn't heard a sound lately, and the silence made him uneasy. Quietly, he opened the door and peeked inside.

He was surprised to see Sarah out of bed and standing at the window. Her floor-length robe seemed to swallow up her petite, frail figure. The swish of the door opening drew her attention.

"Hi." Sam stepped into the room. "Are you supposed to be out of bed?"

Sarah offered a feeble smile. "The nurses had me up a few times today. I won't get stronger just lying in bed."

Sam could see she wasn't having an easy time of it. Dark circles colored the skin beneath her eyes in a deep purplish hue. The telltale puffiness told him that she'd been crying. Her sky-blue eyes were clouded over with pain and perhaps even a little fear.

"It is kind of you to show concern, Detective King." Her voice sounded fragile and tired.

"Please, call me Samuel."

He flinched at the sound of his true Amish name slipping from his lips. Donning Amish clothes had returned him to his roots. But the sound of his given name instead of Sam sealed the deal. He had stepped back in time—and it was the last place he wanted to be.

"Samuel." The sound of his name in her soft, feminine voice drew his attention back to her. She smiled again, but it was only a polite gesture. Happiness never lit her eyes. "What can I do for you?"

"I thought I'd poke my head in and make sure you're all right."

"Thank you, but you needn't bother. I'm fine." A shadow crossed her face.

Fine? He didn't think so. Lost in his thoughts, he

hadn't noticed the puzzled expression on her face until she questioned him.

"Who are you, Samuel?"

She stood with her back to the window and studied him.

Who was he? He'd told her he was a detective. Was her loss of memory getting worse?

Sarah went right to the point. "You dress like an Amish man. Our men are not detectives." Her eyes squinted as she studied him.

She looked as if she might be holding her breath as she waited for his answer.

"I assure you, Sarah, I am a detective."

"And the Amish clothes? Is it a disguise?"

"Yes—and no. I was raised Amish. I left my home in Ohio and joined the police force about fifteen years ago."

"Ohio? You are very far from home, aren't you?" she asked.

Was that empathy he saw in her eyes? She was feeling sorry for *him*. Didn't that beat all?

"I wanted to get as far away as I could." Sam shrugged, and his mouth twisted into a lopsided grin. "Memories aren't always good."

She pondered his words before she spoke again. "Don't the Amish shun you if you leave?"

He found her words interesting. She could pull the definition of shunning from her memory banks but talked about it as if it wasn't part of her own culture, as if the term was nothing more than something she had read in a dictionary.

"I have no family to shun me."

The gentlest of smiles teased the corner of her lips. "Everyone has a family at one time or another, Samuel."

Her words hit a tender spot. She was getting much too personal. He didn't want to open that door for her. He didn't want to share that pain. He was acting as her bodyguard, nothing more, and the less emotional connection between them the better.

Attempting to change the subject, he said, "I'm sure you've been up and about enough for one day. Why don't you let me help you get back into bed so you can get some rest."

She allowed him to hold her elbow and support her as she crossed the room. "It must have been difficult for you to leave your Amish religion behind."

Her soft blue eyes stared up at him.

Sam smiled. He was fast learning that she was a stubborn woman, not easily distracted when she wanted to know something, and right now it was obvious that she wanted to know about him.

"I left religion behind, not God," he replied. "I carry God with me every day—in here and in here." He pointed to his head and his heart. "Memories were the only thing I left behind, painful ones."

Since her left arm was useless because of the sling and the IV bag and pole still attached to her right hand, Sam put his hands on both sides of her waist to lift her up onto the bed. Although tiny and petite, he couldn't help but note the slightly thickening waist beneath his touch. The signs of her pregnancy were starting to show, and the protective emotions that surfaced surprised him.

Her saucerlike eyes shimmered with unshed tears, and he fought not to lose himself in their beauty.

"I wish I had some memories," she whispered.

The minty scent of her breath fanned his face, and

the slightly parted pose of her lips tempted him to lower his head and steal a taste of their tantalizing softness.

Instead, he removed her slippers and, after she positioned herself back on the pillows, he covered her with a blanket.

"Memories aren't all they're cracked up to be, Sarah. I have memories, but no one to love me. You don't have memories, but you have people who love you very much."

She acknowledged his words with a nod and a pensive expression.

Her fragile beauty spoke to him, stirring emotions and feelings better left dormant. Stepping back, he subtly shook his head and reminded himself of his own rules.

Rule number one: never get emotionally involved with anyone in a case.

Rule number two: remember, at all times, that when working undercover none of it is real. You are living a lie.

"So, you didn't answer me. Why are you dressed like an Amish man, Detective King?"

He searched her face, looking for any signs of fear or weakness. He found instead only interest and curiosity.

"This shooter is highly intelligent. He managed to pull off a massive diamond heist without leaving a trace. No images on surveillance cameras. No witnesses. No mistakes. Until now." He took a deep breath before continuing. "This time he left behind a pouch full of diamonds. The doctors found the pouch pinned inside the waistband of your skirt when you were brought into the emergency room."

He heard her sharp intake of breath, but otherwise she remained still and waited for him to continue.

"This time he was sloppy. He left behind a witness. You." His eyes locked with hers. "He believes that you still have the diamonds in your possession. And he doesn't believe in leaving witnesses behind. There is no question. He will be back."

Fear crept into her eyes. "But you told me the doctors found the diamonds. I don't have them anymore, do I?"

"No. But he doesn't know that."

"Then I have to go away. I have to hide. I can't be around anyone who could be hurt because of me."

His admiration for her rose. She was worried about people she couldn't remember, and not about the imminent threat to herself.

"The safest thing for you and for everyone else is for you to return to your community. It will be harder for him to reach you and easier for everyone involved to recognize an outsider."

"Is he a threat to anyone besides me?"

"He is a really bad man, Sarah. He will stop at nothing to get what he wants. He could snatch a child. Harm one of your neighbors while looking for information. He is evil in human form." Gently, he tilted her chin up with his index finger and looked into her eyes. "But you and I will work together, and we will not let that happen. I promise."

Sam couldn't believe he had just said what he did.

Promise? The two of them working together? Was he crazy talking to her like this? Like they were a team fighting against evil?

Had he lost his mind?

"How can I help? I seem pretty useless to everyone these days." She smiled but seemed totally unaware of how the gesture lit up her face like a ray of sudden sunshine.

He liked making her smile. He liked easing her pain and stress. He tried to identify this tumble of feelings she stirred within him despite his attempt to stay neutral.

Pity? No. Sarah Lapp was too strong a woman to be pitied.

Admiration. Respect. Yes, that was it. He refused to consider there was anything more.

"I will be moving back to the farm with you," he said. "I'll be your bodyguard while the rest of the police force concentrates on finding this guy. With my Amish background, it makes me the perfect choice for the job. I can blend in better than any of the other officers. I can help maintain respect for the Amish way of life."

"Move in? With me?" Her eyes widened. Her mouth rounded in the shape of a perfect letter *O,* and a pink flush tinged her cheeks.

"We will both be staying with Rebecca and Jacob. We believe you will be the primary target because the shooter still believes you possess the diamonds. You also saw his face and lived. He can't afford to let you talk to the authorities. He will try to make sure that doesn't happen. If we can apprehend him when he makes his move, then everyone else will be safe as well."

"So I am going to be the bait to hook the fish?"

Now it was his turn for heat to rush into his face. He felt embarrassed and ashamed because she was right. He was using her as bait.

"It's all right, Samuel. I understand. I will do this thing if it will help keep the others safe. When do we begin?"

"Soon." He gave her fingers a light squeeze. "You

will be in the hospital a little while longer. You still need time to heal. But try not to worry. I will not let anything happen to you while you are in my care."

"I am not in your care, Samuel." Her smile widened. "I am in God's hands."

"Then that is a good thing, *ya?* With God on our side, we can't lose." Sam grinned, hoping his cavalier attitude would build her confidence and help her relax. "Concentrate on regaining your strength. Let me worry about all the bad guys out there."

The door pushed open behind them. Captain Rogers and Sam's partner, Joe Masterson, stood in the doorway. "Detective King, may I see you in the hall for a moment?"

Sam released her hand. "I'll be back. Remember, no worrying allowed. Everything is going to work for good, just the way the Lord intends."

Sarah tried to still the apprehension that skittered over her nerve endings when she found herself alone in the room. The police were going to use her as bait to catch a killer. Her breath caught in her throat, and she could feel the rapid beating of her heart beneath her hand on her chest. Was she strong enough, brave enough?

You can do this. You must do this. These people need you to help them.

These people? Where had that thought come from? These were her people, weren't they? Her family? She knew she felt a warm affection for both Rebecca and Jacob. They had been wonderfully kind and attentive to her since she'd come out of her coma.

But as much as she hated to admit it, she couldn't

feel a connection to them. At least not the kind of connection they seemed to expect. They were kind people. Loving people. But were they *her* people?

She tried again to conjure up a memory, even the slightest wisp of one, of Peter. Rebecca had told her that they'd grown up together and were the best of friends. They were happily married. They were expecting a child.

Sarah placed a hand on her stomach, feeling the slight swell beneath her touch. Their child. And she couldn't even remember Peter's face.

A stab of pain pierced her heart. She must be a shallow person to not remember someone she had obviously loved. Love goes soul deep, doesn't it? Love wouldn't be forgotten so quickly, would it?

Maybe it hadn't been love. Maybe it had been friendship or convenience or companionship. Maybe it was an emotion that hadn't claimed her heart at all. She would never know now.

Her eyes strayed to the hospital room door, and her thoughts turned to Samuel.

She was certain if a person were to fall in love with Samuel, it would be a deep, abiding love. It would be two souls uniting before God. It would last a lifetime and not be forgotten by injury or time.

Her heart fluttered in her chest at just the thought that she might be starting to have feelings for Samuel, before she angrily shooed them away.

Foolish notions. That was one thing she was quickly learning about herself. She was often a victim of foolish notions.

Chapter Three

"There's been another murder."

Apprehension straightened Sam's spine. "Another murder? Who? When?"

"Not here. Follow me." Captain Rogers, Joe and Sam strode briskly to the conference room and took their seats. The tension in the room was almost palpable.

Sam stole a moment to study his superior's face. The past seven days had made their mark. He noted his captain's furrowed brow, the lines of strain etched on each side of his mouth, but what caught his attention the most was the bone-weary fatigue he saw in his eyes. The political pressure to find a quick solution to a complicated, ever-worsening scenario was taking its toll.

The captain folded his hands on the table. "There's no sugarcoating this, so I'm just going to say it. Around 2:00 a.m. last night, Steven Miller was murdered."

"Steven Miller?" Sam leaned back in his chair. "Isn't that the name of the second diamond-heist robber?" He threw a hurried glance at both men. "Didn't we have him in custody?"

"Yep. Same guy." Joe's expression was grim. "We

had him under armed guard in a secluded room in a medical center in the Bronx."

"Special Agent Lopez called me first thing this morning." Captain Rogers wiped a hand over his face and leaned back in his chair. "The man was suffocated with one of his own pillows."

"How could something like this happen? He was under armed guard. Did they at least catch the guy?"

"No. He did it on the graveyard shift, when there would be fewer people roaming the halls or in attendance. Once Miller's heart stopped, the monitors went off at the nurse's station. By the time the nurse and crash cart personnel arrived at the room, he had disappeared."

"Any leads? Witnesses?" Sam tried to calm his racing thoughts. This shooter had walked into a hospital and murdered a man in police custody. The degree of difficulty to keep Sarah safe just rose several more notches.

"We believe it was the ring leader of the group," Rogers said. "The same guy we're expecting to show up here. We figure he left here right after the schoolhouse shootings and returned to New York. He spent the week tracking down the whereabouts of his partner in crime, did his surveillance of the medical center and set a plan in motion. He's never left anyone alive who could identify him. He wasn't about to leave one of his team in the hands of the enemy."

"I don't believe this guy." Sam ran his hand through his hair. He could feel his blood throb in a rapid beat on each side of his temple. "You're telling me that he just walked up to a guarded room, slipped inside, killed our witness and left? Why didn't our guards stop him? What did they have to say when they were questioned?"

"Nothing." Joe's expression grew grimmer. "The perp slit the guard's throat. Nobody knows whether it was coming or going, so we're not sure if that's how he gained access or how he covered his tracks when he left. But we think it was on the way out, because a nurse reported that she had stopped and asked the police officer if he'd like a cup of coffee only moments before. She'd just sat down at her desk when the monitor alarm went off."

"What about the surveillance cameras?" The throbbing in Sam's temples became a full-blown headache. He closed his eyes for a second or two and rubbed his fingers on the tender spots beside his eyes before locking his gaze on Rogers. "We're not chasing a shadow. He's a flesh-and-blood man just like the rest of us. Somebody had to see something."

Captain Rogers frowned. "Lopez identified someone he believes is the perp on the tapes. The suspect shows up in multiple camera shots and hides his face every time. Lopez sent the digital images to the FBI labs for further enhancement."

"How did he get into the room in the first place?" Sam shot a glance between his partner and Captain Rogers. "We discussed his security plan with Lopez before he left. It seemed solid."

"It was solid." Rogers sighed heavily. "There was a police presence visible at the elevator banks, both in the lobby and the floor in question. There was an officer at the door of the patient's room as well. Matter of fact, Lopez had created a dummy room with an armed guard, so it wouldn't be easy for someone off the street to easily identify the actual location of our prisoner."

"Yeah, I thought that part of the plan was brilliant

myself," Joe said. "I guess the dog we're chasing is smart, too."

"I don't get it." Sam was finding it difficult to process this new information. When he spoke again, he addressed his captain.

"Lopez told me he had a dual checkpoint in place. Every person entering that room would have had to be cleared—not just the doctors and nurses, but housekeeping and dietary would have had to follow the same protocol. They had to be wearing a photo identification badge, and as a fail-safe that photo ID had to match the image in the guard's laptop.

"Even if this guy did manage to create a fake badge, are you telling me that he was able to hack into the hospital personnel files and upload his picture so he'd pass the guard's scrutiny?"

A slow, steady burn formed in his gut and spread through his body. Sam leaned back and threw his arms in the air. "If the guy is that good, we need him running the FBI, not running from it."

"He found a loophole," Captain Rogers said.

Sam arched an eyebrow. "Ya think?"

Rogers ignored the sarcasm.

"Lopez set up a failsafe plan for hospital personnel. He even went one step further and insured that the same police personnel rotated shifts on the door so anyone would question a stranger in uniform, and the officers would recognize their replacements. The guard would also log the time in and out of the room for each visitor."

Sam leaned forward, waiting for more.

"What Lopez didn't consider was that the culprit would create a fake FBI identity. There wasn't anything on the laptop for FBI because Lopez intended to be the only one accessing the room. Unfortunately, he failed to make sure the guards knew it. That's how we figure he got past the guard. He pretended to be one of Lopez's own."

"I told you," Joe said. "The guy's smart."

Sam jumped to his feet. "Sarah…"

Captain Rogers waved Sam back down.

"Sit down, King. We're taking care of it."

"We need to move her to another floor ASAP," Sam urged.

"I already talked with her doctor," Joe said. "She's stable enough to be moved out of ICU, so they are making arrangements for a private room as we speak."

"Our men will be handling security on the door—not FBI, not hospital security guards—us." Rogers glared at both of them. "Nothing, absolutely nothing, is going to happen to that woman on our watch. Understood?"

Sam's heart started to beat a normal rhythm for the first time since he'd heard of Steven Miller's murder. He didn't know how this guy could keep slipping through traps, avoiding surveillance cameras and sidestepping witnesses, but it didn't matter. No matter what it took, Sam wasn't going to let the jerk anywhere near Sarah or any of the people who loved her.

With renewed determination, he shoved back from the table and stood. "Captain, with all due respect, don't you think we've talked enough? The ball is in our court now. We'd better get busy setting things in motion. The FBI botched this one, but we can't afford to. If he shows up here, I intend to make sure he's sorry he didn't stay in New York—deadly sorry."

"King." The censoring tone in his superior's voice cemented his feet to the floor. "Your Amish background gives you a leg up over my other officers. I picked you because I believe you can deal with the nuances of this case the best. But for that same reason, you need to be careful. You can't let your emotions color your judgment and jeopardize this case. Everything by the book. Got it?"

Sam nodded.

"Good. Now get back to Sarah. I'm going to finalize the room move with the hospital administrator while Joe coordinates the shift coverage outside her door."

Sam didn't need to be told twice. He was halfway down the hall with the door easing shut behind him before the captain had stopped speaking.

The man made a final adjustment to the fake beard that covered the lower part of his face, being sure to keep his upper lip clean, as was the Amish custom. He stared at the reflection in the full-length mirror on the back of the door and admired his handiwork.

The blond shaggy wig brushed the back of his neck. It made him twitch the way one might with an errant insect racing down your arm, and he shivered with disgust.

He was a man who took great pride in his appearance. His chestnut-brown hair was always faithfully groomed in a short, concise military cut. His fingernails were manicured at all times, his clothing choices impeccable. He'd be glad when this distasteful costume was no longer necessary.

He leaned in for a closer look at the blue contacts he'd worn to conceal his brown eyes. He finished off the look by donning a pair of plain, wire-rimmed glasses. The transformation was amazing.

He glanced down at his outfit. His clothes looked like they'd been woven a century ago. What kind of people willingly dressed like this?

He couldn't wait to get out of this outfit and back into one of his expensive Armani suits. He longed to sit in his butter-soft leather chair, sip the prime Scotch from his private collection and gaze out his plate-glass window overlooking the ocean.

He hooked his fingers behind his suspenders, turned sideways and grunted with satisfaction.

One obstacle still remained.

He glanced at his immaculate nails. He'd have to go outside and dig in a flower bed. The thought of dirt under his fingernails actually caused his stomach to roil. But these men worked on farms. He imagined they grew used to the feeling of soil and debris as their manicure of the day. The thought made his lips twist into a frown of disgust.

Well, it wouldn't be for long. Diamonds valued in the billions were definitely worth this ridiculous costume and a little dirt, weren't they?

He sighed heavily. He'd have a very limited opportunity to interrogate the woman. But he wasn't worried. If he couldn't get her to tell him where she'd hidden the diamonds before he eliminated her, then he'd find them another way.

He rolled his white sleeves up to his elbows and smiled with satisfaction. Even his own mother wouldn't recognize him. If she had still been alive, that is. He paused for a moment and allowed himself to remember the look of panic and fear he'd seen in her eyes moments before he squeezed the life out of her.

He'd learned many things in his lifetime. One of

the most important lessons was that when you needed to infiltrate enemy lines, it was best to blend in, give off an air of confidence, act like you belonged exactly where you were.

It had served him well over the years. His enemies had never sensed his presence—even though he was often right in their midst, hiding in plain sight, as the saying goes.

He stepped back, donned his straw hat and headed to the door.

Nighttime in hospitals always gave Sam the willies. Fewer staff. People speaking in whispers. Tonight his "willies alert" was operating on full throttle. Some cops called it gut instinct. Either way, Sam hated the tension that shot along his nerve endings, the fingers of unease that crept up his spine.

The only discernible sound as he moved through the empty corridors was the soft whirring of machines from open doorways, an occasional whimper of pain or a soft snore.

He was tired. Bone tired. He hadn't had more than two hours of uninterrupted sleep in the past thirty-six hours, and it was beginning to catch up with him. He wasn't a kid anymore—thirty-four on his next birthday, and he needed those eight hours of sleep. Or at least six. Who was he kidding? He'd settle for four if he could snatch them.

He glanced into the rooms as he passed by. They'd taken a risk when they'd moved Sarah to the pediatric floor. He didn't want to imagine the uproar the parents of these children would unleash if they had any idea that the bait to catch a killer had just been moved into their midst.

Captain Rogers had arranged the move. He firmly believed this would be the last floor in the hospital the perpetrator would expect to find Sarah. The captain didn't seem worried about the sensitive location. He was certain that even if the killer did locate Sarah, the children would be safe because they weren't his target. Sarah was.

Sam moved past the rooms filled with sleeping children. He offered a silent prayer that the captain hadn't made a horrendous mistake. As he drew near Sarah's room, he recognized the officer sitting in front of the door.

"Hey, Fitch, how's it going?"

The policeman folded his newspaper and grinned when he saw Sam approach. He gestured with his head toward the door.

"You'd think she was a Hollywood celebrity or something. Orders came down from the top that this is the last day allowed for visitation. It's been a steady stream of Amish folks in and out all afternoon saying their goodbyes. First thing tomorrow morning, the only Amish visitor allowed to visit is her former mother-in-law, Rebecca Lapp. No one else. Period."

Sam nodded. "Good. How did everyone else take the news?"

"Truthfully, I think they were a little relieved. They've been taking turns keeping vigil at the hospital all week. I'm sure they want to return to their homes and their farms."

Officer Brian Fitch stood and stretched his back. "I must admit I'm glad they've cut back on visiting. Less work for me. I hear the Amish go down when the sun does, so that's probably why it's been quiet the last few hours." Fitch shot a glance at Sam's Amish attire. "No offense intended or anything."

Sam grinned. "None taken. You're right. The Amish do go to bed early because they are up before dawn each day to begin their chores. Running a farm is not an easy task."

Sam leaned his hand flat against the door and then paused before he pushed it open. "You look beat. Why don't you go stretch your legs? Maybe grab a cup of coffee while you're at it? I'm here, and I'm not going anywhere."

"You sure?"

Sam opened his jacket and patted the gun in his shoulder holster. "I'm still a cop. Remember?"

Fitch grinned. "Yeah, well, you sure could fool me. You look like a natural fit with the rest of those folks. If I hadn't recognized you from our precinct, I'd be checking your ID and trying to talk you out of visiting altogether."

Sam grinned. "That coffee is calling your name, Fitch."

"You want me to bring you something back?"

"No, I'm good."

Taking advantage of Sam's offer to cover the room, the guard nodded and hurried to the elevator banks, not giving Sam a chance to change his mind.

The telltale *ding* of the arriving elevator filled the silence of the night, and Fitch waved. Sam gave him a nod and then entered Sarah's room.

Chapter Four

The night-light above the hospital bed cast the room in a soft, white haze. Sam looked down upon the sleeping woman, and his breath caught in his throat.

With stress and pain absent from her expression, she looked peaceful, young and surprisingly beautiful.

Long blond hair poked from beneath the bandages that swathed her head and flowed like golden silk over her shoulders. Her cheeks were flushed, giving her smooth complexion a rosy glow. Lost in sleep and probably dreaming, her lips formed a tiny pout. For the second time in as many days, he had to fight the temptation to taste the softness of those lips.

She was young and vulnerable and…

And she took his breath away.

Although he'd found her attractive when they'd first met, he'd been consumed with the business of ensuring her safety and nothing else.

But now…

In the quiet semidarkness of the evening, she reminded him of a sleeping princess and, for one insane moment, he felt an urge to awaken the princess with a kiss.

Shocked by that unexpected and traitorous thought, he stepped back from the bed as quickly as if he had touched an electrified fence, and then chuckled at his foolishness.

His eyes fell on a white *kapp* resting on the hospital tray table beside Sarah's bed. Rebecca must have placed it there. Sam wondered why. Rebecca had to know that Sarah's injuries would not allow her to wear the *kapp* for quite some time.

Then he glanced around the room and grinned. The middle-aged woman was sly like a fox. This room was a sterile slice of the *Englischer's* world. Monitors. Hospital bed. Even a television hanging on the far wall. This *kapp* resting in plain sight and at arm's length would be a constant reminder of the Amish world waiting for Sarah's return.

He glanced at Sarah's sleeping form one more time before he forced himself to turn away. Before exiting the room, he stepped inside the bathroom. He needed to throw some cold water on his face and try to wake up. His exhaustion was making him think crazy thoughts, have crazy feelings.

He used the facilities and washed his hands. He turned off the water and was drying his hands on a paper towel when a sound caught his attention. He paused and concentrated, listening to the silence.

There it was again. Just the whisper of sound, like the soft rustling of clothing against skin as a person moved about.

He crumpled the paper towel into a ball, tossed it into the trash can and pushed open the bathroom door.

It took his eyes a moment to adjust to the change from bright to dim light as he reentered Sarah's room. A tall man dressed in Amish clothing stood in the shadows on the far side of Sarah's bed.

A feeling of unease slithered up Sam's spine. Why would an Amish man be visiting at this time of night, and without a female companion in tow? Sam slid his jacket aside for easy access to his gun and stepped farther into the room.

"May I help you?" he asked in Pennsylvania Dutch dialect.

The visitor didn't reply. He removed his straw hat and nodded as a person who was apologizing for the late-night visit might. He sidestepped around the bed.

Sam stood too far from the light switch at the door to be able to fully illuminate the room. He had to rely on the soft glow from above Sarah's bed. Because the visitor held the hat higher than normal, Sam was unable to get a clear view of the man's face. His gut instincts slammed into gear. He drew his gun and aimed for the middle of the man's chest.

"Don't move." Sam made no attempt to hide the steel resolve beneath his words. Slowly, he stepped toward the main light switch. He shifted his glance just long enough to see how much farther he had to go.

The visitor immediately took advantage of this momentary distraction, dived sideways and simultaneously threw a pillow at Sam.

Instinctively, Sam raised an arm to protect his face. He pushed the pillow away, recovered quickly from the unexpected gesture and fired his weapon at the man's back as he sprinted out the door. The splintered wood of the door frame told him he'd missed his mark.

Sam sprang forward in pursuit. He'd almost reached the door when his right foot slid out from under him. He struggled to regain his balance and not fall. When he got his footing again, he glanced down and saw a syringe poking out from beneath his foot. He bent down and picked it up.

Suddenly, the monitor beside Sarah's bed erupted in a loud, continuous alarm. Sam's gaze flew to the screen and horror filled his soul. A flat, solid green line moved across the screen. Sarah's heart was no longer beating.

Before Sam could react, the door burst open. The room flooded with light. A nurse, quickly followed by another, burst into the room and rushed past him to Sarah's bed. While one nurse tended to the monitor and alarms, the other began CPR on Sarah. Seconds later, several other staff members hurried into the room with a crash cart pulled by the doctor close behind.

Sam knew he should be chasing the man who had done this, but his feet wouldn't budge. His eyes flew to Sarah's face. She lay so still, deathly still. He couldn't believe this was happening and, worse, that it had happened on his watch. Feelings of failure were quickly replaced first with fear that he'd lost her, and then by a deep, burning rage that he was helpless once again.

Sam had to leave—now. But he could barely find the inner strength to pull himself away from Sarah's side. This was his fault. But there was nothing he could do for her now. She was in better hands than his, and he refused to let the lowlife who did this escape. Not this time. Not ever again.

Sam pressed his hand on the shoulder of the nearest nurse. When she turned to look at him, he shoved the syringe in her hand. "I found this on the floor. I believe something was injected into her IV."

As soon as she took it from him, he raced for the hospital room door. Before he could pull it open, a woman's scream pierced the air, and the sounds of chaos filled the corridor. Something was terribly wrong. Had the mystery man grabbed a hostage or, worse, hurt one of the children?

Whispering a silent prayer for Sarah, Sam wrenched open the door and darted into the corridor.

A small gathering of people congregated at the end of the hall around the elevator banks. One woman had collapsed on the floor. Sam figured from the shocked expression on her face as he drew near, and from the sobs racking her body, that this was the woman who had screamed. An older gentleman hovered over her and tried to offer comfort.

A man dressed in green scrubs knelt half in and half out of an open elevator. Another man, also dressed in hospital garb, leaned close behind.

Sam pushed his way through the few gathering spectators and up front to survey the scene. For the second time that night, he felt like a mule had kicked him in the gut.

Officer Brian Fitch was sprawled on the elevator floor. One look at his open, sightless eyes and the trail of blood pooling beneath his body said it all. The officer hadn't made it downstairs for coffee.

Sam remembered the sound of the elevator arriving. Their surprise night visitor must have been on it. When the door opened, Fitch was busy nodding to him and must have been caught unaware. One quick, deadly slice across the officer's throat guaranteed that Fitch would never need coffee or exercise again.

Sam pulled out his badge and ordered everyone back, including the hospital staff. There was nothing any of them could do for Fitch now, and he had to protect whatever forensic evidence they'd be able to gather. Sam called hospital security on his cell phone, which he had put on speed dial for the duration of Sarah's hospital stay.

But somebody else had beaten him to it. The second elevator bank hummed to life. He held his hand on his gun and watched two startled guards emerge and stare at the carnage in front of them.

Sam identified himself as an undercover police officer, despite his Amish garb, and flashed his detective's shield and identification. He hoped he hadn't just blown his cover, but at the moment it couldn't be helped.

"Shut down every possible exit," he commanded. "Do it now."

Without hesitation, one of the guards barked orders into his radio while the other attended to crowd control. Sam offered a silent prayer of thanks that if this had to happen, it had happened late in the evening and gawkers were at a minimum.

He hit speed dial on his phone and barked orders the second his partner answered.

"Joe, we have a problem. Get over here, stat."

They'd been partners long enough that when Joe heard the tension in his voice, he was on full alert, and any drowsiness in his tone from interrupted sleep was gone.

"What happened?"

"Fitch is dead. Sarah might be, too. It's total chaos here."

Muttered expletives floated through the receiver. "On my way."

"Notify Rogers and call for backup."

"Okay. Where can I find you?"

"Making sure that every window, door and crack of this hospital is sealed shut so this piece of slime doesn't escape."

Sam ended the call and shoved the phone back in his pocket. He stole one more precious second to glance down the hall at Sarah's door. Every fiber of his being wanted to know what was going on in that room. Had they been able to save her? Or was she dead? The fact that no one had come out of the room yet must be a good sign, right? He had to fight the urge to run back and see what was happening. But no matter what was going on inside that room, he would not be able to help. This time logic won out.

He did what he was trained to do. He compartmentalized his emotions and focused on doing his job. He sprinted down the stairwell, his feet barely touching the stairs, and made it from the fourth floor to the lobby in record time. The sound of approaching sirens and the sight of flashing red-and-blue lights as vehicles slammed to a stop in front of the building told him that both Joe and hospital security had also gone straight to work.

Security guards were already at the entrance. They looked confused and highly nervous, but Sam had to admire how quickly and well they had sprung into action. No one was getting in or out of the building right now except cops.

Sam met with the head of security and asked to see the building's floor plans. Once they were in hand, he began to coordinate a thorough hospital search room by room, floor by floor, while making sure that all exits were covered. For the time being, no one would be allowed to exit, for any reason, from anywhere.

Twenty minutes after he'd called Joe, Sam saw his partner flash his badge and hurry through the front door. He breathed a sigh of relief and stepped forward to greet him.

Joe stopped short when he saw Sam approach. He shoved both hands into his coat pockets and scowled. "Want to tell me what happened?"

"The killer entered Sarah's room dressed in Amish garb." Before Joe could ask, Sam said, "He killed the police officer assigned to guard the door. It was Brian Fitch."

The detectives knew the officer well. A deep frown etched grooves on both sides of Joe's mouth.

"Has anybody notified his wife?"

"Not yet."

"And Sarah?"

"I think the guy injected something into Sarah's IV to stop her heart."

"Is she dead? Were they able to resuscitate her?"

"I don't know. I haven't had a chance to check. I've been organizing the search."

Joe's shocked expression echoed the one Sam was sure he wore as well. "How did this happen? Nobody can be this lucky. The guy's a ghost."

"The guy's no ghost. He's as much flesh and blood as you and me."

"I just don't understand. What happened?" Joe shot a bewildered look at Sam.

"I was there, Joe. Right there." The remorse in his voice was evident. "He got past me anyway and got to Sarah."

"Were you hurt? Did he hit you over the head or something?"

A red-hot flush of shame and embarrassment coated Sam's throat and face. "Sarah was sleeping. I'd stepped into her bathroom to throw some cold water on my face. I didn't hear him come in until it was too late. The room was dark. He threw something at me. It distracted me enough that he was able to get past me."

Joe nodded. "Don't beat yourself up over it. It could have happened to any of us."

"But it didn't. It happened on my watch. Mine, Joe."

Joe grimaced. They'd been partners long enough that Sam knew Joe understood this was about more than what was happening now. This shame and pain and anger stretched back to another time and another place, when Sam had been helpless to save loved ones or bring perps to justice.

Joe patted Sam's arm, empathy evident in his eyes, and then changed the subject. "Where do we stand with the search?"

"The best I've been able to do is get all the exits covered. We're dealing with graveyard shift. We don't have a lot of warm bodies in the security department right now."

"Where do you want me?"

"Downstairs." Sam walked with Joe to the elevator bank. "I don't believe the guy will try to walk out any of the obvious exits. He's got to know they're the first places we'd shut down. Check every single room in the basement. Housekeeping has storage rooms, supply rooms. I think there are even some employee lockers and break rooms down there. And, of course, the morgue and the autopsy rooms. I've sent security guards to the loading platform by the morgue, but I'll feel better if one of us is checking things out."

"You got it."

The elevator doors opened, and Joe stepped inside.

"Be careful. Fitch was found dead with his throat slashed."

"Great. Just what I want to hear." His mouth twisted in a wry grin just as the doors shut.

Within thirty minutes of the initial alert, the SWAT team, special weapons and tactics, arrived, quickly followed by Captain Rogers. Sam shared what he knew, and they took over command of the ongoing search.

They hadn't located the perpetrator yet. But the hospital looked like a military camp in Afghanistan for all the uniformed and armed personnel swarming the halls. They'd catch him.

Sam threw a glance at his captain and saw the man in a deep conversation with both the SWAT team leader and the head of hospital security. Everything that could be done was being done. Finally, he'd have a moment to find out what had happened to Sarah.

Adrenaline hammered through the intruder's blood stream, and the beat of his heart thundered in his chest. Who knew all those morning jogs along the beach outside his home would have prepared him for the race of his life? He'd made it down five flights of stairs into the basement without anyone seeing him and, he was certain, before anyone could even sound the alarm.

What a rush! He thought it had been too simple when he caught the cop sneaking away for a break. But that's why he loved operating during the graveyard shift. People often snuck away or fell asleep. Made his job so much easier.

But when he'd slipped inside the darkened hospital room, he'd never expected someone might be in the bathroom.

The man had been dressed like an Amish guy, but he wasn't any more Amish than he was. Not carrying that 9 mm Beretta he had fired at him. He was probably an undercover cop.

Undercover cop. Undercover villain. Both disguised in Amish garb. The whole situation was laughable—and dangerous.

He stood with his back against the wall of the storage closet, trying to quiet the sound of his heavy gasps.

He could hear the pounding of feet racing down the corridor and hear the anxious, high-pitched whispers the guards shot to each other as they did a quick search of every room.

The sounds grew louder as the men approached his hiding spot.

He pushed into the far back corner of the room and crouched behind a utility cart with a large white mop and aluminum bucket attached. His hand tightened around the pistol grip of his gun, and he waited.

The door to the closet swung open. One of the security guards scanned the room with a flashlight. Just as quickly, he was gone.

Idiots.

They hadn't even bothered to throw on the light switch or step into the room. No wonder hospital security guards had the reputation of being toy cops. How did they expect to find anyone with such a lazy, half-done search?

He grinned and relaxed his hand, lowering his weapon.

Lucky for them they were stupid, or they'd be dead security guards just about now.

He stepped out from behind the cart when a sudden flash of light made him squint and raise his hand to his eyes. Someone had thrown on the switch, illuminating the room, and it took his eyes a second to adjust.

"Don't move! Drop your weapon and slide it over to me. Do it now!"

This wasn't a security guard. He looked into eyes of cold, hard steel. This must be a detective. A smart one, too.

Slowly, he lowered his weapon to the floor and kicked it in the detective's direction.

The detective moved farther into the room, never lowering his gun. He stepped to the side and withdrew a pair of handcuffs with his free hand. "Nice and easy now. Put your hands out where I can see them, and slowly walk over here."

Again, he did as requested.

The detective clasped a cuff onto his right wrist.

With speed resulting from years of martial arts training, he spun, released the blade sheathed on the inside of his sleeve and slashed the detective's throat.

The killer grinned. He always loved the look of surprise and horror on his victims' faces, and this detective looked shocked, indeed.

He removed his Amish clothes and quickly donned the detective's cheap brown suit. His lips twisted in disgust. The pants were about two inches too short, the waist at least two sizes too big, and the sleeves of the suit jacket revealed too much forearm. He shoved some towels under his shirt and cinched his belt tight to hold them in and his pants up.

He glowered at the pant length. When a scenario like this played out in the movies, the exchanged clothes were always a perfect fit. Just his luck this wasn't a movie. But he'd have to make do.

He slipped the detective's badge onto his belt, retrieved both guns from the floor and took one last look around to make sure he left nothing of significance behind. His eyes paused on the dead body.

"Sorry, buddy. You were good. Much better than those security guard wannabes. But I'm better. You never stood a chance."

He used a towel to wipe away fingerprints on the light switch and doorknob. He shut off the light, glanced up and down the empty corridor, stepped into the hall and leisurely walked away.

Chapter Five

Sam couldn't breathe.

He tried. But only shallow wisps of breath escaped his lips.

As soon as he could move…or react…or feel anything but pain, he'd remind himself to inhale deeply.

Yep. He'd do that. Just as soon as the world stopped spinning.

"Do you recognize this man?" A male nurse kneeling beside the body on the floor glanced up at him. "Is he one of yours?"

Tears burned Sam's eyes. His throat clenched, making it impossible for him to speak. The nonchalance of the strangers doing their jobs roiled his stomach. To them, this was just another body. To him…

Sam glanced at the body of the man, dressed only in underwear, lying on the utility room floor. He hated what his eyes relayed to his brain, but he couldn't seem to turn away.

How did this happen? Dear God, why?

"Hey, are you all right, buddy? You look pretty gray in the face. You're not getting sick on me, are you? You're a cop. You see dead bodies all the time, don't ya?"

"Bert, give him a minute." The female nurse gently touched Sam's forearm. "You know this man, don't you, detective? He's one of yours."

One of yours.

Sam nodded.

Yes, he was one of his. His partner. His best friend. His only family. And now he was dead.

"His name is Detective Joseph Masterson. He was my partner."

"I'm so sorry." Her eyes supported the truth of her words. "Is there anything we can do to help?"

Sam took a deep breath and steadied himself. Rational thought returned, and his inner cop took command.

"I need both of you to step away from the body and try not to touch anything else on the way out of the room. This is a crime scene now. Please wait in the hall for a few minutes until I can get your names and contact information." He ushered them out of the room and grabbed the closest officer in the hallway. "Who discovered the body?"

The cop pointed to two women waiting at the end of the corridor. "Guard this door," Sam said. "No one comes in—absolutely no one—until our forensic team arrives. Make sure to take contact information from these nurses while I speak to the women at the end of the hall."

The cop nodded and did as requested.

Sam approached the women and flashed his detective shield. "My name is Detective King. I'd like to ask you a few questions." He glanced at their name tags. The younger female was a nurse. The matronly woman's tag identified her as custodial staff. "Ms. Blake," he spoke to the nurse. "I'm told you're the one who called us."

"That's right." She seemed perplexed at his Amish garb, but accepted the badge at face value.

"Did you find the body?"

The body.

He couldn't believe he was able to treat this like any ordinary crime scene when, internally, he was reeling in pain.

Dear Lord, continue to give me the strength I need to do my job and get through this night. First Sarah. Now Joe. Help me. Please.

"She found the body." Ms. Blake nodded to an older woman sitting beside her. "This is Mrs. Henshaw. She went into the room to get supplies, and then I heard her scream...."

Sam arched a brow and studied the drawn features of the elderly woman. It was evident that the shock of her discovery had taken its toll, and he knew he needed to tread lightly. "Thank you for speaking with me, Mrs. Henshaw. I'm sure you want to get home. I'll try to keep my questions short and to the point."

The woman looked up at him, her eyes glazed and distant.

"How long ago did you discover the body?"

She glanced at her watch. "I'm not sure. Thirty minutes, maybe."

Mrs. Blake nodded. "At least. Maybe a bit longer. We checked the body for vitals before I made the call."

"Do you remember touching anything in the room?" Sam asked.

"No. When I saw his throat had been cut, I knew he was dead, but I checked his carotid for a pulse anyway. Then I pulled out my cell and called it in."

Sam took a deep breath and fought to keep the images she relayed out of his mind.

"Do either of you remember seeing anything or anyone suspicious? Anything out of the ordinary?"

Both women shook their heads.

"Do you remember passing anyone in the hall?"

"Policemen," Mrs. Henshaw said. "There were security guards and police officers running up and down the halls. I wasn't sure what was going on. I waited for the halls to clear before going to get my supplies." A moment passed, and her face crunched in concentration. "There was something…"

Tension tightened Sam's body as he waited for her to continue.

"I didn't think much about it at the time but…" The woman looked directly at him. "I did see a man. He came down the hall after everyone else had already gone."

Sam honed in on her words. "Did he do or say anything?"

"No."

"What caught your attention? Why do you remember this particular individual?"

"Well, he was walking kind of slow, like he was taking a leisurely stroll in the park, and I guess I noticed that because everyone else had raced past."

"Anything else, Mrs. Henshaw?"

She frowned. "Yes. His pants. They didn't fit. They were about two inches too short."

The shooter had changed into Joe's suit.

"Thank you both. If I have any more questions, how can I reach you?" He pulled a small pad out of the inside pocket of his jacket.

Both women gave him their contact information.

"King!"

Sam glanced over his shoulder, then thanked the women for their help and joined the captain. It took only a few minutes to bring his superior up to speed.

The captain wiped a hand over his face and sighed heavily. "I'm sorry, Sam. Losing a good man is never easy for any of us. Worse if it's your partner."

Sam nodded. "Any word, Captain? Has anyone caught him?"

"Not yet. Unfortunately, we suspect he has already slipped past us." The captain nodded toward the utility room. "Everyone's been looking for a man in Amish garb. I've got a BOLO out now on him using Joe's suit, badge and gun as a description."

"That sounds like a plan. Be on the lookout for a detective when every detective and cop on the force is part of the search. Don't want to bet on the success of that one." Sam couldn't hide the bitterness and sarcasm in this voice. "We've got to get this creep. If it's the last thing I ever do…"

The captain clamped a hand on his shoulder. "I've got this one covered. Go home, son. Get some rest."

"I need to call Cindy." The last thing he wanted to do was have to tell his partner's wife that her husband wasn't coming home. His distaste for the assignment must have been evident in his eyes, because the captain slapped his shoulder a second time.

"It's been handled. I sent a squad car and a couple of our most empathetic men over to her place. Didn't want to take a chance she'd hear it from another source. Now get some rest. Go see her after you've gotten some sleep."

"Thanks, Captain."

Sam pushed open the stairwell door and sprinted

up the steps. No way was he going home. Not until he found out what had happened to Sarah.

When he entered the fourth floor, the first thing he noted was the absence of guards in front of Sarah's room. His mind raced with a variety of scenarios on why no one would be posted there, but the only one that made sense was the one thought he refused to believe. Sam's feet felt as if they were encased in cement, each step forward harder than the one before.

He paused outside the room, threw his shoulders back and then pushed the door open.

A black mattress, empty and stripped of its sheets, waited silently for its next occupant.

The air gushed out of Sam's lungs.

Where was Sarah? Was she...

His mind couldn't even complete the thought.

He blinked hard and continued to stare at the empty bed. She couldn't be dead. A sense of failure, mixed with a multitude of other emotions, washed over him.

Oh God, please...

Sam was glad God could read hearts, because at the moment he was totally incapable of completing the prayer.

"May I help you?"

Startled, he spun toward the voice. The nurse's expression registered suspicion, even a tinge of fear, as she stood in the doorway, poised to run if necessary.

"Can you tell me what happened to Sarah?"

The nurse eyed him skeptically. Of course she'd be wary. The entire hospital was in shutdown mode. They'd been told the killer had been dressed in Amish clothes—and here he stood in Amish clothes. The staff had also been told the killer had stolen a detective's badge and gun, so showing his identification probably wouldn't help this frightened nurse feel any better.

"Are you family?" she asked.

Not up to explanations, Sam simply nodded.

The nurse pushed the door wider, but made sure not to enter the room and kept in plain view of people in the hall. Smart lady.

"Sir, I'm sure Dr. Clark will be happy to speak with you. Take the elevator to the seventh floor and ask for him at the nurse's station."

"Can you at least tell me if Sarah is alive?" Sam heard the hopeful tone in his voice and realized this case was quickly becoming more personal than he had intended it to be.

"Please, sir. The doctor will answer your..."

Sam sidled past her and bounded toward the elevator before she had a chance to finish her statement. He tapped his foot impatiently and watched the numbers light from floor to floor. A sense of anticipation filled his senses as he got off the elevator and skidded to a stop at the nurse's desk.

"I'm looking for Sarah Lapp."

Don't say she's in the morgue. Please don't.

The nurse looked up from her paperwork. "I'm sorry, sir. Mrs. Lapp is not allowed visitors."

She's alive. Thank you, God.

A tsunami wave of relief washed over him. Now if he could just get this nurse to give him the information he needed. He pasted on his best smile and tried again. "You don't understand—"

"Sam."

He turned his head at the sound of his name. Dr.

Clark approached, stretched out his hand and grasped his in a firm handshake.

"Sarah made it? She's going to be okay?" Sam asked, not paying any attention to Dr. Clark's quizzical expression at the emotion evident in his voice.

Dr. Clark ushered Sam away from the nurse's desk and asked him to walk with him. As they moved down the corridor, Sam could see a uniformed guard sitting in front of one of the ICU rooms.

"Sarah's going to be fine. Thanks to you. The vial you gave the nurse held the remnants of potassium chloride. A large enough dose can stop a heart. We were able to act quickly and bring her back."

"Will she be all right?"

The doctor nodded. "She's going to be fine." He raised his eyes. "Someone up there must be looking out for her. I can't believe everything this woman has survived over the past two weeks. Unbelievable."

Sam frowned. He felt awkward asking, but he needed to know. "The baby?"

"As far as we can tell, the baby is as strong as the mother. All is well."

It felt like one of those old-fashioned leaded vests had just been lifted off his chest. His lips twisted into a smile for the first time that day.

"Thanks, Doc."

"You're welcome. Please tell me that you apprehended the man who committed these horrible crimes." Worry creased the doctor's forehead into two deep, parallel furrows.

"Not yet."

Dr. Clark's frown deepened. "The best thing we can do for all concerned is to make other arrangements for

Mrs. Lapp. Under the circumstances, the hospital cannot accept responsibility for her safety…or the safety of our other patients."

Sam nodded.

Dr. Clark continued, "I believe that with some medical precautions put in place, moving to a safe house or, perhaps, to a more familiar environment will help with her recovery. Her stress level here is off the charts. Understandably, of course."

They walked the last few feet to her door, but stood outside to finish their conversation. Sam recognized the officer on duty, acknowledged him and turned his attention back to the doctor. "How quickly can we move her?"

"I want to keep her under observation for another twenty-four hours. Barring any unforeseen complications, she will be released then."

"Does the captain know?"

"Not yet. I haven't seen him since the hospital shut down."

"I'll fill him in. We'll start making arrangements on our end. Is Sarah awake? I have a few questions."

"Yes, she's awake. Her mother-in-law is with her. But please keep your visit short and try not to upset her. She needs her rest."

Sam nodded, and the doctor walked away.

Sarah's alive. She's going to be okay and so is her child.

Despite the nightmare this evening had become, he couldn't help but smile as he pushed open the door and stepped into the room. He was going to see Sarah.

Chapter Six

Sarah caught movement in her peripheral vision, turned her head and smiled. "Detective King."

"Samuel." He gestured at his clothing. "It won't do me any good to dress like this if you announce me as an undercover cop every time I walk into a room."

A giggle escaped her lips, seeming to surprise them both. "You're right. Sorry, Samuel."

Sam respectfully inclined his head toward the older woman and acknowledged her presence.

"Do you have any information for us?" Rebecca's face wore lines of concern. "Have they found the man who did this terrible thing to our Sarah?"

"I'm sorry—not yet. But I'm sure we'll hear something soon. The hospital has been shut down. Every floor and room is being searched as we speak."

Rebecca seemed satisfied with Samuel's reply. "My husband went home at dinnertime. I was sleeping in one of those reclining chairs in the family waiting room when Dr. Clark sent a nurse to tell me what had happened." She squeezed Sarah's hand, and tears glistened in her eyes. "God is *gut,* Sarah. He has returned you to us twice, *ya?*"

Sam leaned a hand on the bed rail. "I hate to have to do this now, but I need to ask you a few questions."

"It is all right, Samuel. Do what you need to do." Sarah looked up at him and waited.

"Do you remember anything that happened this evening? You were asleep when I first entered the room. Did you wake up at any time?"

Sarah offered a weak smile. "Of this, I remember, Samuel." She locked her gaze with his. "I had been sleeping, but I started to wake up when you came into the room. I was—what's the word?—groggy? My eyes didn't want to open, but I knew you were there." Her smile widened. "When I did coax them open, I saw your back as you walked into the bathroom. I closed my eyes again. I think I started to drift back to sleep. I know this is not helping you."

"You're doing fine."

Her heart skipped a beat and fluttered like a symphony of dancing butterflies in her chest when he smiled at her. Before she could ponder the strange feelings she seemed to experience in this man's presence, he encouraged her to continue her story.

"The man must have entered the room as soon as I stepped out. Did you see him?"

"Yes."

Samuel's eyes widened, and she sensed his anticipation and tension.

"Can you describe him?"

She chewed on her bottom lip as she tried to bring the memory of the man's face into her mind. "I…I'm not sure. The light in the room was dim. I had been sleeping."

"Do your best, child." Rebecca patted her hand. "Anything you can tell Samuel will help him."

Sarah broke eye contact with both of them and stared at the ceiling as she tried to remember every detail she could. "He had blond hair and a yellow beard that reached the top of his chest. He was dressed in Amish clothes. He looked...ordinary."

"Did you recognize him, Sarah? Was he one of the men at the school?" Rebecca asked.

"I don't remember anything that happened at the school."

"Still nothing?" Rebecca asked. "No one?"

Sarah knew the woman kept hoping that she would someday remember her son, Peter. But today wasn't that day.

She couldn't bear to see the disappointment in Rebecca's eyes or the anticipation in Samuel's. She squeezed her eyes shut and tried as hard as she could to remember something, anything. When she opened them again, she looked from one to the other and knew she had nothing to offer. Sadness almost overwhelmed her.

"I'm so sorry. I can't help you."

"What happened when he approached your bed?" Sam tried to prod her memory. "Did he say anything to you? Think, Sarah. It might be important."

"Yes. I remember that he did speak to me. I knew from his words that this was the man who had killed my husband and who had shot me."

Rebecca gasped. Her hand flew to her chest, but she remained silent.

"Take your time, Sarah. No one can hurt you now.

Try to remember what he said." Sam's calm, warm voice encouraged her.

"He asked me what I did with the diamonds. He said he knew I had the pouch." An increasing anxiety caused her voice to tremble. "I told him I knew nothing about his diamonds." Fear slithered up her spine at the memory. "His eyes were so dark, so cold and…and evil."

Sam reached out and clasped her hand. "Go on. You're doing fine. What else did he say?"

Sarah found Sam's touch strangely comforting, and the way her body trembled with fear, she needed all the comfort she could find.

"He grinned at me," she said. "I remember thinking how perfect his teeth were. Really white and straight and clean. His breath…I remember a cloying, minty scent when he leaned close…almost too minty…my stomach turned. He leaned close to my ear and whispered, 'I will find where you hid those diamonds. I don't need you to do it.'"

Her heart galloped inside her chest, but this time it was fear that caused the pace. "That's when I saw him pull something out of his pocket. He held it against the tube attached to my arm. My chest became tight, like something very heavy was sitting on me. I couldn't draw a breath. That's all I remember." A tear slid down her cheek. "I woke up in this room with Rebecca by my side. She told me what had happened. That is all I know."

"She has answered your questions. You must leave her now," Rebecca insisted. "She needs to rest."

Sam nodded and released Sarah's hand. He stared into those mesmerizing blue eyes. "Thank you."

"I have been of no help."

"That is not true. You have helped quite a bit. Thanks to you, we know that he will stop at nothing to find the diamonds. He was bold enough to walk into enemy camp and risk being recognized as an intruder. In New York, he dressed as an FBI agent, and here, as an Amish man. So our belief that he would return has been proved correct."

Sam sighed heavily. "You have also proved our theory that he would not leave behind any survivors. He tried to kill you. He did kill the one member of his team we had in custody in New York. He also killed the guard who had been sitting outside your door." The darkened intensity in his eyes told her that he had more to say, and it was very difficult for him. "He also killed my partner." His voice broke as he tried to conceal his grief.

Rebecca gasped. "Detective Masterson has been killed?"

Sarah looked into Sam's eyes and thought her heart would break when she saw nothing but pain staring back at her.

"I am so sorry, Samuel."

He hung his head in silence.

"You said the man guarding my room was also killed?"

Sam nodded and didn't seem to be able to meet her eyes. When he did look at her, he reminded her of a little boy in pain who needed cuddling and comfort, but this brief glimpse of vulnerability didn't last more than an instant before the hard-edged detective reappeared.

"I apologize. I let my guard down. It almost cost you your life. It did cost the life of a good officer, as well as the life of my partner."

"This was not your doing, Samuel. You must not

blame yourself." Sarah knew from his reaction that her words held little comfort.

"I was standing in the room with you. Just feet away, and I let him slip by. I promise I will not let anything like that happen again."

"God willing."

Both of them glanced at Rebecca after she spoke.

"God is in control, Samuel, *ya?* He will decide what does or does not happen." Her steady, unflinching gaze caught his.

Sam straightened his shoulders. The tone of his voice was harsher than normal when he replied. "Sometimes God needs a little help to bring the bad guys to justice, Rebecca. That's my job, and that's what I intend to do."

"Justice, Samuel? Or vengeance?"

Sam bristled beneath the censure. "Call it what you want. If I hadn't been there this evening, if I hadn't stepped out of the bathroom when I did, Sarah wouldn't be with us right now."

Rebecca shot a loving glance Sarah's way. "It was God's will that Sarah remain with us. He may have used your presence, Samuel, and for that I am most grateful."

Ashamed of himself for lashing out at the woman, he lowered his head and apologized. "I'm sorry I spoke harshly. You're right. God uses many things to bring about His will in this world...and many people."

Rebecca smiled at him and nodded.

The door opened. Sarah thought Captain Rogers looked even more exhausted than Samuel, if that were possible.

"What are you doing here?" he growled in Sam's direction. "I thought I told you to go home and get some sleep."

"I will. I had a few loose ends that I needed to tie up first, sir."

The captain glowered, but refrained from any further admonishment.

"Have you found the man who did this terrible thing?" Rebecca asked.

The captain's face wore the strains of exhaustion. "No. I'm sorry. He got away."

"But how?" Sarah asked. "There were so many of you looking for him."

Captain Rogers sighed heavily. "He killed one of my detectives and switched clothing with him. When we initially started our search, my men were told to look for someone in Amish garb. They weren't looking for one of their own. By the time we got the word out about the wardrobe change, we believe he had already escaped."

"We are so sorry to hear about the death of your men, Captain." Rebecca folded her hands. "They lost their lives trying to protect us. We will remember them and pray for their families."

Sarah shot a glance at Sam and was again moved by the pain she saw in his eyes. The loss of his partner cut deeper than he was willing to admit.

"Thank you, ma'am," Captain Rogers replied.

"Do you think he is gone for good?" Sarah asked. "No man would be foolish enough to come back again when the whole police force is looking for him, would he?"

"That is exactly what he is going to do, Sarah." The captain's steely gaze and no-nonsense voice held her attention. "He plans on killing you, the teacher and the children who were in that classroom. We've suspected that from the beginning. His actions in the past two days have confirmed it."

Sarah's stomach twisted into a tight, painful knot. The anger and determination she saw in both men's eyes upset her. She didn't need past memory to recognize the tension and fear in the room now.

She was willing to accept God's will for her life, and she trusted Him to protect her. But her throat constricted when she thought about the children. She knew in her heart that God would protect them, too. But she had looked into the stranger's face. Pure evil had stared back.

A chill shivered down her spine when she thought of the stranger's threats.

She glanced at Samuel, and a sense of peace calmed her.

Maybe Samuel was right. Maybe God used people to help carry out His will, and He could be using Samuel. She certainly hoped so. She would pray about it.

"What happens now?" Rebecca asked, swinging her gaze around to everyone in the room.

"Dr. Clark will be releasing Sarah tomorrow," Sam said.

Captain Rogers looked surprised. "So soon?"

"Yes, he told me just a few moments ago. He feels Sarah will be safer somewhere else. And, of course, the administration is screaming about liability."

"I'll need time to get the wheels in motion." Rogers looked at Rebecca. "Can we count on your help, Mrs. Lapp? Will Sarah be going home with you? Are you still willing to let Detective King accompany you?"

"Of course we will be taking Sarah home." Rebecca moved closer to the bed and busied her hands, gently tucking the blanket around Sarah's body as a mother might when tucking in a child for the night. When she finished, she looked at the two men.

"As for Samuel, my husband has already given his permission, and Jacob is a man of his word. Nothing that has happened here tonight will change that." She sent a kind, warm glance Sam's way. "Besides, Samuel has had a great loss of his own. Losing a partner must be a difficult thing, *ya?* Like losing a member of your family? It will be good for Samuel to be in a quiet place where he can reflect and pray and feel the tender mercy of God's healing touch."

He cleared his throat. "Okay, then. Let's get this thing started. We have twenty-four hours to make it happen."

"No. We have sixteen hours," Captain Rogers corrected. "Both of us need sleep. I don't want to see your face for at least eight hours. That's an order."

Sam nodded. "Understood, Captain. I'll be here first thing in the morning to take Sarah home."

Home.

A place she couldn't remember, but just the word made her long to get there. She tried hard to conjure up a mental image. What did the house look like? Did they have a barn? Horses? Cattle? Were they farmers tending fields of grain, or did their fields contain rows of corn? With all that had happened, would the Amish community still gather for celebration and praise? Or would the death of the bishop's son change everything?

Once Sarah saw the house and the farm, would it help refresh her memory? She held current memories of many faces that had come to visit her during this ordeal. They had claimed to be her friends. Would she be able to rekindle those relationships once she returned home? She hoped so. Maybe she wouldn't feel so lost and alone anymore.

In twenty-four hours, she would know the answer to all the questions tumbling around in her head. Somehow the thought of returning to a place where she had once forged roots, a place where she had once belonged to a community and a family, was strangely comforting… and oh so terrifying.

Chapter Seven

Sarah glanced down at her clothing. Gone was the print hospital gown. She wore a black apron that covered a good portion of the light blue dress beneath it. The dress draped her body loosely, fell slightly below her knees and brushed against her black opaque stockings. She smoothed her hand across the material.

Because of the many visitors she had had over the past week, Sarah knew this was typical Amish garb. So why didn't it feel familiar? Why couldn't she picture in her mind another time and place where she might have been dressed this way?

"Is something wrong?" Rebecca's heavily lined face wore a quizzical expression. "Are you feeling ill? Is this task too difficult for you right now?" Before Sarah could reply, Rebecca hurried forward. "Here, let me help you with your shoes."

"Thank you, but I can put on my shoes." But when Sarah bent down for the shoes, her head spun, and pain seized the left side of her temple.

Rebecca leaned over and retrieved the shoes. "You are not yet fully recovered. You are going to need some help with things you used to do for yourself. Do not let pride make you stumble before the Lord."

Sarah accepted the chiding with a respectful nod. But was it pride? Or a fierce determination to get better as quickly as possible and regain her independence?

A knock on the door drew their attention.

Sarah's heartbeat skipped when Samuel poked his head inside. She hadn't seen him for more than a moment or two since yesterday. He'd been making arrangements for her safety after she left the hospital. She'd missed him—and that thought surprised and unsettled her.

Samuel nodded a polite greeting to Rebecca as he entered, and then froze. The intensity of his gaze as his eyes roamed over her Amish clothing made her self-conscious. She smoothed her apron and wondered if some piece of clothing looked silly or out of place.

Rebecca coughed, breaking Samuel out of his reverie.

"Forgive me," he said. "I apologize for staring." He smiled at Sarah. "It is a surprise to see you out of hospital gowns. You look—" he seemed to search for the proper word "—healthy." His smile widened. "You look like you're ready to get out of here and go home."

Sarah smiled in return. "That I am."

Dr. Clark had told her that familiar surroundings might help her regain some of her memory. Sarah was counting on it with an anticipation so intense she found it almost hard to breathe.

"Are you ladies ready?"

"Almost." Rebecca slipped the white *kapp* that had been lying on the nightstand on top of Sarah's bandages.

It was a tight squeeze, but she got it placed properly. She tilted Sarah's face up. "We are ready now, *ya?*"

Sarah squeezed Rebecca's hand. She had grown fond of the woman, grateful that she came every day regardless of how difficult it must be for her. It didn't take black clothes to show that Rebecca was grieving. All someone had to do was look at the pain and fatigue evident in her eyes, body language and facial expressions. Yet still she came, every day, and sat beside her and told her stories of the farm, and occasionally stories of the life she'd shared with Peter.

Sarah learned they had not only known each other since childhood but had been good friends, which was a bit unusual in the Amish community, since boys and girls often had separate activities and chores. But Sarah had been a bit of a tomboy as a child. She loved to climb trees and play baseball and fish. Rebecca's eyes would light up when she'd tell Sarah tales of her escapades— the catfish she'd caught that weighed more than any of the boys' and the tale of her broken arm when she'd been spying on the boys swimming and had fallen out of the large oak tree on the back of their property by the pond.

"You always pushed boundaries. I had to practically tie you down when it came time to teach you how to cook and sew." Rebecca actually smiled for the very first time since this nightmare began.

"Why didn't my mother teach me those things? Why did it fall on your shoulders?"

A dark cloud passed over Rebecca's expression, but she quickly recovered. "That is another conversation for another day, *ya?* Right now I think it is best to get home."

Sarah held her tongue, but she couldn't help wondering why Rebecca seemed reluctant to talk about her mother. Was there some dark secret no one had told her about? And if Rebecca was hiding behind secrets, how could she be sure that what she told her about Peter and their marriage was the truth?

Before Sarah could question the older woman more, a nurse entered the room pushing a wheelchair. "These are your discharge instructions. Your medications are listed. So are signs and symptoms that you should report immediately to Dr. Clark if they occur."

Sam took the papers from the nurse's hand. "Thank you. We will go over these with a fine-tooth comb once we get home." He folded them and tucked them inside his jacket. "Sarah won't be needing the wheelchair. You can take it out with you."

"It's hospital policy that every patient is wheeled safely to the curb," the nurse insisted.

"Her safety is exactly the reason we can't afford to have her leave in a wheelchair." Sam shifted his attention to Sarah. "I was afraid the news media would catch hold of this story. After the hospital lockdown and the two murders, they have. National news crews have been camped outside all night, hoping for a picture for the tabloids or a few quotes for their papers. They've been trying to locate your room and slip in to see you. You wouldn't believe how creative and sneaky some of them have been. Hospital security has had their hands full. If we push you outside in a wheelchair, they'll descend on us like vultures."

"So what must we do?" Rebecca twisted her hands together and looked at Sam with concern on her face. "Sarah is not strong enough for such attention."

Sam looked at Sarah with a steady gaze. "Are you strong enough to walk out of here if I help you?"

Her stomach flipped under his scrutiny. When he looked at her like that, she wanted to please him. She just wasn't sure she could. "I think so but…" She lowered her voice and her eyes. "I'm willing to try, but I'm not sure I can."

"That's my girl. I knew I could count on you to give it a try. Don't worry. I'll be with you every step of the way."

My girl? Had he just said that to her?

He turned to Rebecca. "Do you have any extra Amish clothes with you? Perhaps a *kapp,* and possibly a shawl?"

"Yes," Rebecca replied. "I have some extra clothes with me. I have been sleeping in one of those fancy chairs that tilt back. Jacob brought me a bag from home so I could change and freshen up in the public bathrooms."

"Good." Sam grinned at the nurse. "I think you will look lovely in a white *kapp,* don't you?"

The nurse stammered and sputtered a weak protest as she realized he intended to put *her* in the wheelchair. She glanced at the two Amish women. Their faces were pale with fright and concern. She looked back at Sam and smiled. "Why not? I love pranks. This should be fun. Maybe I'll even make it on national TV."

Sam gently cupped Sarah's elbow, and the heat of his touch sent waves of tingles through her body. When he spoke, his voice was warm and tender. "How do you feel? Are you able to do this?" His eyes locked with hers, and she thought she'd drown in their darkness. "Am I asking too much of you? If you can't do the walking, we will use the wheelchair. We'll try to camouflage your exit."

Her pulse beat like war drums against the soft tissue of her wrist. She wasn't sure if it was the result of her anxiety about evading the press and going home, or whether it was a reaction to the strong, masculine presence of the man standing beside her. The man who had been kind and supportive and…and almost irresistibly attractive from the moment she'd opened her eyes.

"How far must we go?"

"Not far. We'll take the elevator to the basement and slip out the morgue entrance. I will be with you every step of the way."

Rebecca clasped Sarah's other arm. "So will I, child. God will be with us too." Rebecca handed a *kapp* and shawl to the nurse. "I hope these will help."

Sam asked an officer to push the disguised nurse in the wheelchair through the front entrance while they headed toward the elevators.

Just as the three of them were about to make their exit, the door opened again.

"Jacob." Rebecca looked at her husband in surprise. "What has happened? Why are you here?"

"You are my wife. Sarah is my daughter-in-law. You need me. Where else would I be?"

Although there was no physical contact between them, there was a sense of intimacy. They obviously loved each other and it showed…in the kindness of their words…in the gaze of their eyes…in the gentleness of their voices. Sarah couldn't help but wonder if this was what her relationship with their son, Peter, had been like.

A deep sadness flowed over her that she felt no feelings for Peter. Neither good nor bad. She couldn't even draw his image into her memory. The Amish did not approve of pictures, so Rebecca was unable to show her a wedding photo or any other.

Sarah glanced at Samuel. There was kindness and gentleness and something else with this man. She felt more fondness for this stranger than she did for the man who had been her husband. It wasn't the way it was supposed to be, not the way she wanted it to be. And it troubled her greatly.

Almost as if he could read her mind, Sam seemed to assess both the change in the atmosphere of the room and its possible reason. Instantly, he took charge.

"Come." He spoke with authority. "We have to slip out before the press realizes that isn't Sarah we sent out front."

Without a word, they hurried from the room. They rode the elevator in silence. Sam exited first, checked that the corridor was empty then summoned them to follow.

Sarah knew he shortened his steps to keep pace with hers. She moved as quickly as she could down the long, empty corridor, but her rubbery legs had no strength. She feared they would crumple beneath her at any moment. Her heart beat in her chest like a runaway horse, and for the first time in many days, fear threatened to claim her composure.

Sam had arranged for a driver to be waiting for them at the morgue loading dock. The four exited the building and crossed the dock with synchronized movements to the steps to the parking lot.

Beads of sweat broke out on Sarah's forehead. She felt as if the blood had drained from her face, leaving her light-headed and dizzy. Her chest hurt, and suddenly it became difficult to breathe.

"Wait! Please." She began dragging her feet. "I can't...I can't breathe." Her hand flew to her chest, and she gulped for air.

Jacob and Rebecca had reached the car, and they turned to see what delayed them. Sam gestured them on. "It's okay. Get in the car. We'll be there in a second."

Sam faced Sarah. He clasped both her forearms in his hands and locked his gaze with hers. "Sarah?"

"I don't know what's wrong. My chest...it hurts... and I...I can't breathe."

"Listen to me. You're having a panic attack. Dr. Clark warned me that you might, once you left the hospital and the stress hit you." He locked his gaze with hers, the intensity of his stare mesmerizing her. "I'm not going to let anything happen to you." He drew her closer, almost as if he could transfer his strength to her. "You can do this. But you have to trust me."

"There they are! On the loading dock!"

Sam and Sarah looked in the direction of the voices. Two women, each holding a microphone in hand, raced toward them. A couple of men carrying cameras sprinted behind the women.

"We have to get out of here," Sam said.

Sarah's legs trembled as if they were made of gelatin instead of flesh and bone. "I can't." Certain her legs would no longer support her weight, she leaned heavily against his chest. "I'm sorry, Samuel."

Without hesitation, he scooped her off her feet.

She could feel his muscled strength supporting her legs and back as he carried her to the car. She clenched his shirt, its softness rubbing against her cheek. The clean scent of fresh linen mingled with the appealing, warm scent of his skin as she clung to him, and for a crazy moment in time she had no desire to release her grasp.

By the time they'd reached the first step, her heartbeat had slowed and her breathing returned to normal. Raising her eyes to meet Samuel's, Sarah knew that everything would be okay. God would protect her... and He would use Samuel to do it. Peace and gratitude replaced the terror that had been flowing through her veins just moments before. She smiled up at the man who held her in his arms.

"Take me home, Samuel. Please, I just want to go home."

Chapter Eight

It was early evening when they arrived at the house. Looming in the shadows of twilight, the two-story white clapboard house looked much like many of the others they'd passed along the way. A large red barn loomed to the left. They passed a multitude of fenced areas. In the distance, two horses grazed in the meadow.

Once the driver stopped the car, Jacob got out and hurried ahead to ready the house. Sam came around and helped both Rebecca and Sarah out of the vehicle.

Sarah stood for a second and looked around the property. She breathed in the heavy smells of fertile earth, manure and animals common to a working farm. She climbed the steps to the front porch, all the while trying to retrieve memories of times past, but none came.

Jacob met them just inside the door. Several kerosene lamps bathed the home in a warm, soft glow. "It is *gut* to have you home, Sarah." He helped Rebecca take off her coat and then helped Sarah with hers.

"I will make us some hot tea." Rebecca crossed to the propane-powered stove and put the kettle on.

Sarah glanced around the living room. She noted a

sofa, several chairs and scattered tables, but the focal point of the room was an impressive stone fireplace.

"Please, sit. Rest." Jacob gestured toward the kitchen table. "I have to bring in my horses. I will be back shortly."

"Do you need help?" Sam offered.

"*Danki,* no. Sit. Rest. It was a long trip, and I believe you have gotten little sleep in the past weeks."

Rebecca placed hot tea and a plate of fresh, home-made cookies in the middle of the table.

The scent of chamomile and chocolate chips teased Sarah's nostrils and made her realize she had barely touched her dinner.

"There's nothing better to ward off a night's chill than a hot cup of tea and a sweet treat. Come, both of you. Sit. Eat," Rebecca said.

"*Danki,*" Sam answered in the Pennsylvania Dutch dialect, his tone light and friendly. He bit into a cookie. "*Gut.* Did you know the *Englisch* have a saying that the way to a man's heart is through his stomach? These cookies are probably what prompted the saying."

A smile teased the corner of Sarah's mouth when she saw the blush of pleasure stain Rebecca's cheeks. What do you know? She wasn't the only one to succumb to this man's charm.

Rebecca, mindful of Sarah's arm in a sling and her frail health, poured her a cup of tea and placed two cookies on a small plate in front of her.

The three of them sat in companionable silence, enjoying the quiet and the treat, comfortable enough with each other not to feel obligated to fill the silence with idle conversation.

Sarah felt at home amidst the simple, plain surroundings, even though she had no concrete memories of ever being here before. But it only took a glance outside, now that twilight had ebbed to darkness, to remind her that until this man was caught, she would have no safe haven.

The back door opened, and Rebecca waved her husband inside.

"Come, Jacob. Sit. The tea grows cold."

Jacob took a seat and grinned. "I'm coming, *lieb*. I already know the secret that I am sure Samuel has just discovered. A bite of your cookies on a person's lips is a moment of pure joy."

Rebecca's blush deepened, and she placed an extra cookie in front of her husband.

Sarah grinned. Cookies might bring joy to the men, but for her, it was witnessing the strong and loving bond between the two people who were turning out to be the only family she had.

Sam and Jacob kept the conversation at the table flowing. They discussed hopes for the fall's harvest, the farmer's market prices, the plans for next year's planting.

Sarah smothered a yawn with her hand, and immediately Rebecca rose from the table. "You must be exhausted after today's journey, child." She picked up one of the oil lamps. "Come, I will show you your room."

Sam stood, clasped Sarah's elbow and helped her to her feet. His touch sent a surge of energy through her body, leaving tingles and confusion in its wake.

"Rebecca is right." Sam gently trailed a finger down her cheek. "You need your rest."

His eyes darkened with an intensity Sarah didn't understand. As they gazed into each other's eyes, there was an intimate pull between them, almost as though they were the only two people in the world.

More confused and disconcerted about the feelings that were growing for this man, Sarah broke eye contact and took a step away.

They were right. She was more than tired. She was exhausted, weak and disheartened. She'd expected a flood of memories to burst forth once she'd seen the farm, and she could barely hide her bitter disappointment when it did not happen.

Sarah followed close behind Rebecca, her path illuminated by the oil lamp Rebecca had given her. Rebecca paused outside a door to the right of the stairs, opened it and stood aside, looking hopeful and expectant.

Sarah recognized Rebecca's expectation. She was hoping that once Sarah entered the bedroom, her memory would return. She couldn't fault the woman; she longed for the same thing and dreaded that it wouldn't happen.

She stepped inside. The oil lamp bathed the room in a soft glow. She noted the pretty patchwork quilt on the double bed, the plain curtains at the two windows, the rocking chair beside a sturdy table that held a Bible.

Sarah's eyes missed nothing, and her heart grew heavy. She released the breath she'd been holding. Nothing. No memories. No feelings. No past. She could barely turn to face Rebecca.

The older woman forced a smile to her face, hurried to the chest against the wall, pulled out a clean, fresh, cream-colored floor-length flannel gown and laid it out on the bed. "Will you need me to help you dress?" Rebecca glanced at Sarah's sling.

"No. I'll be fine."

Rebecca nodded. "This should keep you warm, but if you find the gown and quilt are not enough, please come and tell me. The nights this time of year can sometimes chill a person to their bones." She crossed to the door. "If you need anything, child, anything at all, our room is only three doors down on the right."

"Danki." Sarah answered in the Pennsylvania Dutch dialect, but she wasn't sure if it was something she was pulling from her memory or something she'd heard so many times over the past few weeks that it felt natural saying it.

After Rebecca left, she placed the oil lamp on the nightstand. It was a struggle to get out of her clothes and don the flannel gown, but she managed. Sitting on the edge of the bed, she glanced around the shadowed room. That's how her mind felt—a mixture of clear images, shadows and darkness. Would she ever remember her former life?

It was frustrating not to remember anything of her childhood, her teens, her adulthood. Questions swirled through her mind.

What kind of person was she? Was she kind and loving, or did she have a selfish streak? Was she hardworking or lazy? Had she laughed easily, loved deeply, or was she more withdrawn and quiet?

Everyone in this small community knew the answers to her questions. Why couldn't she find those answers within herself?

A tear slid down her cheek. She felt so afraid and alone.

But she wasn't alone, was she? The thought brought her comfort, and she began to pray.

In the bright light of morning, Sarah took the opportunity to study her surroundings. The room was clean, neat and simple. A plain wooden oak chest stood against a far wall. Small oval rag rugs rested on each side of the bed to warm one's feet against the chill of the wooden floor. Two hooks hung on the wall next to a small closet. Were they to hold the next day's clothing? Or perhaps a man's hat? Peter's?

The thought reminded Sarah that in the not too distant past, she'd shared this room with someone. Someone she'd been told she loved. She spread her hands over the slight swell of her belly. That love had created this new life.

Even if she had no mental images of Peter, she was certain she'd have a clearer picture of the man when this child was born. She would only have to look at the child's eyes, or the color of hair, or the tiny baby smile, and she would be able to "see" her husband. If nothing else, she was certain that at that moment she would feel love for the man who had given her such a precious gift. But would she ever remember Peter himself, and the life they'd shared?

Dr. Clark had warned her not to expect too much of herself, that memories would come gradually, if they came at all, and not to stress over it.

Easier said than done.

Sarah couldn't deny that she'd had huge expectations when she'd come home. As foolish as it might seem now, she'd believed that once she actually saw her home, her memory would return. Disappointment left a bitter taste in her mouth and her heart heavy. But she wouldn't let it color the day. She would be grateful that she was home and healing.

Sarah followed the rich, mouthwatering aroma

of coffee and freshly baked bread downstairs to the kitchen. "Good morning, Rebecca."

The woman spun around from the sink. "*Guder mariye*. Did you sleep well?"

"Yes, *danki*. The trip home must have tired me more than I thought. I fell asleep as soon as my head hit the pillow."

"Did sleeping in your own bed help you remember anything?"

Rebecca's expression held such hope, and Sarah's inability to give the woman the answers she longed for filled her with guilt and sorrow.

"I didn't remember anything. I didn't even dream last night." When she saw the light in Rebecca's eyes dim, pain seized her heart. "I'm so sorry. I know you were hoping for more from me."

"The only thing I am expecting from you, child, is for you to do your best to regain your health. Nothing more. You will remember in God's time if He desires it." Her brow furrowed. "Should you be out of bed? I was fixing a tray to bring to your room."

"I was just about to ask that same question."

Sarah didn't have to turn around to know that Samuel stood behind her. He filled every room he entered with a strong, masculine presence. Besides, she would recognize the deep, warm tones of his voice anywhere.

The polite thing to do would be to acknowledge him and answer his question. She glanced over her shoulder to do just that, but the smile froze on her face and her breath caught in her throat. He stood closer than she'd expected. Close enough that she should have been able to feel his breath on the back of her neck.

Mere inches separated her from the rock-solid wall

of his chest. She couldn't help but remember how warm and safe and protected it had felt to be held in those muscled arms, cradled against that chest.

She took a step back and stumbled awkwardly over her own feet. Sam's hand shot out to steady her. "See, it is too soon. You should be in bed." Concern shone from his eyes and etched lines in his face.

"I'm fine." She eased her arm out of his grasp. "I tripped over my own feet. I don't know if I was an awkward oaf in my old life, but it looks like I am now." She grinned. "And yes, I should be out of bed. I've been in bed for two weeks. I may not remember much about my old self, but this new self, this person I am now, can't stand being cooped up for one more minute."

Rebecca chuckled behind her. "That's not a new self, Sarah. That's who you've always been. A dervish of activity from sunup to sundown, even as a little one." Rebecca patted her hand on the table. "Come. Both of you. Sit down. Eat."

"I can't remember the last time I sat down to a meal that didn't come out of a hospital vending machine. I'm starving." Sam beat Sarah to the table and pulled out a chair for her before he sat down.

Rebecca laughed. "Good. I like to feed people with healthy appetites." She carried a heavy, cast-iron skillet to the table and filled his plate with potatoes and sausage. Scrambled eggs were already in a bowl on the table. She set out a second small plate filled with slices of warm bread and a Mason jar of homemade strawberry jam.

"Yum." Sam's stomach chose that moment to growl loudly, and both women laughed.

Sarah watched every movement he made while pretending not to notice anything at all. She noted how long and lean his fingers were when he lifted a slice of bread. She smiled to herself when she saw the tiniest bead of jam at the corner of his mouth.

A warm flush tinged her cheeks when she realized how happy she was when he was around, and then she grew confused and unhappy with herself for that same reason. Should she be allowing anything, even friendship, to develop with this man? He was an *Englischer*. She was Amish, or at least that's what everyone told her she was. She wished she felt Amish, or English, or anything from anywhere—if she could only own the memory.

One thing she did know for sure. She was an assignment to Samuel, and he would be leaving as soon as his assignment was over. Didn't she have enough chaos in her life without adding unreturned feelings to it?

She stole another glance at him. She couldn't help but admire his strong, chiseled features, the square chin, the pronounced cheekbones, the angular planes and the deep, dark, intense eyes that seemed to be able to look at a person and see into their soul.

Was she gravitating toward him because, besides Rebecca, he had been the only constant in her life for the past two weeks whom she could rely on in an otherwise frightening, blank world of strangers and fear?

Or was the reason simply a woman being drawn to an attractive, kind man?

Either way she had to learn to dismiss these new feelings in an effort to discover the old ones. She had to concentrate on remembering the past and forget the temptation of daring to think about a future. There was no future for Samuel and her. There never would be.

"Where is Jacob?" Sam smeared jam on a second slice of warm bread. "I'd like to ask him if there is anything close to the house that I might help him with today. Maybe muck the stalls in the barn?"

"Jacob is mending a fence in the back pasture," Rebecca replied. "He left at first light. I am expecting him back anytime now."

No sooner had the words had left her lips than the back door opened and Jacob strode into the room. He hung his coat and hat on the hooks by the door, slid out of his boots and padded in his socks to the table.

Rebecca slid a mug of hot coffee in front of his chair before he even sat down.

"*Guder mariye,* everyone. The skies are clear. The air is sweet. Looks like a good day for working in the fields." Jacob rubbed his hands together in anticipation and took a slice of bread from the basket.

"What can I do to help?" Sam asked. "I know work is never truly done on a farm, but I am limited in how far I can wander from the house. I was hoping you might have something for me in the barn. I can muck stalls, feed animals. I also saw carpentry equipment."

"*Ya,* that was Peter's work. He built cabinets and furniture. He was working on a new table and chairs to present to Josiah and Anna. They are to be married this month."

"Aren't weddings held in November, after the harvest?" Sam asked.

"*Ya,* but this is a special occasion. Josiah has a *gut* job opportunity with an Amish family in Ohio. Peter finished the chairs he was making for them, but not the table." Jacob's eyes dimmed. "I will have to find time in my schedule to finish it for him."

"Let me."

Jacob cocked an eyebrow. "You know woodworking?"

Sam shrugged. "I am better working in the fields, but my father taught me to sand and stain and varnish. I need to be close to the house to protect Sarah, but it doesn't mean I can't share in the work."

Jacob nodded, and a new respect crossed his expression. "That is *gut. Danki,* Samuel. I will accept your help with the table."

Sam glanced out the kitchen window. He tensed and rose to his feet. "A buggy passed by the window," he said in answer to the questioning looks on everyone's faces.

Pounding on the front door drew their attention.

Jacob rose to answer it, but before he could the door opened like a burst of wind had pushed it, and Benjamin Miller stormed into the house. He strode to the kitchen doorway, his demeanor angry.

"Forgive me, Jacob, for entering without your permission, but the matter is urgent."

Jacob's tone of voice was low and calm but stern as he faced his friend. "What could be so urgent, Benjamin, that you could not wait for me to open the door? You have frightened my wife and Sarah."

Sam remained standing. Sarah thought he looked like a panther poised to strike, his hand subtly hidden within the folds of his jacket. He must be wearing a gun. The thought made shivers of apprehension race up and down her arms. She did not like guns, and she did not want to be reminded that Sam was as comfortable wearing one as he was his pants or boots.

Benjamin removed his hat. "I apologize." He pointed an accusing finger at Sam. "But I told you that allowing this man into our homes would only bring trouble to us, and now it has."

"What are you talking about? What trouble?" Jacob asked.

"There is a man in town. He is going business to business asking where he can find Sarah—and the man protecting her."

Chapter Nine

"*Kumm,* sit." Jacob gestured to a vacant chair at the table. "Rebecca will pour you a cup of *kaffe,* and you can tell us what you know."

Benjamin glared at Sam as he stepped past him. After he took a sip of his coffee, he leaned in toward Jacob as if he was the only person in the room to hear.

"I was at the hardware store when Josiah came in and told me. The whole town is in a dither. No one knows what to do or say."

"What are folks saying?" Sam tried not to appear annoyed when Benjamin directed the answer to Jacob as if he was the one who had asked.

"We cannot lie. Everyone has simply said that we cannot help him."

"Did you see this man?" Jacob asked.

"*Ya,* he came into the hardware store just a few minutes after Josiah. He was of average height and dressed in an *Englisch* suit and tie. He had bushy, bright red hair and wore wire-framed glasses."

"Did you hear what he said to the store clerk?" Sam

asked. "Did he have an accent? Any distinguishable features like a scar or mole on his face?"

Still ignoring him, Benjamin finished his coffee and then spoke to Jacob. "He pulled out some kind of wallet and flashed the badge inside. He said he was a police detective."

"But that is a lie." Jacob glanced between Sam and Sarah, who had paled like the milk in the glass in front of her. "If he truly was a police detective, he would know where Sarah lives, and he would know Detective King."

"*Ya,* he is lying. Everyone knows it. He brings trouble to our town." For the first time since sitting at the table, Benjamin made eye contact with Sam. "He is following you. You should not have come here."

"Benjamin, please tell us what else the man said." Rebecca refilled his coffee cup.

"He told the store clerk that the woman he was searching for, Sarah Lapp, had been kidnapped from the hospital by the man who was claiming to protect her. He asked if anyone could tell him what farm or family she belongs to, or if they'd seen her in town."

Sam ignored the accusatory glare directed his way. "Could he have been a newspaper reporter? They have been known to use less than truthful tactics to get a story."

Benjamin shrugged. "The town is full of reporters. They travel in packs like wolves. They carry cameras and climb in and out of big motor vans. They wear their pictures on a badge on their clothes."

"So what do we do?" Rebecca held fingers to her chin, and concern filled her eyes. "We cannot let this man near our Sarah."

"I don't intend to let that happen, Rebecca. Don't worry," Sam assured her.

"Maybe I should leave this place." Sarah joined the conversation for the first time. Her eyes were earnest, her tone anxious. "If I go away and hide someplace else, maybe the man will follow me. Maybe it will keep the *kinner* safe."

"The children will not be safe, Sarah, no matter what you do. It is not beneath him to use them to flush you out, even if you did hide someplace else. It is better for you to stay here. It will be easier to protect you."

"Is there anything we can do to help?" Jacob asked.

"Yes. Talk to everyone you know. Ask them to keep their silence. Tell them it is not only Sarah's safety they will be protecting, but also the children's."

Sarah stood. Her legs wobbled beneath her, and she held on to the table edge for support. "I cannot let this man hurt the *kinner*."

Sam hurried to her side and supported her right arm with his hand. "The only thing I want you to do right now, Sarah Lapp, is to rest. You must get stronger if you expect your memories of that day to return. If they return, that is when you will be the most help."

"Samuel is right, child." Rebecca took Sam's place at Sarah's side. "You've had enough excitement for now. Let me help you back to bed. You haven't been out of the hospital an entire day yet."

Sarah looked at each man at the table, and then fixed her gaze on Sam. "What happens now, Samuel?"

"We wait."

"That's it? Just sit and wait for a madman to come and hurt our *kinner,* or kill me, or both?"

Benjamin jumped to his feet and shouted. "You must

go! Maybe if you go, he will leave and we can all go back to our lives."

Benjamin flailed his arms in anger, but Samuel saw beneath it and recognized the fear. He kept his voice calm and his tone reassuring.

"Tell me, Benjamin. If a wolf stalks a man's sheep, will the wolf go away because the shepherd decides to leave the flock and go home?"

Sam paused while he waited for the other man to consider the wisdom of his words. When Sam spoke again, his voice, though calm, held a note of steel.

"This man will come for Sarah…and when he does, I will stop him."

Sarah thanked the good Lord that the day had ended much quieter than it had started. She gently rocked back and forth on the front porch and watched the sun set over the newly planted fields. Despite the disturbing news at breakfast, once the discussion had ended, the men had gone about their chores, and the day had passed peacefully.

Samuel had kept busy in the barn with the table he had promised Jacob he would finish. Although he rarely left the barn, Sarah could feel his eyes upon her whenever she stepped out of the house. At first it was unsettling and made her uncomfortable, but after she'd had some time to think and pray about it, she realized his intention was to keep her safe, and she was grateful.

Rebecca crossed the porch and sat down beside her. "Let me help with the string beans."

Sarah laughed. "Please, I may not be able to use my left shoulder, but my hand works. I can break string beans into smaller pieces for dinner."

Rebecca glanced into the bowl resting on Sarah's lap. "And it is a good job you do."

Once Rebecca had settled into a soft, rhythmic rocking beside her, Sarah dared to broach the subject that had been weighing heavily on her mind all day.

"Rebecca, tell me about my family. In the hospital you changed the conversation when I mentioned my mother. No one has claimed me as daughter or sister or aunt. Do I have a family? Beside you and Jacob... and Peter, of course."

A shadow crossed Rebecca's face, and her rocking quickened.

"I do not wish to cause you any grief," Sarah continued. "But of course, you must understand how difficult it has been for me not to know who I am, who I come from. I am afraid those memories may not return, and you...you could help me with some of the answers to this darkness inside."

Rebecca dropped her head and remained silent.

"Was I an evil person? Did I come from a bad family? Is that why talking about it is difficult for you?"

Rebecca's eyes widened, and her mouth opened in a perfect circle. "Lord, help us. Where would you get a notion such as that?"

"Because the question brings you pain. I assume it is bad memories I am asking you to recall."

"Nothing could be further from the truth, child. The pain I feel is that of loss and grief for all the wonderful people who were part of my life and are now home with the Lord."

Rebecca reached over and patted Sarah's knee. "Your grandmother and I grew up together. We were best friends. Her name was Anna. She married when she was still in her teens and had a daughter soon after, a beautiful girl named Elizabeth.

"Elizabeth was a dervish of energy, a tornado of sunshine and light…just like you were, child. Elizabeth met an *Englisch* boy and left our community to marry him and live in his world. It broke Anna's heart but…" Rebecca shrugged. "She understood this thing called love."

"When your father was killed in a factory accident, Elizabeth brought you home. You were about five at the time. Such joy! Such happiness you brought to Anna's eyes every time she looked at you." A cloud passed over Rebecca's expression. "And when your mother took ill and died, you were the only thing that kept Anna's heart from shattering into a million pieces."

Rebecca smiled at her. "Your grandmother died just before your tenth birthday. Jacob and I brought you into our home and raised you like one of our own. We were overcome with joy when you married Peter and became a true daughter, not just one of my heart."

Rebecca's eyes glistened with tears, pain, grief—and something else, something she found harder to identify. "You are all Jacob and I have left now. We have lost Anna and Elizabeth and…and Peter…" The catch in her words gave her pause.

"I'm so sorry. I didn't mean to cause you pain."

"Ack. Sometimes life is painful, child. That is what makes it life and not heaven." She smiled broadly. "But it is not all pain. We still have you, *lieb*. And the child you carry is God's blessing to all of us. He knows how painful it has been for me. Not to see my son's smiling face or hear his voice or watch him hammer away on the furniture he crafts in the barn. Part of my heart shattered that day in the school house. But not all of it…"

She cupped Sarah's chin in her hand. "God made sure He left me with enough of a heart so I could fill it with love for you and for my grandchild. He took Peter to be with Him. That was His will, and sometimes it is hard to understand His ways. But He left a little part of Peter with us. For that, I am so very grateful. God is *gut*."

Rebecca stood. "*Kumm*. It will be dark soon. The men will be tired and hungry. I am sure there is something I can find for you to help me with despite your sling. It will be like old times, fixing dinner together for our family."

The two women embraced and then walked together into the house.

Later that evening, Sam saw Sarah standing on the porch. She stared up at the night sky and seemed to be studying the stars.

"For a person who just got out of the hospital, I find you spend most of your time outside." Sam's boots scraped loudly against the wooden floor of the porch.

Sarah turned her head and tossed a smile his way. The light from the kerosene lamp danced softly across her features.

"I've been cooped up much too long. I like to feel fresh air on my skin." She turned her eyes back to the sky. "Have you ever really looked at the sky, Samuel? God is an artist, and He uses the sky as His palette. I watch in awe as the patterns and colors change from dawn to dusk to the inky blackness of night. Even then, He decorates the darkness with stars to light our way and to give us hope."

Sam stepped behind her and wrapped a quilt around

her shoulders. "If you insist on living on the porch, you must start wearing a jacket or sweater. The days are pleasant, but the temperatures still dip in the mornings and evenings. You're going to be a mother. You must keep yourself warm and healthy."

Almost on cue, a rush of cool air brushed past them and he could feel her quiver beneath his touch. She pulled the quilt tighter and burrowed into its warmth.

"You have looked at the sky for hours, Sarah. Even God has gone to bed," he teased her.

Sarah chuckled. "True, I suppose. I find it easier to think when I'm out here."

Sam gestured to a rocker. "I have been standing all day. I would like to sit now, and I can't if I am supposed to be protecting you. How about protecting me for a little while? Sit with me so I can give my legs a rest."

She did as requested. "I think it would be your eyes that need rest, Samuel. They bounced in my direction and then back to your chores so often, I'm surprised you can still see straight."

He laughed hard and deep, the booming sound breaking through the silence of the night. No words needed to be spoken as they rocked together in perfect unison.

"You are right, Sarah," Sam said. "You created quite a dilemma for me. A bodyguard cannot guard a body if he is not watching it, and a man cannot be a man if he stays in another man's home and does not attempt to pull his own weight. So my poor eyes got a workout for sure." He rested his left ankle on his right knee.

"How is the table coming along? I saw how hard you worked. You went over every inch, your movements steady, your attention to detail evident."

"Tomorrow I will do the final touches and it will be

ready." He reached over and squeezed her hand. "Maybe you will take pity on my eyes and sit with me in the barn."

"Breathe in fresh air on the porch, or inhale the smell of hay, manure, animals and varnish in the barn? Sit in shadows when I can be outside and feel the warmth of the sun on my face. Hmm?" She held an index finger to her lips as if seriously considering the proposition. "Sorry, I think not, Samuel. You will just have to finish your chores faster and come sit in the sunshine with me."

"I do sit in the sunshine whenever I am with you."

The unexpected compliment seemed to surprise them both. A heavy silence fell over them. The only sound on the porch was the rhythmic swishing of the rockers. When Sam spoke again, his tone was thoughtful and serious.

"Talk to me, Sarah. What deep thoughts trouble you so much that you stare into the horizon for hours searching for answers? I know the past two weeks have been difficult. I understand. I am just wondering if there is something more…something deeper that troubles you."

A tear slid down her cheek, and she hurried to wipe it away.

"You can talk to me, you know. Listening is part of bodyguard duties and comes absolutely free of charge."

In the soft glow of the kerosene lamp, Sarah saw warmth and empathy in his eyes. She knew she could feel safe baring her soul to this man because he was a stranger. She didn't have to choose her words with care for fear of saying the wrong thing or having something she said cause pain, like it sometimes did when she talked with Rebecca or Jacob. She felt she could talk to him about anything—except the unsettling feelings and questions she had about him, of course.

He reached out and clasped her hand. "Talk to me. I can be a good listener."

She inhaled deeply. Maybe it would be helpful to talk with someone who might be able to understand the disappointment and fear gnawing inside. Grateful for an open ear, she kept her voice low so as not to disturb Rebecca or Jacob inside.

"I thought coming home would end all my troubles. I thought when I saw the house, when I returned to familiar surroundings and slipped back into a normal daily routine, that everything would be okay."

Silence hung in the darkness between them.

"I expected my memory to return. Expected answers to the thousands of questions I have inside."

"I take it you haven't had any flashes of memory?"

She shook her head, oblivious as to whether he could see the movement in the dim light.

"Dr. Clark warned you, Sarah. He said your memories would probably come back slowly, maybe in flashes, and you should be patient. He also told you that they may not come back at all."

"I know." Her voice was a mere whisper on the wind.

"Can you live with that? Can you cope with the fact that your memories may never return?"

The warmth of his voice flowed over her, filled with concern and offering her waves of comfort, but still she felt lost and defeated. "I'm not sure. I don't know how it will be if this is a permanent situation. The only thing holding me together right now is hope…hope that it will all come back, that I will remember again."

"And if you don't?"

The silence became heavy and oppressive, stealing her breath, causing her fingers to tremble and her toes to nervously tap against the wooden floor.

"Calm down, Sarah. You're starting to have another panic attack. Take a couple of deep breaths. It will be all right."

He stopped rocking, pulled his chair around to face her and moved in closer so she could see his face in the dim light.

"You're scared."

She nodded.

"What frightens you the most?"

She thought for a moment, and then locked her gaze with his. "I'm scared to death that I will never know who I am, who I was..." She nodded with her head toward the house. "Who they expect me to be." She lowered her eyes. "They are good people. They have been hurt enough. What if I can't be the person they want me to be?"

A burst of anger raged through her. "Why did this happen? What am I supposed to do with all this emptiness?" She jumped to her feet, held on to the porch rail and stared out into the night.

"Do you have any idea what it feels like to be me?" she asked. "I can't remember the people around me, the same people who shower me with love and gaze at me with such high hopes and expectations." She sighed deeply. "I can't even remember *me*.

"I am told I was an *Englisch* child who was raised by an Amish grandmother and then adopted by the Lapps after her death. But what does that make me? Am I *Englisch* because I was born in your world? Or am I

Amish because I was raised as a child in this one? I can't remember anything about either world, so how can I answer that question?

"I am told I was a dervish of energy. Is that why I want to be busy all the time? Why I long to be outside and moving? Or is it fear and restlessness from thoughts I cannot bear that drive me?"

She paced, and Sam didn't speak or try to stop her.

"Do I like strawberry jam? Scrambled eggs? Sausage? Can I cook? Can I sew? Do I have friends? Do I care about anybody? Am I a person who should be cared about?"

Sarah's fears shone through her eyes.

"I was married to a man I can't remember. There isn't even a picture I can look at so I can try to remember his face. Married, Samuel. Partners in life, in love. I can't remember any of it. Does Peter deserve to be forgotten? What kind of person does that make me?"

Her voice rose. She could hear the frustration and anxiety in it, but she couldn't control it.

"I'm pregnant. I'm carrying a precious gift, a blessing. But what kind of mother will I be? How will I teach this child the ways of the world when I can't remember ever taking the path myself? How can this child grow to love me? How can *anyone* love me when I don't know me well enough to love myself?" Her voice rose an octave. "I have to remember. Everyone needs me to remember. I don't know what I will do if I can't."

Sarah had to physically fight the urge to dart away, to flee into the darkness and try to outrun the fear.

Sam stood and gathered her into his arms. She nestled firmly against the warmth of his chest. The sound of his voice rumbled against her ear. She could feel the gentle breeze of his breath through her hair with each word of comfort.

The words he spoke were not important. They were comfort words. It was the strength of his embrace, the solid wall of his presence that soothed her. He offered her a safe haven to air her fears without judgment. He offered her friendship and empathy. Sarah may not be able to prevent disappointing the people who knew her in the past, but Samuel wasn't a part of her past. He knew her only as she was now. She truly believed that God had sent him into her life to help her when she needed it most…and that thought brought her peace.

"I'm sorry." She eased out of his embrace.

She didn't have a chance to finish the sentence before he cupped her chin with his hand and forced her eyes to lock with his.

"You have nothing to apologize for, Sarah. You are as much a victim in all of this as anyone. Remember that."

He brushed his fingers lightly against the path of tears on her cheek. "You can sit and wallow and feel sorry for yourself. You have the right to do that." He smiled down at her. "Or you can look at this as God's gift…an opportunity to be anyone you want to be."

She arched an eyebrow.

"You tell me you don't know if you were a good person or bad, selfish or kind? Okay, so choose. It doesn't matter who or what you were. None of us can change one moment of the past, no matter how much we might want to. But God has given you the present and it is a gift, isn't it? Decide what kind of person you want to be. Will you be loving and kind to others? Will you be hardworking and helpful? Your choice, isn't it?"

He smiled down on her. "You will be a wonderful

mother because you care for your child so much, and he or she isn't even here yet. Think about it, Sarah. You can take the journey with your child. The two of you can learn to play in the sunshine. You can both decide together whether you like the taste of turnips or prefer the taste of corn. You can read books together each night before bed. You might find that you enjoy them just as much as the child because you will be reading them for the first time.

"Who cares if you can cook? If you can't, you can learn. Who cares if you can sew? Try it. If you can remember the stitches, *wunderbaar*. If not, it is only another lesson to learn. You can start your life over again, Sarah. Many people I know wish they could have that chance."

The truth of his words washed over her, and she felt a new resolve, maybe even a little happiness blossom within. She chewed on her bottom lip. "But what of Jacob and Rebecca? What if I can't be the person they remember?"

He slipped his arms around her waist and drew her close again.

"They loved the person you were. Now they will love the person you will grow to be."

She smiled and allowed herself to burrow against him one more time. She closed her eyes. He felt so warm and comforting and safe.

Suddenly his body tensed. She raised her head and searched his face.

"What?"

He didn't speak but stared hard into the darkness. The tension in his body made his formerly comforting hands tighten to steel. His grasp almost hurt as she eased out of his hold.

She turned her head and followed his gaze. A tiny ball of light shone in the distance. She squinted and tried to focus to get a better look. As she stared harder across the dark, empty fields, the light grew larger, brighter.

"Samuel, what is it?"

His features were stone-cold, his expression grim. "Fire."

Chapter Ten

"Fire? Are you sure?" Sarah grasped the porch post and stared hard at the horizon. What had begun as a tiny glimmer was now an ominous orange light that grew in height and width even as they watched.

The sharp clanging of a bell broke the silence of the spring night. Seconds later Sam's cell phone rang, the musical notes clashing with the continued clang of the farm triangle. He mumbled a few words in reply to whatever he was hearing, shoved the phone back in his coat pocket and raced for the barn.

"Samuel?"

"Stay there. Don't move!" he yelled over his shoulder as he ran.

Sarah watched in alarm as the light became a looming two-story-high monster of flame on the horizon.

Jacob and Rebecca raced onto the porch.

"What's happening?" Jacob stumbled toward Sarah in a half hop as he bent down to pull one of his boots on. Rebecca, tying the sash of her robe over her long flannel nightgown, was close on his heels.

Before Sarah could respond, Jacob yelled, "That's

Benjamin's place! There's a fire!" He turned and clasped his wife's forearms. "I must go. I'll be back as soon as I can." He kissed her on the forehead.

Rebecca nodded. "God speed and keep you safe."

Just as Jacob moved to the steps, Sam ran out of the barn, pulling one of the horses behind him. He brought it to a stop at the base of the stairs. "I thought it would be faster to saddle the horse than hitch the buggy."

"Danki," Jacob replied, throwing his foot in a stirrup and mounting up. The horse, sensing the tension and probably smelling the smoke, pawed the ground and tried to rear, but Jacob took control of the reins and had the steed settled and listening to commands in no time. "Take care of the women."

Sam nodded and watched Jacob gallop away. He climbed the steps and joined the women. They watched in silence as what had been a glimmer of brightness now filled an uncomfortable stretch on the horizon, with ominous fingers of light that seemed to touch the sky.

"Let us say a prayer." Rebecca clasped their hands. They bowed their heads and prayed for safety of all who faced the flames, for strength to deal with whatever lay in wait, for hope that no life would be lost. They knew that material things could be replaced.

"What do you think happened?" Sarah asked. She removed the quilt from her shoulders and tucked it around Rebecca, then sat down beside her.

"I don't know." Rebecca sounded as surprised and confused as the rest of them. "It is late. I'm sure the propane stove was turned off. No engines would be running in the barn at this time of night. Perhaps a kerosene lamp was knocked over. But…" Her words trailed off, and worry lines etched her face.

"But what?" Sarah asked.

"A kerosene lamp should not be sufficient to cause that size flame," Sam said. His hardened features looked like they were carved in granite. He didn't seem able to pull his eyes away from the horizon. "Even if a lamp had been knocked over onto something flammable, the lamp would not have been unattended, and the resulting fire should have been easily contained."

Sarah gasped. "Are you saying this fire was deliberately set? Who would do such a thing?"

Sam stared hard at her. His silence and the truth she saw in his eyes chilled her to the bone, more than his words ever could.

"*Nee*, Samuel. I refuse to believe anyone set the fire." Rebecca rubbed her hands together against the chill that raced through her body. "In your world, you are accustomed to meeting evil every day. I understand your mind jumping to that thought. But in our community, accidents are usually just that—accidents."

Rebecca patted Sarah on the shoulder. "*Kumm* inside, child. You are still recovering and must not stress yourself. You, too, Samuel. There is nothing you can do out here to help. I will make some hot chocolate." She stood and folded the quilt over her arm. "I would appreciate it, Samuel, if you would bring in some extra wood for the fireplace. It is going to be a long night for all of us."

Rebecca stepped toward the door, but spun back around when she heard Sarah gasp.

"Look! Over there!" Sarah pointed her index finger to a spot a considerable distance west of the fire. "Do you see it? Tell me I'm not seeing what I think I see."

Sam and Rebecca huddled beside her. The three of them stared at the small flicker of light in the distance.

Terrifying moments passed as they watched the light intensify and grow.

"It can't be. That's not another fire, is it?" Sarah held her breath. She hoped it was a reflection of something, or that her overactive imagination was spooked and creating worst-case scenarios.

A second bell began clanging furiously, the frantic sound wafting across the night air.

"That's the Yoder farm." Rebecca's voice was little more than an awestruck whisper. "The Yoders have a fire."

The three of them stood in silence and watched the light quickly become an orange wall against the night.

Over the horizon and harder to see, another light appeared. Another clanging bell joined the unwanted symphony of the night.

"Oh God, please Lord, help them." Rebecca's eyes widened, and shock was evident on her face. "It is too far to be certain, but I think that is coming from Nathan and Esther's place. They just had a baby last week. Please God, let them be safe."

"Why is this happening? I don't understand." Sarah tried to keep the panic out of her voice as she counted at least three yellow-orange walls of flame shooting high in the night sky.

Sam wiped a hand over his face and then threw his arms over the shoulders of the two women huddled together in front of him.

"Evil is no longer out in the *Englisch* world, Rebecca. Evil is here."

The sunshine streaming through her bedroom window brought Sarah fully awake. She arched her back like a sleepy cat upon awakening, stretched her right arm over her head, and then used it to push up into a sitting position. She adjusted the sling on her left arm and winced at the pain still throbbing in her left shoulder whenever she jarred it.

Her thoughts wandered to the night before. Had it all been a horrible nightmare? It took her a moment to orient herself. No, it had been only too real.

She'd sat with Rebecca for hours in front of the fireplace, sipping hot chocolate, reading the Bible together and waiting. Sam had paced like a caged animal. He slipped outside every thirty minutes or so to check the Lapp barn and the perimeter of the house before hurrying back inside. He was a man whose emotions were torn. Sarah knew he'd wanted to go with Jacob and help the men, but she also knew he would never shirk his duty of protecting Rebecca and herself.

She dressed hurriedly, pulled the *kapp* over her bandaged head and walked to the bedroom door. It had been almost dawn when Jacob had come home. His body had screamed of fatigue. The haunted look in his eyes told them it had been as bad as they had suspected.

She wondered if anyone else was up yet. She eased the door open and heard the sound of men's voices below.

Padding softly down the stairs, she saw Jacob surrounded by men. She recognized Benjamin, Nathan, Thomas and several others she'd met but still couldn't place names to faces. The deep rumble of conversation wafted up the steps and then ceased when they sensed her approach.

"*Guder mariye,* gentlemen. Please don't let me interrupt." Sarah smiled and nodded as the men returned her greeting. She passed them and headed into the kitchen, stopping abruptly when she saw at least a half-dozen Amish women gathered around the table.

"Kumm, Sarah, join us." Rebecca waved her to the table, lifted the pot and poured her a hot cup of *kaffe.* "We are discussing the troubles of last night and dividing up the workload."

"Ya." Elizabeth Miller passed Sarah apple butter and fresh bread. "Our barn was first, but there were four more barns burned to the ground last night."

"Five barns?" Sarah couldn't keep the surprise from her voice. She'd seen three fires. There'd been two more.

"Ya, five barns. There was no way the fire department could reach even one of the barns in time, let alone five. There was nothing we could do but keep the fires from spreading," Elizabeth said.

"That's how Esther got hurt," Rebecca said. "She ran out to help Nathan. Part of the barn collapsed on her. She got a pretty nasty burn on her back."

Sarah gasped. "Isn't she the woman who just had a baby last week?"

"Ya," Rebecca replied. "We are just discussing a schedule on how we can help with chores and dinner. She will have her hands full taking care of her *boppli.* We will help with everything else until she is recovered."

"What can I do?"

"Sarah, dear, you must work on getting better yourself." Elizabeth patted her hand. "You have only been out of the hospital two days, *ya?"*

"Maybe so, but I'm not helpless. There must be something I can do, especially since…"

"What?" Elizabeth asked.

Sarah felt even worse when she saw the kindness in Elizabeth's eyes. She lowered her gaze. "Since everyone here knows it is my fault the barns were burned."

"Nonsense," Elizabeth said, and the other women at

the table murmured their agreement. "You did not burn our barns. You did not hold our children hostage in their school. You did not kill one of our own and severely injure another of our loved ones." Elizabeth's eyes welled with tears. "This bad thing has happened to all of us, Sarah, and I'm thinking you have suffered most of all."

The other women at the table nodded.

"We will put this in God's hands," Rebecca said. "It is not our way to seek vengeance or punishment. It is our way to help. So let's divide the work, for there is much to do."

"Sarah and I will prepare three *yummasette* casseroles and three pies. We will deliver them to the Yoders, the Burkholders and the Zooks."

"*Gut.* Hannah and I will cook for Elizabeth and Benjamin."

Elizabeth started to protest, but Hannah waved her silent. "*Nee,* Elizabeth, you are not going to work all day, helping with Esther's house and *boppli,* and think you are coming home to your own chores, too. We will have a hot meal for you and Benjamin by the end of this day."

Elizabeth nodded. *"Danki."*

"We will all be working to help each other," Rebecca said. "Now let's finish our *kaffe.* There is much to do."

The men decided as a group to rebuild one barn at a time rather than scatter their labor force. Once that decision was made, Jacob pulled out Peter's wagon and went to town for lumber while the other men left for Benjamin's. The women scattered to their own homes to prepare the meals they'd promised.

When Rebecca returned to the kitchen, she had a surprised look on her face.

Sarah looked up from her preparations. "What? Is something missing?" She glanced down at the bread, soup, ground beef, onion, peas and noodles she had collected on the table.

Rebecca smiled. "*Nee,* everything is there. I am just happy to see you remember."

Sarah froze and then smiled. "I guess I do remember." She glanced at the ingredients in front of her and then at Rebecca. "I don't have a definite memory of making this particular casserole, but when you mentioned it I knew right away what ingredients to gather. Did I make this often?"

"One of your many talents was your cooking. After you married Peter, you took over preparing the main meal for all of us each evening. Rarely would you even let me step inside the kitchen." Rebecca smiled at her. "I suppose that is why I started making huge breakfasts for everyone."

Rebecca clasped her hand. "This is a *gut* thing, Sarah. Soon now, God willing, you will remember even more."

Sarah smiled at the older woman, but it was only a smile for show—it didn't touch her heart. Yes, she knew the ingredients for *yummasette* casserole. Just like she knew how to brush her teeth or wash her face. It came naturally to her, ingrained deep inside like breathing. But she still had no flashes of memory where she could see herself preparing the dish. She didn't want to dash Rebecca's hopes, but she was beginning to fear she would never remember the past again.

Not wanting to give Rebecca any more grief—five neighbors' barns burning through the night had caused enough of that—she squeezed the woman's hand, and the two of them began the day's cooking.

Samuel kept himself scarce for most of the day and allowed the women to work in peace. He was always on the periphery, doing what chores he could while still keeping himself within shouting distance of the kitchen. Every now and then he'd step inside under the guise of getting a glass of water. He'd snitch a piece of sliced apple or a piece of cheese, and Rebecca would puff up like a mad hen and smack at his fingers and scoot him away, but he never strayed far.

Many times through the course of the morning, Sarah could feel his eyes on her. She'd look up to see him gazing in through the kitchen window or pausing in the doorway. It should have annoyed her, but instead it made her feel cared for and protected.

Sarah sensed his discontent. She'd see him gaze in the distance toward the neighboring farms. She knew he was itching to pick up a hammer and help the men. But the moment would pass, and he'd seem to settle into his routine of barn chores and watching the women.

Samuel seemed relieved, even happy, when Rebecca asked him to hitch up the buggy so they could deliver the food.

Rebecca offered to drive the buggy herself and urged Sarah to stay behind and rest, but Sarah would have none of it. She was tired, sure. She was pretty certain they were all exhausted by now after having such little sleep. But her pain level was tolerable, and no matter what the women told her this morning, she did feel responsible for their troubles. No one would stop her from delivering this food. It was the least she could do.

Samuel sensed this. When she glanced his way, he was already standing beside the buggy and extending his hand to help her inside. They'd known each other for little more than a few weeks, and yet he seemed to know her so well—guessing correctly what she would do or how she would feel before she even knew those things herself. How could this stranger become a friend so quickly? How could they be so attuned to each other's thoughts and feelings? And what kind of pain was she going to feel when he left?

When those thoughts entered her head, she shooed them away. Samuel had become a good friend and confidant. He'd sit and talk with her for hours. Although, if she was honest, she did most of the talking.

Samuel was a great listener. He didn't judge. He didn't offer unsolicited advice. He didn't seem to expect her to be anything other than who she was. She could relax with him. She didn't have to be constantly striving to recall the past or deal with others' disappointments when she couldn't.

"Well, are you coming or do I have to carry you to the buggy?" Sam grinned and shook his waiting hand, as though she may have missed seeing it held out for the past few minutes.

"I'm coming. Hold your horses."

Sam jiggled the reins in his other hand. "That's exactly what I'm doing."

Sarah laughed and allowed him to help her into the buggy. She adjusted the basket she carried on her lap and anchored it between the sling on her left arm and her body to keep it from falling.

Sam helped Rebecca into the seat beside her, handed

up the basket she carried and raced around to climb in the left side of the front seat.

"Okay, ladies. This is your last chance. Do a quick mental checklist. Do you have everything? This horse doesn't know how to turn around. It only goes forward."

Both women chuckled and assured him it was safe to leave, and he clicked his tongue and jiggled the reins.

The buggy ride was more painful than Sarah had expected. Each bounce and jolt sent shooting pains into her left shoulder and down the side of her back, but she didn't complain. She kept a smile pasted on her face and offered a silent prayer that the ride would soon be over. Gratitude washed over her when a little while later they pulled up in front of the Miller home. Benjamin's three children hooped and hollered as they raced each other to the buggy.

Rebecca nodded toward the approaching children. "You may not have your memory back yet, Sarah, but the *kinner* remember that you always bring cookies with you when you come to visit."

Samuel helped Rebecca out of the buggy. She took her basket up to the house just as William, Benjamin's oldest boy, squeezed past her into the seat she'd vacated.

"Hi, Sarah. Did you bring any chocolate chip cookies with you?"

"*Mamm* will be mad at you for asking for cookies." The little girl, who was standing on a wheel hub and leaning into the buggy, was adorable. About five or six years old with golden blond hair and brilliant blue eyes, she looked like a living, breathing doll. "But if you did bring cookies, I want one too, please."

Sarah laughed. "Well, lucky for both of you I just happen to have a fresh batch of cookies in my basket."

The children squirmed and bounced in anticipation while Sarah slipped her hand inside and pulled out one cookie for each of them. "Don't you have another brother?" She handed them their treats. "I think someone told me there are three of you."

The girl giggled, and the high-pitched melody sounded like wind chimes on a breezy day. "You're silly, Sarah. You know there are three of us—William, Daniel and me." She hung by one arm off the buggy and swung back and forth.

"You're right. How silly of me to forget." The child was so adorable. Sarah couldn't help but wonder whether her child would be a girl or a boy, and if that child would be as cute and impish as these two.

"I'll take his cookie and give it to him," William volunteered.

Sarah chuckled. Somehow she didn't think it would reach his brother without at least a little nibble out of it, if she gave the cookie to the boy.

"Where is Daniel?" she asked.

William pointed his finger. "Over there, standing by Daed and the other men in the field."

For the first time, Sarah turned her attention their way. Samuel had already joined them. She shielded her eyes from the glare of the setting sun and squinted for a better look. She noted it wasn't just Amish men standing in the field. There were two police cars parked where the rebuilding of the barn had begun, and some uniformed officers stood talking with the men. A large area of field was roped off with yellow tape.

"I wonder what's going on over there," Sarah said aloud.

"The policemen want to look at the words somebody wrote on the ground," William mumbled through a mouthful of crushed cookie.

"I don't like going over there. It's scary," the little girl said.

"It isn't scary," William corrected. "I told you, Mary, it's just spilled paint."

"Messy red paint. I don't like it. It looks like blood."

"Well, it isn't blood. It's paint. It's messy 'cause Daed said the man did it in a hurry after he set the fire in the barn."

"It's still scary. I'm gonna stay here with Sarah... and the cookies."

Her smile warmed Sarah's heart, and she had to fight the urge to pull the child close and squeeze her tight.

"Daed told us not to go over there, anyhow. He said it was adult business and we should stay away. So I'll keep Sarah company, too...and the cookies."

Sarah reached inside the basket. "Okay. You win. I can't resist your beautiful smiles. You can have another cookie."

After handing them another cookie each, she glanced over again at the men. "William, do you know what words the man wrote in red paint?"

"*Ya,* but they didn't make any sense." He bit his cookie.

"Why don't you tell me? Maybe they'll make sense to me."

"It was only four words. I don't know why everyone is so upset about them."

"What did the words say?"

He swallowed his last bite of cookie and then said, "'Give her to me.'"

Chapter Eleven

Sarah gasped and then, not wanting to upset the children, she pretended to cough. "Well, *danki*. Go play now. Shoo. I have to get these goodies in the house while I still have some left."

She slid across the seat, but before she could attempt to climb out of the buggy, Sam had returned and was standing below her. He took the basket out of her hand and placed it on the ground. Instead of offering his hand, he clasped her waist and lifted her high, as if she were as light as a flower in the breeze. Heat seared her cheeks as the firm touch of his hands on her waist sent her pulse flying. The heat deepened when she stared into his eyes and saw he knew the effect he was having on her.

"Danki," she said when he placed her on the ground. Trying to hide her reaction to his nearness, she glanced over at the men still gathered by the field. "William told me about the words written in the field."

Sam picked up her basket, clasped her right arm with his hand and guided her toward the house. "This is why I became a police officer in the first place. The

Amish people are not accustomed to the evil that exists in the world."

"And you are?"

He stopped midstride and shot a look her way. "Yes, Sarah. I have met evil face-to-face many times. The Amish are my people. I chose to devote my life to protecting them because they are peaceful people who will not protect themselves."

"They depend on God for protection, Samuel. Certainly you do not think you are God?"

The words sounded harsh even to her own ears, and instantly she wished she could recall them. She hadn't meant to be unkind. She was just trying to understand what drove a man who loved God, his family and his people to leave them behind.

Sam's hand tightened on her arm, and his body bristled. The red flush on his throat was the only physical sign that she had hit a nerve, and it had angered him. "No, Sarah, I know I am not God." He gestured toward the field. "But He seems to be a little busy someplace else right now, so I thought I'd give Him a hand."

She knew she couldn't take back what she had said or soften its blow, so she continued walking beside him in silence.

"There they are." Rebecca's voice carried on the air. "See, I told you they were right behind me." Rebecca and Elizabeth peered from the doorway and beckoned them inside.

Sam handed the basket to Elizabeth and spoke to Rebecca. "I'll leave Sarah in your safe hands."

Even though his words were light, Sarah knew Samuel well enough by now to feel the anger emanating from him. He didn't even glance in her direction as he marched off to rejoin the men.

Sarah gazed at his back as he moved farther away, and wished she could rewind the past few minutes and eat her words. Since she couldn't, she followed the other two women into the house and vowed to apologize to him later when they could find a moment or two alone.

But the time never presented itself.

The afternoon slipped into evening in a flurry of activity. Jacob and Rebecca drove the buggy home with Sarah in the second seat while Sam brought up the rear with the lumber wagon.

The next few days fell into a similar pattern. The women cooked all morning, delivered the food to various farms in the afternoons, helped with cleanup and returned early evening just in time to finish their own chores, say their prayers, get some sleep and do it all over again.

Their visit to the Yoder farm had the most impact on Sarah. With her left arm still in a sling, she wasn't able to cradle and rock the Yoders' new infant as the other women did. But she had managed to steal a private moment with the newborn.

Sarah couldn't resist tracing her finger across the silken softness of the baby's cheek, and a smile tugged at the corner of her mouth at the strength of the fisted hold the child had on her finger. She counted the ten perfect little fingers and ten perfect little toes. She watched the tiny lips pucker in a sucking motion as the baby slept. She breathed in the clean, fresh baby-powder scent and, for the first time, longed for the day when she would be hovering over the cradle of her own child.

Almost as if the child she carried could read her mind, Sarah felt a slight stirring, like butterfly wings fluttering in her stomach, and she knew this was her baby moving about, letting her know it wasn't a story a doctor had made up, but that this child was very real and would soon be in her arms.

The thought comforted her—and frightened her, as well. She didn't know the first thing about giving birth or raising a child. And she would have to do it alone, without a husband to help and guide her.

Raising a child would be the most important job she would ever have. She offered a silent prayer that God would be with her each step of the way so she could raise the child in the ways of the Lord—with love and patience, without fear or self-doubt.

"Sarah?"

She spun around at the sound of Sam's voice.

"I'm sorry. I didn't mean to startle you." He stood a few feet from her and held his hat in his hand. He glanced at the baby in the cradle and then looked back at her. It was as if he could look into her mind, into her very soul, and he smiled. "Soon you will have a *boppli* of your own. That is exciting, *ya?*"

His features scrunched up as he studied her, but after a moment, a slight smile teased his lips. "I know life has been hard for you lately, but we will find this man. This will be over soon, and you will be happy again. I promise."

"Only God can promise such things, Samuel." Before he could respond, she raised a hand to stop him. "I apologize for the harshness of my words a few days ago. I did not mean to insult you by implying you thought yourself like God. I do not think such a sinful thing, or think you are prideful."

She softened her voice. "I was just trying to understand why you made the choices you did. And if you ever regretted those choices." She lowered her eyes.

Sam tilted her chin and looked into her face. "I had my reasons for leaving, Sarah. Good reasons. And no... I do not regret the choice I made. I am no longer Amish, and I will never return to this way of life. My time here will end when my job is over."

Sarah's heart clenched. She didn't want to be reminded that he was only here for a short time. She didn't want to imagine how empty her days would be without seeing him at work in the barn or sitting across from her at the dinner table. She didn't want to think what it would be like not to sit beside him in the evenings and count the stars. Not to have him near so they could talk.

So she wouldn't think about it. For now she would pretend that he would always be here—and she'd deal with the pain later, when he left.

"What is so important, Samuel, that you sneak up behind me and startle me to death?"

He grinned. "Rebecca asked me to fetch you. She went to join Jacob in the buggy. They are ready to go home."

"Well, why didn't you say so?" She brushed past him in a huff, unable to hide her annoyance. It wasn't his delay in telling her that Rebecca was waiting for her that bothered her. It was the fact that no matter how much she wanted to or how hard she tried, she couldn't forget that soon Samuel would leave.

Sarah gazed out the window. The skies were gray, and the smell of rain was in the air.

The sun did its best to break through the clouds but was losing the battle. It would be dusk soon, and the men would be coming home, looking for a hot dinner and a good night's rest.

She pressed her face against the windowpane. She should be able to see Samuel from here. He'd told her he wouldn't go far. He needed to help Jacob mend some downed fencing before the worst of the impending storm hit, but the barn obstructed her view.

Samuel had not said anything else about leaving since their discussion a couple of days ago. But the subject hung in the air between them. She knew he saw the sadness in her eyes when she looked at him, but she couldn't help it. He had become a dear and close friend. Why would she be happy about his going?

Sarah was pretty certain that Samuel wasn't happy about going, either. She had seen a deep, pensive expression on his face more than once when he thought she wasn't looking. She knew she wasn't imagining it. Samuel liked her, too. They had become friends.

And friends harbored a fondness for each other.

Friends would miss friends if they parted.

And sometimes…friendships deepened. Feelings grew. If Samuel started having deeper feelings, it might be hard for him to say goodbye. Right? She could only hope…and wait…and pray.

She rubbed her hand against the glass, trying to erase the moisture her warm breath had caused on the cold pane. Still no sight of him. She had to stop acting like a mooning teenager and get downstairs and help Rebecca with dinner.

She noticed that she had more fluid movements these days. She wasn't due to see the doctor again for a couple of days, but she was optimistic about the visit. She knew her body was healing. She didn't tire as easily.

Her pain had lessened, and she was looking forward to getting the sling off her left arm and the bandages off her head. All she wanted to do was soak in a hot bath and shampoo her hair. Who would have thought that the idea of such a small thing promised so much pleasure?

"I was just going to call you." Rebecca, her face flushed from standing over the hot stove, waved her over. "I need to go out to the barn. I forgot to bring in the pickled beets and corn. The bread is rising nicely but needs to be watched. The stew needs to be stirred. Will you please watch the meal? I will be right in."

Sarah gestured for her to stay where she was and grabbed her sweater hanging on the hook by the front door. "You're the cook. Who better to tend the food? I'll fetch what you need."

"Are you sure? It's going to start pouring any minute."

"Yes, I'm sure. I've been looking forward to catching raindrops on my tongue."

Rebecca laughed. "I must be getting old. That thought never entered my mind."

Sarah smiled back. "Do you need anything else while I'm out there?"

"Will you be able to carry more than two Mason jars with just the use of one arm?"

"Of course."

"*Gut,* then please bring me a jar of sliced apples, too."

Sarah nodded and hurried out the door before Rebecca could change her mind. She stopped midway between the house and barn and lifted her face to the sky. Thick, dark clouds were rolling in rapidly. A breeze caught the leaves of the trees and teased the dust of the ground into swirls around her feet.

Maybe spring was one of her favorite seasons. She didn't have any specific memories to draw from so it was only a guess, but she was pretty sure she was right. She loved the smell of freshly cut grass, the flowering buds that poked their heads through the last of the winter's snows, the warmth of the day followed by the chill of evening where she would sit in front of a roaring fire and sip a cup of hot chocolate.

Samuel was right. If she still couldn't recover memories of the past, she could decide what pleased her now and form new memories for the future. Today she decided that spring was definitely her favorite season.

She unlatched the barn door. Before she opened it, a sound caught her attention and made her pause. She looked over her shoulder. Had Jacob and Samuel returned?

She couldn't see anyone, but an inner awareness told her that she wasn't alone.

"Hello. Is anybody there?"

Her words were swallowed up in the impending storm. She squinted her eyes and tried to focus as she let her gaze wander around the yard. Darkness was descending on the farmyard and the first, fat drops of rain began plopping on the ground. She knew she needed to hurry with her task, find the items and get back to the house before Rebecca started to worry. But still she hesitated. Her senses told her she was being watched, even if her eyes didn't see anyone.

"Samuel? Jacob?" she called out as loudly as she could. Nothing but silence.

Apprehension crept up her spine.

Hurriedly, she let herself into the barn. The wind had picked up, and she had to exert all her energy to pull the door shut behind her. She briskly walked to the pantry in the far corner of the barn, opened the doors and started to search the shelves for the items. So much food. Rebecca must have cooked and canned all last summer. She had enough stored in here to feed an army.

But of course, being the bishop, Jacob often had people to the house for a variety of reasons. He likely presided over weddings, counseled those in need, met with the elders of the church and occasionally took his turn conducting church services. Plus, Rebecca had told her that she often delivered food to the sick and shut-ins throughout the year.

Sarah found the beets and corn quickly. It took a few minutes more to find the apples since Rebecca had jars of pears, peaches and a variety of berries, as well. She slipped two of the jars inside her sling and grinned at how she was finding many other uses for this sling besides just holding a useless arm. With the third jar clasped in her right hand, she shoved the pantry door shut with her forearm.

She had turned to go back to the house when the sound of metal upon metal froze her in place. Someone tinkered with the handle of the barn door.

"Hello? Jacob? Samuel?"

Someone was out there. It was probably one of them, but why hadn't they answered when she called?

The barn door swung open, and a man stepped inside. She knew with just one glance that this wasn't anyone who should be here this late in the day. This man's dress was *Englisch*.

A shiver of anxiety shook her from head to toe. Why was a complete stranger standing in their barn in the middle of an impending thunderstorm? Panic made her want to run. Logic and common sense kept her calm and standing in place. There had to be a simple explanation.

The storm! That must be it. Perhaps he was afraid he couldn't outrun the storm, and he wanted someplace safe to wait for it to pass. Or maybe he had lost his way and just wanted directions to town. No reason to panic.

"Can I help you?"

The man didn't reply but, instead, took several strides in her direction. Just as quickly, Sarah stepped back. Something was wrong. This man didn't belong here, and he wasn't answering any of her questions.

Her heart thundered in her chest.

Please God, help me. Is this the man who burned the barns? Who killed Peter and shot me? Has he come to kill me?

"Who are you?" She tried not to reveal her terror, but her voice betrayed her.

The man sprinted forward.

Startled by his actions, Sarah dropped the jar from her hand and cried out. She turned and ran toward the back door of the barn. She had almost reached it when she lost her footing and tumbled onto the barn floor. The impact of her body on the barn floor broke the jars hidden in her sling. Glass sliced her skin. The force of the fall shot fresh pain radiating through her arm and shooting into her shoulder.

Dear Lord, protect my child. Please don't let this man kill me.

Stifling a groan, she rolled onto her back to face her assailant. She wouldn't go easily. She intended to fight for her life—for her child's life.

But it was too late. The stranger loomed over her, and she was unable to get to her feet or run. Something was in his hand, but he moved it too quickly for her to identify it.

Please Lord, don't let it be a gun.

The man raised his hand high and pointed the object at her.

She flung her arm up to protect her face, squeezed her eyes closed and screamed.

Chapter Twelve

Sarah tried to prepare herself for the sound of gunfire and the slamming pain she expected at any moment from bullets entering her body. Still, she refused to give up. She crab walked on her back as quickly as she could in a last-ditch attempt to scurry away from the stranger.

Instead of gunfire, she heard a muffled *oomph.*

Sarah opened her eyes and couldn't believe what she saw. As if caught in a tornado, the stranger was lifted straight up into the air. His body flew several feet to her right and slammed hard into one of the barn's support beams. She leaned up on her elbows for a closer look, but before she could react she felt hands pulling on the back of her arms.

"*Kumm,* Sarah, let me help you." Jacob helped her to her feet. "Are you all right? Did he hurt you?"

Sarah brushed at her clothing. "I'm fine, Jacob. Just scared."

The sound of a strangled scream caught their attention, and both of them hurried toward the stranger.

"*Nee,* Samuel, don't." Jacob tried to pull Sam's hands off the man. Samuel had a fisted hold on some kind of binding around the man's neck and was holding the stranger several inches off the ground by it. The man looked terrified, his face red, eyes bulging, breath coming in gasps.

"Stop, Samuel. Let him go." Jacob tried to insert his body between them. "This is not our way."

With a ferocity that Sarah had never witnessed before, Sam pushed Jacob away and refused to release his hold on the stranger. "I am not one of you. Remember? This is my way, so step back."

Sarah rushed forward and gently placed her hand on Sam's shoulder. "But is it God's way, Samuel?"

Sarah wasn't sure whether it was the truth of her words, the sound of her voice or her touch, but Sam froze. He seemed to struggle for a few minutes with his anger, but gradually gained control. He released the hold on the binding around the man's neck and let him fall to his feet. The stranger doubled at the waist and coughed and gasped for breath.

"Who are you?" Sam loomed over the man. His tone of voice threatened more violence if he didn't receive the answers he wanted.

"Roger... Roger Mathers." The stranger started to reach inside his pocket.

Sam drew his weapon with lightning speed and had it aimed at point-blank range at the man's chest before the gasp left Sarah's lips.

"Don't move," he ordered.

The stranger did as he was told. "I was just going to show you my credentials." His voice trembled.

"Do it slow and easy." Sam's tone of voice and stern expression brooked no hesitation.

Roger pulled out a plastic card with his photograph

and name printed on it. His fingers trembled as he offered it to Sam, who snatched it from his grasp and read it.

"A reporter? I don't believe it." He threw the identification back at the man. It bounced off his chest and landed on the dirt floor. "You're working for a sleazebag tabloid?" Sam muttered something unintelligible under his breath. "What are you doing sneaking around out here?"

"I'm sorry. I didn't mean any harm. Do you know how much money I could get for an exclusive picture? Everyone knows the Amish don't like their pictures taken. But a picture like this one…" He hung his head. "My wife's sick. I need the money."

For the first time, Sarah took a good look at the man. She saw the camera hanging from a thick cord at his neck. That's what he'd pointed at her—a camera, not a gun. A wave of relief flowed over her. She noted the bright red marks on the man's neck from the camera strap and felt sorry for him. "What is wrong with your wife?"

"She needs an operation." He looked hopeful. "Just one picture would guarantee that for me."

Sam grabbed the man and slammed him back against the wood. "Knock it off, Mathers. Stop trying to play on her sympathies, you creep. You don't have a sick wife. Tell them the truth." He knocked him back again. "Tell them."

"Okay!" He raised his hands. "So I don't have a wife. So what? Get your hands off me before I press charges."

"Call the sheriff. Go for it. I'd love to see what happens when a trespasser calls in to report his own crime."

Mathers's face contorted into an angry grimace, and he swatted Sam's hands away.

Sarah's mouth fell open. No wife? No operation? How could a person lie so convincingly? Worse, how much evil had Samuel witnessed that he would recognize it so quickly and easily?

Jacob had remained silent through it all, but now Sarah heard low murmured prayers behind her. Apparently, Jacob was uncomfortable in the presence of evil, too.

"How did you find her?" Sam folded his arms over his chest and returned the glare.

"Easy." He moved his hand toward his inside coat pocket, waited for Sam to nod permission and pulled out a folded paper. "The dry-goods store sells these church directories."

Sam took the paper from his hand and looked it over, then he glanced at Jacob. "Why didn't you tell me about this? This paper not only has all the names and addresses of everyone in the community, but it also has a map to each farm."

Jacob blinked and looked confused. "Of course. Many Amish communities publish this information. We do not want anyone who wishes to attend a church service to get lost or to forget who is having the service that particular week." Jacob looked puzzled. "Have you been gone so long, Samuel, that you forgot something as common and simple as this?"

A flush of red crept up Sam's neck. Instead of responding to Jacob, he grabbed Mathers by his coat collar and shoved him toward the door. "Get out of here. Don't set foot on this property again, or you'll get more than my hands on you. I guarantee I'll be the one calling the sheriff. You'll have a one-way handcuffed trip to jail for trespassing on private property."

Without a backward glance, Mathers ran out of the barn.

Sam watched Mathers's back. Not because he wanted to make sure the man was gone. Like the cockroach he was, he knew the man would scurry into the night. No, he needed the few precious moments to gain control of his emotions before he could turn and face Sarah.

The sound of her screams still echoed in his head. His heart hammered in his chest. Adrenaline raced through his blood.

"What's going on? Who was that man?" Rebecca, her coat flapping open and her *kapp* askew, rushed into the barn. "Is everything all right? I came out to check when Sarah hadn't returned."

Jacob slid his arm over Rebecca's shoulders and pulled her close. "*Ya,* everything is as it should be. We are all fine and hungry. Ain't so, Samuel?"

Sam didn't respond. Instead, he turned toward Sarah. He knew he shouldn't, but he couldn't stop himself. As if in a slow-motion movie, he reached out and drew her to him. His arms encircled her waist. He felt her cheek press against his chest. With his left hand, he cradled the top of her head against him.

"Sarah…" It was all he could say—and it said everything. The anguish, the fear, the concern. His emotions coated his words, and there was no hiding the feelings behind them.

Rebecca gasped at the sight of the sudden intimacy.

"Samuel." Jacob's voice was firm and censuring.

Sam couldn't process Jacob's words or his tone. All

he could think about was how close he'd come to losing her—again.

"When I saw that man standing over you, it was like a switch went off inside of me, and all I felt was rage." Samuel loosened his hold enough to let her move a step back. "Not just for the threat he presented. But mostly at myself, I think, because I let you down again."

"Shh." Sarah placed her fingertips on his lips and looked into his eyes. "You did not let me down, Samuel. You saved me."

The shimmering in her brilliant blue eyes and the smile on her perfectly shaped lips clenched his heart as tightly as if it were squeezed in an iron fist. He was developing feelings for this woman. He couldn't deny it anymore to anyone, not even himself.

But he couldn't let it continue.

He was her bodyguard. Her protector. He had to keep his emotions in check, his mind sharp so he'd be able to do the job. There was a definite, though invisible, line drawn between every bodyguard and victim, a line he couldn't cross. Not now. Not ever.

And in Sarah's case, it was more than a line. It was a canyon-size gorge, impossible to bridge. She was a pregnant, vulnerable *Amish* widow. He was an *Englischer* who would return to a world that held no place for the sweetness or softness of Sarah. Whether he harbored feelings for her was no longer the question. He did. But if he didn't want to hurt her, he had to bury those feelings. Permanently. Right now.

"Samuel!" This time Jacob's voice demanded attention. When Sam looked at him, he said, "Rebecca can tend to Sarah. We should go into the house and clean up for dinner."

Their eyes met. Jacob's gaze was stern, clearly showing displeasure in the inappropriate affection Sam had just shown Sarah. Sam's eyes held both shame for dishonoring these kind people, as well as challenge that he wasn't able to express his heart.

It was Rebecca's gaze that made him feel guilt and hang his head. She looked shocked and disappointed and wary…as if a trust had been broken. And it had.

"Kumm." Rebecca rushed past him to Sarah's side. "I don't know what happened, but you can tell me all about it while we get dinner on the table."

Sarah glanced down at her soiled sling and dress. "I'm so sorry, Rebecca. I broke the Mason jars when I fell."

"Were you hurt?"

"I banged my shoulder pretty hard." She grinned humorously. "Just when the pain went away, now it is back again."

"Let's go inside. We'll get you in dry clothes and make sure you didn't do more damage to yourself. It is a good thing you are scheduled to see Dr. Clark in the morning. He will fix you up good as new."

"But the vegetables…"

"It doesn't matter. We have more. Jacob, please bring in some corn and beets." Wrapping her arm around Sarah's shoulders, she ushered her toward the house, but not before shooting a warning glance at Sam that said it all.

Stand back. Keep away. She belongs to us, not you.

And she was right.

Jacob didn't say anything. He didn't have to. He handed Sam a Mason jar, clapped his hand a couple of times on his back as though consoling him, and then the two men walked in silence to the house.

* * *

The following morning Sam offered his hand to Rebecca and helped her out of the back of the car. He wished he'd been able to be the driver that morning when he'd accompanied the women to see Dr. Clark. It would have made the trip go faster and less stressful.

He was sure his cover had been blown, anyway. News travels quickly in an Amish community, and he could tell from the nods and glances sent his way that everyone knew by now who and what he was. It also stood to reason that the stranger in town who'd been seeking Sarah and the "man protecting her" had a pretty good idea that he was a cop and not an Amish farmer.

But undercover meant *undercover*. Until they were certain his cover was no longer in place, he had to act as if it were.

So he had climbed into the backseat and let one of the other police officers act as driver today. He'd been smart and had made sure to sit between the door and Rebecca, setting himself an acceptable distance from Sarah. He had no desire to endure another day of sharp, disapproving glances from Rebecca as he had through dinner last night. It seemed to work. The less attention he gave Sarah, the more Rebecca relaxed.

Once Rebecca exited, he turned to offer a hand to Sarah. He kept his face an unreadable mask. He was certain no one could see in his expression just how lovely he thought Sarah's blond hair looked now that the bandages had been removed from her head. Even tucked beneath her white *kapp,* enough errant strands escaped to glisten like gold and make his fingers itch to see if it felt as silky as it looked.

He didn't allow a smile to cross his lips when, free

of the sling she no longer had to wear, she stretched her left arm across the back of the seat.

And he was particularly careful to keep any tenderness out of his eyes when he noted how her dress stretched across the growing swell of her body as she scooted across the seat.

"*Danki,* Samuel." She smiled that beautiful, sweet smile of hers and he thought he'd melt at her feet. Before he made a fool of himself, she turned away.

Jacob met them in the yard with a horse already hitched to a wagon and waiting.

"Are we going to Nathan Yoder's house now?" Sarah asked when she saw him. "It's our day to help with the *boppli* and the housework, isn't it?"

"*Nee,* it is my day to help," Rebecca replied. "You had a long trip back and forth to the city today. You heard what the doctor said. You are healing nicely and getting stronger, but you need more rest. He does not want you to overdo it."

"But…"

"You can be helpful without coming with me."

Sarah gave her a questioning look.

"It would be *wunderbaar* to come home to a hot meal. I have a pot of stew that needs tending."

"That is not much of a chore, Rebecca, to stir a pot of stew every now and then."

"Your job today is to rest. You can work your fingers to the bone tomorrow."

Jacob finished loading the back of the wagon with supplies. "*Ya,* Sarah. I would appreciate a hot bowl of stew when I finish the repairs on Nathan's barn. I understand that, to you, it does not seem like much of a chore.

To us, it is a task we hope you will do well because we will be looking forward to the rewards all day."

The small group laughed. Sarah nodded and threw up her hands in surrender. "Okay, Jacob. I will stir the stew."

"Danki." Jacob helped Rebecca into the wagon.

Sarah watched them pull away. "Be sure to kiss the *boppli* for me," she yelled as the wagon moved down the lane. Her words were answered with a wave from both of them.

"Should we go into the house?" Sam stood near the porch steps and waited.

"Nee, Samuel. I need you to prepare the buggy for me. I'm going into town."

Sam frowned at her but refrained from offering what he knew would be a useless argument. When Sarah set her mind on something, she was not easily swayed from doing it.

"Where are we going?" he asked.

Sarah opened her mouth to speak and then shut it. "I don't suppose I could convince you to stay behind?"

Sam scowled.

"I didn't think so. We're going into town. A hot, steamy stew should be accompanied by a hot, sweet dessert. I found a wonderful recipe in a cookbook I was looking at the other day. I want to try it, but Rebecca does not have all the necessary ingredients."

"Dessert. Ah, you found my soft spot. I'll have the horse hitched up in no time."

"Good. But we must hurry. I need to get back in plenty of time to tend the stew and make the dessert."

They rode in companionable silence for a good part of the journey. The brisk morning air kissed her cheeks, but she enjoyed the feel of the fresh breeze against her skin. The billowing, uncut grass in the meadows and the bare tree branches rapidly being clothed with green leaves made her smile. She thanked God for such a beautiful day.

"Are you going to give me a hint about what kind of dessert you'll be making?" Sam grinned at her.

"Nee."

"No? You'd really torture me like that? I'm sitting here thinking up one thing after another, each one better than before, and my stomach is growling. Can't you hear it?"

"I won't tell you, but you can try to guess."

He laughed, and the deep rumble in his throat made Sarah's smile widen.

"A homemade cherry pie," he guessed.

"Nee."

"No? Then pumpkin. Or sweet potato, maybe."

"Not even close."

"Apples. You're making crisp apple strudel or baked apples and cream."

Sarah shook her head.

"Give me a hint."

"We are not shopping for fruit, Samuel. Rebecca has more than enough. I need chocolate and heavy cream and marshmallows and—"

Before she could finish, Sam grabbed at his chest as if he was having a heart attack. "Oh, you're killing me. I love chocolate. I am a chocolate fool. It's my deep, dark secret that I can be easily manipulated with just the promise of chocolate."

Sarah giggled at the silliness of their game. But then Samuel always brought a smile to her face, made her feel happy and content, sometimes by doing nothing more than walking through a door.

Suddenly, their horse flung her head in the air and moved slightly right and then left.

Sam stopped the teasing banter and turned his attention to the horse. He tightened his grip on the reins and spoke to the mare. "Easy, girl. Take it easy."

The horse tossed its head again and whinnied.

"Something is spooking her." Sarah checked both the road ahead and the landscape. "I don't see anything that should be frightening her."

Sam pulled back on the reins and continued speaking in a calm, soothing voice. "Whoa, girl. Quiet down. You're okay." He slowed the mare from a brisk trot to a steady walk.

Within seconds, the roar of a car engine sounded behind them.

"What the…" Sam threw a glance over his shoulder and then turned back to soothe the horse, who grew more agitated as the car approached.

"That car is going awfully fast." Sarah clasped the frame of the window and leaned her head out for a closer look. "But Molly shouldn't be scared. She's used to cars on the road."

The driver of the car revved the engine and sped even faster toward them.

"This one isn't operating like the normal drivers Molly is used to," Sam said. "No wonder she's spooked. The fool shouldn't be speeding on a country road like this. It's dangerous." Samuel edged the mare to the side of the road, being sure to leave plenty of space for the car to pass, and then brought the buggy to a stop. "Let's wait and let him go by."

Within seconds the car flew past. His tires spewed an arc of gravel and dust. Samuel ducked as he was pummeled with the spray. Although Sarah couldn't hear the words he muttered under his breath, she was certain he wasn't happy.

Once the car passed, Sam made a clicking sound with his mouth, bounced the reins and eased Molly and the buggy back onto the lane. They'd gone only a few dozen yards when Molly stopped dead in her tracks and whinnied loudly.

One look told Sarah all she needed to know. "Samuel." Her blood froze in her veins. She tried to keep the anxiety out of her voice when she spoke. "He's coming back. Why would he be coming back?"

Sam didn't answer. By now he had done all he could do to control the frightened horse. Again he moved them to the shoulder of the road, and again the car rushed past at a dangerous, accelerated speed, veering toward them like a bull charging a matador.

"Did you see the driver?" Sam asked. The set of his square jaw and a grim frown on his face revealed his own tension regarding this strange and unforeseen situation. "Could it be teenagers playing a dangerous prank?"

"I don't think so, Samuel." Sarah strained her neck to see behind them. "I'm certain I only saw one man in the car."

Within seconds the car came back—faster, closer, more threatening. This time the side of the car actually scraped against the buggy. Molly whinnied, pawed the earth and tried to run to the right. Samuel struggled to keep control of the terrified animal. While he fought with the reins, he yelled, "Get my cell phone out of my pocket. Hurry!"

Sarah didn't hesitate. She scooted over as close as she could get, allowed her hand to slide across the warmth of his chest until she located the small cell phone tucked in the pocket of his shirt. She withdrew it immediately and held it in an outstretched palm.

Once Molly had calmed, Sam chanced loosening his grip on the reins and grabbed the phone out of her hand. Within seconds he had called his sergeant, given their location and asked for immediate backup.

But the call was too late.

Sarah watched in horror, unable to believe her eyes. The car crested the rise and increased its speed until it seemed to be flying. Sarah clutched his sleeve and pointed. "Samuel, look. He's driving right at us!"

Already pulled as far off the road as possible, Samuel had nowhere else to go. The car was to their left and closing the distance between them. The horse, against the fence to their right, whinnied in fear. She reared to her hind legs in panic.

"Get out!" Samuel yelled and pushed hard. She fell between the buggy and the fence.

The horse reared to her hind legs. Seconds later the car smashed into the buggy. Sam flew through the air and landed with such force, he momentarily blacked out.

When he opened his eyes, he pulled himself to a sitting position. He grabbed his head in an attempt to stop the waves of pain and dizziness trying to claim him. Taking a deep breath, he dared to look at the carnage. His brain didn't seem to want to register what he saw. Pieces of buggy were strewn all over the road and well into the fields on both sides of the lane. The car, although it must have sustained considerable damage, had managed to drive off and was out of sight.

Sam scrambled to his feet, stumbling and half running toward the fence. He stopped abruptly when he was only a few steps away, an expression of relief on his face which was immediately replaced by one of anxiety.

Tears streamed down Sarah's face.

"Sarah? Are you all right?" He stepped closer but didn't touch her.

Sarah laughed uncontrollably and she could see by Sam's expression that he didn't know what to make of it but she couldn't stop. Her anxiety level was high and the laughter seemed to be her body's way of coping.

"Look!" Sarah pointed toward Molly, and a fresh wave of giggles erupted from her. "Molly is ready to take us home."

Sam looked in the direction she pointed. The horse stood docilely by, still in harness. The remnants of what was left of the front seat of the buggy were wrapped in the reins. To a passerby, it would look like the horse forgot the buggy altogether and waited for her master to take their seats so she could pull them home.

Sarah took a second glance at him and came to his side instantly. "You're hurt."

"It's just a scratch."

She probed his wound. The soft, feathery touch of her fingers against the heat of his skin was almost his undoing. He clasped her wrist and stilled her hand.

Their eyes locked. Sam thought he would never be able to pull his gaze away from the glistening blue pools staring back at him. Her lips were slightly parted and only a breath out of reach—and he wanted to reach, to taste, to lose himself in a stolen, forbidden kiss.

"Samuel?" The whisper of his name on her lips brought him back to sanity. He was her bodyguard, her protector, and he couldn't let himself pretend or even hope for one moment that he could be anything else.

"It's just a bump." The huskiness in his voice made a lie of his sudden aloofness. But still, he had to try. "How about you? Are you okay? Are you hurt?"

Sarah stared hard at him, searching his face for something, an answer to an unasked question that hung in the air between them. Slowly she smiled—a sad smile, an understanding smile—and she withdrew her wrist from his grasp.

"I'm fine," she whispered.

He knew she didn't understand his emotional withdrawal, and a deep, clenching pain seized his heart with the knowledge that he was causing her pain. But he had a job to do—and a different world to go home to.

Turning away, Sarah crossed the few feet to her horse and lovingly stroked the mare's neck. "Good girl, Molly." She ran her hand along the animal's back and crouched down to run her fingers over all four legs. When she seemed satisfied that Molly was uninjured, she looked over her shoulder at him.

"Why, Samuel?" Her face still wet with tears, her laughter faded to hiccuping breaths. "Poor Molly could have been hurt or worse. We could have been killed. Why would anyone do such a careless thing?"

"It was not careless, Sarah. It was deliberate and premeditated. Just like the shooting in the schoolhouse. Just like the fires on the farms."

He withdrew his gun from his shoulder holster.

"What are you doing?" Sarah looked at the weapon in his hand as if he held a poisonous snake.

"I won't be caught unprepared again. I never should have agreed to Jacob's terms. I will no longer carry an empty gun for fear of offending Amish sensibilities."

"No, Samuel, please. There must be another way." She choked and had difficulty forcing out her words.

The pain on her face seized his heart and made it difficult for him to draw a breath. Right now he hated himself for what he knew she must be thinking of him. She was seeing a side of him she'd heard about, knew existed, but until now hadn't seen.

She straightened and stared hard at him.

"Violence is never the Amish way, Samuel."

He broke his gaze away from her pleading eyes and slammed the clip into the base of the weapon.

"I've told you before, Sarah. I am not Amish. Not anymore. Not ever again."

Chapter Thirteen

Captain Rogers offered Sam a cup of hot coffee. Sam was pretty sure it had been the captain's coffee, but he accepted it gratefully.

"That's a pretty good knot on your forehead. Maybe you should get it checked out. I can put someone else on Sarah's protection detail until you get back."

Sam glanced across the dozen yards that separated him from Sarah. Past the local police and state trooper cars. Past the flashing strobe lights. Finally resting on the ambulance that had pulled up a short time ago.

He could see Sarah sitting in the back as the paramedics checked her out. He'd done a cursory check of her before they'd arrived, and other than suffering a few bumps and bruises from being thrown out of the buggy, she appeared physically fine.

Emotionally, however? She hadn't spoken a word to him since he'd loaded his weapon, and he couldn't help but wonder if she ever would again.

He couldn't erase the memory of the look on Sarah's face. For the first time since they'd met, the reality of what he did for a living had seemed to come crashing down on her. She'd seen him in cop mode, gun in hand, ready to kill—and her look of horror pierced his soul.

"Sam? Did you hear me? Are you okay?"

"Yes, Captain. I heard you and I'm fine. No need to replace me. Thanks."

"Did you see who did it?"

"No. It happened too fast, and I needed to focus my attention on controlling the horse. I couldn't get a license plate number. It was a dark blue sedan. Didn't look like a foreign model, and probably wasn't more than a year or two old. What I am sure about is that the perp held pedal to the metal. This was deliberate." He dumped out what was left in his cup. "Sarah confirmed that it was a sole driver."

Captain Rogers nodded. "Luckily I'd driven up from the city this morning to take a look at the situation for myself. I was with the sheriff when the call came in. We set up roadblocks the second you called it in. He put out a BOLO for any car in the area with body damage, but so far it hasn't turned up anything."

"We both know it was our guy."

Rogers planted his hands on his hips. The scowl on his face as he stared out over the accident scene said it all.

"He's leaving bodies in his wake, and we can't touch him." His superior scratched his head. "He burned down five local barns in one night. He attacked the two of you on the road. And he's still a ghost. No name. No picture. No leads." He rubbed a hand across his face. "He's a cocky character. Always one step ahead of us. No question he knows we've got state troopers, local police and undercover officers in place. Nothing deters him. He's fearless."

"We'll see how fearless he is once I get my hands on him."

"Is that your brain talking, King, or your emotions?" Captain Rodgers clapped a hand on Sam's shoulder. "You've got to keep your wits about you if you're going to catch this guy. He's smart, Sam…and deadly."

"You think?" Sam laughed mirthlessly. "He administered an almost lethal dose of potassium to Sarah right under my nose. He killed the relief cop guarding her door. He killed my partner. You think I don't know the evil I'm dealing with?"

Captain Rogers returned a hard, steady gaze. "Evil, huh? You know, I've never discussed your religious beliefs with you before, Sam. But this time you might be right. If we are dealing with evil personified, it wouldn't hurt if you took a moment and had a conversation with the man upstairs. We sure could use some help on this one."

Rogers walked back to join the sheriff just as Jacob and Rebecca's buggy pulled up.

The two of them spoke briefly to one of the officers, and then Rebecca raced to the back of the ambulance. After another short conversation with the paramedics, Rebecca wrapped her arm around Sarah and ushered her to their buggy. Before she climbed on board, Sarah threw a glance over her shoulder and her gaze locked with his. Without a word, she climbed into the buggy.

Jacob followed her gaze, spotted Sam and walked over to where he stood.

"You've been hurt."

"It's nothing."

The man studied his face, looked as if he was going

to argue that statement and then decided to keep his counsel.

"Please, can you take Sarah home? She's been through a lot and must be exhausted." When Jacob turned to go, Sam clasped his arm. "Make sure you ask the sheriff to send one of his men with you until I finish up here and can get back. And Jacob, keep Sarah inside the house. Period."

Jacob nodded and walked briskly back to the buggy. A police cruiser, lights flashing, pulled out and slowly followed the buggy as it turned and headed back the way it had come.

Sam stood at the side of the lane and watched until they disappeared over the rise. He couldn't erase the memory of what he'd seen in Sarah's eyes when she looked across the distance between them. He saw confusion and shock. He saw vulnerability and fear and sadness. And he saw something else he couldn't quite identify.

Please, Lord, don't let it be disgust.

Sam hung his head. For the first time in over a decade, he wished he wasn't a cop.

Captain Rogers arranged for additional men on the property. Jacob and Rebecca bristled beneath the added police presence. Jacob felt their agreement had been breached. Sam was the only officer who was supposed to be on his property, and Jacob didn't like the betrayal. But at least they were trying to make the best of the situation. Rebecca invited the officers to join them for dinner. Jacob treated his guests with the hospitality of the Amish. The officers sensed the polite but distant ambience of their hosts, and nobody at the table was happy right now.

Rebecca offered a platter of fried chicken to one of the men. "Would you like some more, Officer Jenkins?"

The man smiled and raised a hand in a halting motion. "No, ma'am. I couldn't eat one more bite. Everything was delicious. Thank you for the invitation."

"A man needs to eat." Jacob glanced at his guest. "I wouldn't want you to go away hungry."

The officer hid his chuckle in a napkin. Jacob did little to hide how much he hoped the officers would be getting ready to leave.

Both men stood up. "Thank you again for your hospitality. We'll be sitting outside in our squad cars if you need us. Just call."

The other man, Officer Muldoon, gave a curt nod in agreement with that statement and reached out to grab a chicken leg off the platter. "I'm gonna save this piece for later, if you don't mind." He raised it in the air as he backed toward the door. "I can't remember ever eating chicken so good."

"Will you be staying all night?" Jacob scowled at the men.

"Yes, sir. Our replacements will be here first thing in the morning."

"You can't sit in the car all night." Jacob's gruff tone caught everyone's attention. He placed his napkin on the table and rose. "*Kumm,* I will make a place for you in the barn. I have an oil burner. It will be warm."

"Thank you, sir. That would be much appreciated." They stood and followed Jacob out to the barn.

When the men left, the silence around the kitchen table became stifling. Sam glanced back and forth between Rebecca and Sarah. When neither woman spoke, he turned his attention to his meal. Although the aroma of fried chicken mingled in the air with the scent of cinnamon atop baked apples, Sam found no enjoyment in the dinner. It was simply fuel that his body needed. When he was finished, he thanked them and walked out of the room.

He grabbed a hurricane lamp and stepped out on the porch. Placing the lamp on the table, he sat down in one of the rockers and stared into the darkness.

Waves of pain washed over him as memories of days past entwined with the emotions of today's events. Pieces of buggy scattered and strewn in multiple directions. The sound of screams in the stillness of the night. A frightened whinny of a horse. A racing, reckless driver making stupid, irresponsible, dangerous choices. The sight of blood and lifeless bodies crumpled beneath wreckage as he scrambled through the carnage, begging and praying for survivors, only to find none.

His breath came in short, shallow gasps. Faces, sounds and sights raced through his mind.

He hadn't allowed himself to go to this deep, dark place for more than a decade. But here it was again. As though it had just happened, the pain fresh and intense.

He couldn't take it anymore. He bowed his head, cupped his face in his hands and sobbed.

Sarah helped Rebecca clear the table. She washed the dishes while Rebecca dried and put them away. Rebecca tried to maintain idle chatter, and when she realized Sarah was in no mood to talk—not about what to make for dinner tomorrow or even about how well Nathan's wife was recovering from her injury, and definitely not about the horrible events of the day—she finished her chores in silence.

Sarah couldn't think of anything but the day's events and the haunted look she saw in Samuel's eyes every time he looked at her. What had she done wrong? She knew she shouldn't have tried to stop him from loading his gun. He was a police officer, and that was a huge component of his job. But had that been enough to cause the anger and pain she saw in his eyes?

Still, she couldn't shake the way he had looked at her. Something was terribly wrong.

Once the chores were complete, Rebecca shooed Sarah into the living room. She told her to go sit in front of the fire. She'd make them a kettle of tea as soon as she was finished washing the floor.

Sarah left the kitchen but she didn't sit by the fire. Instead, she donned her sweater and slipped outside to find Samuel. She didn't have to go far. As soon as she stepped outside, she saw him sitting on the far end of the porch. He was hunched over, his face covered with his hands. She couldn't be sure, but from the muffled sounds she heard and the shaking of his shoulders, she thought he might be crying.

"Samuel?" She hurried to his side and placed a comforting hand on his back.

Sam startled at her touch. He jumped up from the rocker, dragged his forearm over his face and turned away.

"What are you doing out here? You should be resting."

She heard the catch in his voice, witnessed the effort it took him to regain control. She waited for a moment before speaking. "Can I help?"

He drew in a deep breath. Slowly, he turned to face her. "I'm sorry. I lost control for a moment, but I'm okay now. Truly, Sarah, go inside and go to bed. You need to rest, if not for yourself, then at least for your *boppli*."

He stayed in the shadows, and she couldn't see his face.

"Are you upset with me? I'm sorry I tried to stop you…"

"This has nothing to do with you, Sarah. Now please, go inside."

She stepped closer. So close they were both swallowed in the shadows cast by the hurricane lamp. She touched his arm. "Talk to me, Samuel. Tell me what torments you so."

For a moment, she didn't think he was going to answer her. When he did, his voice was gruff and harsh.

"It happened a long time ago. More than ten years now. Today stirred up those memories." He made a gruff sound. "Like I told you before, Sarah, memories are not always good things to have."

"Talk to me." She ran her hand down his arm and clutched his hand. "You have been such a good friend to me. Let me be a friend to you." She moved closer still, watching the kerosene light play across his features. "Tell me of this thing that troubles your soul."

He stepped into the light, and she was taken aback by the terrible pain she saw in his eyes. His expression reflected his indecision about whether he was going to talk to her about it. When he finally spoke, his words tumbled out with the force of a breaking dam.

Sarah never removed her hand from his. She smiled gently, encouragingly, and listened—until she thought her heart would break under the weight of his words.

"I was seventeen when I experienced the worst day

of my life. Thanks to *rumspringe,* most of the restrictions my *daed* had enforced in my life were lifted. He turned a blind eye to the radio I'd sneak into the buggy when I'd take it to town. He'd pretend he didn't hear when I'd play music in my room and sing at the top of my lungs. When I'd had a few sips of beer that one of my *Englisch* friends had given me, I knew he smelled the alcohol on my breath. He scowled, his expression telling me he didn't approve, but he kept silent."

Sam turned his face away and stared into the darkness, but not before Sarah saw a tear trace its way down his cheek.

"But the one thing he wouldn't budge on was my curfew."

Sarah remained still, afraid to move, even breathe. She felt as if she was standing on the edge of a deep, dark crevice, and knew that whatever Sam was about to tell her had been buried for a very long time and had cut deep.

"I disobeyed the curfew. I didn't want to lose face with my friends. I was afraid they might taunt me for running home to Daed." He looked at her, and the pain she saw in his eyes seared her soul. "Friends? I can't even tell you the name of one of those boys today. Yet on that night they were more important to me than my father...or his rules."

Her eyes filled with tears. She wasn't even sure why. She just knew Sam was suffering, and there was nothing she could do to help him—except stay strong and silent and listen as he spoke about this thing, maybe for the very first time.

Sam's voice seemed wooden, his tone flat, empty. He stared off into the darkness. He might be standing here on the porch in front of her, but his spirit was gone—to another place, another time.

"It was dusk. Dark enough to trigger the streetlamps along the main street in town, but still light enough to recognize my father's buggy. I can still remember seeing him snap the reins when he saw me standing outside the local general store with my friends. Our horse fell into a trot, and the buggy headed in my direction.

"Some of my friends recognized my father's buggy, too. A few of the *Englisch* teens we were with had been drinking. They thought it was funny that my *daed* was out looking for me. They teased me, taunted me. When I didn't respond, they decided it might be more fun to taunt my father. They jumped in their car, revved their engines and drove down the street toward him."

Sarah's heart seized. She relived today's sound of an engine revving and the fear of watching a car swoop past their buggy. Her pulse pounded in her ears with fear as she remembered how hard Sam had fought to control the panicked horse. Suddenly present and past converged, and Sarah understood Sam's pain.

Today's incident had opened a portal into Sam's past, and everything he'd experienced came flooding back. She wanted to silence him. She wanted to pull him away from what she knew would be ugly, hurtful memories. But it was too late. Sam was already standing in front of that general store, watching a car full of drunken teens descend upon his father.

"I didn't even know those boys. They were friends of a friend. Mere acquaintances. Older than me and the boys I was with." Sam rubbed his hand over his face. "They'd been drinking, and it affected their driving. They didn't mean to hit him. They thought it would be fun to scare him a little. But they were driving too fast and they lost control...."

Sam's words faded away, but it didn't matter. Sarah was with him now, standing beside the teenage Sam as he apprehensively watched his father approach, feeling the panic when he saw the car driving too fast and too close to the buggy. She held her breath and tightened her hold on his hand. She needed him to tell her the rest—and simultaneously wished he wouldn't.

"My father wasn't the only passenger in the buggy that night. My *maam* was with him. I didn't know it at first. I didn't know until after the buggy shattered into a million pieces, and I found their bodies in the rubble."

Sam looked at her. Flickers of lamplight danced across his face, but not even the shadows of the night could hide his tortured expression. "My mother was dead when I reached her. God was merciful. She died upon impact and didn't linger or suffer. My *daed*... his back was broken, his legs twisted at an odd angle beneath him, his breathing shallow and difficult. I remember he stayed awake and alert for a long time. Long enough for the police to arrive. Long enough for the paramedics to confirm my mother was dead.

"He held tight to my hand, and he kept saying the same words over and over again. I heard the words but they didn't really register...not then...not for years to come."

Sam drew his hand out of her grasp and ran his index finger softly down her cheek. His voice fell into a whisper. "My *daed* kept saying, 'I love you, son. Do not blame yourself. It was an accident.'" Sam's eyes glistened with fresh tears. "Isn't that the Amish way? To forgive the person who sinned against you?"

Sam stared off into space for several minutes before he spoke again, but when he did his words carried the pain and guilt of a young, frightened teenage boy who'd been unable to face his past.

"How could he do that, Sarah? Forgive? I killed my own family. Even God will never be able to forgive me."

Chapter Fourteen

"Hush, Samuel, don't say such a thing." Sarah wrapped her arms around him and pulled him close. "God knows our hearts. He can forgive us anything if we ask." She released her hold and cupped his face with her hands. "It is a terrible thing that happened that night. Terrible. But I agree with your father. It wasn't your fault."

"I broke curfew."

"*Ya,* just like hundreds of other teenagers trying to find their own way in this world. That's all you did."

"If I hadn't broken curfew, my parents would not have been in that buggy looking for me."

Sarah smiled tenderly at him. "Ah, Samuel, that is the hurt child inside of you speaking now. The man who stands in front of me knows that we do not have control over other people. Everyone made their own choices that evening. Your *dat* to search for you. Your *maam* to go with him. Those boys to drink and then drive recklessly."

She let her fingers trace a path down his cheek. "It would be prideful and foolish to think that we have power over other people, over life. Only God can claim that right, *ya?*"

"God?" Samuel scoffed. "Where was God that night? He allowed it. How could He permit such a terrible thing?"

"It is not our place to question God's plan. We do not know why He allows these things or how they affect His plan for our lives." The gentleness in Sarah's voice soothed him. "God never promised us that bad things wouldn't happen, Samuel. Just the opposite. The Bible tells us we will suffer many trials in this life. We only know He promises to be at our side to help us through when bad things do happen, and that somehow, in time, He makes all things work out for good."

"How is watching the murder of my parents a good thing? What good came of their deaths?"

Sarah folded her hands in front of her and smiled softly into his face. "I don't know. No more than I understand why Peter was killed or why my memory was erased. I don't understand why my neighbors are being punished because I am still alive. And, *ya,* I know how guilt can creep up on you and make you think that everything is your fault. But aren't you the one who told me everything that is happening now is not my fault? Did I shoot my husband? Terrorize the children in the school? Burn down my neighbors' barns?"

"No, of course not."

Sarah's smiled widened. "You're right. I am not responsible." She waited a heartbeat to allow her logic to penetrate his pain. "And you are not responsible for the tragedy that befell your family."

"You make it sound so easy."

"Easy? *Nee.* Suffering through trials is never easy.

Simple? *Ya.* Put your faith in God, Samuel. Trust Him to run the world. He's been doing it for a very long time."

"How did you ever get to be so smart?"

"I don't know. I can't remember."

Sam laughed at her attempt at a joke, and Sarah joined in. When the moment passed, he drew her close. "Thank you." He wrapped one of the ties of her *kapp* around his finger. "I haven't spoken to anyone about that night. I thought I had dealt with it and buried it long ago. But today…I found myself reliving everything."

Sarah smiled up at him. "I'm glad I could be here for you."

His expression sobered. "I've never had anyone be there for me." He drew her close. His lips hovered inches above hers.

Sarah's pulse raced like birds taking flight, and a delightful shiver danced along her spine. She held her breath in anticipation. She didn't need to wait long.

When Sam lowered his head toward hers, he ignited feelings inside that she could no longer deny. She loved the feel of his breath as it whispered across her skin. She loved the softness and taste of his mouth as he claimed hers in a tender kiss. She loved the warmth and strength of his arms wrapped around her, holding her close, close enough that when she slid her hand along his shirt, she could feel the beating of his heart against her palm. She loved—

A bright light shone in their faces. Instinctively, they broke apart. Sarah raised a hand to shield her eyes.

"Um, sorry. I saw Mrs. Lapp come out onto the porch." The officer lowered his flashlight. "I didn't see you, Detective King. I thought she was alone, and when she disappeared into the shadows… Well, um, I thought I should check and make sure she was okay."

Even in the dim light from the kerosene lamp, Sarah could see a deep red flush on Sam's neck.

"You did the right thing, Officer." Sam stepped forward. "But, as you can see, Mrs. Lapp is unharmed."

The officer glanced back and forth between them. "Well, okay then." He gestured with his flashlight over his shoulder. "I'll just head back to the barn." He took a few more steps away. "And please thank Jacob for us again, Mrs. Lapp. The spring nights are still pretty cool, and that heater made it real comfortable in there."

Sarah watched him walk back to the barn. When he disappeared, she chanced a demure glance toward Sam. Suddenly, she felt awkward and unsure of herself—of them. What had really happened between them tonight? Had it been a simple kiss? An expression of gratitude when his emotions were running high? Or could it be something more? Could he be drawn to her as powerfully as she was to him? Could their friendship be turning into something deeper, something lasting, something that gave her hope for their future?

But she didn't find the answers she sought. His expression was inscrutable. There was no lingering sign of the tears he'd shed for his family. No warmth or tenderness directed to her after their kiss.

"You should go back inside, Sarah. It's not safe for you to be out here at night." His dismissive tone pierced her heart. It was like he could reach inside his mind and flip a switch from being a warm, tender, attentive man—*flip*—to a hard, cold, professional cop. A slow, seething anger surfaced inside.

"Not safe? From whom, Samuel? The man trying to kill me?" She stared hard at him. "Or you?"

She walked away and thought her heart might break because he didn't ask her to stay.

The wedding ceremony of Josiah and Anna had been simple but beautiful. Each time the bride smiled demurely at her groom, or the groom beamed his smile over the congregation, everyone could see how much in love the two of these young people were. At the conclusion of the ceremony, the women gathered to set up the food for the reception. The men moved the benches apart and squeezed as many tables as possible into the small space.

While setting plates and utensils on the tables, Sarah noticed Sam walk across the yard toward the barn. She smiled and greeted people as they inquired of her health and took their seats at the tables. She helped Rebecca carry out the hot casseroles and fresh bread. But her mind was elsewhere. She wondered why Sam had left the reception and what he was doing in the barn.

Sarah could barely squeeze through the cramped spaces between tables. Normally, Jacob would have erected a tent for the reception outside, but the heavy rainstorm from the other night had left puddles of mud and downed tree branches in its wake and changed those plans. Instead, the living room furniture had been pushed to the walls, and smaller chairs stored in bedrooms and outdoor tables and benches were overflowing through the great room, into the kitchen. One even rested at the entrance to a hall.

You'd think the cramped space would have put a damper on the wedding plans and upset the bride and groom, but it seemed to have a totally opposite effect. Everyone laughed and talked and rubbed elbows and laughed some more like one big happy family gathered for a holiday meal.

Then Sarah realized that that was exactly what this small community was—one large happy family. She smiled at the thought, and then gave a wistful sigh. She wondered if she would ever get her memory back. Even though everyone had been kind and helpful, she had no memory of them, no relationships with them, and she couldn't help but continue to feel like an outsider, always watching and never truly belonging.

She was making her third trip from the kitchen into the great room when she glanced out the window and saw Sam. Now she understood why he'd left the group and gone to the barn. A smile tugged at her lips.

Sam waited while the groom pulled his wagon up to the barn entrance, and then jumped out and circled around the back to help. He removed the protective sheet he'd put on top of the table.

Josiah moved a hand lightly over the waxed-to-perfection table. "*Danki,* Samuel. You honored Peter's memory with this fine work."

Sam, embarrassed by the rare compliment, acknowledged it with a curt nod. "I hope Anna is pleased."

"Ah, how could she not be?" He stepped back, hands on hips, and studied the table. "It is a fine piece of furniture, is it not? Simple and plain, but sturdy and attractive too, *ya?*" He helped Sam cover the table, and then the two men lifted it into the back of the wagon. "This table will serve us well, Samuel. As our family grows,

God willing, it will be the focal point of our home for prayers, meals, conversations. *Ya,* this is a good table."

They shook hands, and then both men headed back to the reception in the house.

Sam couldn't stop thinking about the table and the words Henry had spoken. It was true. The table was sturdy, well built and would service the family for years to come.

Peter had been the carpenter. He'd carved the wood lovingly with his own hands, building a piece of furniture that would withstand a baby banging a cup against it, support children doing their homework, bring a family together with hands joined and heads bent for prayer.

Sam wondered if Peter had thought about his own family when making the table. Jacob had told him that Peter was planning to start building his own house on the property in the spring—a place he was certain God would bless with the laughter and love of many children. Sarah and Peter had endured the emotional pain of two miscarriages. Sadness tugged at Sam's heart because Peter hadn't seen that prayer answered.

Sam was glad he could finish the gift that Peter had made for his newlywed friends. But now there was one more thing he could do in honor of the man's memory. He could find the man who had taken his life and threatened to end the life of his wife and unborn child. This is why he'd left his Amish ties so many years ago. To protect those unable to protect themselves. And with God's help, he would.

"Hurry, *kumm,* you are letting all the cold air into the house." Sarah laughed, braced the door open with her hands and ushered Sam into the house. "Josiah moved as quickly as a jackrabbit to get inside. You have been poking along like a turtle, and all the while I'm holding this door open for you."

Sam hung his hat on a peg by the door. "Do you know the rest of that story, Sarah? I believe it was the turtle who won the race."

Sarah's eyes widened with bewilderment. "What nonsense are you saying? When did you ever see a jackrabbit and a turtle race each other?"

Sam threw his head back and laughed. "Never mind. Go stand by the fire and warm yourself."

Sarah's smile was all he needed to feel warm. He watched her weave in and out between the tables, stopping for a quick word and always sharing a smile with many of the folks who spoke to her on her way. When she reached the fire, she shot him a quick look and then rubbed her hands together near the open flame.

"She looks happy today, *ya?*"

Sam had been so absorbed in watching Sarah that he hadn't heard Rebecca approach, and the sound of her voice startled him.

"Hello, Rebecca. Yes, she looks very happy today. It must be Josiah and Anna's wedding. The festivities seem to have lifted everyone's spirits."

"Not everyone's spirits were lifted today. Some of our hearts are still heavily burdened with loss." Her eyes glistened. "Let me ask you, Samuel. This man—the one who kills our loved ones, who burns our neighbors' barns…" Rebecca's voice choked as tears threatened to fall, but she took a deep breath and held them at bay. "How much longer do you think it will be before you find this man?"

"Soon, Rebecca." He hurried to reassure her and ease her pain. "He is getting careless and sloppy. He is out of his element now, in the country, not his familiar city setting, having to work quickly without help and not having the luxury of time to plot and double-check and plan. He is getting careless and frustrated and desperate. I believe it will be very soon when he will make a mistake that he will not be able to fix. Then we'll get him."

Rebecca considered his words and nodded. "*Gut*. Sarah needs this to be over. We all do."

Sam glanced in Sarah's direction and smiled. "Meanwhile, she is getting stronger and healthier each day."

Rebecca nodded. "*Ya,* that is true. Because she is home now, where she belongs—with her family and her community surrounding her, loving her, supporting her."

Sam straightened and tried not to bristle at the poorly veiled meaning behind her words.

Rebecca folded her hands in front of her and spoke just loud enough for him to hear. "I see the way you look at her, Samuel. More importantly, I see the way she looks at you."

He opened his mouth to protest, but Rebecca raised a hand in a silencing motion. "It is natural for her to have feelings for you. You are a *gut* man, strong, kind, protective. She feels vulnerable and afraid, and she has no memories of the man she loved…of the man whose child she carries…so she turns to you. I understand."

Sam didn't want to have this conversation, didn't want to hear what he knew Rebecca was about to say, but he remained silent and showed her respect by listening.

"You must be the strong one, Samuel. You must be the man whom all of us have come to know and respect. You must find this man—and I believe with God's help, you will—and then you must leave. Quickly. To ease her pain at seeing you go. We will take care of her when you are gone. After all, we are her family."

Rebecca locked her gaze with his. Sam almost had to look away from the pleading look in her eyes. "I have loved her as my own daughter since she was a small child on a neighboring farm. Often, she would come to our farm to play. I watched her grow into a beautiful young woman. I was so happy when Peter fell in love with her and asked her to be his wife."

She paused and stared off into space, reliving those distant memories. When she turned her attention back to him, she wore her pain like a heavy shawl.

"She carries my grandchild, the only part of Peter that I have left. Sarah's world is with us, and your world—" She shrugged her shoulders. "You made your choice many years ago, *ya?*"

Pain ripped through his heart as physically as if she had struck him with a dagger. But she was right. He had no intention of returning to the Amish community—and they would shun Sarah if he tried to take her with him.

"Be a *gut* man, Samuel. Be strong. Protect her from the evil of your world."

Anger bubbled beneath the surface and raced through his body. "Do you want what is best for Sarah, or what is best for you? Have you discussed this with her? Would she leave with me if I asked her to go?"

Rebecca sighed deeply. "No, Samuel. We did not speak of such things." Her gaze wandered to the other side of the room. Both of them watched Sarah as she teased and played with some children at a nearby table. Her laughter floated through the air like the tinkling of wind chimes and hovered over the rumble of conversations at the tables.

Rebecca turned her attention back to him. "I am not too old to remember what it feels like to give my heart to a man. When Sarah looks at you, I see it in her eyes. I think she has already given her heart. I think maybe she would go with you if you asked."

Rebecca stepped closer. "But just because someone *can* do something, Samuel, does not mean they *should* do it. Sometimes the wrong decision brings only heartache and pain. Be a *gut* man. Help Sarah make the right decision. You may not like my words, but you know my words are true. Sarah belongs here with her people, not in your world of evil and killing and pain."

She patted his hand like a mother who had just scolded her child, but wanted to assure the boy that he was not bad, just his actions.

He hadn't felt that motherly admonition for many years, and it was just that action that made him face the truth. She was right. He had to leave—soon—and if he loved Sarah, then he would be leaving alone.

Overcome with emotion, he grabbed his hat, donned his coat and stepped outside. He checked in with the other two officers watching the house, told them he would be out of contact for a bit and to keep a sharp eye on Sarah.

With bent head and heavy heart, he walked away.

The man's teeth chattered, and he salted the air with a string of curses. He should be home. He envisioned himself standing before a roaring fire with a snifter of brandy in his hand as he looked through the wall of glass to the ocean below. That's where he belonged.

Not here, perched in a tree, hidden by leaves and clinging to branches so he wouldn't fall to his death.

He cursed John Zook. Why had he ever allowed the man to join his team? What a colossal mistake that had been, and he wasn't a man who made many mistakes.

Who would have ever believed that stupid Amish lout would find the backbone to steal his diamonds? Steal! From him!

He should have cut his losses and called an end to this long ago. After all, he certainly didn't need the money. His expertise at ridding the rich of their wealth had served him well over the years. A smile bowed his lips when he pictured some of the art and fine gems in his collection.

No, it was not the loss of the diamonds. Money could always be replaced. And what did it matter, since none of it had been his in the first place?

It was the betrayal he couldn't forgive.

No one betrayed him and lived.

So he'd followed Zook and punished him appropriately. He hadn't anticipated the resulting mess. The Amish husband rushing to his wife's defense. The woman surviving—twice—but unable to remember. Yet.

He definitely had a mess on his hands, and he didn't like messes.

But it would soon be over.

If he killed the woman, then none of the others would dare come forward. He'd read that the Amish were big on forgiveness. They often didn't prosecute offenders and rarely testified in courts. Yep, kill the woman and the others would be so afraid for their children— and themselves—that he would feel safe to return home, where he belonged. He couldn't bear being away for even one more night.

Today it would end.

He glanced at the sky. The sun would be setting shortly. The party at the Lapp residence would soon be over. He'd have to act fast. He'd thought it over and decided it would be easier to strike when hundreds of people milled about the place rather than try to isolate her when she was on her own.

He wasn't worried about the cops. Oh, they kept watch over her, sure. But they could be easily distracted. They weren't as invested in her well-being as that one who'd followed her here from the hospital. There was probably something going on between the two of them. But he didn't care. He hoped the guy got what he wanted from his lady friend because their little romance was coming to an end real quick.

He lifted binoculars to his eyes for another surveillance of the party and couldn't believe his good fortune. That cop—the undercover one who thought he could fool him by dressing Amish—was leaving.

He adjusted the lens and took a second look. He watched him consult with the other two cops and then walk off. He watched his hurried gait, his bent head, his stooped shoulders.

Uh-oh. Something had happened. A love spat, maybe? This guy didn't look happy, and he definitely didn't look like he was coming back.

It was time. He smiled in anticipation. Soon this would be over. He would be home and safe. He could almost taste the brandy on his lips.

With agile movements, he lowered himself to the ground. He had to move fast—and it had to be now.

Chapter Fifteen

"William, you forgot your sweater." Sarah stood in the doorway, waving them in front of her. The boy rushed back, took the sweater from her with a hurried *"Danki,"* and ran off to join the mass of children playing in the yard.

Benjamin came up beside her in the doorway. *"Danki,* Sarah. I worry about that boy. His head is always in the clouds."

"He is young still, Benjamin. He will settle down soon enough."

Benjamin frowned. "Sometimes he seems so distracted, I worry he can't walk a straight line across the yard." Benjamin shook his head. "Always getting into trouble, that one. Not bad behavior. Just foolish behavior from not thinking things through."

"How old is he now? Seven? Eight?"

"Seven. Old enough to stop all that daydreaming."

"Who knows? Maybe William will use his creativity to be a great writer or painter."

Benjamin frowned. "Sarah, you should know by now

that the Amish do not take great stock in those foolish things. I will be happy if he is a great farmer."

Sarah chuckled. "Ah, but Benjamin, think about it. The good Lord created all of us. Each one of us is the same, yet different. It is those differences, those individual talents, that make us unique and special, *ya?*"

Before he could reply, both Benjamin and Sarah ducked as a baseball flew past their heads and crashed through the front window.

"Sorry, Daed. I was trying to throw the ball to you." William, wearing a worried expression, stood at the bottom of the steps looking up at them.

Benjamin frowned. "Throw it to me? Did you call my name? Did you let me know the ball was coming my way? Look what you've done to Bishop Lapp's window. Think what you could have done if you had hit me in the head!"

William hung his head. "I'm sorry, Daed. I will do chores for the bishop to help pay for the broken glass."

"That you will!" Benjamin looked at Sarah. "See what I mean? Now I must speak to Jacob about this." Sighing heavily, he reached down to retrieve his hat, which had fallen to the ground, plopped it on his head and went back inside.

"I didn't mean to hit the window," William said, his gaze trailing after his father.

"I know you didn't." Sarah lowered her voice to a whisper. "But next time you aim for your father, William, make sure he knows it is coming. Now go back and play." She shooed him away.

Sarah stepped back inside the house. Most of the adults were preparing for their trip home. The women finished washing dishes and wrapping up leftover food.

The men carried the benches out to the wagon used to transport them from farm to farm for services, and then they collapsed and stored the long plastic picnic tables for future use.

"Anything I can do to help, Mrs. Lapp?"

Sarah glanced at Officer Muldoon. He looked too young to be a cop. She bet his *maam* found it difficult to watch him don the uniform and walk out the door with a gun strapped to his side each day. Sarah placed a hand on her swelling belly and thanked God she would never have to carry that worry in her heart for her child. The worst that could happen to him or her was to be kicked by a horse or hurt by some farm equipment.

She'd found it difficult to see Samuel carry a gun. He hadn't liked it, but had complied with her wishes when she asked that the gun be put away for this occasion. There were so many women and children attending today's wedding. This was not a time or place for guns.

Sarah glanced around and then looked back at the officer. "Have you seen Detective King anywhere?"

"He left about an hour ago. He asked us to keep an eye on things."

"Left?" A frown twisted her lips. "Where did he go?"

"Don't know. Didn't ask. But you're in good hands, don't worry."

"I'm not worried, Officer Muldoon. I am sure you will do a good job."

Sarah smiled and then walked away.

How strange. Even in the hospital, Samuel had barely left her out of his sight. Since they came home from the hospital, he'd never been farther than the sound of her voice. So why would he suddenly leave without a word of his whereabouts to anyone? It seemed so unlike him.

Seeing the bride and groom preparing to leave, she hurried over to offer her congratulations and best wishes for their future together. En route, she said her goodbyes to several other families that were heading out. When she'd accomplished her task, she sat down in front of the fireplace to rest—and think.

She still couldn't understand Samuel's sudden disappearance. She knew he didn't owe her any explanation—but still. She thought back to the last time she'd seen him, and then remembered him standing by the front door speaking with Rebecca. Maybe he'd said something to her.

Sarah found Rebecca in the kitchen putting away the dishes. "Do you need any help?"

"*Danki,* child, but no. This is the last of it. Many hands made the work disappear fast." Rebecca sent a puzzled look her way. "Is everything all right? You look troubled."

"Everything's fine. I was just wondering if Samuel might have said something to you before he left. I saw him talking with you earlier, and I haven't seen him since."

Rebecca's cheeks flushed a bright red, and she averted her eyes. If Sarah didn't know better, she would have thought the woman felt guilty about something. But that certainly couldn't be the reason for the flush, could it?

"Rebecca?"

The older woman tucked pots into lower drawers on the stove, and then pretended to wash an already clean countertop.

"Do you know why Samuel left? Or where he went?" Sarah asked.

Rebecca turned and planted her hands on her hips. "I think you pay that young man much too much attention. We both know that his job brought him here, and when the job is done he will leave. It is best you remember that and go about your business."

Stunned by her harsh tone, Sarah simply nodded and stepped away. She'd never heard Rebecca utter a stern word before, and it shocked her. Of course, she couldn't remember if there had been any harsh words spoken between them in the past. She could only base her opinion on her experience with the woman now.

Maybe the stress of the past month, along with everything that happened since Sarah had come home, was catching up with Rebecca. Yes, that must be it. The woman was tired and still grieving. A bit out of sorts. Anyone would be. She'd have to be a little kinder, a little quicker to offer help.

But still…

Something didn't feel right. Sarah thought Rebecca knew much more than she was saying.

Wrapping a shawl around her shoulders, Sarah stepped onto the front porch. Maybe a little walk would do her good, make her feel less restless. She told herself that she was just getting some exercise. She would not allow herself to believe she was looking for Samuel.

"Going somewhere, Mrs. Lapp?"

"Officer Muldoon, please call me Sarah. I have trouble remembering to answer to Mrs. Lapp."

"Yes, ma'am."

Sarah smiled. "And please don't call me ma'am. In our language, that means mother." She squelched a giggle at the bashful and embarrassed look he sent her way.

"Yes, ma'am…uh, Sarah." He looked around and

then asked, "Are you walking alone? Would you like me to accompany you?"

"No, that won't be necessary. I'm not venturing far. I just feel the need to stretch my legs."

As they spoke, Officer Jenkins appeared. "Everything okay here?"

Sarah laughed. "How could it not be with so many attentive gentlemen watching over me?" She folded her hands in front of her. "I just wanted to stretch my legs. You can both sit on the porch. I promise I won't leave your sight. I just want some time alone with my thoughts."

"Seems to be a lot of that going around lately."

Sarah raised an eyebrow in question.

"Detective King told me the same thing not so long ago." Jenkins nodded toward the porch. "We'll wait over there. But please don't leave the yard."

Sarah acknowledged his words with a nod and continued her walk.

Samuel needed time alone with his thoughts?

Once again the niggling feeling that Rebecca knew more than she was saying returned. She'd only strolled a few yards when the ground shook beneath Sarah's feet, and the sound of an explosion deafened her.

Children who had still been playing in the yard raced for the safety of their parents' arms. Screams rent the air. Men's voices of alarm and concern added to the cacophony. The police officers scrambled off the porch. Jenkins ran to their vehicle. Muldoon hurried to her side.

Jenkins shouted to Muldoon. "Get her back in the house, and don't let her come out until we know what's going on!" His voice brooked no argument. Muldoon nodded.

Sarah watched the patrol car, lights flashing, speed down the lane.

"C'mon, Mrs. . . . Sarah, let's get you inside."

They were hurrying toward the house when Jacob rushed past. Sarah reached out to stop him. "What's happened?"

"I don't know." Jacob pointed in the distance to a large plume of black smoke. "There's been some kind of explosion in the west end of my cornfield. But nothing is there to cause such a thing. Stay calm. It will be all right. We will follow the police officers and find out what is happening. Stay inside with the rest of the women." Before Sarah could respond, he hurried to a buggy hitched at the rail, climbed aboard and snapped the reins, leading the horse in the direction of the smoke.

When they reached the bottom step of the porch, Officer Muldoon released her arm. "Go inside, Sarah. I'm going to make a fast check of the perimeter of the house and the barn, and then I'll be right in."

Before she could reply, he disappeared around the corner of the house.

Sam leaned against a bale of hay and glanced toward the house. The loft of a barn had been his favorite spot as a child to find a quiet, private place to be with his thoughts, and he found it worked for him as an adult, too. The slow, steaming anger he had felt toward Rebecca at her blatant request for him to leave slowly dissipated.

She was right. How could he be angry with someone who spoke the truth? So he cooled down and gave her words some more thought. It didn't take long for him to realize that he'd never really been angry with Rebecca. He was angry with himself.

What had he been thinking? He knew better than to mix his professional life with his personal life. That was rule number two in undercover work. Rule number one was to stay alive at all costs. He should never have allowed himself to get too close to Sarah, to care about her. He shouldn't have—but he did.

He rubbed a hand over his face. He couldn't deny it anymore. It had begun as sympathy for a wounded widow, then admiration for her spirit and determination. It had progressed to appreciation of her gentle nature and enjoyment of her sense of humor until, without knowing exactly where or when, he'd fallen in love with her. When he looked into her eyes, he could see that she had fallen in love with him, too. That was the worst part.

The fact that he had never intended to hurt her didn't mean much when he knew that he would. There was no future for them. He couldn't return to the Amish way of life. He'd left it more than a decade before, and although he still retained a love for the Amish people, it was no longer his world.

And Sarah…

Even though she had no memory of this life, she still had strong, loving ties. What was he supposed to do? Take her away from the people who loved her? Ask her to sit in his small apartment all alone because he was off for days, weeks, sometimes even months on undercover jobs? What kind of life would that be for her? For her child?

No. Rebecca was right. If he loved her—and he did—then he needed to leave as quickly as possible, just as soon as this was over. One broken heart was enough. Best it be his.

Satisfied that he was making the right decision, he began to crawl out from behind the bale of hay. He intended to climb down the ladder, relieve the other two officers and have a heart-to-heart talk with Sarah.

The sound of an explosion froze him in place.

He scrambled toward the ladder, but stopped when he saw a stranger enter the barn. It was the stealth of the man's movements, the way he kept looking over his shoulder, that made Sam pause.

Mary and William Miller were playing on the barn floor below.

Sam couldn't believe what he was seeing, and he had to force himself not to move when the man grabbed Mary roughly by the arm and dragged her toward the far end of the barn. The intruder stood just below him, which made it difficult for Sam to get a clear view of what he was doing without exposing his presence and putting Mary at greater risk.

Sam's brain raced a million miles an hour. Who was this man dressed in Amish clothing? He'd seen him before. It definitely wasn't Benjamin. As strict as Benjamin was, he loved his children and would never treat them in such a rough, unkind way. Sam was just about to speak up and reveal his presence when recognition slammed into him with the force of a semi truck.

This was the man he'd fought in Sarah's hospital room. Even though it had been dark and he'd only seen him for a moment, he was sure it was the same man.

This was their killer.

As he watched in horror, trying to formulate a plan, William ran to Mary's defense. Like a charging bull, he pushed against the man, then yelped like an injured puppy and pulled his hand back. The man had sliced the palm of William's hand with a knife.

Fury seethed within him. It took every ounce of strength he had to stay where he was. But he'd seen the silver glint of a blade pressed firmly against Mary's throat. Sam knew this man wouldn't hesitate to use the weapon if he were startled or if he discovered his presence.

Sam dared to lean forward. He took another glance at the situation. His heart melted when he saw tears streaming down Mary's cheeks. He hoped she'd do what she was told and remain still. This particular intruder had no conscience. He wouldn't care in the least that the life he ended would be that of an innocent child.

As quietly as possible, Sam crept back into the shadows. He needed to signal for help. He moved to the loft door to see if he could spot the other officers. He didn't catch sight of either one of them. But what he did see turned his blood to ice.

Sarah had reached the top porch step when she thought she heard someone calling her name and turned around. William stood at the base of the steps, looking up at her.

"William?" Sarah's heart clenched. The boy's face was as white as the sheets on the line, and his entire body trembled. She hurried down the steps, crouched in front of him and placed a comforting hand on his shoulder. "What's wrong?"

The little boy's lips trembled. He spoke in a whisper, and she had to lean closer to hear. "He…he told me to get you. He told me to bring you to the barn."

Sarah glanced toward the barn and then back to the

boy, who was literally shaking in his boots. "Who told you, William? What man?"

"A bad man, Sarah. A very bad man." William's eyes were wider than she thought his little face could hold.

"Okay, honey. Let me get Officer Muldoon, and we'll come into the barn."

As Sarah started to rise, the boy grabbed her arm with both his hands. "No! The man said nobody could come but you." Then the boy collapsed into her arms and began to cry.

"Shh, William, everything will be okay." She held the child against her, rubbing his back in comfort while searching the yard for help. Seconds ago there had been people everywhere. Since the explosion, there wasn't a person in sight. Sarah continued to pat William's shoulder. "Your parents are inside. Let's go talk with them."

"No!" William looked terrified. "We can't tell my parents. We can't tell anyone or he'll kill her. He told me so."

Sarah felt the blood in her body drain away. "Kill who? William, tell me everything, please, right now." She tried to remain calm and keep her voice controlled so the boy wouldn't panic. The strength seemed to drain out of her legs, and she didn't know how much longer she trusted them to hold her up.

"We were playing in the barn when a man ran in, grabbed Mary and pulled her into one of the horse stalls. He held her real tight so she couldn't run away. He told me to come and get you. He told me to make sure we didn't bring anyone else."

"We don't listen to bad men, William. Of course we are going to bring people with us to help Mary." Sarah placed one foot on the lower step, but William threw himself at her, almost as if he were trying to tackle her.

"Please, no." His eyes pleaded with her. "If you tell anyone, then he said he will cut her worse than he cut me." He held out his left hand.

Sarah took hold of his tiny hand. Her eyes could barely pull away from the sight of the thin red line slashed across the boy's palm.

"Dear Lord, help us. Why didn't you tell me that he'd hurt you?" For the first time, she noticed the stark droplets of red on the ground at the boy's feet. She quickly untied her apron and used it to tend to the boy's wound. She applied a steady pressure against his palm.

After a moment, she lifted the material and breathed a sigh of relief. The cut had been superficial and not deep. The bleeding stopped immediately. No permanent damage had been done. He wouldn't need stitches or even have a scar.

"Danki, Lord."

William couldn't hold back tears anymore, even though they both knew his father would find it a sign of weakness for a boy to cry. His breathing came in hiccups. "He...he is holding a knife against Mary's throat. She can't even try to run away, or he will cut her. Please. You have to help Mary."

Sarah hugged him close. When she released him, she held his forearms and stared hard into his eyes. "I am going to go into the barn and try to help Mary, but you must help me. Do you understand?"

The boy nodded.

"Good. You stay here. You count to ten very slowly. Then you run inside and tell your father everything. Counting to ten will give me time to get into the barn. After the bad man sees that I am alone, he won't be expecting anyone else. It will be safe for you to tell your father and let him bring people to help me." She gave William's shoulders a gentle shake. "This is important, William. Do you understand? Count to ten slowly, and then go inside and get help."

Although the boy nodded, she didn't like the dazed expression on his face. This was not a time for William to get distracted or daydream as he frequently did, but she didn't have a choice except to trust him. If this man had used a knife on William, she had no doubt that he'd use one on Mary, and she couldn't let that happen. She offered up a silent prayer that the boy would do as she'd requested, and she hurried to the barn.

Stopping right outside the entrance, she took a deep breath to steady the trembling that seized her body. She glanced over her shoulder. William stood right where she'd left him, his eyes riveted on her. She did her best to smile reassuringly. She nodded in his direction and then, slowly pushing the door open, stepped inside. Her breath caught in her throat the moment she spotted the stranger. He stood at the far end of the barn in the entrance to one of the stalls. The knife he held pressed against the little girl's throat was clearly visible.

"Don't cry, Mary. Everything is going to be all right. Try not to move, honey." Although the beat of her heart galloped like a wild stallion on stampede, Sarah kept her voice steady and her outward composure calm.

Please, God, be with this child. Please keep her as still as possible until William can bring help.

"Come in, Sarah. Shut the door behind you." The tenor of the intruder's voice rose and fell in a singsong rhythm. "I've been waiting for you."

Chapter Sixteen

Fear danced up and down Sarah's spine. "Please. Let her go." She took several steps toward the man. "She is just a child. She has nothing to do with any of this."

The man stepped out of the stall, dragging the girl with him. He sneered, and for a moment Sarah couldn't believe she was even looking at a human being. He seemed to have no heart, no compassion. She found herself looking into the eyes of pure evil.

"Where are my diamonds?" he demanded.

Sarah had to take several breaths before she was able to calmly answer. "I have never seen your diamonds. The police told me they found them on my body when they took me to the hospital. They must still have them."

"Police, huh. Figures." He yanked the child closer, and she whimpered with fear. "So what are you going to do to make it up to me, Sarah? What can you offer me in exchange for my diamonds...and for the life of this girl?"

Sarah's legs shook so badly that she felt they would dump her on the dirt floor at any moment. Her mind raced, but she couldn't come up with any plan of action that would ensure the girl's safety, and she knew there was little hope for her own. She prayed that William had done what she requested and that help would be racing through the open barn door at any moment. She moved closer so she could throw herself against the man and try to save Mary as soon as she heard help coming.

"Stop right there!"

The command in his voice froze her in place.

"Do you think I'm stupid? I can see exactly what you have in mind. It's written all over your face. You think you can wrestle this knife from me and save the child. I may even let you do it." He let out a maniacal laugh. "I'll even do one better. I'll give you a choice. I can slit this child's throat right now…or you can step forward so I can claim the life of the child you carry."

In horror, Sarah's hands flew to her belly, and for a moment she couldn't move, couldn't think.

"That's what I thought. So it will be the girl." Before he could move his hand across her throat, a small voice echoed in the barn.

"No! Let my sister go!" William had crept into the barn behind Sarah and now stepped out into the open, drew something from his pocket and, before anyone could blink, launched an object into the air.

It took only seconds for Sarah to realize that William had a slingshot in his hand, and his stone had hit its mark.

The stranger groaned and automatically lifted his right hand to his forehead, freeing the knife from Mary's neck. The girl dropped to the barn floor and scrambled away on all fours. Sarah and William raced forward to help her. At the same time, a large, dark object fell out of the loft and landed on top of the stranger.

"Help! Somebody help us. Help!" Sarah screamed at

the top of her lungs as she pulled William and Mary toward the open barn door. It wasn't until they'd cleared the barn and were standing safely in the yard that Sarah sent the children racing to the house for help and dared to turn and look behind her to see what had fallen on the intruder.

Her eyes widened in horror. It wasn't a thing. It was Samuel. Both men were in the fight for their lives as they wrestled on the dirt floor of the barn.

Glancing over her shoulder, she saw the children burst into the house.

Sarah ran back into the barn, grabbed a pitchfork and hurried toward the men. She never had to wonder whether or not she'd be capable of piercing the man with it. She couldn't get a clear poke at him. His back would be toward her for a split second, then just as quickly it would be Sam's.

Sarah danced around the two men looking for an opportunity to help, but she needn't have worried. After a few well-aimed punches, Sam had the situation under control. He straddled the man, holding the stranger's hands behind his back.

"Sarah, place that pitchfork on the back of this man's neck."

Nausea rose in Sarah's throat.

"Do it. Now," Sam commanded.

It took a moment of supreme trust in Samuel, but Sarah did as he asked.

Sam grabbed the weapon from Sarah's hands. "I'm holding this pitchfork now, and I will not hesitate to use it on the likes of you. Understand?" He exerted a little more pressure, and the man stayed absolutely still. "Smart decision," Sam said. Then he glanced up at Sarah. "Find Officer Muldoon and get him out here. Then go and get my gun."

Sarah ran from the barn just as a half-dozen Amish men rushed past her into the barn. When she returned, the gun held at arm's length in front of her and hanging gingerly from her fingers, Sam looked like he was trying not to laugh at her. The Amish men, armed with sticks, baseball bats and a second pitchfork, had formed a circle around him and the intruder. They seemed to be doing their best to look threatening, but Sam knew that not one of them would connect a blow, and the entire scene was staged for support, not protection.

Sarah hurried forward, and he took the gun from her fingers. He loosed his hold on the pitchfork, ordered the other Amish men to step away and hauled the intruder to his feet.

Officer Muldoon stumbled into the barn. The back of his head and the shoulder of his jacket were coated with blood. Despite his injury, he moved forward, drew his weapon and stood next to Sam.

"I'm sorry, Detective King. I was checking the perimeter of the house when someone got me from behind."

"Meet the somebody who clocked you. You okay?"

"I will be."

"Good. Cuff him and get him out of here."

Sam supervised the cuffing and had started to walk with Muldoon to the car when Jenkins raced into the barn, assessing the situation in an instant. He stepped forward, replaced Sam's hold on the perp's arm and helped escort him to his patrol car.

Sam thanked the Amish men for their support and watched as they filed out behind the police officers. Sam smiled again.

Finally, he had a chance to focus his attention on Sarah. He clasped her forearms and felt the trembling beneath his fingers cease. Her eyes, filled with concern and caring, caught his gaze and melted him to the spot. His heart thundered in his chest. His pulse raced.

Before he could give it a moment's thought, he pulled her into his arms and kissed her. This kiss wasn't tender or tentative. All of the emotions he had tried to hide surfaced in an embrace of passion and fire and need.

And she kissed him back.

She fit in his arms as naturally as if she'd always belonged there. She threaded her fingers in his hair and wrapped her other arm tightly around his waist. She tasted of strawberries and coffee and tears.

It was a delicious, intoxicating kiss—and he wanted more. When he lifted his mouth, the flush of her skin and the brightness in her eyes made him smile.

"Are you all right?" he asked. "Did that man hurt you?"

"*Nee,* I am fine." She smiled so widely it barely fit her face. "Samuel, you saved us."

"I wish I could have done something sooner, but he had too tight a hold on Mary for me to take the chance. If it wasn't for William's bravery..." He directed the words to Benjamin who had just reentered the barn, closely followed by Jacob and the others. "That is a brave, fine boy you have."

Benjamin's voice croaked. "*Danki,* Samuel. William was very brave today, it's true."

Although the Amish try not to show favor, pride shone from Benjamin's eyes, and Sarah believed God would forgive this moment of transgression.

"Who was that man, Samuel?" Aaron Miller asked from the middle of the crowd.

"That is the man who shot Sarah and killed Peter. He is a career criminal who has made a lifetime of stealing art and fine gems to support his expensive lifestyle. He made fatal mistakes when he entered a world he was not familiar with. No one will have to worry about him again."

"What happens now, Samuel?" Jacob stepped forward. "What will they do with that man?"

"He will go on trial. Based on the evidence we have against him, he will spend the rest of his miserable life in a cell. He will never be a threat to you or your family again."

Jacob nodded. "*Danki,* Samuel."

"Don't thank me. Everyone worked together. The children, Sarah, yourselves. You graciously allowed the intrusion into your home and into your lives. But it's over now."

"Yes, it's over." Rebecca stepped out of the shadows and stood beside her husband.

Sam took one look at the expression on her face, and he knew that she had witnessed the kiss.

"We must say a prayer of thanksgiving to the Lord," Rebecca said. Her gaze locked with his. "God is good. Sarah is safe. The man has been captured. He will be punished in an *Englisch* court under *Englisch* law. And our lives can return to what they should be." Rebecca stared hard at him. "Isn't that so, Samuel?"

Sam's stomach clenched. His arms still ached with the feel of Sarah within them. His lips still tasted her lips. He knew what the woman expected of him. Now he had to ask himself if he was man enough to do it.

Sarah watched the exchange between Samuel and Rebecca. She heard the words. Nothing out of the ordinary had been said, but something unspoken hung in the air.

Seconds of silence stretched between them, and then Samuel nodded. "Yes, Rebecca. Now is the time for your lives to return to normal."

"Gut." She stepped forward and hugged Sam. "You are a *gut* man, Samuel. God bless you."

Sarah wasn't sure what she had just witnessed, but a sense of dread overcame her.

Rebecca ushered the others out of the barn to re-group, check on the children and have a cup of coffee before their departure. Sarah had started to go with them when Sam's hand shot out and stopped her.

"Sarah…"

She stared into his eyes and almost had to look away from the pain she saw looking back at her.

Gently, he cradled her face with his hands.

"Sweet, sweet Sarah."

His eyes glistened, and for a brief moment she thought he might cry.

When the others were out of sight, he pulled her to him. He kissed her again—a passionate kiss, a desperate kiss—and suddenly Sarah knew. It was a goodbye kiss.

She lifted her eyes and searched his face, hoping she was wrong, but the shuttered look in his eyes told her she wasn't. Still, she tried to deny the inevitable. She offered him a tentative smile. "When you are finished with whatever you have to do for your job, you are welcome to join us for dinner. Rebecca is making a pot roast, and I still have some of your favorite apple pie left."

"Sarah…"

"If you can't make it back this evening, that's okay.

We understand you have many things to do. You are welcome to join us tomorrow night."

He placed his hands on her waist and held her in place.

"It's over. My job here is done. It is time for me to go home."

Her breath seized in her throat, and her heart refused to beat. She had known this moment would come, but she'd hoped…she'd prayed…

"Your home could be here, Samuel. You are Amish. You could return to your roots, study, get baptized. Our community would welcome you."

"I am not Amish. I haven't been for more than a decade." He trailed a finger down her cheek. "You are a very special woman. A loving woman. Smart. Kind. Brave." Boldly but gently, Sam placed his hand on her stomach. "God knew what He was doing when he chose you to be the mother of this child."

She placed her hand on top of his and clasped his fingers. "Samuel…please, don't…"

"I will always cherish the moments you allowed me to share with you." He removed his hand. "We both knew this time would come, and now that time is here. I must return to my world—and you must stay in yours."

"But is this my world?" Sarah's eyes filled with tears. "I have no memories of this life. I have no memories of *any* life. As you told me yourself, I can be whoever I want to be. The future has not yet been written."

He smiled sadly. "You will have a wonderful future here with your family—raising your child and surrounded by the people who love you."

"What about who *I* love?" She challenged him with her eyes. "Don't my feelings matter?" She hesitated and then took the chance and spoke. "I…I don't remember Peter. You are the only man I know. You are the only man I…I…"

He placed a finger against her lips before she could finish.

"Shh. Think, Sarah. You love Rebecca. You love Jacob. And they and all the people in this community love you in return. They are your family. You belong here." He drew her into his arms and hugged her tightly. His breath was like a gentle breeze through her hair. "Go with God, Sarah. Be happy. It is best you do not dwell on everything that happened in this past month. Try to put it all behind you and move on."

"Is that what you truly want, Samuel? For me to forget you, too, as I have forgotten everything else?" She stared defiantly into his eyes, daring him to look away.

He released her. He tilted her chin up and kissed her on the forehead. His tenderness ripped at her heart. "In those quiet moments of the evening, when you sit on the porch and stare at the sky, I want you to know that the feelings we had for each other were real. The respect. The friendship. The warmth."

"The love?" Sarah could barely whisper the question.

He dropped his gaze from hers. "Our time together was special. Something to be cherished. A memory, Sarah. A memory that no one will ever be able to take away."

He placed a gentle kiss on her lips, and Sarah could have sworn she tasted the salt of his tears. When she opened her eyes, she stared at his back as he walked out of her life as suddenly as he had swooped in.

Chapter Seventeen

"I wish you had stayed home," Rebecca scolded as she stepped down from the buggy and turned to help Sarah down as well. "Soon you will be delivering that wee one. These bumpy carriage rides cannot be helping."

Sarah grasped Rebecca's hand and used it to steady herself as she moved her cumbersome girth and stepped down. Her foot twisted, and she started to fall.

Rebecca gasped and reached out to try to grab her, but her hold was too weak to help.

Before Sarah hit the ground, two strong hands grabbed her from behind and righted her. When she regained her footing, she turned with a smile to thank the person who had helped her, but the words locked in her throat.

Tears welled in her eyes. She had truly believed she would never see him again. But here he was. Not an apparition or a dream, but a flesh-and-blood man standing mere inches away from her.

"Samuel?"

He shuffled his feet and stared at the ground. It was

obvious he was as uncomfortable with their encounter as she was.

"What are you doing here?" She held her breath and waited for his answer.

"I quit my job in Philadelphia. I got a job here with the Lancaster Sheriff's Department." He dared a quick glance her way and shrugged. "I kept telling everyone I became a cop to protect the Amish community. Figured if I planned to really do that, then I belonged here with the Amish."

His sheepish grin tugged at her heart.

He was back. For good.

What did that mean? Did she dare hope?

"Are you telling me that you live here now…in Lancaster, I mean?"

"Yes." He tucked his thumbs into the utility belt on the waist of his police uniform.

Sarah's eyes couldn't get enough of him. He looked tall and dangerous and absolutely delightful. And he was back.

"I bought a place not far from town," he said. "The older couple who had owned it couldn't keep up with the repairs. I'm fixing it up little by little on weekends and any hours I have away from work."

"Are you talking about the Townsend farm?" Rebecca asked. She hid her shock at seeing him as well, but the tremor in her voice gave her away. "I'd heard they'd sold their property to a young investor and moved away."

Sam laughed. "I don't consider myself an investor. Don't know if I'd qualify as young these days, either. But yes, I bought the Townsend place."

The sound of his deep chuckle sent a wave of warmth through Sarah's veins.

He's back. Sam came back.

"The Townsend place…isn't that the farm down the hill from ours?" Sarah asked.

Sam locked his gaze with hers. "Yes."

Had he come back for her? And if he had…

Sarah glanced at Rebecca and saw the question and fear residing in the older woman's eyes.

Myriad emotions raced through her. Could she leave the Amish community knowing they would shun her? She'd never be able to continue her relationship with Rebecca and Jacob. Could she bear that? Would she be any happier in the *Englisch* world than she had been in the Amish one? Since her memory had never returned, how would she be able to answer the questions tumbling through her mind?

And then she knew.

It wasn't her mind that would answer those questions. It was her heart…and her heart belonged to Samuel.

She stared at him, waiting for him to say the words she longed to hear. She tried to understand his silence, searched for a hidden message in his eyes, an invitation, but she didn't see one. Her exhilaration and hope quickly faded.

"It was good seeing the two of you again. I expect we'll bump into one another now and again. Give Jacob my best."

He was getting ready to walk away…again.

Please, God, not again. Please.

"Well, you ladies have a nice afternoon."

Sarah couldn't believe it. He hadn't returned for her. He wasn't here to ask her to be his bride. She stared at his back in silence and wondered just how many times her heart could break before there wouldn't be any pieces left.

Walking away from Sarah for the second time was one of the hardest things he had ever had to do. He loved the woman. He'd always love the woman. And that's how he found the strength to leave.

She belonged with Rebecca and Jacob. She was close to term with her pregnancy, and the birth of this baby would seal her role within their family.

He knew he should have stayed in Philadelphia. What had he been thinking?

Sam hadn't been thinking. He'd been feeling. He knew he couldn't have a life with Sarah, but he couldn't live a life without her, either. So he satisfied himself with the occasional glimpse, the few idle words spoken on the street. And he prayed, something that hadn't come easily to him but was now part of his daily life. He prayed that somehow God would perform a miracle and find a way for them to be together, and that He'd give him the strength to continue to do what was right if that miracle didn't come.

And Sarah...

Her weekly jaunts into town became almost daily buggy trips. She seemed to have the same need he did to see each other on the streets, to nod at each other in passing, to steal a few spoken moments and words.

Sam leaned against his car door in the parking lot of one of the local restaurants and watched the buggy approach. When it came to a stop beside him, he approached the driver.

"Are you sure about this?"

Benjamin shrugged. "We have to try. Get in."

Sam walked around the horse, and he climbed into the buggy. The irony of the situation did not escape him. He settled onto the seat beside the man who had once been against his presence in this community, and now not only welcomed him but wanted to help.

Benjamin snapped the reins and turned the buggy onto the open road.

"How is Sarah?" Sam could barely wait for Benjamin's reply. He had been on pins and needles since he'd received word that she'd gone into labor.

"The midwife is with her, as well as Rebecca. I am sure all will be well."

Sam's stomach clenched. He wished he could be as confident.

Benjamin laughed. "You would think, the way you pace and worry, that you are the papa. Relax. The women know what they are doing."

Sam tapped his fingers against his knee and looked out over the fields they passed. The harvest complete, the fields stood empty and waiting for the first taste of winter's snow.

It was time for rest, renewal and hope.

Sam's stomach twisted into knots when they turned into the lane leading to the Lapps' farm. As they approached the white clapboard house, his pulse raced and his knees literally knocked together. He hadn't felt so unsettled and unsure of himself since he was a teen.

Benjamin pulled the buggy in front of the barn. Sam hopped out, circled around and met Benjamin as he climbed down.

"I don't know if this is a good idea. Maybe I shouldn't be here, especially today."

Benjamin tilted his head and studied Samuel's face. "Where else should you be on the day Sarah delivers her *boppli?*"

Sam began to pace. "What if this idea of yours doesn't work?"

Benjamin laughed, and the sound startled Sam. He didn't think he'd ever heard the man laugh at anything.

"Where is the brave man we all came to know?" Benjamin asked. "You can capture killers, *ya?* But you cower at the thought of seeing the woman we both know you love?"

"I shouldn't have come. The situation is impossible."

"Nothing is impossible with God." Benjamin put down the reins and gestured with his hand. "I have been praying. I believe God has given me an answer to those prayers."

"What if it doesn't work?"

"Have faith, Samuel. It is in God's hands. Whatever He wants will be. Now let's go inside."

The men had turned toward the house when Benjamin reached out and grabbed his arm. "Wait…"

Sam faced him.

"I think I hear Jacob's voice coming from the barn. It would be best if we spoke to him privately before approaching Rebecca or Sarah."

Sam agreed, and the two men quietly entered the barn.

Jacob's voice drifted from inside one of the far stalls. "I can't believe you are coming to me with this request. Do you know what you are saying? Do you know what it would cost us?"

"Of course I do." Rebecca's voice, timid and filled with tears, reached their ears. "It is all I have thought about…all I have prayed about for weeks. Ever since Samuel came back to town."

Sam knew he should make his presence known and not eavesdrop, but something about the serious tone of the conversation stopped him. Apparently, Benjamin felt the same way. The men glanced at each other and remained still, continuing to listen.

"When Samuel left, everything changed. You know that. Sarah did her best. She is a good and obedient child. She tried to adjust to his absence and commit herself to the Amish life. She did chores, attended services but…"

Rebecca placed her hand on Jacob's arm.

"She can't hide the longing in her eyes from us, Jacob, or her pain. She is still a stranger to herself. She is a stranger even to us. This is *not* our daughter-in-law, Jacob. Not the Sarah we knew."

"What nonsense do you speak? Of course it is."

"No." Rebecca shook her head. "I love her just the same, but she is different. You know what I say is true. Sarah stayed for us so we could see our grandchild. But her heart…it left with Samuel."

Sam's heart constricted when he heard Rebecca's words.

"That will change with time."

"Will it, Jacob? It has been months, and I have seen no signs of this change. It is even worse now that Samuel has returned."

"Ah, but now she has a daughter. Peter's daughter. Our grandchild. Now she will be happy again."

Sam grinned widely and gave a friendly slap to Benjamin's arm. Sarah had given birth to a baby girl. He wondered if the child had hair the texture of golden silk like her mother. It was all he could do not to run into the house and see for himself.

"Sarah stayed for us, Jacob. She didn't want to hurt us, and with time I believe she has even grown to love us. But asking her to continue to stay for us would be wrong."

Sam's breath caught in his throat. Sarah had missed him. Sarah had had as much trouble letting go of him as he had of her. Maybe there was hope.

"What are you asking of me, Rebecca?" The pain in Jacob's voice was evident in the harshness of his tone.

"I'm asking you to love her, Jacob...as much as she has come to love us. I am asking you to love her enough to let her go...to let her find her heart again...to let her be happy. Hasn't she been through enough? Isn't it selfish to keep her here when we know her heart is elsewhere?"

"But the *boppli*..."

"I know, Jacob. I know." Rebecca's voice choked on sobs. "But she is not happy, and without Samuel I don't believe she ever will be."

As Benjamin and Sam slowly moved forward, they saw Jacob throw his shovel to the ground.

"What you are asking of me is too much. If she leaves, we must shun her. We could not speak to her again. We would have to turn away if we passed her on the street. We would lose Sarah forever, just as we lost Peter, and we would lose our only grandchild. I cannot, Rebecca. I cannot do this."

Rebecca stepped into his arms and held him tightly. "But you will, Jacob. You will let her go because you love her. You will let her go because it is what is best for Sarah."

Sam's throat constricted, and his admiration and affection for this couple grew. He saw the tears and pain etched deeply in Jacob's expression, and it tore at his heart.

"Perhaps there is another way."

Jacob and Rebecca startled at the sound of Benjamin's voice and stepped apart.

Benjamin entered the stall with Sam close behind. "Excuse us for this surprise visit, Bishop, but I believe what I have to say might help."

Jacob blinked in surprise. "Benjamin, what is this about?"

He glanced between the two men. "What are the two of you doing here?"

"Forgive me for the intrusion in what is obviously a private conversation, but I think it is time to speak the truth," Benjamin said.

"What truth?" Rebecca asked.

"The truth that we all lost Sarah the day we lost Peter."

Rebecca gasped, and her hand flew to cover her mouth.

"It's true." Benjamin hurried to finish what he wanted to say. "Do not misunderstand me. We love this Sarah. She is kind and sweet and loving. But she is not the same woman who stepped into the schoolroom that day. She has no memories of that Sarah. She has no memories of us or our way of life. All of us have watched and waited for many months for that woman to return, and she hasn't."

Benjamin stepped forward and placed a comforting hand on Jacob's shoulder. "You know I speak the truth. This is a new woman—in Sarah's body, *ya*—but it is not the Sarah we knew. It is not the woman who was married to Peter. It is not an *Amish* woman."

Jacob opened his mouth to protest, but Benjamin raised his hand to stop him.

"Listen to me, Jacob. She speaks *Englisch* and can only remember some words of our language. She attends our services but can't participate because she does not understand the words of the songs or service. She is not Amish, Jacob. She is *Englisch*. She was born and raised *Englisch*. And after the shooting…" Benjamin looked steadily into Jacob's eyes. "It is the *Englisch* woman who came back to us."

"What are you saying?" Jacob shook his head and stepped away from the three of them, his expression showing how hard he was trying to deny what he knew he had to do. "You are telling me that I should let her go? That I should shun her?"

Benjamin smiled widely. "We do not shun the *Englisch,* Jacob. We befriend them. We welcome them into our homes for visits. We welcome them to join us in our services and gatherings, *ya?*"

A smile creased Rebecca's face as understanding dawned on her. "And this would be acceptable to the community, Benjamin?"

"Forgive me, but I have already taken the liberty to speak to the elders. They agree that the woman residing in Sarah's body is more *Englisch* than Amish. They love her but…" Benjamin shrugged his shoulders. "If God has wiped away her memory, if God has erased the Amish part of her and replaced it with her *Englisch* roots, then it must be God's will, *ya?* And who are we to question God's will?"

All four adults stood in silence as each processed the conversation.

Sam's heart pounded so hard in his chest, he thought it might burst. This was it. The moment of truth. If the bishop and the elders decreed that Sarah was not Amish but *Englisch,* then they would not have to shun her. She could remain an active part of their lives.

Hope filled every pore of his body. Sam bowed his head and prayed. He prayed harder than he had ever prayed before. And he waited.

When an eternity seemed to pass, Rebecca clasped her husband's hand. "Jacob?" Her eyes never left his face as she waited for his answer.

Jacob brushed the tears from his face. "It is true that Sarah was born and raised an *Englisch* child." He turned to face them. "It is also true that since that horrible day in the school, she has no memory of the Amish ways. She does speak the *Englisch* language well, and she struggles to learn ours. It is true that she loves God, but she does not know or understand our *Ordnung,* our Amish rules and laws."

Jacob smiled widely. "What happened to Sarah was God's will, and I will never go against God's will. Sarah is *Englisch.*"

Rebecca flung herself into Jacob's arms, and even though public displays of affection were frowned on in Amish life, this was an exception that all four adults could live with.

Jacob slid his arm around his wife's waist and faced Sam. "Sarah is inside. I am sure she would like you to meet her daughter."

Chapter Eighteen

Sarah couldn't tear her eyes away from her daughter. She traced her finger across the baby's soft skin. When she saw the child's lips pucker and suck in sleep, she smiled with joy. She examined the exquisite, perfectly formed little fingers. She grinned at the way her tiny golden tufts of hair stood up at attention, and she wondered if it would remain that way as she grew.

For the hundredth time today, she offered a prayer of thanksgiving to God for blessing her with this tiny miracle.

A light rap sounded on the door. She made sure she was properly covered with the blanket and then called, "Come in."

The door opened.

"Samuel."

The word escaped her lips as a gasp of surprise. Her mouth fell open. Her pulse raced. She must be dreaming. This couldn't be real. Her eyes took in every inch of the apparition standing in front of her. The dark brown hair that still wanted to fall forward across his forehead. The rasp of a day's growth of beard. The dark, compelling eyes that stared back at her with such longing, she didn't think she could draw another breath.

"Can I come in?"

Unable to speak, Sarah simply smiled and nodded.

Sam fell to his knees beside the bed and gazed at the tiny infant held in her mother's arms. The touch of his index finger to the child's fist caused the baby's fingers to startle open, and then they fisted tightly around his finger.

"She's so beautiful, just like her mother."

A warm, tingling sensation flowed through her body when his eyes caught hers.

Thank you, God.

Samuel had come. He was here with her on one of the most important days of her life and was meeting her daughter. Her eyes welled with tears.

"Samuel, what are you doing here?"

"Where else would you have me be?" The baby still clutched his finger, and Samuel seemed hard-pressed to claim it back. He glanced up at her, and the look of awe and joy in his eyes stole her breath away.

Sarah glanced at the open doorway and then back at Samuel. "Do Jacob and Rebecca know you are here?"

"Yes, of course. They are in the barn with Benjamin. They gave me their blessing and sent me in to see you."

Sarah's mouth fell open, and for a moment she didn't have any words. When she finally found her voice, she could no longer hide the tears that flowed down her face.

"I don't understand. Gave you their blessing? What does that mean?"

Sam grinned and placed the index finger that wasn't being held in the baby's fisted grip against her lips. "It means God has answered our prayers, *lieb*. He in His infinite wisdom devised a way for us to be together, and I will fall on my knees in thanksgiving every day for the rest of my life."

He replaced his finger with his lips in a kiss so sweet, so tender, that she thought she'd never forget this moment of absolute joy.

This wasn't an apparition. This was real. The feel of his touch on her skin. The taste of his kiss on her mouth. Samuel was here, with her, on one of the most important days of her life. He was crooning over her baby. He was smiling down into her eyes and stroking her cheek. She didn't understand it all, but at that moment it didn't matter.

"We have much to talk about, Samuel."

"We do, *lieb*. But we also have time…lots and lots of time."

Why had Samuel suddenly appeared at her door? How could he possibly have Jacob and Rebecca's blessing? But Sam had proved himself to be a man of his word. For now, just seeing him was enough.

Overwhelming waves of emotion gripped her. Tears tracked down her cheeks like streams escaping a dam. But they were good tears, happy tears. For what could make this day more perfect than to be sharing it with her newborn daughter and gazing at the man she loved with all her heart?

She swiped the back of her hand against her face. *Must be hormones setting off these endless tears.*

Sarah quietly watched Samuel interact with her daughter.

"Hello, little one," he whispered in the deep, caring voice she had come to love. His tender expression as he gazed down at the baby touched Sarah's heart. When he glanced up, his eyes glistened. Hmm. *Was he having a surge of hormones, too?*

They spent the next few hours sitting, the three of them—talking, laughing, enjoying their first day together.

Rebecca had come into the room twice. Once just to see if anyone needed anything, and then hours later with a tray laden with sandwiches, fruit and tea.

Samuel took the time to repeat the conversation that had occurred in the barn. He told her that Benjamin had approached the elders, and after several hours of deliberation, they came up with the solution that everyone believed was the right one, one all could happily live with.

Once again Samuel fell to his knee beside Sarah's bed. This time he wasn't focused on the sleeping child in her arms. This time he clasped her hand and looked deeply into her eyes.

"I love you, Sarah. I think I have been in love with you from the very first moment you opened your eyes in that hospital room. You were so vulnerable and lost and frightened." He grinned widely. "But you were also strong, resilient and determined." He drew her hand to his lips and kissed her palm. "From the moment I looked into those beautiful blue eyes of yours, I knew my life was about to change."

Samuel reached into his pocket, extended his hand and opened it.

Nestled softly on his palm was a simple silver band with a small diamond stone. "I know the Amish do not exchange wedding rings. But neither of us are Amish,

Sarah. We are *Englisch,* and I would be honored if you would accept this ring and agree to be my wife."

Sarah stared at the ring.

Was this really happening? Had God truly answered her prayers?

She smiled such a wide grin that her face hurt. "Yes, Samuel. I will wear your ring. I will be your wife."

He slipped the band on her finger and clasped her hand in his.

"The repairs on my house are almost finished. I think you will like the house, Sarah. It has a large kitchen and lots of windows for light. There is a stone fireplace in the living room, and there are four bedrooms upstairs."

"Four? Are you planning for us to have several children, Samuel?"

Sarah almost laughed out loud at the embarrassed flush that colored his neck.

"Would that be acceptable to you?" He looked at her earnestly.

"More than acceptable, my love. I want to fill our lives and our home with many, many children."

"I do have one thing I must talk to you about."

She was surprised by the seriousness of his tone, and she waited for him to continue.

"I am a cop, Sarah. I've been a cop my entire adult life. I don't know any other way of life." He gazed deeply in her eyes. "But I'm willing to try to be something else. A farmer, maybe. Or perhaps I can learn woodworking. I did a decent job on that table I finished."

Sarah cupped his face in her hand. "I do not know Samuel the farmer. Nor have I met Samuel the woodworker. I only know the man I met and the man I love with all my heart…and that man is a cop. A very good cop, I might add. And I wouldn't want him to try to be anything that he is not."

"Are you absolutely certain? I want you to be happy, Sarah. I do not want you to have any regrets."

"No regrets. But one ironclad rule."

He arched an eyebrow in question.

"There are never to be guns in reach or sight of the children. Not ever."

"I promise." Samuel leaned forward and sealed the promise with a kiss.

"Speaking of children," Sam said, turning his attention to the sleeping infant in her mother's arms. "What have you decided to name this precious one?" Sam gently stroked the wisps of golden locks that continued to stand straight up in the air.

"I don't know yet," Sarah replied. "I've been holding her for the last few hours and trying to decide what name best suits her."

"I know what we should call her."

We? Did he say "we"?

Sarah's heart felt like a bird thrashing in her chest. The three of them were going to be a family. She didn't believe it was possible for a person to be so happy.

"Faith." Sam's eyes locked with hers. "Let's name her Faith."

When Sam's lips touched hers in a passionate kiss full of promises for the future, Sarah knew he was right. Faith was the perfect name. Sarah had complete faith that they had a long and happy future stretching out in front of them. Their future was in God's hands—and God was good.

Epilogue

Jacob snapped the reins, and the horse and buggy cleared the curve and approached the white house on the hill.

"What time will Samuel be joining us?" He glanced over at his passenger and smiled. "Rebecca has baked a fresh apple pie, and she will not allow anyone near it until Samuel arrives."

Sarah grinned. "He won't be long. He got called over to the Millers' farm. Someone tampered with his fencing, and his cows are scattered up and down the road."

Jacob chuckled. "That must be a sight. Cars and cows on the same roads. Perhaps the cows will win, and the *Englisch* drivers will go away—permanently."

Sarah laughed. "You know you don't mean a word of that, Jacob. The tourists provide an excellent market for your produce and Rebecca's pies."

Jacob pulled up to the hitching post.

"I know. I know." He waved his hand dismissively. "But I cannot help but wish I could steer my buggy into town without horns blasting and my horse being skittish each time the cars rev their engines or rush past."

Jacob jumped out of the buggy and tied the reins to the post.

"*Kumm, kumm,* everyone has been waiting." Rebecca beckoned to Sarah and stretched out her arms. "Let me have the *boppli.*"

Sarah smiled as she handed her sleeping daughter down into her grandmother's waiting arms. Jacob came around and offered her a hand getting out of the buggy.

Sarah followed the two of them to the grove, where picnic tables covered by white tablecloths dotted the horizon. Even from this distance, Sarah could recognize most of her neighbors already socializing.

"Sarah, Sarah!" William and Mary raced across the lawn in her direction. "Did you bring any cookies with you?"

Sarah laughed. "Get the basket off the floor of the backseat of the buggy. Carry it over to the table, and I will let each of you sample one cookie apiece."

The children dashed off.

Benjamin followed them with his gaze. "They should not be asking you for cookies, Sarah. I will speak with them."

"Nonsense, Benjamin. They are children. Let them be."

"Only if I am also allowed to sample the wares."

Sarah's eyes widened with surprise, and she laughed. "Well, Benjamin, if I didn't know any better, I would swear you are just a big kid yourself."

The sound of her daughter's voice caught and held Sarah's attention.

"Looks like someone just woke up from her nap."

Faith squirmed in her grandmother's arms and tried to get down.

"No, precious. If I put you on the ground, you will get dirt all over your hands. Let's sit down at the table, and Grandmom will fix you something to eat."

A car approached, kicking up dirt and dust as it sped closer.

Jacob shook his head from side to side. "There's something about cars and speed that appeals to Samuel, but I am afraid I will never understand."

"I understand it, Jacob. Samuel doesn't want to miss Faith's first birthday party. Why don't you and Benjamin join the others? I will wait here for Samuel, and we'll be over in just a moment."

The warmth of the sun beat on Sarah's face, and the light breeze ruffled the wisps of hair framing her cheeks. Sounds of laughter and conversations wafted on the air. The party was in full swing, and from her vantage point she could see her daughter basking in the love and attention.

Sam kissed her on the back of the neck, and Sarah startled and squealed.

"You saw me coming, *lieb.* How could I startle you?"

She wrapped her arm around his waist, and he encircled hers. "I was so lost in the beauty of the day, I didn't hear you approach."

As they walked toward the others, Samuel asked, "Have I missed anything? They haven't sung or cut the cake yet, have they?"

Sarah grinned. "You haven't missed a thing. We just got here."

Samuel nodded, happy that he'd made it in time.

"I can't believe it's Faith's first birthday. It seems like only yesterday we were sitting together in this very house and trying to decide on a name for our daughter."

Our daughter.

A flash of warmth and love flooded her being. Samuel had always treated Faith as his daughter from that very first day, and the child adored him.

"Have you told them?" Samuel asked.

"Without you? How could you think such a thing?"

Samuel's smile widened. "Let's tell them now." He steered her toward the gathering of friends and family.

After pleasantries were exchanged, Samuel clasped Sarah's hand and pulled her toward him.

"This is a very special day," Samuel said. "Faith is one year old today."

Everyone cheered and fussed over the child.

"It has been a good year, *ya?*" Benjamin asked. "Good weather. Good harvest. Good friends. And now time to eat good food!"

Everyone laughed as he reached for a chicken leg and Rebecca shooed his hand away.

Rebecca tilted her head and stared hard at Sarah and Samuel. Then a grin broke out on her face, and she clapped her hands together. "You have news, *ya?*"

Her words silenced the group, and all eyes turned toward them.

Sarah smiled up into her husband's face. It was a good face. Strong features. Strong jaw. Eyes that shone with intelligence—and love.

Her heart overflowed with emotion. God had brought such blessings into her life. Her smile widened so much, she thought it would no longer fit her face.

"You tell them," she whispered.

"Tell us what?" Jacob asked.

"They don't have to say a word. It's written all over their faces, Jacob. Can't you see?" Rebecca rushed forward, Faith wrapped in her arms and clinging to her neck. "Faith is going to have a little brother or sister, *ya?*"

Sarah smiled and nodded. The crowd cheered and congratulated them.

"That is great news," Benjamin said. "Now let's celebrate by eating."

Laughter filled the air as friends and neighbors resumed talking while filling their plates.

Sarah's gaze drifted to the horizon. From this distance, Peter's headstone was a mere shadow on the rise. A twinge of sadness touched her heart that no memories of the man had returned. But the sadness was immediately replaced with happy thoughts. She had a pretty good guess now what he must have looked like. She saw glimpses of him every time she looked into her daughter's face, and felt nothing but fondness and gratitude toward the man.

Sarah could feel the warmth of Samuel's breath on the back of her neck.

"Penny for your thoughts."

"I was thinking what a perfect day today is."

He spun her around and smiled down at her. His lips brushed hers softly and tenderly. She could smell the fresh, clean scent of mint and could taste a trace of coffee on his lips.

"Now it is a perfect day," he whispered.

Sarah reached up and cupped his face with her hand. She smiled into his eyes. Without a word, she stood on tiptoe and kissed him back, long and passionately, expressing all the love and joy her heart could hold. "Now, my love, it is a perfect day."

Samuel's eyes glistened. "How did I ever find some-one as wonderful as you?"

"I was gift wrapped in bandages and express-deliv-ered to your care by God," Sarah replied.

Samuel laughed. "That you were. And I will be for-ever grateful to the good Lord for such a wonderful gift." He clasped her hand and tugged her toward the picnic tables. "Speaking of gifts, Faith is waiting for us to open hers. Let's go and help our daughter eat her cake."

Sarah offered a silent prayer of thanksgiving as she crossed the lawn to join her family and friends. God makes all things good…and Sarah's life was good, in-deed.

* * * * *

WE HOPE YOU
ENJOYED THESE
LOVE INSPIRED®
AND
LOVE INSPIRED®
SUSPENSE
BOOKS.

Whether you prefer heartwarming contemporary romance or heart-pounding suspense, Love Inspired® books has it all!

Look for 6 new titles available every month from both Love Inspired® and Love Inspired® Suspense.

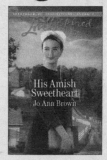

Love Inspired®

Save $1.00

on the purchase of any Love Inspired®, Love Inspired® Suspense or Love Inspired® Historical book.

Available wherever books are sold, including most bookstores, supermarkets, drugstores and discount stores.

Save $1.00

on the purchase of any Love Inspired®, Love Inspired® Suspense or Love Inspired® Historical book.

Coupon valid until January 31, 2017. Redeemable at participating retail outlets in the U.S. and Canada only. Limit one coupon per customer.

52614314

`5  65373 00076 2   (8100)0 12222`

LIINCICOUP0916

SPECIAL EXCERPT FROM

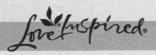

When Macy Swanson must suddenly raise her young nephew, help comes in the form of single rancher and boys ranch volunteer Tanner Barstow. Can he help her see she's mom—and rural Texas—material?

Read on for a sneak preview of the first book in the
LONE STAR COWBOY LEAGUE: BOYS RANCH
miniseries, THE RANCHER'S TEXAS MATCH
by Brenda Minton.

She leaned back in the seat and covered her face with her hands. "I am angry. I'm mad because I don't know what to do for Colby. And the person I always went to for advice is gone. Grant is gone. I think Colby and I were both in a delusional state, thinking they would come home. But they're not. I'm not getting my brother, my best friend, back. Colby isn't getting his parents back. And it isn't fair. It isn't fair that I had to—"

Her eyes closed, and she shook her head.

"Macy?"

She pinched the bridge of her nose. "No. I'm not going to say that. I lost a job and gave up an apartment. Colby lost his parents. What I lost doesn't amount to anything. I lost things I don't miss."

"I think you're wrong. I think you miss your life. There's nothing wrong with that. Accept it, or it'll eat you up."

Tanner pulled up to her house.

"I miss my life." She said it on a sigh. "I wouldn't be anywhere else. But I have to admit, there are days I wonder if Colby would be better off with someone else, with anyone but me. But I'm his family. We have each other."

"Yes, and in the end, that matters."

"But…" She bit down on her lip and glanced away from him, not finishing.

"But what?"

"What if I'm not a mom? What if I can't do this?" She looked young sitting next to him, her green eyes troubled.

"I'm guessing that even a mom who planned on having a child would still question if she could do it."

She reached for the door. "Thank you for letting me talk about Colby."

"Anytime." He said it, and then he realized the door that had opened.

She laughed. "Don't worry. I won't be calling at midnight to talk about my feelings."

"If you did, I'd answer."

She stood on tiptoe and touched his cheek to bring it down to her level. When she kissed him, he felt floored by the unexpected gesture. Macy had soft hair, soft gestures and a soft heart. She was easy to like. He guessed if a man wasn't careful, he'd find himself falling a little in love with her.

Don't miss
THE RANCHER'S TEXAS MATCH by Brenda Minton,
available October 2016 wherever
Love Inspired® books and ebooks are sold.

www.LoveInspired.com